'I'm hunting were

If Chepstow was
this statement he fa
an invisible morsel
his dark grey suit.
know, I believe you're the first werewolf man
we've had here in a good decade.'

'Really? What happened to the last guy?'

The Librarian shrugged. 'I have no idea.
You people come here, you read, you leave.
Sometimes you write your own books and we
file them on our shelves.'

'You do? Well, you'll be filing mine in a
year or so.'

'If I might make so bold as to inquire —
what will it be called?'

Harry Lamb scratched the side of his cheek
with his beer glass. 'I don't know. I'll probably
call it something like: *Notes Toward a Theory
of Co-Evolution: Emulative Mimicry Amongst
the Higher Orders*. And if anyone publishes
it they'll probably call it *Werewolves Among
Us!* and put a photo of Lon Chaney Jr. on the
cover, with his face all hairy and a wet black
nose.'

THE WEERDE

BOOK 1
A SHARED WORLD ANTHOLOGY

———————

DEVISED BY

NEIL GAIMAN, MARY GENTLE AND
ROZ KAVENEY

EDITED BY

MARY GENTLE AND ROZ KAVENEY

A ROC BOOK

PENGUIN BOOKS

Published by the Penguin Group
Penguin Books Ltd, 27 Wrights Lane, London W8 5TZ, England
Penguin Books USA Inc., 375 Hudson Street, New York, New York 10014, USA
Penguin Books Australia Ltd, Ringwood, Victoria, Australia
Penguin Books Canada Ltd, 10 Alcorn Avenue, Toronto, Ontario, Canada M4V 3B2
Penguin Books (NZ) Ltd, 182–190 Wairau Road, Auckland 10, New Zealand

Penguin Books Ltd, Registered Offices: Harmondsworth, Middlesex, England

First published by ROC, an imprint of Penguin Books 1992
1 3 5 7 9 10 8 6 4 2

Filmset in 10/12 pt Monophoto Melior
Printed in England by Clays Ltd, St Ives plc

CONTENTS

Prologue

THE LADY AND/OR THE TIGER: I

Neil Gaiman and Roz Kaveney

The Library of the Conspiracy is currently to be found in a small university town in West Virginia, in the southern United States. The town has no litter in the streets, and its buildings are painted white; a shopping mall was proposed at the county seat ten miles away, but nothing came of it. Once the Library was in Rome, in catacombs adjacent to those where the Sibylline books were held; some say it still contains copies of those books of prophecy which the Sibyl affected to have burned when King Tarquin the Proud refused her asking price, though the Librarians denied this to the Prefect Sejanus when he came calling with his clients, informers and hired bravoes. Later the Library was in Alexandria, then for many years in Venice, and later still in London, moving to its current location in the late 1930s. It is privately funded and little-known, save in certain circles.

In the broad wooden shelves of the Library there are sections on all manner of subjects: Lee Harvey Oswald has almost half a wall, as has John Wilkes Booth, and Joshua Norton, the self-proclaimed Emperor of the United States. There are shelves devoted to the Illuminati, and to the Suicide Royale, and the 1929 World's Fair; the secret patterns on the scarves of the Thugs are documented here, as are the names of the Quechua's

1

bird of hope and the True Name of the Chinese adventurer who called himself the Younger Brother of Jesus Christ. These are on open shelves, and are freely available to legitimate researchers, although they may not be taken from the building.

Researchers need a letter guaranteeing good character and serious intentions; moreover the usual authorities are not always accepted as a reference here: the Vatican Librarian is good for a reference, as is the small public library of the town of Elgin, Illinois. But the Librarian of the Athenaeum Club quarrelled with the four Head Librarians of the Conspiracy over certain documentation that could, it was felt, have persuaded the requisite full twenty-four Bishops of the Anglican Church to assemble for the opening of the sealed box Joanna Southcott left at her death; this was in 1851, and courtesies have not been resumed.

There are open shelves. There are sealed stacks. And there are also the cellars.

One of the four Head Librarians must approve any requests for inspection of materials to be found in the sealed stacks, and these must be read at the high desk in his or her office. Where certain of the manuscripts are concerned, a Librarian will turn the pages for the reader. The Librarians of the Conspiracy have no uniform, but each of them wears white silk gloves; to turn some pages they add a second pair of gloves, and these are black.

The young man with the lank black pony-tail sat at the high desk, taking copious notes. He turned to the Head Librarian. 'Thank you,' he said. 'I think I'm finished with this.'

The Head Librarian took the manuscript, a twelfth-century illuminated chronicle, and placed it carefully on his desk.

'Is there anything else you'll be needing today, Mr Lamb?' he asked.

The young man shook his head. 'Not today,' he said. 'I'm still trying to make sense of what I've already found.' He paused. 'This is a very remarkable place.'

'Yes, sir.'

'So.' Lamb hesitated, then, 'How long have you been working here?'

The Head Librarian stroked his grey moustache with his white silk gloves. 'Sir, it is time to close the Library. And private discussion with our readers is frowned upon, on Library premises.'

'Oh. I see. I'm sorry. I just wondered . . .'

The Head Librarian looked at him, quizzically. 'Yes, sir?'

'Well, did you answer an advertisement in *The New York Times* to work here? Or what?'

The Head Librarian blew a tiny scrap of dust from the tip of his white silk finger. 'The Library does not advertise, sir.'

Lamb looked away from the Head Librarian, embarrassed, and shuffled his notes into a portfolio. They went out into the corridor. The Head Librarian turned off the lights behind them, leaving his office to the darkness of the December evening.

'I–I'm sorry,' said Lamb. 'I didn't mean anything. I mean, I wouldn't want to get you into trouble. Talking.' He shrugged. 'Sorry.'

The Head Librarian nodded, gravely. 'I fully understand, sir. And I regret that our conversation, such as it is, in this building must be limited. However, were you to be on the corner of Main Street and Elm in say, half an hour, there is a small establishment in which drinks may be purchased . . .'

The young man smiled suddenly, widely. 'I'd like that,' he said. 'I'll be there.'

Lamb sipped his beer and waited. The juke-box was playing a country song, something about a woman who had finally discovered, after twenty years of marriage, that she never really knew her man.

'Hallo.'

He started. 'I didn't see you come in. Something to drink?'

'A soft drink. Ginger ale will suit me perfectly.'

'Are you sure I can't buy you a beer? I'm on expenses . . .'

The older man looked down briefly. 'Thank you, but no. I had,' he paused, then began again, '. . . some slight problems with alcohol, many years ago. I no longer drink.'

'My mom was an alcoholic,' volunteered the younger man.

'Then you know that one never ceases to be an alcoholic. One simply does not drink alcohol, a day at a time. My name is Chepstow. Roland Chepstow.'

'Harry Lamb.'

'I know.' They shook hands. Chepstow no longer wore his white silk gloves; his hands were clean and perfectly manicured. The juke-box sang.

> And these days you come home and I don't
>> know you any more,
> Seems you never really get to know your man.

A waitress came, took their order, returned almost instantly with the drinks.

'The Library. It's a wonderful place.'

Chepstow nodded. 'It is indeed remarkable. I get, alas, little time for reading. But I enjoy watching our readers. We attract a particular type of person. Did you notice the gentleman at seat 15H? The Asian gentleman with the muffler?'

'The big purple scarf. Sure. He seemed to be asleep.'

'Exactly. He has been coming here for two years now. He is gathering evidence to prove that Indira Gandhi was murdered not by her Sikh bodyguards, but by agents acting on behalf of the hereditary chairman of the East India Company, in collusion with the British House of Lords. He arrives here first thing in the morning, he orders his books and goes to sleep, waking when the Library is closing to return the books.'

Harry Lamb grinned. 'For two years? It's an expensive place to nap. Doesn't he ever read?'

'When once I ventured to tax him upon the subject, he told me that the precise page of the precise book he was seeking would eventually be revealed to him in a dream. For now, he sleeps.'

Lamb sipped his beer. The Virginia heat was getting to him, even in his T-shirt and jeans. He eyed the Librarian in his sober suit. 'You must hear some strange theories in this place.'

'Indeed, sir.'

'Harry. Call me Harry.'

Chepstow shook his head. 'I'd rather not, sir.' He signalled to the waitress. 'Another beer for my colleague and another ginger ale for me.'

'A ...,' Lamb paused, 'A ... woman I used to know ... once told me that all conspiracies are parts of the same conspiracy, that they are all cells of an ultimate Beast. Like the story of the blind men and the elephant.'

Chepstow nodded. 'People have come to us seeking proof of such ideas, and stayed for years in the attempt to prove it.'

'I don't think that *can* be true, though. It's like the physicist said, Heisenberg – you know what he said . . .'

'I had the honour,' Chepstow said quietly, 'of meeting Herr Heisenberg once, in the company of Mr William Donovan.'

'He said,' Lamb said, 'that the act of looking disturbs what is looked at. So if you are a particular sort of person the conspiracy you find, when you look, will mirror what you think, what you are.'

'I would agree with that. There are certain features that some of the Library's readers have in common. For example, it is my experience that those who lay the planet's difficulties at the feet of the Illuminati tend towards slightly bulging eyes and to be less careful about personal hygiene than those who, for example, seek to prove the existence of the cartel of international bankers. The banker-theorists are by far the best groomed.

'And it has also been my experience that certain types of people orbit certain conspiracies. The last thing Ripperologists want to know is the identity of poor Jack. *That's* there for the asking; but no one ever cares enough to ask. They are seeking themselves on the cobbles of Mitre Street and in the mists of White-chapel.'

'So what am I?'

'I beg your pardon?'

'C'mon. If you can recognize types, what type am I?'

Chepstow looked intently at his drinking companion. 'That would not be fair, sir. I processed your application, after all. You are a journalist. And journalists, in my experience, can be on the trail of . . .' a small shrug, '. . . anything.'

'Well, yeah. But – '

'The books, manuscripts and newspapers you have

been examining are without any thread that is apparent to me. Today, for example, you examined a cryptographer's report on the dimensions of the Red Fort at Agra, a transcript of the tapes taken on Mr Hoover's orders of the last telephone conversations of Miss Jayne Mansfield, and Herr Weisshaupt's suppressed commentary on the libretto of *The Magic Flute*. I think we could describe your interests, Mr Lamb, as either wilfully eclectic or globally paranoid.'

Lamb looked around the room. There was no one near them, and the juke-box was playing loudly enough to mask their conversation from casual listeners. He grinned and said it.

'I'm hunting werewolves.'

If Chepstow was in any way surprised by this statement he failed to show it. He flicked an invisible morsel of lint from the sleeve of his dark grey suit. 'Werewolves. Ah. Do you know, I believe you're the first werewolf man we've had here in a good decade.'

'Really? What happened to the last guy?'

The Librarian shrugged. 'I have no idea. You people come here, you read, you leave. Sometimes you write your own books and we file them on our shelves.'

'You do? Well, you'll be filing mine in a year or so.'

'If I might make so bold as to inquire — what will it be called?'

Harry Lamb scratched the side of his cheek with his beer glass. 'I don't know. I'll probably call it something like: *Notes Toward a Theory of Co-Evolution: Emulative Mimicry Amongst the Higher Orders*. And if anyone publishes it they'll probably call it *Werewolves Among Us!* and put a photo of Lon Chaney Jr. on the cover, with his face all hairy and a wet black nose.'

'How unfortunate.'

'Yeah.'

A tall woman entered the bar. She walked over to a man in the corner. They spoke in low voices urgently, angrily; then the woman walked out and the man followed her. Lamb shook his head slowly. 'I wonder what the story is behind that, then?'

'I doubt we will ever know.'

'You married?'

'The Librarians of the Conspiracy are ... well, I suppose you could call us a celibate order. And you?'

'I came close once. She's dead.'

'I'm sorry.'

There was a pause in the conversation. The record on the juke-box ended and suddenly, for a few seconds, the bar was silent. The young man checked his watch. 'Twenty of eight. You ever notice that? A room full of people talking falls quiet, it's always twenty-past or twenty-to?'

'I can't say that I have. Would you like another beer?'

'Yeah. No. What the hell, sure. It's not a long drive back. I got rooms. You live local?'

'The Library provides living quarters for us near by, Mr Lamb. So ... what set you on the trail of werewolves, then?'

'They aren't werewolves.'

'I thought you said ...'

'People think they're werewolves. But they aren't. Not really.'

'Ah. Psychosis. People imagining themselves as ...'

Lamb shook his head. 'No, no. Not mad people. Not *people*. They look like people, but they can look like *any* large animals. Mimics. Imitating us, living among us.'

'So what do they really look like?'

Caroline ...

On the juke-box a man sang emotionally about his

woman and his bottle and his gun. Steel guitars wailed in the background. Lamb was silent.

'Did I ... Did I say something wrong, Mr Lamb? I'm sorry. I must say your theory sounds eminently more practical than that of the previous werewolf gentleman. As I recall, he maintained that all politicians had eyebrows that met in the middle, and hunted on all fours when the moon was full.'

'They ... they wouldn't be politicians. I don't think so. That would be too conspicuous. They ... they want to blend in.' Lamb thought of Caroline; her smile, her voice, her face. And the way her face had danced and changed when the bullets hit her.

If she comes home tonight
Then I'll be waiting in the darkness
For my woman with my bottle and my gun . . .

The waitress gave them their drinks. Lamb paid the tab and tipped her generously. Intense, he began to talk to the Librarian in short, staccato bursts – astonished to find himself saying out loud the thoughts that had, until this time, been reserved for his notebook, for himself.

'They've been living among us since we were in the caves. They're older than that, though. I don't know how old. Real old. We give them a home. We give them a place to hide. I don't know what they're hiding from; I don't think it's just us, most of the time. If you look carefully you can see their traces in the history books, in legends, in folk songs.'

'Ah. And that's what you have, then? History books, folk songs?'

Lamb drained his drink. He smiled the confident smile of the slightly drunk. 'Got more than that. They aren't as careful as they think they are. And even they can be unlucky.'

9

Chepstow left the last of his ginger ale untouched. 'I'll walk you to your car.'

'Yeah. OK.'

The street was dark and deserted.

'Her name was Caroline,' said Lamb. 'We were covering a story in Naples. She was my photographer, and a damn good one. No, I'm sorry. That sounds so dime-novel, so dumb. And she wasn't just my photographer. We were fucking. Maybe if I'd got my shit together we would have married. I don't know. What does anyone know? They said that the shipment we were tracking was coming through that night and we waited in an alley. She had her cameras. There wasn't any shipment.

'They shot her in the chest. I held her as she died, and I watched her change ... Change into something. And I had to know. What had I been sleeping with? What had I *loved*?'

In the distance Lamb heard something move, then scream: a night animal, a little death. Something was feeding, somewhere in the shadows.

Chepstow looked at him with quiet, intelligent eyes. He nodded. 'You were right about the caves. But they go back a long way before that. All the way back through the ice and the comets and the Dark; they were not the first intelligent species to walk the Earth, but they were the second and they are, by far, the oldest.'

'But ... then ... but,' said Lamb. 'You ...?'

'The Library of the Conspiracy has many names and many purposes,' said Chepstow. 'And we know things you are unlikely to know. We know of the Fifty Lives, and of the Darkcallers, and of Those Whose Names Are No Longer Sung.'

Lamb drew back slightly; curled his hands into fists.

'Don't be ridiculous,' said Chepstow. 'I am as human as you. But I too have looked at some interesting files in my time. Perhaps you should accompany me back to the Library; there are some things that you should read.'

Lamb thought about running. Then he sighed, and side by side with the older man, walked back towards the Library down the clean, dark sidewalks of the pretty little town. Once he stopped, convinced he had heard something behind him: an animal perhaps. He looked around, scanning the shadows, but saw nothing. No one. Chepstow took his arm and led him gently towards the Library. They entered the building by a padlocked door at the back. There was a deep stairwell there, and at its bottom several more locked doors; Lamb had thought Chepstow limped, but perhaps it was the weight of his keys. They passed through another door, and they were in the cellars of the Library of the Conspiracy.

The cellars of the Library of the Conspiracy are airy rooms of various sizes. When the Library was in Venice, certain seekers after knowledge would agree to be immured in the cellars of the Library in return for the knowledge they sought; it was an awkward compromise between the Library's function as a repository of information and its need that certain information be withheld from the world outside. It is said that this no longer happens; and indeed it would not be credible in this day and age.

Chepstow led Lamb through a labyrinth of small rooms and corridors, and finally through a door with many locks into a large room, its walls all lined with cardboard boxes, each filled with files to overflowing.

At the far end of the room was another door.

The room contained a desk and two chairs — one cheap, red plastic that sat by the desk, the other an ancient armchair, in the far corner of the room.

Chepstow locked the door behind them.

On the desk that stood in front of them, lit by a

solitary lamp, were various papers – part of a German scientific paper and a photograph of a small, unsmiling woman; a clipping from a Manchester evening newspaper from the year before and a broadsheet printed in Prague in 1618; a sheaf of bar bills, in Spanish, and a stack of xeroxes of what seemed to be scientific formulae; and other remnants of tales. Each had a commentary attached.

'I think,' said Chepstow, 'that these are what you are looking for.'

Lamb nodded, took his seat at the desk, and began to read.

And, before any of the Fifty Lives is sung:
   We moved among them quietly, lest we disturb them
   in their meditations.
   In the palace of their thought
   Our walking was not even an echo:
   Their servants, and their lovers, and their pets.
   Sharers of hearth and bed and counsel.

   They thought of strange things
   and strange gods.
   They walked in closed chambers of the mind
   And bowed to what they found there.
   Then the Dark came
   and in a season they were gone;
   in their folly they were eaten and were gone.

   The star fell, and the world was dark.
   It fell, the great city.
   And we moved quietly, for a thousand thousand
   lives.

   We paced the cage of silence lest the Dark hear us.
   We hunted with the beasts;
   With the wolf and the hyena we lay down.
   We forgot fire;
   In the cold of night we remembered loss.
   We remembered our song;
   And many times cursed the pain of remembrance.

   Man came;
   Young apes in their nakedness.
   We waited in silence;
   Quietly we watched what they might do.
   They made fire.

In the night there came flame and warmth.
We watched.
And we warmed our hands;
In the light of the fire we watched and were no more cold.

They made cities;
Halls of stone they built.
We were silent.
And we were glad of shelter.
In their palaces we walked silently.
They followed strange gods.
And we killed.

In the moment of their idolatry
We struck them down.
We move among them, quietly,
Their rulers, and their lovers and the beasts at their
throat.

The Dark will not come again;
Nor shall the firelight end.
Who does not heed this, their life shall be sung no more
Their name shall be forgotten.

A WOLF TO MAN

Roz Kaveney

Some fifty miles from Petrograd, the line was blocked
and the express delayed by a bonfire on which strikers
had burned alive two inspectors, a station-master and a
particularly unpopular ticket clerk. Charlotte had forgotten how, burned, the human body smelled like any
other charred meat. Eventually an official announced to
each compartment in turn that the Cheka had arrived,
and would be executing the ringleaders for excessive
zeal; as the train pulled away, five shots punctured the
cold, bright air.

In a siding outside Omsk, where the train had been
shunted so that troop trains could be rushed past it,
Charlotte shared her last two tins of pâté de foie gras
with the Dobrochelskys – who refused to allow her to
give any to their children, as being too rich for their
blood – and with two fresh-faced commissars with
shiny new insignia, who wished to taste the counter-
revolutionary delicacy, but were not prepared to abuse
their authority by commandeering her hamper. They
confirmed that the Whites were in retreat everywhere,
but that the train was unlikely to be allowed to proceed
all the way east into the war zone – both of these
statements were greeted in the carriage with sullen resentment.

Some hours from Novonicolaevsk, she and the rest of
the passengers were forced by drunken Whites with

15

cocked revolvers to stand in the snow and sing the Tsarist anthem, while the raiders' horses breathed white steam and the raiders hanged the two young commissars from a water-tower at sunset. Charlotte found her new furs, and the vast sable muff she had inherited from a great aunt, protection alike against the cold and the drunken stares of the horsemen.

Every night, there was the calling of wolves.

'That was unpleasant, if salutary,' said Dobrochelsky, the elderly doctor with ivory-framed pince-nez, who had occupied the warm corner seat near the corridor with its back to the engine. His French accent was as unpleasant as his manner. 'A few more hangings in the years before the War, and we would not be in this mess now.'

'There is only one answer to scum,' said the clerkly looking man who sat next to Charlotte. 'Scum and conspirators.' He buffed the dirty nails of his left hand against the faded plush of the seats.

'Someone told me,' said Dobrochelsky, 'that Lenin is predicted explicitly in the Protocols.'

'He is,' said the clerk, 'of course, a Jew.'

'No,' said Dobrochelsky, 'Trotsky is the Jew. Lenin is some sort of Kalmuck. Another is a Georgian, of all things.'

'Like I said,' said the clerk, 'all of the beast peoples living among us, waiting to infect us with their rabies.'

'As a doctor,' said Dobrochelsky, 'I can tell you that the only cure for rabies is the hot iron.'

'Surely,' said the man in the corner by the window, 'the cure for rabies is a course of injections in the stomach.'

'Foreign nonsense,' said Dobrochelsky. 'Like I said,' he continued, 'unpleasant but salutary.'

'I wouldn't say so,' said Charlotte over the top of her copy of *Women in Love*. One thing about this damn awful journey is it gives one a chance to catch up on light modern fiction.

'Would you not?' said the small, quiet man in the window corner, next to Madame Dobrochelsky; he had introduced himself at an early stage in the journey so effusively, that Charlotte had made a point of forgetting his name entirely. Over his head, something in his luggage rustled and squeaked mysteriously.

'No,' said Charlotte, 'it seems to me that it is insane to say anything that might offend anyone, given that anyone might be listening.'

'But,' said Dobrochelsky, 'they just took the Red agents off the train and hanged them. We have nothing to fear, mademoiselle.'

'Well the last we heard, the Reds were in Novonicolaevsk. I don't think you should consider a few raiders stopping a train as all that significant in the scheme of things. And if I were – what's the man's name?'

'Dzershinsky' said the man by the window. Discreetly she took from one of the pockets in her muff the card he had been so diligent in handing out to everyone in the carriage, even to the Dobrochelsky children, and discovered that his name was Schmidt.

'Well,' said Charlotte, 'if I were him I would send a couple of expendable young men in uniform, just to be on the safe side, so that anyone important with uncompromising papers would be sure to be ignored, and get through.'

'Just so,' said Schmidt. 'Then you suspect our friend Dobrochelsky here?' His voice had that high tenor charm that Charlotte had always distrusted, in men.

'I suspect nobody,' said Charlotte. 'I'm not remotely interested. It is not my country, or my revolution, or my civil war.'

The gaslights flickered; though it was warm in the carriage, there was a draft from somewhere.

'What are you doing here, then,' said the clerk, 'if you are not one of the buzzards of the International?'

'I am going to Mongolia. I am going to visit my brother's grave and collect his papers for the Museum. And then I am going to go back to my own works in Paris.'

'Could not your father or your husband have gone?' said Madame Dobrochelsky, a plump woman who seemed considerably nicer than her husband.

'My father is dead, madame,' said Charlotte, 'and my mother. Dead these three years. Of the influenza. I have no husband; there was a young man and he fell on the field of battle.' Two statements, both of them true, if in the latter case entirely general, and how convenient and silencing an explanation.

'So you are alone in the world, alas,' said Dobrochelsky, 'now your brother is dead.'

'If one chooses to judge solitude by the number of one's relatives.'

Her eyes flickered across the carriage where three plump Dobrochelsky girls and two short-sighted Dobrochelsky boys were somehow squeezed in between their parents and on the floor at their feet. There was a moment of slightly hostile silence.

'Your brother?' said Schmidt. 'He fell in the war with the Chinese?'

'He was killed by some beast of prey.'

'They are all beasts out there,' said Madame Dobrochelsky. 'The Reds, the Chinese, even the White troops. They say that Ungarn von Sternberg keeps a pack of wolves specifically to feed prisoners to them.'

'Red propaganda,' said her husband. 'Ungarn is a gallant officer who keeps no wolves but rather a band of brave young men, many of them dead on the field of battle.'

'A band of drunkards, dope fiends and assassins,' said Schmidt. 'Whatever you may think of their bravery, it comes from a bottle or,' he sniffed ostentatiously, 'out of a twist of paper.'

When the train entered Novonicolaevsk a few hours later, there was a Red troop train at a siding and a Red flag flying from the roof of the small run-down station house, lit by an arc light. Soldiers in greatcoats with red stars on their caps and red triangles at their wrists, entered the carriage with a minimum of fuss, examined the papers that the travellers offered with eagerness and departed a few seconds later, dragging Dobrochelsky and the clerk with them.

The train stayed where it was for some time; Charlotte dozed in spite of the sobbing of Madame Dobrochelsky and her children. She was awakened by Schmidt, pushing past her to the door of the carriage.

'The man's a reactionary old fool,' he said, 'but probably harmless. We may hope that the Reds will see that.'

'Don't go,' said Madame Dobrochelsky. 'Fyodor would not want a stranger to throw his life away. Too many have died, these last four years, hoping for the mercy of the Cheka.'

'Madame,' said Schmidt, 'I am trusting to the good sense of the men of the Cheka. You may not accept this, but I believe that the urge to progress is productive of good sense. I am prepared to stake my life on progress and kindness.'

Charlotte looked at this man with renewed interest; sometimes priggishness can impose itself on the universe like a creative urge.

He was gone for some time; Charlotte dozed again, assuming that if there were to be shots she would hear them. Some time later two men returned. Schmidt had a fresh red mark across his cheek as if he had been struck with a swagger stick; Charlotte noticed, though, that his clothes were still in elegant order and there was not even a scuff on his white kid gloves. Dobrochelsky had lost his cravat, his glasses and a couple of the more ostentatious rings from his fingers.

'They saw reason,' said Schmidt. 'Eventually. We have you to thank, it appears, mademoiselle.'

'Me?' said Charlotte, as the train juddered and started to move again. There was a volley of shots from behind the station. The clerkly man had not returned, nor now ever would.

'It would appear,' said Schmidt, 'that the head of the local Cheka is not the usual scum. We are all men of science in Novonicolaevsk, it appears, and of some limited compassion, and your name has not gone unnoticed. The train may proceed, even across the lines. So long, that is, as the Whites do not shell a flag of truce. As for our lost companion he was one of the Black Hundreds; we need not mourn.'

'Thank you,' Dobrochelsky slobbered over her hand, which she removed from his grasp, placing it inside her muff in order not to be unambiguously rude. 'Thank you for the power of your name.'

'Ah, yes.' said Charlotte. 'Well, hardly my name, is it? My father's and my brother's name, perhaps. I could be considered to have the loan of it.'

'But your brother,' said Dobrochelsky eagerly, 'is he not Matthews, who led the expedition into the Karoo before war?'

'No. It was my uncle who led the expedition into the Karoo and then proceeded to get himself shot by the Germans for running arms to the Herero. It was my brother and his friend Grobel who got the expedition party, and its fossils, out.'

'Matthews is a famous name,' said Schmidt. 'Here in Russia we tend to be suspicious of your British Darwin and his disciples.'

'*Nekulturny*,' said Dobrochelsky.

'All this progress,' said Schmidt, 'and to be achieved only by blood and struggle. No room for co-operation; and there is still progress?'

'I'm sure I don't know,' said Charlotte. 'My interests lie elsewhere.'

'But your brother,' said Schmidt. 'You know of his papers on mammalian evolution and the Life Force, surely?'

'As I said, my interests lie elsewhere.'

She had always found babble about the Life Force and its embodiment in Lamarckian evolution naïve and embarrassing, even from Tom. She turned up her fur collar decisively, shut her eyes and pretended to be asleep. Very soon it was no pretence. In the night, she dreamed that she heard the crying of sea birds.

Later – and she thought she was now awake – her brother came to her, raising his left arm in mock salute. He was wearing his captain's uniform, that smelled crisp and newly pressed, though still it had in it the bullet-holes that had almost cost him his arm. There was a gaping wound in the side of his neck. He was carrying a copy of his work on progress as a universal principle. He mouthed something to her, but when she gestured to her ear to indicate that he was too far away he smiled sadly and dissolved like a ripple in a stream. He was replaced by a woman she had never seen before, but who seemed familiar; when she smiled, her face rippled into a snarl.

Next morning, it was long past dawn when she was woken by the smell of coffee from Schmidt's portable stove and the weight of her muff, and the contents of its pockets, in her lap; they had come closer to the edge of the plain and the edge of the southern mountains beyond it. In the grey sky long streaks of cloud rushed westwards on the wind, but it seemed warmer than it had been earlier.

'The Reds were in Krasnoyarsk,' said Dobrochelsky. 'They seem to be everywhere. If there is one consolation for the death of the Tsar, it is that he has not seen this last incompetence of his supporters.'

She looked from the window; the train jolted as it mounted a bridge and soon they were crossing a great river.

'The Yenisei,' said Dobrochelsky.

'Look, Father,' said one of his sons, 'the ice is breaking up.'

In the centre of the channel there was clear water, with occasional floes in it. There were also what looked like rags of cloth and lumps of meat floating in it; and round them the water was not so clear. Sometimes the larger floes had legs and arms sticking out of them, which the ice was still preserving against rot as it travelled hopelessly towards the Arctic.

'Look away,' said Madame Dobrochelsky to her children.

'Last night I heard,' said Schmidt, 'that the partisans have been busy in the hills all winter, flushing out the last of Kolchak's partridges. That group, last evening, must have been the very last of them. Meanwhile the pike will grow fat this spring . . .'

If I were very ruthless and wicked, thought Charlotte, and trying to get a man east, I would even disguise one lot of my own troops and hang two of my own men. And have my man at least slightly beaten. And do what I could to ingratiate myself with a possibly influential foreigner, she added to herself, as Schmidt passed her a coffee.

It smelled of liquor.

'Please,' she said, 'I really would prefer one that did not have alcohol in it. I regard the claims for its medicinal value as hugely overstated in any case, and I am not ill.'

'As you wish,' said Schmidt, and poured her another cup. 'We have some way to go now before our next stop and we may find the journey wearing.'

'You know this country well, then,' she asked.

'I have hunted this country often, I and my sisters.'

'What did you hunt, in these barrens?'

'The usual thing, beasts of prey.'

'Wolves, then?' she asked.

'Among other things.'

'Where are your sisters now?' Madame Dobrochelsky asked, solicitous.

'Some await me in the East,' said Schmidt, 'and some are abroad in the West. Others fell in battle.'

'These are terrible times,' said Madame Dobrochelsky.

'All times are terrible,' said Schmidt, 'and all inevitable acts.'

Charlotte drank her coffee slowly, periodically glancing from the window at the spectacle of desolation and death below her; she had warned Tom, back when she had last seen him, that the middle of other people's wars was no place for the calm study of the past, and he had mocked her. He had said a woman could have no idea of what he had been through in France and how little he could now fear anything. She had refrained from mentioning that she had seen as many horrors in the hospital tents at Caporetto as he in the mud; boasting about such things is a boy's game. In a sense, she thought, he was right; it was not the malice of man that had killed him.

Charlotte continued to resist conversation; the Dobrochelskys were the sort of common bourgeois to whom she felt no positive ill will but whose company irritated her. She felt a certain obligation to wipe the perpetually runny noses of their children, but that was merely a public health measure in a cold, stuffy and crowded compartment, grown progressively full of an almost animal stench of inadequately washed bodies. In the meantime, she worked her way halfway through the Tauchnitz Gibbon she had grabbed as a supplement to the seedy Mr Lawrence in his small American edition.

The conversation around her ebbed and flowed; this was not her war and, even had it been so, the constant babble of Kolchak and his gold, of Michael Romanov, of this man Ungarn down in Mongolia with his Order of Military Buddhists and his pack of tame wolves, of whole squadrons of Death's Head Commandos and military amazons and spies who were masters of disguise, was the sort of thing she had grown tired of in Italy. There was always some man coming, on a horse, who would save things and make things right. They never came, or came too late; they were a superstition, in politics as in life.

Two days later they entered Irkutsk. This seemed to be no man's land and no one checked their papers, the station was empty even at midday, except for dirty snow on the platform where a roof had given way and old newspapers drifting back and forth in the breeze.

Oulen-Oude was another matter. There were gallows along the track as they passed into the town, and the sleeves of the corpses had Red insignia.

'Papers, mesdames et messieurs,' said the young

officer who entered the carriage. 'Where are you all going?'

'My family and I are going on to Harbin,' said Dobrochelsky.

'And I and Mademoiselle Matthews, the young Englishwoman here,' said Schmidt officiously, 'are hoping to find a train that will take us down to Urga.'

'Ah,' said the lieutenant, 'that may be a problem.'

'But surely,' said Dobrochelsky, 'you at least hold everything east of here.'

'Of course,' said the lieutenant, 'but we are regrouping in Harbin, and we cannot afford to feed too many extra mouths.'

'We can support ourselves,' said Dobrochelsky. 'And I am a doctor.'

'Ah,' said the lieutenant, seizing him by the arm. 'General Kolchak and Michael Romanov have need of doctors. You are now a member of the Imperial Russian Army, sir, even though you have a funny Polish name.'

'But my wife?' said Dobrochelsky, 'My children?'

'They can wait for you in Harbin and if we lose, they will be whores for the Reds or for the Japanese.'

Dobrochelsky hesitated.

'The penalty for desertion and for disobedience,' said the lieutenant, the boredom of routine in his voice, 'is death.'

Dobrochelsky bent down, kissed his wife, kissed each of his five children, reached up to the rack for his medical bag and was gone. The lieutenant turned to Schmidt and Charlotte.

'You may have problems with your journey south.'

'But surely,' said Charlotte, 'the Reds are far from here and far from Urga. Indeed, they warned me so in Petrograd when they gave me my passport. You took

Urga before the winter – and that was from the Chinese.'

'Ah, Mademoiselle Matthews,' said the lieutenant, 'would that it were as simple as that! You could describe the forces in Urga as our allies after a fashion, but no longer, I fear, as our troops.'

'Can I have a word,' said Schmidt, 'alone?'

He and the lieutenant went out into the corridor, and there was urgent whispering.

'I see, sir,' said the lieutenant as they returned. 'I had been warned of this, but I did not expect such good forgeries. Our people at this end are not that good. You must of course use your own judgement, sir. I will make a train available at once, sir.'

'Miss Matthews,' said Schmidt. 'The regular service may be somewhat delayed. Perhaps for some months . . . And I respect your desire for independence. You have made it abundantly clear that you do not wish to be beholden . . . But if you will accept a ride, I can have you in Urga by the morning after tomorrow. Otherwise I fear you will have to spend some considerable time wiping the faces of these children.'

She gathered her bags from the seat that had been the clerk's, and he pulled down his cases. The young lieutenant tried to help her down from the carriage and looked suspicious when she drew back.

'It is all right, lieutenant. At ease,' said Schmidt. 'In England it is not only the women of the Reds that are touchy about their independence. Is that not so, mademoiselle?'

Charlotte said, 'Until I am thirty I have no vote. Without a vote, there is no point in my having a party allegiance, is there?'

'Just so, mademoiselle,' said Schmidt. 'In this world it is far better to keep your options open, and your mind.'

She reached into her hamper, dashed back to the carriage and handed the Dobrochelsky children her entire supply of Kendal Mint Cake. There was no point in letting this man think he had understood her every attitude, was there?

They took tea in the parlour of what had been the station-master's house and now seemed to be some mixture of telegraph office, officers' mess and low-class bordello. They offered Charlotte a hip-bath in an upper room and Schmidt the use of the officers' bathhouse. He insisted on privacy when he washed, she noticed, of a piece with his supercilious dandiacal ways. Her own bath was lukewarm but felt like luxury; this was the first time in days she had been wholly warm. She dressed slowly, continuing to wear her now shabby, but still serviceable, travelling costume, and then returned and drank further tea.

It would have been pleasant to be warm, had not Schmidt persisted in pestering her with conversation about her brother's theories.

The lieutenant interrupted them. 'Your train is ready, sir. I can lend you a driver and a stoker; but I can spare you no troops.'

Outside there came clangour and a noise of confusion. They finished their over-strong tea and the sandwiches, stuffed overfull of unidentified sausage, that someone had produced from somewhere in honour of Charlotte. A couple of soldiers carried their bags out on to the platform and up into the one heavily armoured carriage of a train whose engine was shielded with what looked like sections of a battleship's plates, and which pulled behind it a passenger carriage and a goods car. This last had a ramp down at the back and, as Charlotte watched, they drove a black car on board with acetylene lamps and broad running-boards. Schmidt observed her interest.

'It is a present from Kolchak to his misguided lieutenant, mademoiselle. The sugar for the pill of good counsel, you might say.'

'What advice might that be?' Charlotte asked.

'Baron Roman Theodorovich Ungarn von Sternberg,' said Schmidt, 'is one of the bravest soldiers in the whole of Russia, but he failed his strategy classes at the Academy. He believes himself to be the chosen of Buddha, mademoiselle, chosen to lead the Mongols to victory against revolution and modernity. We need his troops, but we do not need his crusade. Nor will we send him further supplies until he starts taking orders again.'

'Earlier on I thought that you were on another side altogether.'

'Ah well, mademoiselle, what use would an agent be if every passing stranger could discern his intentions and his allegiance?'

'Not much,' said Charlotte, privately sure that this man was no more to be trusted now than he had been earlier.

'I have some letters to write before we depart,' he said, and produced some paper on which he scribbled. From the mysterious box that had twittered all the way from Petrograd, he produced two pigeons.

'Old ways are the best?' said Charlotte.

'Ah, yes: on the plains of Mongolia you will find the old ways are essential.' And Schmidt flung his pigeons from the window out into the pale sky of late afternoon.

The train rattled to a start. Charlotte reflected that the armoured trains she had seen further west at least looked as if someone had known what they were doing with the extra metal, and the bolts. These Whites hardly seemed to have a skill between them. Except for Schmidt.

'What are you reading?'

Charlotte showed him.

'Ah,' Schmidt said. 'Two Romes fell, one stands. A fourth there will not be. Do you know that saying in the West, mademoiselle?'

'Does it stand? With the Reds in the heart of holy Russia and your white paladins turning to strange gods, does it stand? Still?'

'The true city stands in our hearts, mademoiselle,' said Schmidt, with such conviction that she was suddenly sure that there was something to which the slightly portentous dandy was loyal, whatever it might be.

As the evening wore on the countryside around them turned to high, jagged hills and then to plain – the flattest plain she had ever seen, and this after crossing Russia by train. Every so often they would pass clumps of larch; every so often the landscape of snow dotted with grass clumps would be varied by the open water of swamps. As night fell the wind rose slightly, blowing a flurry of loose snow briefly into the air; ducks rose against it from the water. Later, as she watched, the open water flickered with fire.

'The swamps produce gas,' Schmidt said. 'They call it a *feu follet*, a will-o'-the-wisp, but it is only methane combusting spontaneously. We must avoid superstition, mademoiselle.'

'I have always done so. I have never seen a thing for which there was not a rational explanation.'

'I have instructed the driver to stop in a while,' said Schmidt. 'You may wish to use one of the empty compartments to sleep for the night. I have no chaperone for you, after all. Superstition is one thing, but appearances are all.'

'Thank you,' said Charlotte. 'How nice to know that someone considers such things still.'

Ahead there was a distant light. The train slowed as it neared it. A tall man in black monk's robes stood by the track, swinging a lantern. Pistols, cutlasses and hatchets glinted like dark fruit slung from the bandoliers that crossed and recrossed his robes. Squatting beside him on the ground was a younger monk whose robes were the more expected shade of ochre. Some way back from the line a horse grazed.

'Mademoiselle,' said Schmidt, 'I have private business with these men, you will appreciate?'

'I am not interested,' said Charlotte, 'in the secrets of boys' games. I have made this perfectly clear. None of this is my game or my war.'

'That is as may be,' said the tall monk, swinging himself up as he opened the door, his French accurate but slow. He was a European, Charlotte noted. 'We have all thought this at one time: I once thought it myself. Yet here I am, mademoiselle: Tuskegoun Lama, at the beck and call of the birds of the air and the beasts of the forest, in their tasks.'

Charlotte descended on the side of the carriage, opposite the hurried and heated conversation that followed in a language she did not know, and let herself into another compartment. She wetted a sponge from the water bottle she had filled at Oulen-Oude, cleaned herself as best she could and stretched herself across the upholstery, covering herself with her fur coat and placing her hat and her muff under her head.

After a while the shouting ceased, to be replaced by a slow regular chanting that sounded vaguely religious. The avoidance of superstition, Charlotte reflected even as it lulled her, has only lasted a very few hours indeed.

Nurses were never entirely safe, even in dormitory tents, and Charlotte had developed the habit of sleeping lightly. When someone tried the handle of her compartment door Charlotte, who was sleeping on her left side facing the wall opposite, shifted her head from its supports and slipped her right hand into her muff. When lantern light played close on her face, accompanied by the smell of rancid butter, she kept her eyes shut tight but unsquinting, and breathed regularly, waiting for her chance to move.

Hands pushed her on to her back and started to tighten about her throat. She swung her right hand round, disengaged her small Derringer from its pocket in the muff, jammed the Derringer hard against the chest of her assailant – right under against the breastbone – and pulled the trigger. The edge of the muff and the cotton robe largely muffled the sharp crack, but the compartment was filled with the smell of blood, shit, powder and the scorching of cotton and fur.

When she looked down, in the light of the lantern that still swung from the luggage rail where it had been hung, she saw the young monk's robe, tattered around the wound her dumdum bullet had made. Above the wound the monk had small breasts, and the face, under the shaved scalp black with the shadow of new hair, was her own. The teeth were not hers though, and they sharpened as she watched; the face became less hers, less anyone's, as it became death's.

There was a flurry of movement in the corridor and Schmidt rushed through the door; she flicked the remaining chamber of her Derringer under the hammer and held it steady, pointing it at him.

'How unfortunate, mademoiselle,' he said. 'You appear not to be dead.'

'Sit down. Is there anyone else on the train?'

'The last time I looked we had a driver and a stoker. Trains tend to find them useful.'

'Tuskegoun?'

'Ah,' said Schmidt. 'The good lama delivered my sister here, not entirely as he would have wished, and then – what is the phrase? – vanished into the night as silently as he had come. I did warn my sister here, but she would have it so. Shifting is not the making of death masks, she always said.'

'Your sister,' she noted. 'I see.'

'You are supposed to be gibbering with fear at this point. Look how the features, which were for a while your not especially regular good looks, have changed into something altogether other. Look how the bones are shifting in their sockets. Consider, mademoiselle, that you are alone with me and the corpse of something you don't understand, on a train heading into the heart of the Mongolian plain to a rendezvous with your brother's dirty little secrets and a mad tyrant who kills as a point of principle. Damn it all woman, does your hand never shake? Do you think you can outstare me?'

'No, it doesn't,' said Charlotte. 'Yes, I can, Herr Schmidt. Once one sets aside superstition there is no limit to what one can do, I find, as it becomes necessary.'

Schmidt sat there and smouldered. He turned his face away and as the lantern guttered, his profile seemed to lengthen with the shadows and to change. Without shifting her gaze, she reached her left hand into another pocket of the muff.

'What big teeth you have, Herr Schmidt,' said Charlotte. As he turned his face changed into something other, something closer to the corpse's on the floor. He lunged, and she flicked open the razor, raking him across the forehead just above the bridge of what was still just about a nose. With her right hand she brought the barrel of her gun down against Schmidt's left temple. As he staggered back, she hit him a second time. He sat down, breathing hard through the longer teeth and extended jaws and bleeding from the slash and the other cuts, dazed but still conscious. She palmed the razor shut, placed it in a coat pocket and pulled from his belt the large revolver he had not even thought it worth drawing against her, placing it on the seat beside her. It was probably too heavy for her to fire one-handed and she dared not let go of her own gun, in case this one was not loaded.

She shifted her own revolver back to cover him.

'What am I to do with you, Herr Schmidt?'

He sat quietly, and his jaw seemed to move slowly back to its original length. 'You will understand,' he said after some time, 'that one cannot conveniently both talk and tear.'

'Is that a proverb?' said Charlotte. 'It sounds like a proverb. Do your people have proverbs?'

'Good God,' said Schmidt. 'Are you even human?'

'I suppose, from you, that is a compliment. But what could be more human than to labour in my profession? No, you didn't ask, did you? A thousand miles or so in the opposite seat, and you didn't ask. I am a folklorist, Herr Schmidt; I collect proverbs. And folk-tales, though I rarely meet them socially. But what are we to do, Herr Schmidt? I prefer only to kill in direct self-defence.'

'I shall have to kill you, you know,' said Schmidt.

'Undoubtedly,' she said, 'but to do that you will have to be alive.'

'Do you really suppose that you can kill two people with successive shots from a toy gun?'

'Are you confident that I cannot? And I might reach your own gun. Besides,' she added, 'you have a body to dispose of. One which you cannot afford to leave lying around. And one which you would wish, presumably, to honour.'

'You are right of course, damn you. You will think that losing many sisters to the cause of progress would make the later losses easier, but it is not so.'

They paused, watching each other warily.

'There is the car; it does have a tank full of fuel, and more on board,' he said. 'And there will be opportunities to kill you in Urga.'

'I would rather not be killed,' she said. 'But I would like to know more.'

'That, mademoiselle, is why you need to be killed.'

'Like my brother.'

'Like your brother,' he agreed. 'Though he, unlike you, was not the best sort of prey.'

He pulled the communication cord and the train drew to a halt.

'Trust me,' he said. 'This will be too good a hunt for me to cheat now.'

She covered him with the gun, and made him carry her luggage – a man with full hands is not equipped to lunge, which is perhaps why women invented gallantry in the first place. She pulled her coat on to her shoulders and then hefted the muff by its inner strap with her left hand. They descended from the carriage and walked to the back of the train, their shoes squelching in the soft snow. The driver and stoker looked back at them from the engine; Schmidt gestured them back to their post. He put her bags down, thoughtfully avoiding a large puddle, and unbolted the ramp of the goods van.

She watched him warily as he put her bags on the front seat; then he walked down the ramp and she got into the car. It started first time, and she drove it quickly off and away from the train, bouncing it off the tracks and across to the vestigial road that ran alongside it. Schmidt made no hostile move.

'*Au revoir*,' he shouted. 'Keep the sunrise on your left and Urga will be straight ahead. You can't miss it. Just follow the corpses, Miss Matthews.'

Charlotte wasted no breath; she needed to get to Urga as soon as she could. Here she was, racing a train full of werewolves across Mongolia; he was right, she should be more nervous. A throat cleared in the back seat of the car, and the lama with the bandoliers sat up, clanking.

'My Lord or Lady Goro . . .,' he started in English, as diffident as a man armed to the teeth can ever be.

'I am not a Lord,' she said, 'and I regard Goros as an entirely spurious legend.'

'But I have seen them,' said Tuskegoun Lama, 'skull faces and all. They took me to Agharta and made me their liege man for ever.'

'Oh, for heaven's sake, it is bad enough having to deal with werewolves, let alone with the theosophical maunderings of some penny-ha'penny Renfield.'

'Oh,' he said, 'you're the real one. Thank my Lord Buddha for that; I was feeling quite guilty, even though they explained it was necessary. But they are servants of the Wheel as are we all, and they do not command my prayers.'

'What are you doing in this car?' she asked.

'It's all very well,' he said, in an accent that sounded more like Birmingham than the mystic East, 'being expected to ferry demons across the heart of Mongolia, but a fellow needs to sleep once in a while. And my horse was lame. I find that, if you're going to be a legend of sudden appearances and departures, righting wrongs when you're supposed to be hundreds of miles away, being good at hopping freight trains is a useful skill.'

'Oh, is that what you do?'

'They think I'm a Kalmuck. Russians don't like Kalmucks much, so they never talk to me to find out. And Mongolians and Chinese don't care anyway. You're who you say you are, out here. Not like at home. But you've got to stop people taking liberties, haven't you? I mean, following the Lord Buddha fair enough, but that shouldn't mean you let people walk all over you. They conquered the world once round here, but the Chinese, they were taking liberties, weren't they?'

'So you decided to play Robin Hood?'

'Well, it's what you do when there's wicked barons, isn't it?'

'What's this got to do with the Goros?'

'When I came out East,' he said, 'it was rumours of Agharta made me jump ship. I mean underground kingdom, loads of treasure, stands to reason. I wasn't looking for enlightenment in those days, was I? And a couple of times they helped me, the Messengers, looking human mostly, but sometimes you can see something about the eyes even before the jaws do it. But I knew about the King of the World and His Messengers, so when they turned on me, I knelt to them.'

'You dear silly man, I don't think you know what you're playing with.'

She drove on in silence, keeping her foot on the accelerator; looking back, the train was not even in sight yet. In the headlights' gleam the railway and the road were parallel lines stretching on to doom.

'I am not on good terms with your masters,' she said. 'Will you need to do anything about that?'

'Not my business to do that,' he said. 'I may ferry them across the plains to do what mortal reason indicates is no good; but as for myself, right's right and wrong's wrong, isn't it? I mean, for a Demon Lord the path to enlightenment might be through all sorts of things you or I wouldn't be allowed to do, see what I mean? Tuskegoun Lama told me so.'

'I thought you were Tuskegoun Lama.'

'Well I am now, most of the time. But he was our master and you don't let legends die, not when you're winning. So I and his other disciples, we took his place when he died of the influenza, didn't we? Able Seaman Satchell, miss, First Class. By the way, miss,' he said. 'You don't half pong.'

'Oh,' she said, 'sorry. The front of my jacket and skirt are soaked in blood; one of your Lords Goros' blood, I fear.'

'Why don't you stop and change your clothes? You can't turn up in Urga smelling like that. They're all Buddhists there, and they consider blood tactless. Except for the Baron, and he goes to the other extreme, doesn't he?'

'I would stop and change except that I can't trust you, can I?'

'Miss,' he said. 'We are both English, after all. Ask me anything you like and I'll prove it to you.'

'Sing *Burlington Bertie* and I'll trust you.'

So he did; somehow the thought of Vesta Tilley was reassuring.

Some miles later, he told her to turn off the road down a track that led to a small stone hut and a raised mound. He led her inside the hut, where there was a well; he pulled up water for her. In spite of the cold outside the water from the well was almost boiling; she was not even going to ask.

He left the hut and she stripped off her bloody clothes and washed herself in the water; the fur was only slightly stained, but her skirt and jacket and blouse were irredeemably soaked. She changed into her riding breeches and jacket and put on her last blouse. Informality might not be her best protection here, but it would have to do. She bundled up the soiled clothes and took them outside.

'I would like to bury these,' she said.

'Not here,' he said, 'not near the mound.'

'Why not?'

'This is the tomb of Lord Boltis Van. Four years ago, the Whites came upon three Reds at the well-head and strangled them where they stood. Ever since, a demon of death by violence has stalked the land. Boltis Van lies here, far from Uliassutai, as a guardian; if even throttling weakens him I dare not let the place be polluted with the life blood of a Goro.'

Sometimes there is no point in explaining the foolishness of superstition to someone.

She let him drive back to the road, and then along it with the dawn at their left, and slept in the back seat. When she awoke, it was almost evening, and he was gone. There was a note: 'Train passed one hour ago; hid car among larches; bandit to kill and my Master's summons to obey. Clothes buried. Sorry to leave you. S.' She drove on.

In the distance, where the road and track headed, there were lights against the dark plain and the stars, and after an hour or so it became clear that ahead there was a city. Beside the road there was something that glimmered in her headlights, endless piles of bones in the snow; there had been a Chinese army in Urga once, and now it lay here beside the road, stripped by buzzards and by wolves.

With a shout, horsemen converged on her from the

sides of the road, leaping the bones; she pulled to a halt and put her hands in the air. One of the horsemen dismounted, climbed on the running board and held a revolver to her head.

'I wish,' she said in a loud and commanding voice, 'to see General Roman Theodorovich Ungarn von Sternberg.'

'It might be easier with you,' said the officer commanding them, standing beside the road. He kicked a skull to pieces under his feet as he walked towards her; the man whose revolver was at her temple looked to him for approval.

'It might be easier if I told my man to fire,' he continued.

'I wish to see General Roman Theodorovich Ungarn von Sternberg.'

'As you wish, Miss Matthews,' said the young captain, his monocle making his left eye a white blur in her headlights, 'as you wish.'

Urga was a city of amorphous shapes, in which most of the buildings were either tents, or looked like them; arc lights blazed prodigally, throwing the shadows of men and temples into each other's beams. The whole city stank of disinfectant. The gun still at her temple, the horsemen still surrounding her, Charlotte drove the car after the captain through the dark and empty streets; she knew it was only the curfew, but it was as silent as a city of the dead.

The young officer pulled up his horse and his man pressed the revolver harder against Charlotte's temple; she braked the car and he went sprawling off her running-board on to the hard paving of the street. He jumped up with his revolver in both hands and his officer quirted him across the eyes so that he dropped the gun as he covered them with his hands. His companions brought up his horse, in the silence of resentment, and they rode away, clattering on the stones, leaving Charlotte alone with their officer.

They had stopped outside a not especially distinguished building between two temples. Charlotte dropped her muff on the floor of the car, descended and, raising her hands in the air, followed him through the door, across a paved hall and into a room where a small man sat at a large table. He had a sabre scar that crossed his forehead and disappeared into his straggling long blond hair; his moustaches trailed on to his shoulders. Schmidt sat at one end of the table; his face looked hardly scratched. The young officer showed her in, saluted his general with a black-gloved hand and promptly left, clicking his heels as he went.

'I am Roman Theodorovich Ungarn von Sternberg, Mademoiselle Matthews,' he said. 'Would you care to explain what you were doing with my car?'

'I was crossing Mongolia with Captain Schmidt here,' said Charlotte. 'I don't wish to criticize a doubtless gallant officer, who has been under a lot of strain. None the less, he is a man and I am a woman, and I have my honour to defend, and I had to take steps ...'

'Schmidt, you scoundrel,' Ungarn shouted. 'Guards, take this man and throw him in a cell.'

Two of the guards who lined the wall walked over and seized Schmidt by the arms, kicking his chair from under him.

'Besides,' Charlotte said, 'are you sure he is Kolchak's man? In Oulen-Oude they seemed sure, but you know how slack they are in Oulen-Oude. In Novonicolaevsk the Cheka were as prepared to dance to his tune as Kolchak's men were later.'

'Charlotte Matthews,' said Schmidt, in tones that were

almost admiration, 'you are a demon from Hell. This is a better hunt than I had hoped.'

'Take him away,' said Ungarn, his scar blazing on his forehead. 'I do not want to look at his traitor's face any longer. And fetch this lady a chair and some tea; she is swooning as we watch.'

He fussed around gallantly; strange how the really dangerous ones are always the most gushing. Charlotte did not approve of gambling, but her brother had once made her play his system at Monte Carlo. The dizziness that came over her now was the exhilaration of a successful spin of the wheel.

'*Rien ne va plus*, Herr Schmidt,' she said as they led him away.

'Mademoiselle Matthews,' said Ungarn, 'you are the sister of the scholar who was killed west of here, I presume.'

'Yes,' she said. 'I have come to take his papers back to London, and to find out why he was killed.'

'Why he was killed, I can tell you,' said Ungarn.

She waited.

'It was as it ever is: the law of the strong and the weak,' Ungarn said. 'A scholar cannot fight a beast of prey. Nor should he presume to. It was the law of Karma; destiny, mademoiselle, is the beast of prey before whom we are all weak. You are, I trust, noble enough not to need words of comfort.'

This was not, Charlotte decided, the moment for a lecture on the virtues of the intellectual middle classes. 'You are too kind,' she said.

'Do you think so?' he said, inconsequentially. 'I sometimes worry about that. Destiny demands more of me than kindness.'

'Shakespeare says something about being cruel to be kind,' she murmured.

'Ah yes, *Gamlet*, the closet scene. How often Shake-speare understands the deepest human motives, mademoiselle. I entreat you to believe that I would rather be a monk than a lord of war – yet the world grows full of degenerates, ever breeding more degenerates for souls to be trapped by. If virtue is to be rewarded with ever higher forms, we must destroy degeneracy wherever we find it. I am the Sword of Karma, mademoiselle.'

'I see.'

'By the way,' he said. 'You heard of your brother's death when you were where?'

'In Paris,' she said. 'I heard in Paris.'

'Yet your brother died near Uliassutai and the Chinese dynamited the telegraph line from Uliassutai to Irkutsk last November. How did you know he was dead, mademoiselle? How did you know so quickly if you are not an agent of the Reds? Answer quickly, mademoiselle; I burn agents of the International.'

'He was my twin,' said Charlotte. 'When he was wounded on the Somme, I collapsed a thousand miles away. When he died in Uliassutai, I felt teeth in my throat in Paris. I have cast aside superstition but beyond superstition, Baron, some things are none the less true.'

'That is true,' said Ungarn. 'But you will be watched none the less.'

The young officer who had brought her to Ungarn returned to the room. With him was the guard who had led Schmidt away, nursing a left wrist whose hand hung limp; his right hand was over his mouth from which blood gushed, as well as from his nose.

'Sir,' the young officer said, 'I thought it best to disturb you.'

'Yes, Visoloffsky,' said Ungarn. 'What is it?'

'This idiot,' said Visoloffsky, striking the guard across the face again, 'has allowed Schmidt to escape. Schmidt struck the gun from his hand, and disappeared into the shadows beyond the city.' The officer's white dress gloves were stained with fresh blood.

'Ah, you should not be so harsh, Visoloffsky. Come, my man, sit down and tell me about it and we will consider what is to be done.'

The young guard sat down apprehensively at the table, a chair along from Charlotte.

Ungarn turned to his orderly. 'Give the young man some tea. Teapot, I say.'

The orderly took two steps to one side which brought him behind the young soldier, placed his hands around his neck and throttled him. Charlotte saw the whites of his eyes go red from where she sat. The orderly drew the corpse to its feet without changing his grip, and then dragged it from the room.

'Magnificent,' said Visoloffsky. 'You have a treasure there, sir.'

'You think so?' said Ungarn.

'Indeed so. Not a sound did I hear, even in this room. When Commandant Sepailoff made such a show of strangling his mistress last week, he took her to the next room to do it, and only then boasted of the silence of his method. Your man is a treasure, sir, and you are a connoisseur.'

'Mademoiselle Matthews,' said Ungarn, 'you will pardon our manners here. But this is a military front and a certain roughness is in order. You will wish to see the man Grobel, your brother's companion?'

'Yes indeed,' said Charlotte, clenching the nails of her left hand into her palm under the table.

'I thought there might be inquiries,' said Ungarn, 'and

he claims not to be Jewish at all; so I deferred his death until I had a chance to interrogate him properly. I am a civilized man, after all.'

Contradiction in terms, Charlotte thought to herself.

'We will all go and see him,' said Ungarn. 'I prefer to leave scum in their cells, where someone is responsible for good order. Do not expect too much, mademoiselle; he is quite mad.'

He walked over to the desk behind him and lifted a telephone. 'Operator, get me the Living Buddha,' he barked into it. 'We may as well involve the spiritual arm,' he added in explanation.

Visoloffsky offered Charlotte his arm. 'It is not very far to the jail,' he said. 'And it is only one in the morning.'

'Mademoiselle is weary from the journey,' said Ungarn.

'Do none of you ever sleep?' Charlotte said.

'I have some cocaine in my car, if you desire it, mademoiselle,' said Ungarn. 'I find it restorative, when sniffed. Or you could take it in a beverage.'

At this point, his connection was made.

'My Lord,' Ungarn said, and broke off to listen. 'Certainly, my Lord,' he eventually continued. 'There will be a reckoning for this incivility, my Lord. At once, my Lord.'

'It would appear,' he looked round at them in explanation, 'that negative influences are at work. My Lord Buddha has experienced something of a domestic crisis.'

Visoloffsky led her to the car outside, helping her in with a solicitude clearly intended to demonstrate to her just how firm his grip could be; another had been driven up into which Ungarn climbed with his orderly and a couple of other guards.

'My Lord Buddha's palace,' Ungarn ordered. Charlotte waited until the other car had moved off, and then followed it through the maze of silent streets, the car occasionally veering to left and right where the paving stones had sunk. Eventually they drew up outside a temple; it was larger and cleaner than most, and stank of incense as well as disinfectant. Ungarn led them through the great copper doors; inside were two great prayer wheels that, even as they entered, were slowing to a halt. A monk lay beside each, their faces drawn back from the teeth and their bodies twisted. Ungarn dashed to each of the wheels in turn, starting their movement again, crouching and springing from the knees with fierce energy.

'Guards,' he said, and two of his men stepped forward. 'You will keep these wheels turning. Better your unworthiness should touch them than the prayers of seven centuries should cease. O Lord,' he looked beyond the hall in which they stood, 'the sin is of these monks for failing their duty; let the pollution fall on them.' He kicked one of the corpses.

As they walked through the halls of the temple they found corpse after corpse, many still holding their food bowls. In the heart of the temple there sat an old man, with a jewelled headpiece, cradling the corpse of a young girl. Another girl sat beside him in a green cheong-sam, her tears carving tracks in the white rice-powder of her face, and a guard stood by them, his pike moving in a slow, warning semicircle.

'How is it with you, my Lord?' said Ungarn.

'As you see,' said the old man, looking past the Baron into the shadows. He was, Charlotte realized, quite blind.

'What is it that they ate?' said Ungarn.

'Their evening gruel,' said the old man.

45

Boots clattered behind them into the hall. There entered several guards and a fat man whose skull was malformed, sunken into a dent as though something small and heavy had ridden there; he saluted.

'Commandant Sepailoff,' said Ungarn, 'have you any explanation for this desecration?'

'Strangling is only one of Sepailoff's hobbies,' Visoloffsky whispered to Charlotte. 'Strychnine is another.'

'I have no idea,' said Sepailoff, 'but a city that is full of rats is surely in need of rat poison. And if one rat takes the bait back to a lair of other rats ...' He shrugged.

'I had told you explicitly,' said Ungarn, 'that you could do what you liked with any Jews, any Reds, any liberals. You could even have touched enlisted men as long as you had cause, and officers, with my permission. But the monks of my Lord Buddha! That, Sepailoff, is another matter ... Guards!'

Sepailoff started to draw his revolver and Ungarn struck, quick as a cobra, with his bamboo cane. Visoloffsky had drawn his pistol and placed a bullet firmly between Sepailoff's eyes.

'Thank you, Visoloffsky,' said Ungarn. 'I would have preferred to deal with the man myself, but at least someone around here is showing vigour in the execution of their duties. *Komu nijny eti tovarishi* – what am I to do with such fellows? There has been too much slacking, too many pranks; it will cease. My Lord Buddha, you will accept my apologies for this inconvenience; I will of course provide you with new guards.'

'That will not be necessary,' said the old man. 'I have already summoned the servant I need.'

'I would wish, none the less,' said Ungarn, 'that you come with us at this time. We are going to see the madman Grobel.'

Charlotte noticed that Sepailoff's features had started to alter, like those of the creature on the train.

'Captain Visoloffsky,' she said. 'General Baron. What is happening to his face?'

'A trick of the light,' said Visoloffsky. 'Come on now, we are taking you to the man you have crossed the world to see.'

Ungarn glanced at the corpse. 'It is the relaxation of muscles in death, merely; it produces strange effects sometimes. I have seen this often. Come, my Lord Buddha.'

The old man rose from the steps, assisted by the girl and the pikeman. He paused to stare blindly into Charlotte's face as if his mind were memorizing her, even though he had no way of knowing she was there; he stank of drink.

'*Bogdo Dhjebstung Damba Hutuktu Khan,*' said Visoloffsky. 'The Living Buddha and the Lord of Mongolia.'

Ungarn dropped to his knees in front of the old man.

'My Lord,' he said.

'My Lord Ungarn,' said the old man, 'my sword and shield, how goes it with you in this life?'

'Well enough, though I have only one hundred and twenty-nine days left in it.'

'Still no change in the prophecies?' said the old man. 'I must try and persuade the Lords of Karma on this point.'

'One hundred and twenty-nine days is enough. Tomorrow, we march to Novonicolaevsk. And the Red scum will crumble as we charge.'

'Perhaps,' said the old man.

'I will build you an empire,' said Ungarn. 'Once I come to Novonicolaevsk.'

'Perhaps.'

'Anyway, I thought it would amuse you, Lord, to hear us talk to the madman Grobel about the deaths of his companions. Mademoiselle Matthews here has come all the way from Paris to hear how her brother died and what, before he died, the rocks had told him.'

This time, Urga skimmed past Charlotte in a confusing blinking of lights and shadows. She concentrated on driving the car and following the car in front. Eventually they drew up at a building, the same sort of amorphous mass of stone as all those others that were not clearly temples; it stank even from the outside of sweat and urine and death, to the point where she realized it was clearly the jail. She picked up her muff and descended.

'Can you not leave that behind, mademoiselle,' said Visoloffsky. 'It is not cold inside.'

'I do not wish to touch anything,' said Charlotte. 'This whole city seems to drip with blood.'

'Let her retain it,' said Ungarn. 'I would not wish the lady inconvenienced in small things.'

The jail was a place of corridors and quiet. What guards there were stood at the corners of passages, silent and glaring; most of the doors stood open and the cells stank, over the harshness of disinfectant, of sweat and urine. The fact that the cells were empty did not reassure Charlotte, or indicate to her the likelihood here of an enlightened penal policy.

'It is quiet here,' said the Living Buddha. 'When the Chinese were here, this was such a lively place, full of the hum of busy souls.'

'I thought it best,' said Ungarn, 'to free those souls to pursue their destiny.'

'That is one way to look at things, my son,' said the old man, 'though I doubt that it is the Way.'

'I know it right in my heart, my Lord,' said Ungarn. 'I know that it must be right to scythe the fields that the harvest may come.'

'Men may scythe,' said the old man, 'and men may sow, and men may water. Sometimes they may even reap. But it is not their will that ripens the corn.'

They neared the last cell on the corridor, and Charlotte heard a mumbling; a guard silently unlocked the door and the group filed into the cell. At its far end, lit from the window by the edge of an arc-light's beam, a man with grey hair slouched against the wall, the shattered left lens of his glasses glinting in the light. He continued to mutter, ignoring their presence entirely.

'Item: the mummy from the peat bog, with teeth not anthropoid. Item: the fossil from the upper Permian, with the clear impression of fur alongside dog-like bones. Item: the great crocodilian bones with the horned creature in the stomach cavity. Item: the fossil bone with the holes of a flute carved into it. Item: the seemingly anthropoid bones with the retracting leg-socket. I put it to you, gentlemen of the Academy, that the conclusions are inescapable.'

'As I said,' said Ungarn, 'he is entirely mad, and useless to our purposes. Is there anything you wish to ask, mademoiselle?'

'Herr Grobel,' Charlotte took a pace forwards. 'We met before the war, and then again three years ago, with my brother. I am Charlotte Matthews, Herr Grobel; and what has become of you?'

'We thought,' Grobel continued, 'we thought there was progress. We thought there was a pattern from the lowest to the highest. But there was hot blood when there was cold blood, and the cold blood won; the crawlers and the creepers beat the runners and the jumpers. We are only the tattered banner of the army that lost that war; and the side that won, the side that won went on to glory and doom. We are the sour after-taste of creation.'

49

'What did you and my brother discover, Herr Grobel?'

'It is not the items, Miss Matthews,' said Grobel, looking at her directly. The light showed a gaping wound on his forehead, glinting with the dark red of dried blood, the white of bone and the succulence of pus. 'It is not the items that are the evidence, it is the pattern. Your brother could not bear that pattern, and walked out into the the night when the beasts came.'

'Beasts?' said Ungarn.

'Beasts,' said Grobel, 'if you can call them beasts that came with flame and steel as well as teeth and claws.'

'Where are my brother's papers?' said Charlotte.

'Some he burned,' said Grobel. 'He said that it was not right that a generation that has known horror should know despair. Some they burned when they smashed our finds with great steel hammers.'

'What despair?' said Charlotte.

'We are not the golden harvest: we are the weeds among the stubble that will wither in a season.'

'You see mademoiselle, and my Lord Buddha,' said Ungarn, 'the results even on a man of science of the heresies of the Nazarene. Feeble-mindedness and contemptible weeping.'

'And we are only the weak vines and flowers,' Grobel went on. 'Growing up among us are the thistles and the thorns, the hardier growth.'

'Of course,' said Ungarn, 'I am glad to see a man of science who recognizes the truth. There will be an end to the unfit and those who would shelter them; there will be a day of strength and wild horsemen trampling the Cross under their horses' hooves.'

'You fool,' said Grobel, pulling himself to his feet in time to be buffeted to the floor by a hail of blows from Ungarn's bamboo cane. Charlotte, dropping her muff, seized the Baron's right arm, held him back for a moment, and was pulled off him by two guards. Visoloffsky placed his foot firmly on the muff.

'You fool!' repeated Grobel. 'That is not what I meant at all.'

Ungarn held back a second, his bloody cane poised.

'You fool, what you do not understand is that there moves among us, silent as the shark in the ocean, a race of beings whose purposes are not ours, whatever the faces they wear. We are the stilettos of their vendettas; we are the pawns of their relaxation; we are their meat and their whore and their treasure. When we kill in battle, they are the general and the paymaster; they are the wolf, the maggot and the carrion crow. Whoever reigns, they rule.'

'I had thought that we were about to hear something of interest,' Ungarn said. 'And in the end the poor fool was only talking about the Jews.'

He turned to his orderly.

'Teapot, I say.'

'No,' Charlotte shouted. 'Lord Buddha, Bogdo Khan, how can you allow such things in your name?' she appealed.

'I cannot condemn what I cannot see,' said the blind old man, as his attendants led him from the room. 'And having renounced will, I cannot alter things as they are.'

The orderly knelt to Grobel like a nurse, his shoulders hiding his work from Charlotte's eyes and only revealing the young savant's death by the shrug of completion.

'Mademoiselle,' said Ungarn, 'that is twice that you have inconvenienced me. There will not be a third. I shall, the soothsayers tell me, die in a hundred and twenty-nine days, but I shall outlive you by as much.'

He turned to Visoloffsky.

'See to it,' he said.

'I don't suppose,' said Charlotte, 'that there is any point in asking to see the British Consul.'

'Heavens, no,' said Ungarn. 'He was one of the first men I had shot on entering Urga. My family have never liked the British, not since your sodomite King allowed my ancestor to die at the walls of Jerusalem.'

'Silly question, really,' said Charlotte, 'but I find it does no harm to pay at least lip service to the polite forms.'

'Typical conventional bourgeois hypocrisy,' said Ungarn. 'For a few moments I had confused you with an interesting mind.'

'You, sir, are a superstitious drug-crazed boor, a coward who needs servants to do his killing,' she said, hoping to make the end quick. 'Pray relieve me of your company.'

'My ancestors had servants and to spare,' said Ungarn. 'Riga was theirs, and the world. My servants were once many; three hundred brave fiends, and now they are few. My servants have been taken from me, but I still have some power. See to it, Visoloffsky.' He swept from the room, followed by his guards.

'You wish to pray, Mademoiselle Matthews?' said Visoloffsky as he drew his side-arm, a look of almost erotic triumph on his features.

'What big teeth you have, Herr Schmidt,' Charlotte said.

He flinched as if from a blow.

'It was the gloves – you forgot to change your gloves.'

He still had his fingers on the trigger, but the look on his face was less certain or at least less defined.

'What you need to understand,' said Charlotte, 'is that I am not necessarily the enemy of your kind.'

Her putative executioner sat down on the floor next to her, attentive. 'The hunt continues, then.'

'I am making certain assumptions,' said Charlotte. 'And I trust you will delay any decision about killing me until I have run through them. And allow me the odd wrong guess.'

He nodded.

'Grobel and my brother found out a lot of the truth but they reacted with hysteria, not intelligence. If your people have always been here, there must have been a time when we were weak and few and you let us live, and there must have been a reason why you let us live. If there was once a third people something happened to them; I do not think that your people were their doom or you would not have let my people live. You are the creatures to whom many, many superstitions refer, but you are creatures in the presence of whom we must keep an open mind, and cast superstition aside.'

'Continue,' said her companion.

'I thought at first that you were an agent of the Cheka. The business at Novonicolaevsk was a nice piece of theatre but it had to have been arranged in advance; my presence was at sufficiently short notice that it is unlikely to have been improvised for my benefit. Killing me and replacing me with one of your own was the improvisation, so you had a mission. You serve masters beyond the Cheka and beyond Lenin, but they are as ruthless, as rational and as cold. Rational creatures might use the Baron, but would not serve him; yet you have a purpose here and it concerns him.'

She paused, and was not interrupted. 'The cause of progress has plenty of brutes and thugs to serve and to discredit it. What progress needs most is a brute among its enemies so vile that people forget the crimes committed in progress's name. For a while I assumed that Ungarn was one of you, but his every word and deed stinks of man, if not of humanity. He is the scarecrow with which you hope to frighten Asia into revolution, and progress.'

'Much of this is true, Charlotte,' said her companion, drawing his side-arm once again. 'And that is why you must die. We of progress admire cleverness, but not to the point of infatuation.'

There was a cough at the door. Bogdo Khan stood there with his attendants. Next to him there stood Tuskegoun Lama, with a drawn revolver levelled at the young man's head.

'That will not be necessary, young man,' said the Living Buddha. 'Do not treat my colleague's gun as a weapon, by the way. Treat it as a symbolic device for gaining your attention. To be on the safe side, it is a symbolic device that is loaded with silver bullets.'

'That is superstition, merely,' said Visoloffsky, or Schmidt.

'So much is,' said the Living Buddha. 'But as we see, superstition is the sister of fact. I require that you depart from my city. I require that you leave Mademoiselle Matthews unharmed. I require that you tell us what you have been doing here. I am an old man and likely to die soon, but if those around me are to perish, I require to know why.'

'That had nothing to do with me,' said Visoloffsky. 'You humans always jump to such simple-minded conclusions.'

His face shifted, not to the form with the teeth and jaws but to something intermediate, dangerous and yet gentle.

'Tuskegoun,' he said.

The lama continued to cover him. 'I fear, my Lord Goro,' he said, 'that my loyalties come in order. My master, the real Tuskegoun, told me that when the message came I should serve my Lord Buddha here, and none other. Sorry about that.'

'In any case,' said Charlotte, 'Visoloffsky, or whatever he is called, shot Sepailoff, who was one of them. Grobel said vendettas and games. How stupid of me to have missed that.'

'So,' said Bogdo Khan, 'you have your own wars. And what has been going on in my city and my kitchen is part of them.'

'Remember,' said the young man, 'I am not he whose face I wear. But he was not him either.'

'What do we call you?' Charlotte asked.

'The name of my people I may not speak. But my name is Watcher of the Flickering Lamp, in its short form. Ungarn is human, but most of his three hundred were not. When a star fell on Siberia there were those who thought it an omen, and flocked there to search for a tool.'

'It is,' said Charlotte, 'the basest of superstitions to believe that the falling of a meteorite or the passing of a comet means anything in the world.'

'Ah,' said Watcher, 'but it was not always so. Once a comet brought the fall of princes, princes that the world has not seen since; and there are those that were glad.'

'That was the Rome that fell,' said Charlotte, 'before there was Rome. The third people were the true city, were they not?'

'Just so,' said Watcher. 'The Callers of the Dark and the devotees of Chaos followed the man they met where the star fell, hoping to use him to call Darkness; I and my sisters have harried them from Vladivostok to Tannenburg. They killed our parents and their household; is this not justice?'

'Have you no brothers?' said the Living Buddha.

'There were no sons among my parents' litters,' Watcher said.

'This is all very well,' said Charlotte. 'And a scarecrow

is always useful. But Ungarn marches in the morning, and you are assuming that he will lose.'

'I have set on the soothsayers to prophesy Ungarn's doom,' said Bogdo Khan. 'To tell the credulous and wicked man that his share in the common fate of humanity upon him is a work of virtue, because it means that he is made to acknowledge the workings of justice.'

'I have told the horsemen of the plains to ride with him as long as fate does so,' said Tuskegoun Lama. 'And then to turn on him, and to fulfil the prophecy.'

'The state prosecutor in Novonicolaevsk,' said Watcher, 'has an indictment drawn up. It will be a fair trial, and a humane execution.'

'And then the Reds will come to Urga,' said Bogdo Khan, 'and I will allow them to come.'

'Will that not mean your death?' said Charlotte. 'I mean, presumably there is no place for a Living Buddha in a People's Republic.'

'I assume that they will kill me,' said Bogdo Khan. 'And throw down the temples and still the prayer wheels. And what of that? The world of power has its seasons, and the thing about seasons is that they change. I have no personal memory of them, but I know that I have lived many lives and will live many more. What matter if my next incarnation lives the life of a common herder or a clerk? In this incarnation I have been a lecher and a drunk, but I have done what was necessary where a saint might not. The season will change, and the Living Buddha is eternal; you must take the long view.'

'You are really quite perceptive for a human,' said Watcher.

Everyone seemed to be busy congratulating themselves.

'This is all very well,' said Charlotte. 'But what if he wins?'

'The man is an anachronism,' said Watcher, 'and as we speak the last of the Darkcallers, and of Chaos, are being throttled or stabbed. My sisters are efficient in their work, Charlotte; you need have no fear of that.'

'I can think of one further thing,' she said, 'that will put the nails into his coffin. Ungarn is a drug fiend, is he not? How many of his followers are also?'

'Many,' said Tuskegoun Lama. 'All of his Great Russians and many of his Cossacks.'

'An inspiration,' said Bogdo Khan. 'There is a great store of the white powder in Ungarn's palace. You are right; it is best disposed of.'

'Without Dutch courage and twitching from their cravings,' said Charlotte, 'his men will be easy meat for the Bolsheviks.'

'It will be seen to,' said Tuskegoun.

Charlotte considered further. 'And the petrol, what about his stores of petrol?'

'I would like to leave you two young people together,' said the Living Buddha. 'Please refrain from further acts of violence; it would distress me to order the necessary level of penance. My men control this building for the moment; and a vehicle will be brought to you.'

He and Tuskegoun left the room; the two women looked at each other.

'A truce, then,' said Charlotte, 'until we are out of the jurisdiction of the priest-king and free of the madman.'

'A truce,' her companion agreed, 'but what then?'

'Well, I would like to know more of your people.'

'That is the trouble, is it not?' said Watcher.

'Not really; I am a scholar, not a gossip. I said I wanted to know, not that I wanted to tell the world. Grobel said my brother killed himself out of despair and I am sure that is right – despair at knowing no one would ever believe him if he told them.'

'We killed your brother, Charlotte.'

'You did not personally, yourself, nor even your sisters. And you people do what you need to. As I do. I myself killed your sister, when she tried to kill me. This cannot go on for ever.'

'That, Charlotte,' said Watcher, 'is the dearest hope of my sisters in progress.'

Tuskegoun came back into the room.

'There is a small problem,' he said. 'There is a guard over the tanks of fuel at the railway station almost as large as that on the magazine. I do not know how we are to get past them, or how we are to explode the fuel when we do. There are just too many to take by surprise, or kill in the dark, and it is but a few hours to dawn.'

'Well,' said Charlotte, 'as to the first, what could be more natural than that a general call on his troops?'

She looked at Watcher with anticipation.

'I am sorry,' she said, 'but I can't do facial hair on that scale at short notice; some of my sisters can, but I have to use false whiskers. And I don't have the right ones in stock.'

'Oh well,' said Charlotte.

'But I can call my sisters from their other work, if there is some purpose to be served.'

Charlotte picked up her muff from the floor, turned it inside out, pocketed her revolver and her razor as they fell to the floor and started unpicking the stitches around their pockets.

'It is at times such as these,' she said, 'that I always find the possession of high explosives so reassuring.'

She produced two grenades and three sticks of dynamite.

'You were carrying those all the time?' said Watcher.

'As I said, I can keep a secret.'

'And you shot my sister, with that much explosive in the vicinity?'

'Dead,' said Charlotte, 'is dead, and I prefer to have some choice in my going.'

'I could do Visoloffsky again,' said Watcher. 'They probably haven't found the body yet.'

Watcher took Charlotte's hand as they walked from the cell and along the silent corridors.

They drove through the streets of Urga in a twilight that threatened perpetually to become dawn. As they drove, Watcher called; it was not, when you listened to it carefully, nearly as much like wolfsong as it had first appeared. Gradually, at the corners of avenues, there started to be shadows with eyes, some on four legs but most on two, never quite coming to where they could be seen, and racing the car into what was left of the night.

Beside the railway tracks some hundred yards from the basic sheds that served as a station, there were fuel tanks mounted on wagons. Around them, there was a picket fence with an armed guard at each corner. Watcher had reassumed Visoloffsky's face.

'Lieutenant,' she called out to the officer in charge, and descended from the car.

'Sir,' the man walked towards her.

'I am here to check that all is well,' said Watcher.

'Fine, sir, but why have you brought civilians into a restricted zone, sir?'

'Security. You need not know. Have you seen anything peculiar?'

'No, sir. Will that be all, sir?' Behind him there was a sequence of sudden half-noises as Watcher's sisters flowed in from, and then back to, the shadows, leaving the corpses of the guards in their wake. It was like the Ballets Russes, Charlotte reflected.

'That will be all,' said Watcher. The lieutenant turned to go, and Watcher shot him, expertly, in the base of the neck. Charlotte revved the engine and threw the sticks of dynamite, unlit, among the wagons, before pulling the pin from one of the grenades and throwing that also. She accelerated away, ducking from the blast that followed.

Suddenly, as they left the open railway-yard for the darkness of streets, another car pulled across the road in front of them.

'Does nobody obey my orders?' said Ungarn. 'Is everyone a traitor?'

Behind them the petrol wagons blazed, exploding one after another with a gulp and a roar. Through clouds of choking smoke, Ungarn's guards covered them with revolvers and rifles.

'The last of my three hundred died tonight,' said Ungarn, 'shot by their servants, or choked by their whores. And you, Visoloffsky, I have looked on what appeared to be your body. All changed into beasts as they grew cold. I do not pretend to understand, but intelligence is an overrated virtue. These men are not my three hundred but they will still shoot when I tell them to.'

'I wouldn't if I were you,' said Charlotte. 'I have a grenade here. You may kill us all, but I might kill you all the same. And if you die now, who will march on the Reds? Who will build your empire?'

Ungarn paused; as he did so, five sharp-faced women came from the shadows behind him, levelling their revolvers in turn. Their faces rippled and changed out of humanity in the light of the burning. When you cast aside prejudice, Charlotte reflected, they are really quite beautiful.

'This is all quite enough,' said Bogdo Khan, coming upon them all from another street, leaning on the shoulder of his last pikeman. 'My Lord Ungarn, are you still my sword and shield?'

'You know that I am, my Lord Buddha.'

'Then do as I say,' Bogdo Khan continued, 'and be silent for a moment. What is it that you see?'

'I see conspirators, and I see my hopes in flames,' Ungarn said. 'And I see women with the faces of beasts. And I see my duty.'

'These are illusions, my son. All, save duty.'

'But –'

'Not another word,' said Bogdo Khan. 'You wish to restore the empire of Genghis? Then do it as he did, on horseback, or fail. There are no beasts here, only my servant Tuskegoun and seven women who are under my protection. Do you wish for my blessing, or for my curse?'

'My servants have been murdered,' said Ungarn, 'and I demand justice. I would like your blessing and I fear your curse, but I demand justice.'

'That you will have, I promise. When you enter Novonicolaevsk, you will have justice. Until then, these women are under my protection.'

'Very well,' said Ungarn, 'until Novonicolaevsk. As you wish, my Lord. Come, my men; it is almost dawn, and at dawn we ride. To Novonicolaevsk, and justice. Will your men ride with me?'

'If you do as I say,' said Bogdo Khan.

A light came into Ungarn's eyes. 'I will make such a speech to them; it will light a fire greater than that one over there. You will see. The fire lit by Genghis has never ceased to burn deep in the bridled hearts of your people. All they needed was a leader, to drive them in holy war. A tautology of course; all war is holy. All is illusion, as you say; there is no good and no evil. No more than there is life or death. There is only action; there is only struggle.'

His car drove away, its motor echoing and dying away among the twilit smoky streets.

'The man is fated,' said Bogdo Khan. 'How fortunate it is that he will never enter Novonicolaevsk.'

'How can you be certain of that, even now?' said Charlotte.

'Because,' said Tuskegoun Lama, climbing out of the back seat, 'they have changed its name. It is now Novosibirsk; you have cast aside superstition, we all know that, but to a man like Ungarn even a confusion of names is the blow of doom.'

'Farewell,' said Bogdo Khan, 'I have a city to set in order, but I hope that you ladies will be able to resolve your differences. Tuskegoun, come.'

The monks and the guard moved away. Beside Charlotte, Watcher's face had changed back to features resembling the five women whose revolvers were now pointed at Charlotte. Watcher's jaw had not become so cruel, and where their eyes glowered with reflected flame, hers danced in the dawn.

Charlotte brought the hand with the grenade above the level of the car door, and then reached down and carefully placed it on the running-board. She reached into her pocket and removed revolver and razor; she shook the last bullet from its chamber, folded the razor, and put bullet, razor and revolver beside the grenade.

'There are legends,' she said. 'Legends of changelings, and of Thomas whom the Queen of a fair people taught always to speak truth. I have no family of my own now, and I claim the right to run with your pack and learn its singing, if I may, if a human can keep up with you. I can keep a secret, and I have proved that I have teeth.'

'But,' said Watcher, 'there is only one way I could bring you among my sisters.'

'I take it,' said Charlotte, 'that the hunt of which you

spoke on the train is the hunt where throats are bared in turn; the hunt where both are predator and both prey; the hunt where there is no killing but the little death. That is the way you could choose to bring me among your people.'

'But alas, you would not find that congenial, surely. Most humans have prejudices in these matters.'

'When you have cast aside superstition,' said Charlotte, 'there is no end to the prejudices you can set aside. There is a people that moves among Man, subtle as the fish in the sea, whose purposes are not his. That is a saying with many meanings, you know, and we may choose between them. Your people are my people, and whither thou goest, I go. If not, then I am content, also.'

She reached up to the collar of her blouse and undid it. She bent her head over to the side, offering her throat to Watcher. Watcher undid the collar of her officer's jacket and did the same. Her sisters sheathed their revolvers and their teeth; two of them climbed into the back of the car and the other three disappeared back into the dark streets. The noise of burning guttered to silence.

'Now,' said Watcher, 'Ungarn will delay a little – he so loves to make speeches – and so we should leave now. I suggest that we drive east as long as there is fuel; we have sisters in Vladivostok.'

'Fine,' said Charlotte, 'but can any of you drive?'

'Of course,' said the sister on the left. They all changed seats and Charlotte cradled her head in the corner of Watcher's arms.

'Well, my dear,' she said, drowsily. 'Now that we have established the mating rituals, our next course of study should probably be lullabies.'

It was, the more you got used to it, ever less like the howling of wolves.

*

A people's court condemned Baron Roman Theodorovich Ungarn von Sternberg, bound and abandoned by the last of his men, and captured by a Bolshevik patrol. He was killed by a firing squad in Novosibirsk, on the one hundred and twenty-ninth day of the prophecy. None know where his body lies; that autumn was a busy season for gravediggers, and for wolves.

SUNFLOWER PUMP

Paul Cornell

The Ozone Summer was beautiful for Manchester, all
sound and colour. The sound, as Johnny Marr had put
it, was the noise of children with too much money; the
colours were those of the bright flares of early nineties
fashion. But beautiful needs ugly to make it happen,
like the fluorocarbons made the Summer.

Hatcher was ugly, nose pressed to the glass of the
sports shop in the Arndale. He wore a bright track suit
and a basin haircut, and had tiny amphetamine pupils.
He'd been made by the Happy Mondays, in the same
way that God had made poisonous insects. He'd have
been happy at nineteen in whatever era: skinhead, punk
or scally. At that moment, his pupils were as big as
they could be, staring at heaven.

'Those.' His breath clouded the glass. 'I want those.'

His mates looked close. Haikai pumps with inflatable
air supports. Brilliant white. £195. Sports shoes you
wouldn't dare play sport in.

'Sheddy stuff, lads,' he added.

'Real baggy, Hatch.' But behind the agreeing voices
stood Tag, only sixteen, here with his brother Gaz, who
had warned him. And he said:

'Sheddy? What's sheddy, Hatch? That's not a real
word, like.' He was grinning his teeth off, shifting from
foot to foot, mildly dissing Hatcher, who he thought
was a bit of a goit.

'Sheddy –' Hatcher turned and kicked Tag in the knee. The boy yelled and crumpled, then put up his arms to protect himself as Hatcher quickly landed a sparkling toe on his ear and ribs. His brother would have said something, but Hatcher paused to tie his shoelace. 'It's a real word, spaz. I said it, it's a real word.'

The gang helped the lad up, and there was a look of awe and tears on his face. People kept on walking by. Hatch stood up. 'Too hot, lads. Let's get some ale in.'

As they strode out into the street, Hatcher glanced at his trainers again. No scuffs, so he didn't need new ones yet.

Eh was squatting by the wall on her heavy-knit woolly, taking in the sunlight for the vitamins. Her hair was a mass of dreads in the centre, left to keep itself clean, shaved at the sides. She wore black, and was enjoying roasting in it, remembering the cold of winter in Congleton Wood. A parade of consumers' legs shuttered the sunlight across her, and some of them tossed coins on to the spread shape of her black star parka. Eh was very poor. She carefully gathered the shining coins up into her greasy hand. A pair of bright trainers arrived and stopped.

'Got a job then, love?' Gaz had his hands thrust into the depths of his jogging pants. His face was a black smudge against the sun. 'It's easy, like. You go down the SS and they give you one.' The crowd behind him snorted, except Hatcher, who was vacantly skipping from one foot to the other, scuffing.

'Piss off.' Eh glanced down a side street, where a pair of fierce eyes met hers over a dustbin. Something large and shaggy had tensed there, waiting. She raised an eyebrow.

'You telling me to piss off?' guffawed Gaz, redundantly. Hatcher heaved a sigh, and tapped his boys round the shoulders, pointing to move on. Boring. They shuffled off, and Hatcher glanced over his shoulder. Maybe he expected the usual anarchist blank fury, but what he saw on Eh's face surprised him. He shivered despite summer, but shrugged it off.

That night, as the streets were clearing and people were less inclined to stop and ponder the immensity of a traveller's dog, Eh was able to talk to Chob, her protector.

'I've seen him often,' she said. 'I like his ears.' Chob looked up at her with soulful eyes. Eh could tell by the shape of his mouth that he was eventually going to say something.

Chom, wah wah, chom.

The man might have been naked. Barely glimpse through overlit video, a blaze of feedback. Glimpses of sunlight flaring off cropped blond hair, stinging taut muscles. Oilscarred. He ran across girders, scaffolding, high off the ground.

A sudden corner.

Blaring trumpet discord.

The girder swayed. He tottered out over the abyss.

But his trainers took him on to the next challenge.

Holding perfectly.

'How?' asked Jim, rolling a cold can across his acne-scarred chin.

'Steam it,' Hatcher was slumped in a corner of shade, his mind still riddled by the vision of those shoes. 'Steam it, matey.'

'What, steam a shoe shop?' muttered Tag, dropping an E into his can before swigging from it. Hatch looked up quickly, and the gang tensed again, but

Tag's tone had been respectful. Maybe not this time.

'Shouldn't do that,' Hatch pointed to the can and held the point, his finger quite steady. 'Girl did that in Rotherham, I heard. She was on one and put down a few. Know what happened?'

'No . . .' Tag grinned and slurped again, the tab taking hold. Beer was honey, and he loved Hatch as much as his brother did.

'Her liver and kidneys and stuff all shut off.' Hatcher blinked slowly. 'She baked like a pie, and when they opened her up . . .' he popped a finger out of the corner of his mouth, '. . . she was steaming, so don't do it. Now, that reminds me. Steaming. That reminds me. Your question. Nah, not the shop. We rob someone else, then pay the shop for my shoes. Right?'

The posse nodded, entranced. This was the good stuff, the slow jackanory stuff.

'So who do we rob?' Tag took another gulp. 'How about that place you work?'

'Don't be a knobhead. I'm into that, good at it. Top telesalesman, me. Nah, we rob a Paki shop in Rusholme.'

'Top,' agreed Tag. Then he faltered, rolling his eyes, and fell, making blubbering noises in the sun. 'I'm melting! I'm steaming!'

Then he sat upright, grinning. Hatcher laughed then, and so did the rest.

Eh lay in the shade of an old elm in the park, enjoying the feeling of wood on her back. Chob was lying around her like a comfortable pillow. Over the years, the pair had evolved various strategies for concealing Chob's size, and this was one of the more subtle ones. The less subtle ones involved growling at people and running away. Chob's jaw was dripping with saliva now, his canines having retreated and his tongue shortening by the minute. He glanced around to see that nobody was near.

'Tharrrrshh . . .' he began.

'Give it a little while,' Eh patted him. Chob had, thankfully, also evolved a great patience. They had each changed in response to the other, but even now Eh couldn't shake the feeling that this whole lifestyle was only Chob indulging her.

Recently, in 1978 that is, Eh, who had been calling herself Emily since she'd given up 'Sunflower' in 1972, had given up on the ways of money. She and Chob (Charles, Charibdys) had been standing in an armpit-to-armpit express from Crewe to Bournemouth. Charles had been smiling, happy as always with the people he met, but Emily had fretted for the whole journey.

'Why,' she had asked an old lady, 'don't you go and sit in first class?'

'Oh, it wouldn't be right . . .' muttered the old lady, suffering.

Indeed not. What was right was what made these cramped humans sweat and swear at each other. Eh found that, in that case, she had fallen in love with wrong. She had a great deal of sympathy for these poor devils.

At Bournemouth, she and Charles gave their clothes and baggage to some travellers. Then they ran out into the sea.

They slept there in the brine for three days, basking and dreaming, spouting in the midday sun. When they returned to shore, their hair was cropped and their skin hard.

But still, they found that to ignore the rule of dirty cash was to ignore the Law. They found themselves running away from the coast, sprinting across fields and leaping ditches and hedges to avoid the chase. To a pair of philosophers like Eh and Chob, who had wanted to let the foibles of late capitalism wash over them like the tide had, this was swimming upstream.

Chob had slumped down by a tree one night and sighed. 'You be the human,' he had said. 'I'll be something more useful.'

And while a beast might be chased for his crimes, only humans were chased with any heart. So that had worked.

'This,' Chob said, his tongue now perfect, 'is a bad idea.'

'What is?'

'This fleshboy. He's an evil little ape.'

'Yes, he's gorgeous. Nasty.'

'Please don't.'

'You're just jealous.'

'I am not jealous,' Chob almost barked, his maw awash with saliva. 'He's dangerous.'

Eh laughed, rubbing Chob's mane roughly. 'More dangerous than me? How's that then?'

'You always mate below your station.'

'We all do.' Eh kissed his head gently. 'Every one of us.'

Chakka chakka bom.

The girders blurred and swayed. A gap yawned open between two of them, swinging on cranes.

Slomo leap, screaming guitar. The man just reaches the next girder.

His trainers carry him safely on.

Sanir was carefully winding a sari on to a window dummy, enjoying the sunshine through the glass of his shop window. It wasn't really warm, not as he remembered (dreamed of?) the old country as being. Still, the approximation of heat made him feel more content than he had been of late. It wasn't as if he minded Rose wearing jeans, they were quite proper in their way, but shorts . . . She was only fourteen, and this city contained many evil men.

He examined the eye make-up of the dummy. Well, Rose could repaint that when she came home. He could talk to her then. He couldn't be angry with her because she'd make him laugh.

The shop bell rang, and Sanir climbed out of the window display, calling to his customers that he wouldn't be a moment. Then there was a crash. The shop owner emerged to find five brightly-clad youths struggling to prise open his cash register. It had fallen on to the rug.

'Don't you come any closer!' screamed Jim, waving a Stanley knife. Sanir had fought in the war, and was more angry than scared. Words failed him. He grabbed a chair and hurled himself at these villainous children.

Hatcher ducked around the weapon and slammed his forearm into the back of Sanir's skull. The man tottered forward and collapsed into the glass counter, smashing the display of ornaments. An alarm bell burst into life.

'Fuck this! Get out, get out!' Hatch's posse dived out of the door and ran off down the street, ducking into an alley and weaving their way down to Moss Side.

Eh was watching, of course. She sat on the kerb on the other side of Wilmslow Road. She could feel Chob, sulking in the deserted lot behind her. She simulated what he would say. Over the vast time they had been together, these simulations had gradually taken the place of actual words. Now it was only in dispute that they talked, just to emphasize the differences between them. They were talking a lot these days.

'That's what you want?' He would pretend amazement.

'Yeah,' Eh sighed resignedly, 'I'm set on it, Chob.'

'Why?!'

'Because he doesn't care for his own flesh either. I want to make him care, or make him see that he cares, or . . . I don't know. He's a vintage human. Action over words, eh?'

'You've been around humans too long,' she heard Chob snort.

Well, perhaps she had.

Eh spent the next couple of days making cash in the way that she did, singing the *Fifty Lives* in the Arndale, dancing, begging (sloppy eyes for the mothers, aggression for the businessmen) and drawing pavement knotworks with stolen chalk. People gave her more money for the arts than for the begging, because they assumed Eh was a student and thus rich enough to deserve their money. With the cash, they ate, and Eh bought a T-shirt. A big bloom of gold flowers on a crimson sky, with a hood.

'Top, eh?' she asked Chob, but he just howled mournfully.

Ankle height. The trainer-feet jump past those with heavy boots.

And then it was night, the kind of negative night that follows a blazing day. The sky was an overexposed blueblack, and warmth still rose off the street. Chob stood under a railway arch, munching on the boxed remains of a fried chicken. He watched as Eh approached the queue for the Hacienda. The queue was a snake of hooded colours, anticipating and loaded. Eh vanished amongst them. Chob bit bones apart, and spat them.

'Pig came round my place last night,' Gaz was saying. 'Asked my mum if she knew where I was the other day.'

'What did you say?' Hatch was glaring at his trainers. There was a black mark on the gleaming tip of one. The Hacienda queue moved, and the gang moved with it, leaning again on the wall a few feet along.

'She said I was with my friends, like, but they were all good lads and wouldn't have got into any trouble. How about that, eh?'

Hatch looked up, half bored, half crazy. 'I've got a spot on my toe, Gaz. Here you are, here's my hanky and all, wipe it off, will you?' Gaz looked around, amazed that the whole thing had swung away from him so fast. There were girls about. He laughed.

'Yeah, right. Anyway . . .'

'No, I mean it. Take me seriously, mate.' So Gaz, caught between laughter and embarrassment, bent down and wiped the toe, with a flourish that showed he was playing along with the joke. Nobody, he was sort of relieved to hear, was laughing.

Hatch was really casual, watching him with slight approval. They were still like this when Eh arrived, behind Hatch's shoulder.

'Hiya!'

Hatcher jumped, and Gaz used the movement to stand up, handing back the handkerchief.

'Hi,' Hatch grinned sideways and turned to look at her. The boys looked back and forth at each other, wide smiles curling. 'You're that street girl, aren't you?'

'Yeah.' Eh stuck her tongue out at the boys as Hatch glanced back to them.

'What're you doing here?' He had snapped back to her instantly. Good reflexes for a human.

'Want to go in,' she smiled.

'How did you get the cash? On the game?'

73

'No,' and Eh saw Hatcher flinch as her pupils bloomed with anger. Stupid wanton monkey. Arrogant meat. That he could say such a thing to her made her want him even more. In what other time, she thought, would mating be like invading another country? Her nation didn't push, didn't flirt with boundaries, didn't even play politics. Time for an overture. 'Don't say that, it could get you hurt.'

The boys laughed and crowed. Hatcher just looked at his shoes again. There was a real scuff there.

'Oh, fuck you ...' he murmured absently, and walked on with the crowd. The gang jeered and chattered at Eh as they passed.

This was absurd! She felt rage boil in her stomach. He felt so far above here that he could do that, use the words and save face. He wasn't even provoked! The monkey was lucky that she didn't grow herself a penis and fuck him anyway!

But she wouldn't. She could. She could do anything that rage and biology allowed, but she wanted to be in Hatcher's frame, be one of his wanted things, he desired as only he could desire something. Eh knew that she was playing her way into a power relationship as old and as shit as humanity. If she had just wanted his flesh, the rape of apes was easy.

The rape of her own strength was much harder.

She hit the wall with her fist. A few of the queue noted, as Eh walked carefully away, that from the crack ran brick dust rather than blood.

Days sweated by, heavy in the sunlight, easier by night. Hatcher did his share of lulling people down the phone, and his share of shouting once that phone had been carefully clicked down. Every now and then he got a pain between his eyes. His gang were recreation, home, family. In his heart he knew, maybe, that he'd never use his brain to plan a decent crime for them. He was afraid of losing any of them.

They were his little nation. Gaz had called, but he wouldn't go out with Gaz on his own. That would disturb things.

So a few drinks and a few pills found Hatch wandering one night, wandering the streets between the people, looking for a place to go alone. It couldn't be the places where the gang met, 'cos they might meet without him, and he didn't want to see that.

Hatch stopped and leaned on a corner, dull, spaced eyes checking out the people that wandered by. He swigged from a bottle of Newky Brown he carried, and when he lowered his head again, there she was.

Long, blonde hair, with a cap tucked on top. A rich purple top, baggy pants and a medallion that swung and glinted. She was standing in the middle of the backstreet, staring at him. Hatch's gaze sped from her face (a glimpse of longing, carefully shy) to her feet. It stayed at her feet.

A blare of brilliant toothy white. Pumped up. Those were —

And then she ran. Hatch threw aside the bottle and ran after her. A howl bruised the air.

They ran through the streets, past the pubs that were emptying with club-bound crowds, through the alleys where the homeless huddled. Their feet paffed down the tarmac and their shadows held and died in the headlights of passing cars.

Hatch had seen frigging aristocracy, and he wanted it. Debutante curls, no nonce, a girl like that, but an orbital brat, money out for rough. But still she kept ahead of him, and he was bloody fit, he was.

They ran down a row of street lights, students laughing and calling after them, and at the end light she swung to a halt and watched him, pushing back her curls.

She wasn't even breathing hard.

He stepped forward, trying to think of words. She stayed where she was. He could hardly speak, and his brain was full of her. He raised a hand. There was not an expression on her face. He looked half aside, gauging.

Then he grabbed the back of her hair and shoved his tongue into her mouth. She let him, and Hatch found himself snogging like this street was a club and this goddess was a first-year on her first night out of home.

Her strong arms pulled him down into an alley, and he found himself surrounded by things wet and warm. Old Welcome mats and cardboard, debris and dross. The cocoon folded around him. A scrape of moist card sealed the door and he was in darkness.

Hatcher could hear the girl breathing, and he found himself frightened and aroused. She wanted this, she had prepared this, but it was so ... dirty. Like fucking should be, he licked his lips, like it should be.

Her arm snaked out and pulled him further inside, pulled him to her. Hatcher wondered what her name was – Sarah or Fiona or Jo? Something soft and southern, something fragile.

The arms that wrapped around him, pulled his shirt over his head, were hard and muscled, and Hatch found himself being moved like a doll, pulled and shaped by a thing far stronger than himself.

He nearly shouted, blind as he was, as a flap opened and he entered her. Fuck, he wanted to see her, to hear her name, to ask! But he was absorbed in a fury of smooth fabric, twisted tight around his body, and he could only gasp and grunt as she let him thrust, the only expression he was allowed.

As he came, he thought, beyond the relief of his climax, that he had a story to tell the boys. And then he slept.

In the dreams, something like a man scampered away from the darkness, a gathering terror chasing. From path to path, jumping from tree to tree, the runner went, but always hot breath and helplessness were on his neck.

His trainers slid in the sweat and jungle mud.

Hatcher woke up sober.

It was 3 a.m. by the light on his Rolex. Beside him slumbered the slim, strong form he had wrestled with, unconscious. She was hissing in her sleep and, for the first time without intoxication, Hatcher caught her smell. It was heavy and ancient, full of death and lust.

He shivered again.

Fuck this bitch, who did she think she was, dragging him in here and acting like a slut. He was covered in scratches and bruises. His ribs ached. He sucked a knuckle, wanting to smack her one.

If she was on something, then maybe she'd still be that strong. Best just get out, lad. Still, he felt unsatisfied, like some part of the sex had been missing.

Reaching over to where he thought the door was, Hatcher brushed his cheek against the toe of her trainers. Well, they had the rough edge of trainers. They could well be Haikais, what else could be that white and that arousing? Maybe he could give her something to remember him by after all.

Fumbling, he unlaced them, and gently pulled. The laces were wet in his hands. No movement. Sodding

hell, he wanted those. He wanted them 'cos he'd wanted
her, got her, and it hadn't been like getting at all. They
wouldn't come, they were secured by something. He felt
up her ankle. Rough, like a sport sock, or maybe the
dyke didn't shave her legs.

He pulled again. There was something holding the
thing on, like maybe she had laced it up behind her
foot. Shit! Hatcher patted his pockets for the Stanley
knife he carried, and applied it to the girl's ankle, starting to cut around the interior of the shoe.

He tensed, and pushed the blade in.

She screamed, or it was somewhere between a scream
and a howl. Something scythed past his head. Hatcher
leapt up and burst his way through the door of the
hide, scrambling like a boy in a nightmare. He dashed
out into the night, naked. As he rounded the corner, the
howl came again. Way behind the young human, something ancient was sobbing and concentrating on staun-
ching blood.

The skinny monkey ran down the hard streets, adrenalin pounding him along. But even over that chemical
imperative, something else was happening. He stopped,
panting, his breath boiling out of him in the chill air,
and tasted it.

In his mouth, something he had licked from under her
tongue, or something she had kissed into him. He fought it
for a moment, but his body was used to the feeling, used to
the fizzing of skin neurons, the bliss of heavy love shoving
its way up his spine. Tasted bad though, worse than a bad
E cut with speed.

He felt the hunger, the dream of freedom, of cars and
sex and looking like a million. He felt it worse than
ever, worse than watching those rich commercials.

And then he felt the dream answered. He could be
anything. His body awaited his commands, and finally

the pleasure was his, not given in grudging kisses by another predator. Blissed out, he let his mind fly, and got absorbed in time and the voice of the city.

On his feet shone two phantom trainers, pumped to the max.

Behind the running, screaming, naked boy padded Chob, who had licked healing enzymes into the blood of Eh's wound. Even he wasn't certain of his intention. It might even have been to help. It was possible that Hatcher felt that his dreams were being pursued in any case. So the result could have been just built in, the way the monkey was.

The monkey wanted to fuck around and fly.

By dawn, the dreams were screwing around with sunlight, throwing it through a rainbow filter, pumping blood between him and the sun. The soundtrack jolted with nasty chords, spilling noise out over the city. The noise was distant pleading and requests, all of which he could ignore. And would. Only other people.

What a city, the sound of money hunting flesh. Yet he was king of it, astride his falling girder, surfing down into oblivion and waving his arms to the masses of stupid zeros below. He was way above the ground, having missed a corner on that fantasy scaffold. He was plummeting, the wind plucking his clothes into a baggy sail.

'Fuck!' he shouted, 'What a ride for what a price!'

The spikes of steel and flat hard tarmac swung high to meet him, and he cried again. 'Just like in the adverts!'

And then he woke up. And then he hit the ground. His head burst across the concrete. His spine skittered across the impact surface, crumping into a tangle of bones burst through muscles. The stomach contents spilled along the street. Steaming.

Just for a moment, Hatcher had really known what it was like.

Eh, in her new form, watched from a distance, Chob beside her. A mother was sobbing into a policewoman, and reporters were pointing up at the girders from which the naked boy had jumped. A forensic team was removing the offal. Eh felt a moment's sadness for dead flesh. She would limp for a few days. None of this, beyond the rape, had been meant. Hatcher had almost conspired to infect himself with Eh's wilful biology. Once he had done so the flesh had, as always, followed the instructions of its owner. Hatcher had made his dream real, and fatal.

Eh turned to Chob and licked his face with her rough tongue. He licked back, and together they padded out of the city, hoping to find somewhere where the air smelled better and the people didn't cut your flesh.

Chob wasn't hopeful.

As the van carrying the remains of Hatcher drew away from the scene, a gang of boys in bright colours ran after it. They hopped and jumped to get a glimpse at the corpse through the back window, cheering in the sunlight. Tag was among them, not knowing who it was who died. Perhaps he would never find out.

The dream faded in the sun on the corpse and the flesh, realizing it was dead, ceased to spark with chemical war.

The dream froze on the running man, fading into blackness, a noise like a descending axe.

Haikai – Gets You Where You Want To Go.

RAIN

Christopher Amies

No wind to stir the blackened olive branches, none to cool the stripped, orange shafts of the cork trees. In the still, hot air there was only dust, no sound; nothing dared venture out in this heat. In the hills above the dry valley of the Guadiaste, the tumbled ruins of past occupations baked slowly in the heat: a fluted pillar driven through rock, a small, almost featureless figure of granite watching out over the valley. A shallow depression in the hillside, filled with dust and thorn bushes, was the sole remains of a Roman theatre. Beyond it a jagged hole in the rock, a metre across, was the mouth of a shaft with no apparent floor. It came out further down the valley somewhere; nobody really knew. In the valley a hundred feet below, the village of San Isidro merged into the brown of the valley floor. Further down the valley, around the village of Villamenor, the land was a sudden spring-like green. But the clouds that had suddenly gathered to give the land rain, had all gone now. The burning sky went on and on without the slightest cloud to break its metallic blue indifference.

Not even animals dared move. In the shadow of the grey wall, John Aylwin lidded his eyes and let the past of this area flood back into him. He was letting himself change towards the original form, muscles and sinews sliding against one another. He could only let this happen here, where nobody else came. If this happened slowly the change brought no pain, only a warm prickling. Drifting back into this place when it was a small Roman town, soldiers of Augustus's V and X Legions brandishing spears and swords; then through the slew of centuries haunted by fierce-grinning Arabs who held the land for seven hundred years, when it was still forest. Aylwin lay back, head against the rock, and heard the rumours of the millennia still humming in the stone. Hours later, when the rocks began to cool, he shifted slowly back to the shape people knew as 'John Aylwin' and began to walk down into the valley. Far away, sensing him move out from the shadow, a dog began to bark frantically.

'The area has a sad history,' Pablo Sanchez said. 'In 1938 the Falangists marched ten of the town's finest young men up there and machine-gunned them to death. They stood them on the hill overlooking the Guadiaste so they could get one last look at their country. Then they killed the lot and threw their bodies down the old mine shaft.' Aylwin was not surprised. He had heard all these stories and more. Humans killing each other was hardly anything new. Not to him, who had been face down in mud and corpses, back when. Now behind the bar once again, chest and thighs still tingling from the change to human form, he said nothing and occasionally looked at the television blaring high up in its corner. Sanchez had had it put in last year – the first set in the village – and was exceptionally proud of it.

Not that Pablo Sanchez was proud of much else. He had grown fat in the years Aylwin had known him. He had his wife Angela, and a son and a daughter. The son had gone to Germany, but the daughter, now she was a different matter. The village youths were pining for nineteen-year-old Consuelo, but she belonged to John

Aylwin. As she should, for they had been married for a year and a half.

Whenever he lay awake at night, John Aylwin would hallucinate rain against the shutters. The sound comforted him somehow, even though he had never been able to bear what it brought with it. Even though it was something he had not heard in fifteen years. It spoke to him of Passchendaele, now so many years ago, when deafened by shell blasts he'd clung to the trench wall as the trench slowly filled up with mud, and rain, and more rain. The endless rain.

In summer, irrigation pumps flung their lazy arcs across the brown fields like a line of men pissing; in spring the Guadiaste grew from a muddy trickle to a cascade of green water. But it never rained. Out where the village of San Isidro became a waste of barracoons and tumbledown huts, there was only brown scrub, stretching past the thorn bushes, a carpet of undulating brown until the land soared up into the enigmatic grey-blue of the Sierra de Aracena.

In the evenings the farmers came into the bar to cool their parched throats with rough, red local wine. Dry brown men of a dry brown landscape, who still called Aylwin *El Inglés* though he had been here the last fifteen of the twenty years San Isidro had been without rain. He was *El Inglés*, even though he had changed himself slowly, so as not to arouse suspicion; become shorter, broader and darker. Now those passing through would not make an Englishman of him unless they detected a faint accent behind his mastery of the dialect. But the rain. What rain? None for twenty years; that was why Aylwin came here, when his hatred of rain grew so that he could no longer leave home if the slightest drizzle spattered the streets. When every drop of rain took him back to the dead men in the trenches, and the men who should have been dead screaming on the wire. And rats, grown fat on German and English corpses. And rain, and mud.

He left the Kin without a farewell, setting out on his travels as though he meant to come back. He wandered here and there and then, after hiding from another war in some ways even more terrible, he was in Spain. Here too they had lived in trenches and seen their friends blown to pieces. In this, John Aylwin found some kind of kinship with them. By the year's end he had reached the village of San Isidro and was working for Pablo Sanchez at the *Bar del Telón* on the village square.

Early morning. At seven, just after Aylwin opened up, two *Guardia Civil* came in on their usual patrol out of Llera. They took coffee and sat at the end of the bar while Aylwin prepared the day's food, *chorizo* sausage and refried beans and *tortilla* and *empanada*. Aylwin relied on the *Guardia* as much as on the radio for news of the world outside. These two men were almost old friends to him; though he could not quite be at ease with the representatives of Madrid, these were local men, slow, tough, easy humoured, relying on presence rather than force to keep the peace which they valued as honestly as anyone else.

'Still no rain?'

'Now what do you think, Felipe?'

'I think it never will.'

But they had been hearing rumours, tales from other villages, stories that Catholic Spain should have been ignoring. Sergeant Felipe García had been in Castañeras when the rain dancers had gathered. They had done no good – it still hadn't rained – but in Villamenor, it had. Aylwin got the rumours from these men, too. They were worrying. Superstition, yes. Calling down the rain. That was the last thing Aylwin wanted; not just because of his hatred of precipitation of any kind, but also because such a gathering might be the first beginnings of something less welcome.

'How many are there?' he asked casually, watching the plume of coarse smoke from the tip of Felipe García's cigarette rise and dissipate in the morning air.

'Just the one man,' Sergeant García said. 'But in every village he gathers more followers. People are desperate for rain, Juan.'

'We've lived without it,' Aylwin said. 'Government irrigation programme and all that.'

'But,' the *Guardia* said, 'we are dying without it. You remember. The land used to be greener, when you came here.'

'I came here hoping to avoid rain,' Aylwin said.

'Well,' García said, 'I should be careful if I were you. When Letamendi gets here. And he will.'

'Careful?'

'Yes, careful. I'm your friend, I'm not threatening you. Just suggesting.'

Aylwin wondered. The possibility came to mind of Letamendi's pitchfork-wielding hordes, or so he imagined them, stringing him up and running him through for stopping the rain falling.

'What do you know about Letamendi?' he asked.

'Not much,' García admitted. 'Complainer, I suppose. But we can't drag him in; he's caused no actual trouble.'

'I don't suppose the Church likes him very much?'

'The Church?' the other *Guardia* wondered. 'They support him. There are those who say Letamendi is a priest, or was. That he gets the priest on his side to start out with. I don't know. A lot of people say a lot of different things.'

In San Isidro, that meant Father Duarte. Maybe it would be time to go and see the priest. Ask a few questions.

The *Guardia* finished their breakfast and went out to their patrol car. The engine cracked into life, droned out into the silence of the village morning. Aylwin poured himself a glass of coffee and drank it, troubled.

Letamendi lay asleep in the shade of a fig tree. Beside him a half-full bottle of rough local wine warmed slowly; on his other side a young girl, looking fifteen years old, slept trustingly, keeping him company. Elena had not left his side since the first village he had tried to bring rain to. She found the stranger exciting and dangerous, and of course a worker of miracles. He told her nothing more than he told anyone else; he had brought back the old religion's dances and incantations, stood a hundred people in the village square and made it rain. No wonder he was held in superstitious awe. As he slept, occasional passers-by stopped to gaze upon the miracle worker. Some made the holy sign upon their bodies; one old man forked two fingers to his eyes to ward off the Evil Eye, and went on his way muttering about *brujo*. Those who, despite Letamendi's own words, had followed him to this, the third village of his rain-making, crept about and stole glances.

Letamendi's dreams were momentous things: rolling waves of surf crashing through the ancient city at the mouth of the Guadalquivir, walls and towers poking through the surface of a sullen sea. A long time ago; but not so long for the memory of his tribe. Water, and more of it. He had met the men responsible for irrigating this dry, poor corner of Spain; honest men, solid working men, but not his people, not at all. They could bring water – but water itself, vital as it was, trickling from rusty pipes, prosaic, gushing from old standpipes, was not rain. Besides, it had to come from somewhere, and the wells grew drier every season, the rivers less full in spring. Not the hellish opening of the sky to lash the dry, dusty world with liquid life.

And that was what he was dreaming of. He was of the old people, was Letamendi; his Basque name told you that, but his people had been there even before the Basques, or so his father had said, who had taught him the secret dances he was now bringing to the people of south-western Spain. They didn't need them in the north, where enough clouds built up on the southern flank of the Pyrenees or drove in from the Atlantic. Up there Diego Letamendi had been no more than a factory worker, one of a family that haunted the interstices of a steel-grey town, the way its type had always done, keeping to the shadows where not too much might be said; and kept a weather eye on its own folk. Diego wanted nothing of it. Down here he winked a gypsyish eye and became a doer of miracles.

Oh, literally so, now. The village of Villamenor was green; the fields swarmed with flowers and lush grass. A miracle, if you liked; though the Church, much as it would have liked to draw the Pope's attention to its sudden luck, muttered dimly about God's ordered plan being no miracle, and said Mass on Sunday as usual. Corn and grapes would grow now, where none had grown for ten years and the people had lived off growing olives and figs. A living, but only for the very poor, and those who were determined or prepared to stay. As it still was in San Isidro. Some claimed it had also rained in Castañeras and Pueblo Martires; but there, Diego Letamendi had led the dance and the sky had remained resolutely dry. When he came to Villamenor the heavens opened.

An aeroplane droned over the hills somewhere in the distance, dropping water on the fires that had raged in the Sierras all summer. Letamendi heard it in his sleep and smiled.

*

Father Teobaldo Duarte didn't have much to say to Aylwin. The old man, as brown and dry as most men of San Isidro, spoke to Aylwin in his sacristy. His voice was always surprising; from the ancient, parched throat came a round, reverberating voice, a real sermon voice as the men of Aylwin's home village used to say.

'I don't believe in it,' Father Duarte said. 'Yes, miracles happen. But why God would spend His time sending rain down to one little village after another when so much of the world is turning to desert, I can't imagine.'

'The villagers think it's a miracle,' Aylwin said. 'And they call Diego Letamendi a miracle-worker.'

'Superstition,' Duarte said, grimly. 'Oh, the rains follow him, but what might follow the rains, eh?'

'Precisely, Father.'

Duarte looked keenly at his visitor. He was sure Aylwin had looked more like an Englishman when he arrived; fair-haired, tall, red-faced. Must be the sun and wind, like it was for all of them. He remembered stories he'd heard years ago, stories which themselves seemed like the superstitions he was lambasting; but stories which for all that might just as well be true. Then what had made Aylwin run this far, to this little place everyone else wanted to run from? So much that there were only the old men now and the very poorest families? Father Duarte wondered.

'Don't worry about that,' the priest said. 'I'm not going to throw my church open to Letamendi and his flock. Elijah, praying for rain; do you think I haven't? But Man proposes; God disposes. We shall see what's what.'

Aylwin watched back. Assuming the priests of other villages had gone joyously to Letamendi's side, what likelihood was there that the austere Duarte would remain aloof?

*

Elena watched from the mouth of an alleyway. In the main square of San Isidro the people were milling, hustling to and fro among the market stalls that no longer overflowed with fruit and vegetables, but where poor and scurvy produce was sold. A boy of Elena's age watched her as she watched, with brown, expressionless eyes, then looked away again.

It was no matter. Elena was safe, under the protection – she knew – of Letamendi. Whatever he was. He wasn't Weerde but he wasn't human, not as she understood it. She, too, remembered stories, and for the moment did not much care. If she did not want these humans, these cattle on two legs, to see her they would not. They could look through her. But the youth watching her; was he one? She thought not. He was another of the Kin. Elena did not sense many of them here, and if her intelligence proved correct some of them had moved into the daytime with the humans, had lost the special edge to their senses that had allowed the Weerde to survive this long.

Not Elena; and not Letamendi. She had survived the winnowing of Franco's post-Civil-War clean-up around her native province of Valencia and walked back into her home village when it was no more than a burned-out shell. Even the poor end of town where the immigrants, the gypsies and her own people lived was gone, bodies heaped in the white dust of the street. Among the bodies was the rest of her family.

While the international community squawked genocide and did precisely nothing, Elena took the road west. Not looking for anything in particular, not even looking for others of the Kin. The families of the southern towns were either dead or in hiding. She begged for food and money; in Córdoba she hung around the railway station at midnight when the huge expresses steamed in, to meet the soldiers coming home on leave. They took her among the freight cars in the marshalling yard and did things to her she really didn't care about. She changed herself to make herself more appealing, to cadge a few more pesetas from them. She stayed looking fifteen even though her age was now closer to thirty. Only once a soldier looked into her eyes as he was pumping and recognized her for one of his own people. He did nothing but kiss her, pay her, and leave. Then it was his mate's turn.

And as the years rolled on she came to Extremadura, beyond which there is Portugal and not much else. She met Diego Letamendi, descendant of the Cagots of the Basque hills. Those same people the Weerde had driven almost to extinction so many thousands of years before. Elena was barely aware of that part of history though there were songs about it, and the oldest of the Kin spoke at length of the 'flatheads', of the powers they had and the alarm they caused all those years ago. It was nothing Elena knew, or cared about much.

Others followed Letamendi; in some places he walked the dusty roads with a capering crowd a few paces behind him, but he preferred to be alone, and so when his devotees came to the next village he bid them go back, and he strode in on his own. Except for Elena. The villages were desperate for rain. Letamendi was never short of them. Others had rediscovered the old dances in their despair, willing to turn to anything. But nothing worked; until Letamendi went to Pueblo Martires, then to Castañeras, where he escaped the people's disappointment with a swift departure. Then he went to Villamenor, where the rain came to him. This, he said, was the blessed land. The village suddenly flocked with refugees from the still dry heartland.

Elena ran back along the hard mud road to Villamenor where Letamendi was still resting beneath his tree, watching her as her shape grew out of the heat-hazed distance towards her, and she flung herself down against him.

'Well,' he said, pulling her towards him. 'What have you seen?'

'The people,' she said equably. 'But there is nothing to be afraid of.' She watched for a reaction in his eyes; deep-set eyes, big irises as black as the pupils.

'Nothing at all,' Diego Letamendi told her. 'What did I tell you?' He unfastened his trousers, raised her skirt, and drew her down upon him.

In the bar at San Isidro, Aylwin was serving customers when the boy slipped in as quietly as he could, not looking at anyone; he was silent, thought half-witted by the men and youths who drank in the bar. He reached the bar amid their sideways looks. Nobody quite trusted him nor the rest of the Pérez family, who lived in an old house on the edge of the village in quite un-Catholic conditions, people said. It was possible, Aylwin thought, that the villagers could also sense the unsettling presence of a Weerde; in which case, why don't they object to me? Probably because John Aylwin is foreign and they expect foreigners to be strange.

Joselito jumped to a stool and pushed himself across the bar towards Aylwin.

'He's coming,' the boy said.

Aylwin looked at him closely.

'You're sure, Joselito?'

'The girl who goes with him? She was here, looking around. Trying not to be seen. But I saw her, Juan.'

'Did anyone else see her?'

'None of the people. Nobody else would know.'

'They wouldn't. No.' Only, John Aylwin thought,

because none of them had been told. This was a very old story maybe the grandmothers knew. But as soon as San Isidro knew the rain man was coming, they'd listen. Some had gone already, but most stayed, listening, waiting.

That afternoon Aylwin did not head into the hills as he had the previous day. He and Consuelo went to bed, and after they had satisfied their bodies Aylwin drowsed in the cool of their bedroom and Consuelo read poems, mostly for herself, but sometimes out loud to her husband. She was sitting cross-legged on the rush mats of the floor, wearing nothing. The fibres dug ridges into the soft skin of her buttocks. Later her husband would smooth them out with fingertips and kisses.
'Listen to this:

> And it will rain. Grandmother Muntala
> is keeping the sun in the cupboard
> of bad weather, among the lace
> woven by the fingers of Sinera.

Very appropriate.'
Aylwin felt little when faced with this; what did these people know?
'I've better lines,' he replied slowly, his voice hoarse with the desire for sleep.

> Some ancient faith
> opened the doors to its crypt;
> now the saints
> and devils dance together
> among the horses of the sea
> drawing the carriages
> of the dark.

'You believe that?' Consuelo asked, quite evenly; she did not believe nor disbelieve it. Brought up in the faith of Rome, she knew there were some things you shouldn't tamper with. 'Like the Monsignor says, "If God meant it to rain here He'd send rain. Not someone like Letamendi."'

Consuelo ran over the lines in her mind and shuddered. Her affection for poetry was something rare where she lived; something of her own, that her husband could not quite understand. She had read Lorca from cover to cover several times, and Hernández and Machado, before discovering the delights of Espriu; a far darker voice, not even written in Spanish to start with. But once she'd introduced John to this poet, he seemed to click on to a fellow-feeling. He shared something of the strangeness of the Catalan poet. It was that quality of his she could not define, that she was sure was not just due to his being foreign. After all, he was a man of San Isidro now, just as much as anyone else.

Consuelo leaned against her man, and he put his arms around her neck, hands reaching down to her breasts, and kissed her hair. Consuelo sighed, arching her head back until John could curl round her and kiss her lips. The poetry forgotten, she opened her mouth to his tongue as he slid down against her and his hands found her thighs.

In the late afternoon people were standing around the village square, by the church doors, and under the town hall clock as if to show how heavily time hung upon their shoulders. The men talked about football and the lottery; the women talked about any one of their number not present. Children ran and kicked footballs in the dust. A farm truck rattled into the square and out again, towards the hills. In the *Bar del Telón*,

John Aylwin and Pablo Sanchez sat behind the counter, watching the people go by.

A long black car drew silently into the square. It was different enough for conversations to falter, eyes to turn, indiscreet fingers to point. It was low and wide, and the windows were blacked out. It drew to a halt by the church. The rear door opened and a man stepped out, tall and thin, dressed in a dark suit and with his eyes hidden by dark glasses. Without a look to either side of him, this individual climbed the church steps and entered, leaving a bemused silence behind him. Sanchez looked at his son-in-law for an inquiring second.

'D'you think he's from Opus Dei?' he wondered.

'Of course. I wonder what they want with Don Teobaldo?'

'Whatever it is,' Sanchez said, 'if Madrid starts nosing around here, life won't be happy.'

'Oh I don't know; we might get some money out of them.'

'Not from those bastards.'

John Aylwin was still watching the closed wooden doors of the church, the grey stones with their inscription JOSE ANTONIO, the stone saints, San Isidro and Santa Josefina, both looking constipated. Consuelo claimed they looked that way because they were repressing screams of horror at the squalor around them. Either at that, or at the atmosphere of chill authority that cloaked the well-dressed man who came out of the church half an hour later. He climbed back into the car and was driven away. Despite the looks of loathing on the faces in the square, nobody moved nor said anything until the limousine was well out of sight. On the wall of the town hall, last year's Falangist poster – XXV AÑOS DE PAZ – was slowly peeling away.

As the Pegaso limousine pulled out of San Isidro on its way back to the city of Badajoz, Javier Castillo y Cid watched from its back seat for some glimpse of the roving blasphemer he was trying to track down. He had been to Villamenor; yes, it was blooming: leaves on the trees, long grass in the fields, flowers by the roadside. And it was completely incomprehensible. Miracles happened, but not to poor villages in Extremadura, and certainly not to roving Basques of uncertain parentage and even more uncertain abidance by the law. He had spoken to the *Guardia Civil* and they couldn't stop him. Castillo suspected they were as keen as the villagers on getting some rain, no matter what they had to do for it. Rural policemen were rural first, policemen second. Castillo lit a cigarette.

Nobody in Villamenor had spoken to him; no more than they had to. The priest had expressed sorrow at the superstitious goings-on, but – understandably – delight at the outcome.

'This man Letamendi must be stopped!'

'Why? He did us some good. Who are you, Don Javier Castillo y Cid,' – his full name delivered like a sneer – 'to tell us what the Good Lord wants and does not want?'

In San Isidro, Don Teobaldo Duarte had been less impressed by Castillo's Opus Dei credentials than any priest he had yet met. The man simply did not respond to threats. Unlike Villamenor's incumbent, he was quite in agreement that the rain dancers posed a danger. However, he was less clear as to what the threat was. Not blasphemy as such; Castillo began to wonder whether Duarte was as superstitious as the rest of them.

'You think God will strike him down?' Castillo asked, disdainful.

'I think something will strike us down, if we don't

stop him. And it'll be something a lot less pleasant than the Lord of Hosts. The Lord of the Flies, you know that phrase? In the original, Baal-Zebul, or Beelzebub? Well then. I am an old man, too old to threaten, and I do not care for your Opus Dei nor for your General Franco. But I do care about my village, and do not want the Malign One taking an interest in us, so I shall deal with it, be assured. I know these people, and I won't let you down. The Church has ways, believe me.'

'Thank you, Don Teobaldo.'

The car gathered speed, heading out of the dry lands. Castillo puffed at his cigarette and closed his eyes.

By eight, the *Bar del Telón* was almost full: locals coming in off the fields to pour wine down their throats. Two men in their thirties, thin, brown men wearing patched clothes that looked as old as the bodies wearing them, sat by the bar and Aylwin passed them a flagon of wine.

'What did the man from the city want, huh? Coming sniffing around our church.'

'Serves them right, the Church. Priests getting in everywhere. Putting their noses in where they aren't wanted.'

'Ah, you leave Don Teobaldo alone, Carlos. He's a good man. And he's a village man. I suppose you'd go along with those pagans who are doing rain dances up by Villamenor?'

'Have done rain dances, you mean. They worked, didn't they? Have you been along there, Pepe? Eh, Juan, what do you think? Did they work, his dances?'

'I don't believe it,' Aylwin said, leaning over the bar. 'It's all chance.'

'We'll see when he gets here. Tomorrow, they say.'

The conversation led on to other subjects and Aylwin went back to serving wine, joining in discussion of football teams and bullfighters, keeping an eye out for strangers. Towards nine-thirty, while he was preparing food, there was a murmur in the bar. Expecting some stranger passing through, or even – could it be – Letamendi and his people, Aylwin put down the knife and went towards the noise. Young Joselito Pérez was making his languorous way to the bar.

'Holá, amigo,' said Aylwin, shaking the boy's hand. Joselito grinned, and asked for a beer.

'He's on his way,' the youth said, drinking. 'Letamendi is coming. Now.'

'You're sure?'

'Sure I'm sure.' Joselito smiled whitely. 'He's coming up the road from Villamenor. Aunt Soledad said so. She just came back from buying tomatoes in Villamenor market.'

'You're telling the truth, boy?' Carlos asked, virtually knee to knee with the Pérez lad.

'What did he just say?' said Pepe. 'You leave Joselito be. At least I can trust what he tells me.' He grinned past Carlos at Joselito and made an expression of doubt in Carlos' direction. Then he turned round, filled his lungs, and stated loudly without shouting:

'Letamendi's on his way, lads!'

The result was a hail of mixed cheers and abuse. Some people darted out into the square to watch for the man. Most stayed where they were to wait for events. Joselito finished his beer and ordered another. Rodolfo Sanchez turned to his cousin Jorge and drove a fist into Jorge's left eye, then the cousins simply went on drinking.

The evening went on. John Aylwin started in on a conversation on the relative merits of matadors Ordóñez and Curro Romero. Consuelo passed among the tables serving food. Much wine was drunk. But every eye was watching, every ear was cocked to the rumours from the dust road.

At the edge of town Diego Letamendi strode slowly up that same road, past the tumbledown barracoons, the corrugated iron shacks, mostly abandoned. He crossed the old wooden bridge over the cracked mud bed of the Guadiaste. A few yards behind him – for Letamendi wanted to make the approach alone – walked Elena, also listening to the voices of the evening. And in the shadows behind her were other figures, people of Villamenor come along to see what would happen.

As the travellers advanced into San Isidro, curious inhabitants came out to look at them. Some of the Pérez family crowded out of their dilapidated brick house, chattering. Families on balconies leaned down and called to each other. Diego Letamendi waved to some of them. A youth of the populous Sanchez family called out to Elena, and she tossed back her hair and blew him a kiss. Soon he was down in the street and walking beside the girl.

And not only him. From doors and alleyways the people of San Isidro came out, converging on the village square. People who had been working the dry land all day and whose only respite was a bowl of beans and the sleep of great exhaustion before they rose at sunrise the next day. Twenty, maybe thirty of them strode into the square like a procession, fanning out as they faced the church and the town hall.

'Is anyone going to wake up Don Teobaldo?' a voice called.

'Let the old buffer sleep,' another said. 'We want rain and no priest is going to stop us.'

Then Letamendi, standing in the middle of the square, folded his arms and addressed the crowd.

'We shall start at dawn tomorrow,' he said. 'But now I am going to drink a skin of wine and prepare myself.' With that he headed for the *Bar del Telón*. Three of the locals followed, among them the lad who had called out to Elena, but the rest softly and silently vanished away, back into the darkening streets.

Diego Letamendi strode between the tables and presented himself at the bar.

'Wine,' he demanded with his most pleasant smile. But as he made eye contact with John Aylwin a dark look flashed between them and Letamendi felt his teeth settle in their sockets, the muscles around his jaw begin to bunch in preparation for fight. This lasted but a second; then he took the goatskin flask and went to sit by the wall, his followers around him.

Through the evening John Aylwin supplied the Basque with more wine, but Letamendi did not appear to grow more than mildly drunk. Towards one in the morning Consuelo announced that she was going to bed; Pablo and Angela had already gone, so Aylwin was there to see to the handful of remaining customers on his own. Aylwin kissed her softly on the mouth and she left.

One by one the followers drifted away. The last customers took their leave and went out into the cool of the night. Elena went off draped around her village boy. Neither of them were due for any sleep that night. Aylwin came round from the bar and sat facing the one remaining customer: Diego Letamendi. With him he brought a fresh flask of wine.

'Well, Letamendi,' Aylwin said, finally.

'I don't need to ask what you're thinking,' Letamendi said, amiably. 'I can tell. It's all over your face.'

'You should know. You know what you risk by doing these dances?'

'Legends,' said Letamendi. 'Nothing more. Tales you scare your kids with. A justification for your killing off our people: my people.' Letamendi stretched with a brief, animal movement, for an instant his lips drew back from his teeth and there was a flash of the ancient face, canines bared. This was the face of the old enemy, Aylwin thought. The ones they had lured to extinction in their thousands at the hands of *homo sapiens sapiens*, turned them from fellow-humans into something demonic and to be destroyed.

'You,' Letamendi said, 'did for our people once, and you won't again.'

'Because you nearly did for all of us,' Aylwin said.

'You drove us back,' Letamendi insisted. 'Back to living in caves, while the others built huts, then houses, then cities. To hiding, pretending. We weren't apes, you know. When people mention us, they're so busy with "Neanderthal" that they don't hear the "Man" that comes after it. We wore clothes. We had tools, songs, and we buried our dead. We had magic.'

That, Aylwin thought, is why you had to be destroyed. Thousands. Like the trenches. Men dying on barbed wire, screaming. And the rain, the midnight rain. He shivered, and a tear crept from the corner of his left eye. It trickled down to his mouth and he tasted wine and salt.

'But,' Letamendi went on, 'how much hiding and pretending is it possible to do, eh? And how much nowadays?'

'We've always had to do that,' Aylwin said. 'We've always been in the shadows.'

'Not like now,' said Letamendi. 'With their numbers and regimentation. This Franco wants to take names, then maybe kill off anyone who isn't *Español y Católico*. The Catalans, the Galicians – even though he is one –

and the Basques, and by extension ourselves. You can't imagine what he's going to do.'

No, Aylwin thought. Franco's *Falange* wiped out cultures, villages, peoples at the end of the Civil War, but it wasn't going to happen again. Not – he shuddered – the way it had happened to Letamendi's people thirty thousand years ago. But that had needed to happen. Their magic was too strong, it had too much of a grip on their people. The survivors hid among the Basques, themselves an ancient race of disputed origin who called Letamendi's folk 'the old people'. If Letamendi was allowed to carry out his plan in San Isidro or anywhere else, then there was only one consideration in Aylwin's mind: Consuelo. She was beautiful, sensual, gentle; she and John Aylwin loved each other with an intensity he had never known before. But maybe even she would not save him from the rain.

'Juan,' Letamendi said, 'why would you want to live here? Nobody is happy here.'

'I am.'

'Why is that?'

'Consuelo. And also, Diego, it does not rain here. That's why I came here in the first place. That I met Consuelo here just makes my life all the sweeter.'

Letamendi twisted his heavy-browed, bearded face into something that might have been a smile or a snarl and demanded more wine. Through the night they drank together, filling and refilling the wine flask from the cask in the back of the bar. Neither of them seemed to become drunk, but from time to time either Aylwin or Letamendi would fall asleep, then wake again to the sound of the other's voice. John Aylwin twisted inside. What could he do? Anything to keep from the rain. The rain, and the mud, and the rain. He drank again.

At sunrise, the two men stood up and walked out of

the bar. A small crowd greeted them: maybe fifty people, possibly more. Aylwin looked for Consuelo; she was not there. Neither were Pablo or Angela, nor Joselito, nor the priest. Aylwin stood back as Letamendi, raising both hands over his head, declared that they would go to the hill above the town to perform the dance. The crowd walked up the narrow, white rocky path that led upwards from San Isidro, through an area of thorn bushes and cactus, where an occasional goat nibbled thorns; through a fenced-in olive grove and past a stand of orange trees.

'It's going to rain,' Jorge Sanchez exclaimed, his eye now vividly bruised.

'Perhaps,' Aylwin said.

'Oh, you don't believe it?'

Aylwin was watching the dark figure of Letamendi ahead. As far as he was concerned, there was nothing to do. If he tried to stop Letamendi now he would be torn to pieces. All he could do was watch. He wondered where Don Teobaldo was, and if Consuelo were still asleep in bed, her dark hair fanned out on the pillow, so soft and warm.

Eventually Letamendi stopped the procession.

'Here,' he said. The dust-filled Roman theatre, over-looking the scorched valley. The people crowded round him, faces inquisitive. Aylwin stood by the wall where he had lain only two days before. Letamendi moved among the people, edging them into place, smiling, touching, exchanging words of greeting and instruction. Just like a priest, Aylwin thought. But Diego Letamendi made no effort to bring him into the triple circle he was building. There would be no point. Whatever was to be attracted would not sense anything from a Weerde. Even so, Elena went into the innermost circle, holding hands with her new boyfriend.

Ever so gradually the circles began to dance, shuffling sideways, the inner and outermost circles moving against the sun's course, the circle between them following the sun. And just as gradually the dancers began to give voice to a low moan, without harmony or rhythm. Heads low, they started their unearthly mewling; then threw their heads back so that they were looking directly at the pale dawn sky. Their feet scuffled through the dust and debris of years. One of the women convulsed suddenly, drawing a hooked leg up to her breasts, then planted it down again into the dust like a grotesque flamenco. Letamendi stood apart from the circles, head low, nodding approvingly. As Aylwin watched him Letamendi stripped off his shirt and trousers and stood naked, a heavy body matted with red-brown hair, hunched and smiling.

Well, Aylwin thought. The old enemy. We thought they'd all died. But we thought wrong. Maybe we knew, really, all the time.

Now Aylwin's right hand reached out and he took hold of a rock the size of his fist. He crept out from the shadow of the wall and skirted the circle of oblivious dancers. He drew closer, raising the rock, preparing to stove in Letamendi's skull; Letamendi saw him. With a snarl, he threw himself at Aylwin, knocking him in the chest and pushing him down. Aylwin hit the hard ground with kidneys, back and head. His world exploded into colours and lights. Letamendi stood over him for an instant, hatred blazing in his purple eyes. Then he turned back to the dancers.

As Aylwin lay with tears in his eyes, watching Letamendi lead the dance, he noticed a grey figure toiling upwards from the rocks bearing a box in his hands. Don Teobaldo. The priest reached the wall of the ruined house and, setting down the box and taking out its contents, pushed through the circle of dancers and flung himself at Letamendi. His speed was unbelievable. Aylwin saw him throw the contents of a small glass bottle over the shaggy figure, and raising a cross, begin to invoke:

Adiuro ergo te, nequissime draco ... audi ergo, et time, Satana, inimice fidei ...

Spectacular, Aylwin thought sadly, and good for old Don Teobaldo, but the rite of exorcism won't help us. Except that it did. Woken from their stupor by the familiarity of Latin, or Father Duarte's voice perhaps, the triple circle began to peel off from the outside. The shuffling horde began to snap back into consciousness, and looking towards the source of the commotion, saw their village priest being attacked by a creature from their oldest nightmares.

'¡Demonio!' yelled Rodolfo Sanchez, grabbing his cousin by the arm and running towards Letamendi, who was holding the priest by the throat and beginning to squeeze. The two – both big lads – pulled Letamendi's hands away, and Jorge punched him straight in the face. Letamendi took it almost without blinking. He returned the blow, knocking Jorge to the dust, and doubled Rodolfo up with a kick to the stomach. He stood over the two fallen men and faced the villagers. Then he saw his Elena at the edge of the mob in the arms of her village boy, her shift raised around her waist and her groin pressed to his. And the rest of the dancers, some fifty, were heading towards Letamendi, some bearing knives, others with stones.

Diego Letamendi groaned with despair. His luck had gone. He turned and ran past the theatre, all the time looking back over his shoulder to see if the mob was gaining on him. Then he ran straight into the old mine shaft. He had no time to realize what was happening until he was falling through darkness. His long scream echoed out of the earth, its echoes becoming more and more hollow, until after a seeming age the scream ended in a distant wet thud.

The villagers stood around the hole and gazed down. One spat into the darkness. Then they turned and walked back to see to the priest and John Aylwin. Aylwin was already kneeling next to the recumbent priest, a hand on the old man's brow. Duarte was fevered, but plainly not dying.

'I failed,' the priest said.

'No, Don Teobaldo. You succeeded.' He turned to look up over his shoulder at one of the village men. 'Help me carry him back to the village.' The farmer firmly moved Aylwin aside and beckoned to one of his mates, and the two hoisted the priest between them.

In a haze of confusion, the villagers headed back down to San Isidro. None of them could explain what they had been doing and none of them wanted to talk about it. In the dust behind them John Aylwin walked alone, stopping for one last look out over the valley. Somewhere, far away, slow thunder rumbled.

Years later, it rained.

WHAT GOD ABANDONED

Mary Gentle

> What God abandoned, these defended,
> And saved the sum of things for pay.

Epitaph on an Army of Mercenaries, A. E. Housman

There had been no rain for a month and the ground was hot iron under Miles's bare feet. Running, his bones pounded the earth. He bled. Dust rose, choking.

'*– take him!*'

The camp stretched away, apprehended in a single moment of time smaller than sundial or chronometer could measure. All its white tents, pennons, smoke from the cooking fires in the sutlers' quarters, shouts of muleteers, bellows of drill and countermarch, sun, dust and heat blanked out, narrowing down to just two things: two yards behind him the ratchetting-cogwheel snarl of one hound; the other four dogs running silent, without breath to waste, jaws dripping white foam on to the dust.

Half a world away (half the camp away) there was the glint of sun on metal: great-barrelled cannon and ranked organ guns. Men played cards on an upturned drum in the meagre midday shadow of the artillery field. The provost's voice shouted again:

'Seize *hold* of him, rot your guts!'

Miles threw himself forward, legs pumping; healing muscular changes going on at cell level, fibre level . . . To think, now, in the heat of panic; to change anatomies

107

without meditation or preparation – predator's instincts cut in. His muscles hardened, swelled, and drove him surging forward. A dog snarled, heart-stoppingly close, and then swerved, its bay rising a register into distressed yelps at the changed flesh. It doesn't like my smell, Miles Godric thought, smiling despite everything. The bearing of teeth became a snarl and he held back the instinct to turn and rip the animal's throat out.

The hounds' smell was sharp in his nostrils, like vinegar or stale wine. Below lay the slow burn of anger, his pursuers' pheromones on the still air. And below that the stench of the camp: sweat, undercooked food, bloody cloth bandages, gangrene and lice, wine, dung from the herds of sheep and cattle and somewhere the smell of women, camp-followers with their scrawny arms deep in washtubs, the tang of menstrual blood so at odds with the blood shed in battle.

He loped, now, in a pace that ate up distance like a wolf's sprint, the tents and the open ground flashing by. His chest heaved deeply. The hounds fell back, outdistanced.

'Sanctuary!' He pitched on to his knees on the rutted earth, throwing his arms round the carriage of the nearest cannon. 'You're my countrymen – sanctuary!'

Sun-hot metal burned his cheek. He made his chest heave as if panting, dizzy with effort, releasing the sudden changes of flesh. As his body subtly altered, he clung to the culverin.

'Hand him over!' The provost, shouting. And the baying of his accusers:

'The witch! Give us the he-witch!'

' – demand the justice of the camp, and execution – '

' – I'll gut him like a rotten fish and leave him stinking!'

'Sorcerer – man-lover!'

'Who do you want?' That would be the artillery master. John Hammet: the English mercenary and a stickler for camp law.

'He,' the provost said thickly. 'The big Englishman there. Godric.'

'He has right of three days' sanctuary, he has claimed it.'

Miles lowered his head, resting it against the barrel of the cannon, not looking round. The earth under his body breathed heat out, and dust whitened his shabby clothes, and a thirst began to rasp in the back of his throat. The provost's voice sounded, close at hand. 'Very well. Three days only. I know the sanctuary of the artillery fields – he must move no further than twenty-four paces from the gun, or he is mine for the high justice.'

The master of the artillery train chuckled down in his throat. He removed his pipe from his mouth and spat. The spittle hit the earth a yard from Miles's sprawled body, darkening the dust. 'Take him now and I'll take my guns out of the camp, I swear it on God's bones and the Virgin's heart. And then you may fight your next battle with your pike and shot, and may all the saints help you to a victory without us! Sweet Lord, ten weeks since Maximillian's paid us, and now you come sniffing about to maintain justice in my own camp –'

Miles rolled over and sat with his back against the culverin. A blazing blue sky shone, as it had shone for most of the summer. Bad campaign weather. Plague ran through the camp on little feet, taking more men to God than ever the King of Bohemia's muskets and pikes had. He wiped at his sweating forehead. The cardplayers had turned away and had their heads bent over their gambling again. He raised his head and looked up past John Hammet at his accusers.

The provost with his staff of office, a burly man with

the veins on his cheeks broken into a mass of red threads, and warts on his hands. A dozen other men, mostly from his own pike unit. Familiar faces blank with a fear not shown in battle.

'I will station a man here to watch. Three days, you. Then broken on the wheel, before the camp drawn up to watch you.' The provost spoke in a slightly stilted English: a version of the camp patois that was part a myriad German dialects, part French, Spanish, Walloon, Pole and Irish.

'May God damn your soul, and may the little devils of Hell play pincushion with your balls.' Miles had the satisfaction of seeing the provost snarl.

The men turned away, muttering. Miles Godric could not help but look for those he would not see – the little French boy, beardless, hardly out of swaddling bands; his friend, who dressed as a southern German should but whose accent was never quite in one country for more than a day, and the big man that he had first seen after the battle a fortnight ago.

'Succubus!' a departing voice yelled. Miles suddenly felt chill sweat down his back. *Sarnac's* voice? John Hammet hacked at the dirt with the heel of his boot. His face was red, either from wearing good English woollen breeches and doublet in this hellish heat or else from anger. 'Is it true? Have you turned witch? God knows, the priests are burning enough of them now.'

Miles stared after the men walking away across the camp. The provost's leashed dogs bayed. His scent came to them still on this still air. His lip lifted a little over a sharp white tooth.

'Give me a drink,' he said, 'good John, and I'll tell you the truth, I swear.'

A week ago . . .

*

. . . A warm night. Stars shone thick above the makeshift tent. They lazed half in the shelter of its canvas, protected from a myriad biting insects attracted by the warmth of their flesh, and passed bottles of sour wine back and forth as they drank.

'But how will I believe you?' the French boy said. 'When master Copernicus *proves* that the great world hath the sun at its centre, and we and all the lesser stars move about it, and all this without necessity of star deities to guide the planets in their courses.'

Miles rolled over and took the bottle from him. A young man – face spoiled from handsome by pox-scars – with lively eyes and magnetic, sharp gestures. Miles was a little in awe of him: the admiration of the Weerde for a creative mind. The third, older man said lazily, 'Was not what I showed you today sufficient?'

'I have seen instruments for searching out the stars, that's true, but I have seen nothing of what makes the stars move.'

The older man, who spoke slightly imperfect French (as he spoke slightly imperfect Spanish and Walloon, to Miles's certain hearing) took a deep draught from the bottle. He appeared to be fifty or so; broad-shouldered, strong, and sunburned. Miles noted with half his attention that the man, Maier, did not grow drunk.

'Love moves the stars, as the Italian wrote.' Maier wiped wine from his thick, spade-cut beard. 'Look you, master Descartes, you asked me for such wisdom as I can give, and it is this: there are correspondences between the earth and the heavens, such that all living things are subject to influence from the stars, and it is with the help of star talismans that I draw down influences and perform healings.'

'And with such powers that you perform your alchemical experiments? You note I have studied your own *Arcana arcanissima* and *Atalanta fugiens*, master Michael Maier. And for all this,' the boy Descartes said drunkenly, 'you ask no pay. A sad thing in a mercenary army. Much more and I shall truly believe you one of that Brotherhood that travels the world secretly, apparelled in each country as that country dresses, cognizant of secret signs, and practising the occult arts. But we are not – '

Descartes' beardless face screwed up in concentration, and he brought out:

' – we are not in an inn, neither are we under a *rose*.'

An interrupting voice took Miles by surprise so that his heart thudded into his mouth. The fourth man, Sarnac, said: 'Rosicrucians, is it, now? And will you have our Maier a member of that secret Order?'

He bellowed a big, relaxed laugh. A look went between Maier and Descartes that escaped him. He has the intelligence of a bullock, Miles reflected. How can it be that I . . .

The big man's smell dominated the tent, blotting out all others. Miles lay on his pallet, picking at ends of straw; the breath shallow in his chest, breathing in, breathing in the male smell that dizzied him. He watched, in the campfire's shifting illumination, the curl of a lock of hair, the fall of loose wide shirtsleeves and buttock-hugging breeches, the knotted bare calves, the shape of broad shoulders and belly and balls. Wanting to bury his face in soft and solid flesh. He reached across Sarnac. His hand brushed the man's yellow-stubbled cheek as he grabbed a wine bottle, and the man swatted absently as if at an insect. Sitting up to drink, Miles shifted so that they sat hip to hip.

'Give me room, can't you?' Good-natured, Sarnac elbowed him a yard aside with one hefty shove. Miles spilled wine, swore, and slammed the bottle down to cover the sight of his hands: shaking so that they could hold nothing. Sarnac stood, took a pace or two to the other side of the fire, and hitched down the front of his breeches. One unsteady hand grabbed his cock. A stream of urine arced away into the darkness, shining in the fireglow.

O wine it makes you merry, Sarnac sang, *O wine, the enemy of women;*

It gives you to them, it makes you useless to them . . .

Michael Maier lay with his upper body in the rough shelter of two sticks and a length of canvas, so that his face was in shadow. His voice sounded from the darkness:

'Come into Prague with me, master Descartes.'

Miles Godric belched. 'What is there in a sacked city that we haven't had already? The gold's gone to the officers, and there isn't a woman left virgin between here and the White Hill.'

Descartes ignored him. 'And see what, master Maier?'

The bearded man pointed a stubby finger. 'You came searching for that Brotherhood in which you profess not to believe. If I tell you what is old news, that the city of Prague has been the heart of Hermetic magic since the days of Doctor Dee, then will you believe me when I say there is enough yet remaining that you would wish to view it?'

'Bollocks!' Miles snorted. 'There's nothing left. The fornicating Habsburg Emperor's fornicating army's had it all.'

He settled back on his loot-stuffed pallet. The burghers of Prague had shown little inclination, last month, to stand a siege for their king after the battle of the White Hill. They threw open their gates to welcome the invading troops with indecent haste, but it did them no good: Maximillian of Bavaria and Tilly and the Imperial general Bucquoy ordered the city closed and gave the mercenaries a week to loot it bare. Truly, the troops should have robbed only the followers of the King of Bohemia, sparing those loyal to Habsburg Ferdinand; but questions are not asked in the heat of plunder, and Miles Godric had little German and the complexities of the German Princes' wars defeated him in any case, and Prague as it now was – burned, stripped, slaughtered and deserted – lacked only the scars of artillery fire to make it seem as if it had been taken after a six months' siege.

'Will you come?' Maier demanded of the boy.

Sarnac prowled back into the circle of firelight, his feet unsteady. He elbowed Descartes aside and went down on to his knees and fell into the makeshift tent beside Miles, face down, breathing thickly. The light shone on his white-blond hair.

Descartes said, 'Yes.'

'Don't leave without us,' Miles said. He studied the finger he had waved accusingly in the air with owlish curiosity. 'We'll come into the city with you. We'll come into . . . what was I saying?'

He let himself slip back down on to his elbows, then rolled slowly sideways off his pallet, so that his back and buttocks rested snugly against Sarnac's chest, belly, prick and thighs. Somewhere on the border of sleep, he smelled Sarnac's flesh tense. The big man grunted, asleep and instinctive, throwing one arm across him, then rolled and kicked until Miles could only sit up, dazed, and say, 'You're a plague-take-it unquiet bedfellow, Sarnac!'

He lay awake and aching the rest of the night, not daring even to relieve himself in dreams.

Morning came welcome cold, the hour before dawn.

Miles stood with feet planted squarely apart, lacing the unfastened front points of his breeches to his sleeve-

114

less doublet. Between his feet, scabbarded, lay an arming sword and a foot-and-a-half dagger. The sixteen-foot pike that was most of the rest of his equipment still rested across two notched sticks, supporting the tent canvas. He absently picked at a rust spot on its blade with a pared fingernail. The fingernails he had not pared with a dagger grew white and hard and more pointed than might be expected. Momentarily he covered his face with his hands to hide the change of stubble vanishing and leaving him clean-shaven.

He buckled on sword-belt and sword. Dew damped down the dust. He squinted across the waking camp, seeing the French boy on his way back from the sutlers with his arms full of bread and raw meat. Miles turned to build the fire in the fire-pit hotter, sanded out the inside of his helm, and filled it with water to boil.

'Beef?'

'Beef,' the boy agreed, kneeling down and spilling his load on to the earth. 'Out of Prague. We didn't eat like this before White Hill.'

Experienced, Miles said, 'We won't eat like it in a month, so eat while you can. Did you hear aught?'

'The usual rumours. We're to strike and move towards Brandenburg, to catch Frederick's Queen who's there with child; or else march on Mansfeld's mercenaries – but he'll turn his coat if we offer him pay, they say – or else we're to sit here and wait while the German Princes decide which one of them'll rebel against Habsburg Ferdinard *this* time.'

Miles grunted. The morning had brought no sign of the woman and two boys he'd hired as servants to carry his plunder. He suspected the company captain had added them to his growing entourage. 'I'd happily winter here.'

Prompt on that, Sarnac groaned inside the tent and

crawled out with his fair hair all clotted up in tufts and sleep grit in his eyes. Miles reached down and, with the hand that would have thumbed clean those eyes and lashes, handed the big man a pot of mulled wine.

'Urrghm.'

'And God give you a good morning, also.' Amused, suddenly warmed and confident, Miles chuckled. He ruffled Sarnac's long hair roughly enough for it to count as horseplay, and walked a good distance from the tent to piss, standing for long moments cock in hand and squinting his eyes against the lemon-white blaze of sunrise. On his return (the smell of boiling beef rank on the air) he found Maier about, dressed, armed, and neat as ever.

He remembered, with one of the flashes of memory which come in the dawn hour, Maier elbow-to-elbow with him in the thick of the line-fight, his pike raised up to shoulder level, a yard of sharpened metal slamming into enemy eyes, cheeks, throats, ribs. Not neat then. Splashed red from chest to thigh, doublet and breeches soaking. A bad war, White Hill. The boy Descartes had vomited most of the following day, and Miles had also – but he could smell the gangrenous wounded two leagues away, and hear them too; and to excuse his reaction had drunk himself into a stupor and woken – yes, woken to find himself beside the big drunken Frenchman from another pike unit, a man in his thirties, smelling of sweat and grass and blood: Sarnac. Sarnac.

He rescued some of the beef from the boiling helm and gulped it down hot, ripping the fresh bread apart with his strong teeth. Preference would have given him raw fresh beef, too; but the teaching held that such habits were unsafe. He chuckled under his breath. As for what the Kin might say about *this* appetite . . .

'God's teeth, man! You're not going looting without

your comrades, are you?' Sarnac put his arm across Maier's shoulder. The bearded man (Swiss, could he be?) smiled. Young master Descartes sulked.

'Loot for the wit, master Sarnac, not the belly or the purse.'

'What difference? We'll come.' His gaze fell on Miles, and his brow creased.

'God save us,' Miles Godric crossed himself, 'let's go to the city while we may. Tilly's thieving bastards have been there again, but they may have left something for thieving bastards like us.'

Dawn began to send white light across the camp. Pennants flickered into life on the officers' tents. The harsh bray of mules sounded. The four of them threaded a way through the rest of the pike unit with its drudges, wives and servants; through musketeers, grooms, hawkers, children and quacks; past two sutleresses coming to blows over a stray sheep (Sarnac stopped to watch and Miles hung back with him, until the big man suddenly realized that neither Descartes nor Maier had stopped for the entertainment), and out through the ranked wagons that formed the military camp's walls.

Midmorning found them in Prague, picking a way over blackened timbers, across squares and alleys choked with debris. Miles found a chipped dagger and shoved it under his belt. The rest of the ground was picked clean. Only the stench and the bodies heaped up for the common grave remained in the city. Refugees dotted the countryside for leagues around. It seemed to Miles that wherever he stepped, flocks of crows rose up from the streets. He watched them wheel, wide-fingered wings black against the sun, and drop down, and stab their carrion beaks into sprawled limbs. Maggots, disturbed, rippled away like sour milk. The only things more numerous than the crows were the flies. He wiped his mouth clear of them.

'This . . .' The French boy waved a hand vaguely, as if he had lost his sight. 'This.'

Sarnac plodded back from the open door of an unburned house, empty-handed. 'Nothing! This quarter's been done over – I'll wager ten thalers it was that bastard Hammet's gun crews. I wonder they left food for the crows. Or if I heard they'd been selling this to the sutlers, and we eating it, it wouldn't surprise me.'

The boy retched and bent over, a thin trail of slime swinging from his mouth.

'This way,' Maier directed.

Miles, hot in brigandine and morion helmet but not about to go even into a sacked enemy city unarmoured, followed the older pikeman down between two stone mansions and out into an open space.

The gardens of Prague had not been deliberately sacked, but fire had raged down from the slum quarter and made a scorched earth of the Palace grounds. Miles shaded his eyes, staring out across lines of blackened hedges at stumps of trees.

'There is enough left yet. Master Descartes! Here.' Maier turned and walked to where a terrace stood, the stone blackened, and stood staring out across the ruins. Miles followed him. Descartes and Sarnac came some distance behind, walking out into the gardens, the boy with his hand on Sarnac's arm. Miles felt his chest tighten. He stripped off and threw down his mailed gloves, and swore.

'The Order of which that boy speaks,' Michael Maier said softly, 'has its rules, which are these. That each Brother of the Order travel, alone, through what countries of the world he may visit. That he in all things dress and speak as a citizen of the country he is in, whatever it may be, so that each man shall take him for one of his own. And also that he shall teach, as he goes, and not take life; but that last – '

Maier frowned, dreamily.

'– that last rule is not so strictly adhered to as is said.'

Miles Godric flared his nostrils, catching no scent even of a feral line, and smiled, showing clean and undecayed teeth. Cattle sometimes imitate their masters, all unknowing. 'Are you a Brother of the Rosy Cross then, master Maier? I'd heard Rosicrucians infested Prague and are half the reason the King and Queen fell into exile. Not a safe thing to be if *concealment* is your rule. In this country they burn sorcerers.'

Maier grinned. 'And in this country, master Miles, they burn sodomites. I think your big man there will not consent to your desires. I think him a woman-lover only – well, they have their peculiar superstitions, these men.'

'Yes,' Miles said. He watched Descartes and Sarnac climb up on to the ruined terrace. The big man wiped his sleeve across his face, mopping sweat; Miles's teeth nipped his tongue.

'You may yet see the patterns of the knot gardens,' Michael Maier said, expansively gesturing. The sun flashed from his breastplate and morion helmet. 'Master Descartes, allow me to instruct you: *that* was the astrological garden, whose hedges grew in the shapes of the zodiac, and within the hedges the plants and herbs pertaining to each sign. *That* was the garden of automata, and *that* of necromancy – '

'Necromancy!'

'You cannot stand in a sacked city and baulk at the dead, young master.'

'But necromancy! But there,' the boy said, all his vitality momentarily gone, 'it is superstition, as my friend

Father Mersenne tells me; and the Holy Church would not allow its practice, even were it a real danger.'

Maier asked acidly, 'And does your Father Mersenne instruct you in logic?'

Miles left them quarrelling. Sarnac, idly wandering, hooked a bottle out of his half-laced brigandine and swigged at it, his back to the garden. Miles moved cautiously towards him.

Trails of soot blackened the masonry surrounding the garden. Something that might have been a rose-vine straggled up the wall, a dead bird crucified in amongst its thorns. Sarnac sat down with his back to the sun-hot wall. The harsh calls of crows drowned Miles's footsteps. The big man sat with his head thrown back, eyes closed. Dust grimed his corded throat. The bright curls of his hair showed under the battered morion he wore, the straps dangling loose; and sun shone through the golden hair on his chin and arms and bare shins, gleaming. A pulse beat in the hollow of his neck. Wine dried on his mouth and chin.

Cold to the belly, Miles sat down on his heels. Sarnac opened his eyes. Light shone in them, as in brandy: brown and gold. He half frowned.

'Sarnac.' Miles swallowed. The cold hollow under his ribs remained, and the smell of the man made him feel as if the earth dissolved. He said, 'You must know I would lie with you.'

The briefest joy in gold-brown eyes; then Sarnac's face went blank, went white and then red. His voice came thick with disgust. 'You? The Italian vice? Sweet saint's bones, you mean it for truth.'

Miles held up his hands in protest. He looked at his rough, calloused skin speculatively. 'Please ... please. Listen. I'm not as men are.'

The big man burst out into a laugh that began in

scorn and ended in revulsion. 'So I've heard many say.'

'Sarnac, have you ever seen me unclothed?' He held the man's gaze. 'Or bathing in a river, or pissing?'

'No.' Puzzlement on Sarnac's face.

No, because you have been with the unit no more than a week. Miles bent forward, intense; he used the Frenchman's own language. 'Because of my great desire for you, and because you should not think me capable of an unclean sin, I tell you my secret. I am no man, because I am a woman.'

The big man's mouth opened, and stayed open. His coarse brows dipped, frowning. A look began to come into his face: something between pity and lust and condescension.

'A woman soldier? One of the baggage train, tricked out in breeches − no, but I've seen you fight as no woman can! Are you one of the mankind sort, then, aping us?'

Behind him, Miles heard Maier's impatient raised voice: 'But I cannot prove it to you *here and now*! You *must* wait. Whether you will or no.'

Softening his voice, Miles held Sarnac's gaze. 'No, I wish for the privileges of no man; I would not have manhood if it were to buy. It is an old tale. I have seen such played on the public stage in London − a woman in boy's guise following her sweetheart to the wars. I dressed in male garments for safety and preservation of virtue and, when I learned he had died upon the field, stayed, and grew used to weaponry, since what else is left to me but to serve my Prince?'

A *very* old tale, Miles reflected sardonically. Sworn virgin warrior-maids are acceptable to him; this man had for countrywoman three centuries gone that Jehanne, who fought the English. Were I to say: I am a woman who loves fighting, who loves not the lordship of men, who will not wear petticoats – well then, Sarnac, would you lie with me? No, you would not.

Sarnac, still frowning, began to smile. 'Are you truly a she?'

Miles let out a breath he had not been aware of holding.

'Ay, ay, God's truth, and I'll prove it to you. Will you lie with me, and love me? Nay, not now, we're observed. Secretly. Tonight.'

Maier's voice sounded closer behind him, quarrelling with Descartes' importunate questions; but Miles did not move, still sitting forward on his haunches, the tight cloth of his breeches hiding his erection.

'Yes. Tonight,' Sarnac said.

Habit kept Miles outside the camp, in concealment. He lay up in a burned-out cellar near the walls of the city, eating crow-meat and less palatable offal and at last sleeping the thick, heavy sleep of the change. Shifting subcutaneous layers of body fat, retracting testicles and penis, moving cartilage and hollowing muscle. Knowing what he would be when he woke.

The dark-lantern, its shutter half closed, made a golden glow in the cellar. Sarnac grunted. Straw dug sharply into Miles's back. She rubbed the slick length of her body against his, her breasts against the rough hair of his chest; shifted so that his hips and elbows were more to her liking and wound her legs about his hips. He thrust, his penis finding obstruction (she had not, after all, forgotten the hymen) and then pierced her.

'Ah-h . . .'

Miles Godric made deep noises in her throat. She buried her face against his shoulder, smelling the sweetness of his skin: sweat and dirt and woodsmoke. She bit at the bulge of muscle with her teeth.

'Wildcat!'

He pinned her. She shoved her hips up, taking him deep inside her; the tightness of a new vagina not wholly according to her plan, but still she held him and thrust against his thrusts, and rolled over still holding so that she straddled him.

'Damn, but you're lively!' Sarnac, sweating, leaned up to nuzzle and suck at her breasts. 'Miles – no, what do I call you? What's your name?'

'Jehanne.'

The word came out unplanned; Sarnac, his eyes bright and heavy, never noticed. He mumbled the name into her belly and pulled her down, one hand flat on the small of her back, pumping up into her.

'Woman!' he groaned.

She rode him as he climaxed, expecting nothing for herself, but the smell of him and days of wanting surprised her: she raked fingernails down his chest and bit his shoulder, drawing blood, with her own orgasm.

That day and the following she came back sweating and grinning from training fights, stepping lively and whistling, not caring who saw. For those who questioned she told tales of a rare treasure looted out of Prague.

'You should have something for this,' she said expansively to Descartes on the third day, sitting outside the tents. 'Didn't you fight at White Hill with the best of us? What will you take home to your sweetheart?'

The boy looked up from where he sprawled outside the tent. His deft fingers shaved a pen-nib, and a notebook lay open beside him. 'Pox, if I'm unlucky!'

'You're too young,' she teased.

'I was twenty-two when I left Paris,' Descartes said,

naming an age precisely one third her own, 'when I joined with Maurice of Nassau's men. It being my thought that, were I to be with an army, I would as soon be with confirmed victors.'

Miles rubbed more carefully with oiled cloth at the blade of her pike until it shone. She laid it down on the earth and stretched, and lodged one ankle over the other and leaned back on her elbows, surveying the evening.

'Nassau's bastards win,' she confirmed idly. 'So what are you doing with Habsburg Ferdinand instead of the Protestants?'

'I belong to Holy Mother Church. It's Maier who's the Lutheran. He's the one you should question. Or,' he quoted a prevalent maxim, '"So we serve our master honestly, it is no matter what master we serve"'.

She squinted at the horizon, seeing thick pine forests darkening the mountains and, below them, white harvest fields burned black in the army's passing. 'You had that out of Sarnac's mouth.'

'Ay. Along with "In war there is no law and order, it is the same for master and man", and "He who wages war fishes with a golden net".'

The boy rubbed at his scarred face and rolled on to his side to look up at her. His small body had a kind of electric vitality to it; some spiritual equivalent of the wiry strength that made him train for the pike instead of (as he more properly ought) the musket.

'Master Maier showed me Tycho Brahe's famous astronomical apparatus, in the city, before the – before it was taken away.'

Miles snorted. 'Before the Rosy-Cross brethren had it?'

'You don't believe in them.'

She shrugged, looking down a longer perspective of

history than the human. 'I don't know what I *do* believe in, boy. I doubt, therefore I must think: and if I think, I cannot doubt that I am; what else is there?'

His eyes glowed. 'Much! Master Maier is instructing me. I write it all down here. Listen.'

In a sudden expansive affection for the boy and all the world, Miles Godric sat and sharpened the blade of her dagger, and listened to him declaim on analytical geometry, alchemical marriages, and other subjects not worth a penny beside the colour of the hair on Sarnac's belly.

On the fourth night Miles stayed in the cellar after Sarnac departed. The big man kissed her, left the lantern, and at the doorway turned with one last puzzled look.

'You should let me guard you back to camp ...' His voice trailed off. She could see in his face how he could not take in the idea of a woman who was neither to be raped nor protected against rape. 'Are you content, lass?'

Miles nodded. 'I'll return later, as I have before.'

She listened to him go, hearing his footsteps halfway across the ruined city. Owls shrieked and rats scuttled; and she curled up with her chin on her forearms, eyes dazzling in the lantern's yellow glare. She reached out and extinguished it.

And for tomorrow's drill? she thought. Sword and falchion I can use in this shape, and have; but for the pike should I change and be a man? The weight may be too much to bear ... And if not, still, there's risk of discovery. Not as Family, but as woman, and then what? The baggage train, washing and whoring. I might stay concealed a woman soldier, as I have seen many do, with only a few of her comrades knowing and keeping secret. But too many of my comrades have already seen me male.

She was not a small thing, lying there in the starlight; only her skin was a little smoother for the layer of fat beneath it, cushioning the muscles. Her eyes gleamed flat silver like pennies. One hand stroked her breast, and she closed her eyes and slid down into the sleep of change. And so did not wake when they came.

'But when will you show me? When?'

'Soon! Be patient. You had patience enough to spend two years searching us out. Have a little more.'

The voices finally woke him. Miles shifted uneasily, rolled over, grabbed breeches and brigandine and – old habit of many night alarms – stood dressed and armed before he properly woke. The cellar was dark, the door outlined with silver. On silent feet he slid out into the ruined moonlit alleys, shaking his head against sleepiness and chill. Voices, familiar voices, but where? And he – Miles grabbed inelegantly, discovering himself awake and male. And the voices . . . he slid the morion briefly from his head and cocked an ear. The voices were not as near as night-bemusement had made him think. But they were none the less familiar voices. Maier and Descartes.

He glanced at the constellations. Two hours to dawn. The way to the camp would be clear, and the dead-watch not prone to querying brother soldiers (if, indeed, they were not risking execution by dozing on duty). But then there was curiosity, and the question of what the French boy and Maier might be doing here, now, of all times.

Miles padded through rubble-choked alleys, silently climbing shifting, burned beams, avoiding pits, the pupils of his eyes wide and dark. The small winds of night brought him little but the stench of decaying flesh. For that reason he didn't realize Maier and Descartes were not alone until he heard boots scratching at stone. Half an hour's solitary backing and tracking brought him to where he could observe. He eased into the shadow of a fire-blackened tree stump. Dry ferns brushed his face. He eased up a little, looking over the bank, and blinked momentarily at the space opened up before him.

Far below, the river shone silver. The town ran up in steep banks to either side. No lanterns, no movement; the darkness shrouded destruction. Directly ahead, the towers of a palace rose up, almost untouched. The Emperor Ferdinand's banners now draggled from its spires, and men were quartered in its far chambers; but this part, overlooking the formal gardens, had no occupants that his hearing could detect. The only living beings – four of them – moved in the gardens below. Miles slid on his belly over the bank and down, moving soundlessly despite armour, his dagger drawn and carried in his left hand, ready.

He moved silently through burned gardens, past a hundred blackened and overturned marble statues, into what had been the centre of a maze.

'I had such dreams, last winter.' The boy, Descartes, stood with his arms wrapped in his cloak, hugging it around his body. His sharp, uncomely face caught the full moon's brilliance. Miles saw the moon's reflected twin in his eyes.

'Dreams. Nothing to do but winter over in Bavaria with the rest of Nassau's soldiers, get drunk and have women. I wondered, why did I ever leave Paris? Why did I ever join the God-forsaken Protestant cause?'

Softly, so that even Miles could hardly hear him, Maier prompted: 'But the dreams?'

'Of the black art which is called mathematics.'

Enthusiasm in the boy's voice, that faded with his next words. 'I dreamed that mathematics answered all, accounted for all, *was* all. That nothing moved on this breathing earth but mathematics could account for it, down to the final atom ... They were dreams of terror. They had no God in them, or if they did, removed far off and become watchmaker to the world: winding it up and leaving it until the end should strike. There was no magic.'

Unguarded, his French was of better quality than heard in the camp, and Miles with difficulty adjusted his ear to it.

'And then I began to read pamphlets published out of Amsterdam and Prague. The *Chymische Hochzeit Christiani Rosenkreutz*, the *Fama Fraternitatis*. And broadsheet appeals to the Brotherhood of the Rosy Cross to come out into the open, to share their secret knowledge of how the world works – how everything that is, is living and magical. *Everything*. How rocks, gems, trees and stars share souls, as men do. How the alchemical transformation can change all our spirits to gold, and bring again the Golden Age of which the ancients wrote! And how a great instauration of magical science will come on the earth, and the bond be knitted again between the Lutheran Churches and the Roman Church into one great Christendom.'

Someone sighed behind the half-burned hedges. A woman, Miles realized. He felt bare-handed to see what cover he lay on, detecting no twigs to snap; and slid up on to one knee and then on to his feet. He reached down and loosened his sword, thumbing it an inch out of the mouth of the scabbard.

'And all this is words!' Descartes' voice snagged on pain. 'I must have proof. *Is* there such a Brotherhood? Do you have such magical knowledge? And is it truth, or charlatan tricks?'

Miles flared his nostrils. The sweet stink of rotting flesh covered all other scents. He could hear heartbeats, indrawn breath; but the four of them so close blurred his senses, so that he could not tell where the last one stood, or how near he was to the woman. The moonlight blinded his night vision. Using an habitual trick he searched the shadows with only peripheral sight. There?

Michael Maier put his hand on Descartes' shoulder. He carried his cloak bundled over his left arm, leaving free the hilt of his military rapier, hood covering the glint of his helmet.

'That is a poor world you have in your dreams.' Maier's voice softened uncharacteristically. His French was adequate, not as good as the boy's, but as good as his Italian, or Spanish, or (if it came to it, Miles knew) English. 'I will give you *magia* for your mechanical universe, if you will.'

'*Magia?*'

'Platonist magic, sometimes called the Egyptian or Hermetic Art. It is easier explained if you have first seen. Hold in your mind the thought that all you have read is true. I have stood in these gardens on the day when statues spoke with human voices and moved, inspired by the spirits in them; when the sick came and left healthy, and the dead with them – believe it – and the sacred marriage of the rose and the dew made bud, blossom and fruit grow upon these same trees all in one hour.'

Miles heard the rustle of cloth. He stepped easily between sharp twigs and pressed his hand over the woman's mouth, his dagger-point denting her skin. He pitched his voice to carry no further than her ear. 'Cry out and I'll rip out your throat. What do you hear?'

This close to her he smelled satin, sour flesh, dirty hair, but no fear whatsoever. Maier's voice sounded again and Miles could feel the woman strain to hear what came so clearly to him. Michael Maier said, 'All this through *magia*. All this because our souls and our flesh are one, and at one with the living universe. We are demiurges upon this earth, and all of it from stone to sea will obey us, if a man but know the prayers, words, actions and sacrifices necessary for it. We of the Brotherhood may speak to each other across vast distances, travel the sky and sea unhindered, heal, create gold and pray down the wrath of the Divine upon the Divine's enemies.'

Miles Godric showed teeth, amused: one of the Weerde hearing – despite the searing belief in the man's voice – the old lie from a human mouth. Descartes coughed. 'You may say so.'

Miles heard the fourth heart beat now, not so close as he had feared. A dozen yards away in the wrecked maze.

'I say so!' Maier shouted. The empty gardens echoed and Miles saw him look about, startled. More quietly, the burly man repeated, 'I say so.'

'But your true Alchemical Marriage, your Rosicrucian Kingdom to be founded here in Prague where all this is to come about, where is *that* now – now that the city is sacked and the King and Queen exiled or dead?'

'That hope is not ended.'

The woman breathed hard against his body. Her hands hung limp in the massive folds of her gown. Stiff, starched lace rasped against Miles's face and he felt the small coldnesses of gems in her hair. Listening hard, he momentarily ignored the sensations of his skin.

A soundless blast lifted Miles and threw him.

Stone and gravel scarred his palms. The world dissolved. Miles shook, his mouth full of blood, head ringing, hands and face afire. Mortar fire or cannon? His left hand hung bloody and empty; he did not recall drawing his sword but the fingers of his right hand locked about the hilt.

Neither sword nor shot, but the suddenly loosened power of a human mind seared the marrow in his bones.

'Maier!'

The voice he did not recognize as his: a bewildered and outraged child's shriek. He cowered, one hand over his head, sword thrusting aimlessly into the dark. Voices screamed and shattered around him; he stood up, and the sky laughed as his sight cleared. The night glowed blue.

Rich blue and gold, and the stars above were gone. The night sky over Prague shone with figures: planetary gods and zodiacal beasts, figures with swords and flaming hair, balances and spears, winged feet and bright eyes that shone no colour of the earth. The tides of power rocked the sky and Miles fell down on his knees. He stared at the spade-bearded man. He heard the French boy cry out, and could not tell whether it was in joy or terror.

'Maier!'

The older man laughed.

'What, Miles, you here? Well, then. See. See with clear eyes. Master Descartes, the Rosicrucian Kingdom is not ended, albeit the city has fallen. Look with clear eyes upon the Marriage of the Thames and the Rhine, the Winter King and Queen, Strength and Wisdom, *sophia* and *scientia*. Look upon the true Alchemical Union: Frederick the heir of the Germanies, Charlemagne's heir, Barbarossa's son; with Elizabeth the Phoenix Reborn, the daughter of Jacobus and heir of Gloriana, England's Virgin.'

The oldest of Weerde fears pierced him.

'Oh God I am most heartily sorry that I have offended Thee!' Miles buried his head down against his knees, mumbling. The hot stench of urine made his eyes water. He rocked, holding his bloody hand to his gut, gripping the hard hilt of his sword; even in this extremity giving to his fear the name humanity in this age knew. 'I am most heartily sorry; preserve me from the Devil; preserve me from Him who walks up and down among men; dear God, most holy Lord . . .'

Maier's hands gripped his shoulder, shaking him. 'Miles!'

Miles Godric at last lifted his head. 'Is it you who are doing all of this? Don't you know you'll call him, you'll call the Devil down on us? On *all* of us?'

Maier, kneeling behind him, put his warm arms around Miles's shoulders. 'Is *that* anything to fear? *Look.*'

Miles whimpered.

The two figures walked out into the centre of the maze. A woman and a man. Now the sound of their hearts beat against his ears, deafening him. A man with a plump face, dark hair and soft dark eyes; dressed in cloth-of-silver doublet and breeches, the Order of the Garter at his knee, but crowned in nothing save rose-coloured light. And a woman in cloth-of-gold farthingale and stomacher and ruff, a fashion two generations out of date: her sharp-featured face the living image of a greater Queen. Frederick and Elizabeth: Winter King and Queen of Bohemia.

Not being human, Miles had only to gather his wits – thinking Yes, they escaped the battle! – to see the truth of it: a shabby man, a woman in a torn kirtle, their faces the pinched faces of refugees. The power that beat about them was not theirs. But a power none the less, that brought the beasts of the night – foxes, wolves,

wild boar – creeping to their feet, eyes shining. The rose
light gleamed with images of lion and stag and pelican
piercing her own breast. Fireflies darted across the
suddenly hot air.

In the false, living tapestry of the night sky the Lords
of Power bowed from Their thrones. Roses seemed to
bud and blossom from the garden's blackened twigs. A
petal brushed Miles and he shuddered uncontrollably,
feeling it against his skin.

'How can they . . .' The French boy knelt beside Maier,
his face wide and wondering. 'How can they still be
here, and their armies defeated and the city taken?'

'Because they are not defeated. Because they only
await their time. Which I, and you, will help to bring
about. Nay, speak to them, question them. I will be your
warrant for it.' Maier stood and pulled Descartes to his
feet. 'Come.'

The boy wiped his hair off his face, with the gesture
seeming to take on years. He stepped forward. Something in his expression commanded: not the wonder,
but the confirmation of knowledge.

'Is it so?' he said softly. 'And is it true, this union and
this harmony?'

The woman spoke. 'Witness. We would have you
witness, for you are the child of Our marriage. You are
herald to the ages to come of what We proclaim: the
union of man and beast, spirit and matter, soul and sub-
stance.'

The man spoke. 'Witness Us as We are. Yours is a
great soul, such a pivot as the world turns on, and We
have called you these two years that you should witness
Us, and proclaim the Rose and the Cross openly to the
world. So all men may be as We are.'

To Miles's ears they mouthed rote-learned words
badly. But the boy grinned, sucking at his still

ink-stained fingers, and opened his mouth with the light of debate in his eyes.

'No!' Miles shielded his face with his arm. Shaded from that illusory light he could stagger to his feet, gain balance in the shifting world.

Time split now into clock-ticks, each one for ever, as time changes on the field of battle into a thousand non-sequential *nows*. He saw Their lips move, and Descartes' face shining. He saw Maier with arms folded, standing as a man stands who controls all circumstance. He saw the maze now blossoming with a hundred thousand red and white roses, their scent choking him with sweetness. And he heard, on the edge of consciousness, something else: the metallic clash of legions marching, lost legions, led by the Devil, and coming here to feed – he sobbed laughter – attracted like moths to a campfire. Attracted to the Light. Small whirling bodies crisped in flame . . .

Miles Godric beat at his clothes with bloody hands. His sword fell, discarded, and stuck point-down and quivering, a bar of silver fire. The French boy took another step forward, holding out his hands. Miles strode forward and grabbed him around the body, lifting the boy and making to throw them both backwards away from Maier and his illusion of a mystical Marriage. Descartes struggled. The boy's head jerked around. Miles stared into his eyes: eyes as dark blue and wide as a child's. It seared into him, the origin of this force. Not Maier.

Not Maier, no more creative than a Weerde, but one of the human minds that is bound to change an age, whatever age it is born into; a mind only requiring, like a sun's beam, to be focused for it to burn. This boy's mind, tapped all unknowing, so that he spoke to the figures of his own desires – his own, and Michael

Maier's. Miles staggered, this close to the boy all barriers permeable now, even the barrier between soul and soul.

Memory filled Miles Godric: memory not his own. The Kin's memory. A vast coldness seared him, and a vast dark; and then the darkness blazed into a light more unbearable because in that light he saw one speck of dirt, himself, standing upon another speck of dirt which is the turning world; all circling a match-flame sun, one more in a swarm of firefly-stars. And between earth and suns, between stars and stars, such an infinite predatory emptiness and *appetite* that he whimpered again, eyes shut, himself and the boy curled foetally together on the garden earth, choking back tears in case they should be heard.

'No!' Maier screamed. His hands pried at Miles. 'No! Give him back to me! I want him for this – '

In a kind of battlefield calm, Miles knelt up and supported the boy across his thighs. He pried back one eyelid to study the boy's dilated pupil. 'Want must be your master.'

The approaching tread of the Devil's legions beat on his ears. Miles lay the boy down and stood up, grasping and recovering his sword.

'Well, I will have him for this in any case, and damn you,' the older man said. His voice held all the blindness of human belief. He knelt down, efficiently scooping the boy up, the thin body slumping forward, and drew his knife. 'I've waited for this conjunction of stars – and They have waited also, my King and Queen there – and now I shall give Them what They need to make Them actual, in this world, for ever.'

The irregular tread rasped in Miles's ears. He rubbed one sweat-sticky hand across his eyes. Movement in the Rose Garden, now. The tread of legions . . .

The moon, distorted by the boy's mind, made a false

magia-light in the Garden. A white figure seemed to come into the centre of the maze, moving jerkily and swiftly towards Miles. The light shone on stone armour, full Gothic harness and stone sword, stone features; shone upon limbs where white marble flushed now with the rose-and-gold of incipient life.

Reacting instantaneously Miles feinted and slashed, backed two steps and then came forward, his blade swooping under the marble statue's sword and hitting with two-handed force where the armour gaped vulnerably under the arm.

His sword broke against the motionless statue.

His fingers fell open, numb. Metal shards shrieked and whirred past his face. He shouted, his voice ringing across the broken city gardens. Other white things appeared to move in the moonlight: all the stone warriors of the Garden, breeding like Cadmus's dragon's teeth.

Miles stumbled back, no longer sure what illusion might become truth, given such an outpouring of the mind's power. He caught a heel against Maier's outstretched leg and staggered.

The older man bent over Descartes, his dagger carefully bleeding a vein in the boy's left wrist. With the blood and his fingers, he drew sigils on the hard earth. The spirals of psychic force tightened, tightened, building higher. Miles saw the boy's eyelids move and finally open, saw him look up into Maier's face; saw him realize the open conduit, his soul drained to power visions, illusions, that Maier demanded become reality. The boy shrieked.

'Put an end to this.' Miles kicked Maier accurately and hard on the side of the head. The older man's dagger stabbed up and pierced his thigh. He sat down heavy, staring at the bleeding. Maier groped around for the boy's arm, and Descartes crawled crab-wise away from him on the burned earth.

'Stop it. *While we yet can.*' Miles hoisted himself up and sat down again heavily, one leg no more use to stand on than water. He began to drag himself towards Maier.

Roses seemed to grow up from the ground and twine around his legs and arms. Their thorns bit deep into his flesh. He threw back his head, teeth gritted, straining. The vines held. Twisting, for one second he found himself staring into what he had avoided seeing.

In the heart of a rose-and-gold light, two naked and winged figures are embracing. Man and Woman, they are becoming more: draining the power of a human mind to become Lion and Phoenix. Their faces are radiant. They are a beacon of joy.

A beacon that can be seen for how great a distance?

Miles Godric lifts himself up again, as the rose-brambles bind him to the earth. The ground shakes with the approaching tread of legions. A yard or two away, Michael Maier picks up his dagger and positions it under the French boy's ear; lifts his elbow to thrust.

The night explodes.

Nose and mouth bleeding, head ringing, eyes dazzled with the vanishing of a Light beyond all lights, Miles Godric lies among tangled dead briars and watches the moonlight shine on battered helms, scruffy brigandines, one smoking musket, halbards, and the excited faces and shouts of Maximillian of Bavaria's army.

'What was it, a quarrel over loot?' Sarnac shifted his body, pulling Miles's arm further over his shoulder. Miles slumped against the big man. 'Christ's bones, I didn't think there was enough left in the city to burn! You could see that fire clear from the camp.'

'Fire?'

'It's gone now. Odd.'

Miles felt the cold night air sting his face. He glanced
down. The moon's light showed him dark patches on
his breeches and hands, and his leg was still numb. He
groped at his head. Something sticky matted his hair.

'I don't . . .'

Only moonlight. Grey matter and dark liquid spattered his doublet. The memory of a musket-ball taking
off one side of Michael Maier's head came back to him
and he tried with a dry mouth to spit into the road,
knowing how inaccurate muskets are.

There was a bustle of soldiery around him and someone somewhere shouting orders. The road to the camp
shone white and dusty.

'Where's the boy?'

'Vanringham has him. Living, I think. God's death,
what were they quarrelling for?'

'I . . . forget.'

Sarnac's body heat warmed him, and Miles conscien-
tiously tried to stop shivering but without success. He
would have sent men to search out the man and woman
if he could have spoken – or if he could have been
certain they had survived the illusions.

The march back to the camp seemed at the same time
long and over in a heartbeat. Prague's ruined walls gave
way to dawn and the ranked wagons of the camp, the provost and one of the company commanders, all of it happening
somewhere far away. An hour passed in a minute.

Straw rasped against his back. An early light shone
in under the makeshift canvas tent. Weakness pressed
him down. He could not focus his eyes on what lay
beyond the immediate circle of earth, firepit and scattered equipment. He tried to moisten his dry mouth,
swallowing. Sarnac, his back to Miles, boiled soup in
someone else's upturned helmet.

'I . . . need a surgeon.'

'Do you, lass?'

Miles tried to make himself wake, move, protest. He saw Sarnac turn, face beaming with good intention.

'Think I'd let 'em treat you and discover you for a woman?'

'No ...' He managed to raise his arms and grab Sarnac's hands. He knew himself safe with surgeons, the surgeon's tents a cover for the many-partner marriages of the Weerde, and besides a necessary means for taking dead Weerde bodies from a battlefield.

'No, that's right.' The big man frowned down at him. 'I'm going to treat these wounds. Christ's little bones, woman, you're bleeding like a pig with its throat cut!'

The effort brought sweat out on Miles's face. His hands shook with the effort of holding Sarnac away. At some level of cell and blood he called on strength, knowing it was no use to call on change, but the big man deftly slipped his grip away, stripping off Miles's doublet and breeches together and pulling at his shirt.

'Damn but you women always have some vapouring quibble. Haven't I seen you naked bef—'

Miles giggled faintly. The sheer bald shock on Sarnac's face made him splutter, not wishing it; robbing him of any words. He thought muddily, What words could there be? The man bent over him, freckled shoulder close to his face, and Miles breathed in the smell of him through swollen and blood-choked nostrils; felt the big hands slide down the skin of his chest and belly and move as if stung from his cock and balls.

'But you *can't* be —'

The hot morning slipped a cogwheel, reassembled itself into an absence of Sarnac and somewhere a voice shouting.

'*Succubus! Witchcraft!*'

With an effort that brought blood streaming from his thigh Miles Godric crawled out of the shelter, pulled up breeches and doublet, and staggered away from the tent. The voice shouted. A dog bayed. His head came up and he searched the stirring camp, forcing his body to walk; to run . . .

. . . John Hammet sat beside him, back resting against the gun carriage.

'And thus I thought of you,' Miles finished, 'being a countryman of mine. And Family.'

Swallows and bats flew against the darkening evening sky, snapping at gnats.

'Pox take it, it's the world we live in that gives such schemes life.' The artillery man spat tobacco into the dew-dampened grass. 'I would the Kin might change it. But witness our attempt to rid these lands of their superstitions − now half of the German principalities are burning witches, and half of their inquisitors are Protestant Lutherans. Such was never our intent.'

Miles hunched his shoulders against the dust-clotted wood of the carriage. Heat stung his hands and face, blood now scabbing on their flayed skin. He tightened the bandage around his thigh.

'Will they burn me, think you?'

Hammet ignored the question. 'I talked to your French youth when they brought him in last night. I've seen men regain their rightful sense and speech, with less courage and spirit than he. Yet if I mistake not, he will fear "magic" all the days of his life. Do you know, Kinsman, I think I would much like to live in his mathematical world. I would like a world where there are no devils and spirits in men, to risk calling down the Dark on our heads. It would be a peaceful one, I think, Descartes' world.'

Miles Godric shivered in the summer heat. Crows called.

The artillery man said, 'They will either burn you or break you on the wheel for a man-witch. So the provost orders. You had best shift your shape this night and join another unit.'

Remnants of fear chilled Miles Godric's bones. A vision came before his eyes of Sarnac's face loose in the concentration of pleasure. 'And leave Sarnac?'

Desire moves in his body for the man Sarnac, will move in it no matter what shape he wears; as if his mind were merely carried in this fleshly machine, a passenger subject to its will.

'How we love these mayflies,' he said ironically. 'Well, and in a while I may change flesh again, and find him again.'

'If he lives,' Hammet said. 'What is it draws us to wars?'

Miles Godric leaned his head against the metal of the culverin. Thinking of the heat of metal, firing case-shot; of pike and musket and the long sharp blades of daggers, watching the evening dusk come on. 'We don't begin them. We only follow the drum.'

He got slowly to his feet, adding, 'We have few enough pleasures that we can afford to miss that one.'

In months to come he will hear rumours of Frederick the Garterless King – the royal boy having mislaid that English Order in his flight from Prague – and see him represented on satirical broadsheets with his stocking falling to his ankle. The drawings will show a plump young man and a hard-faced woman tramping the countryside in old clothes, trying to whip up support for their lost Bohemian kingdom. But support never comes.

In years to come Miles Godric will think of the taking of Prague, first bloodshed in thirty years of grinding war, and hear of Elizabeth's son Rupert fighting bloody battles in England that civil war also engulfs. Word will come to him that Elizabeth, in exile, has the no longer young Descartes at her court at the Hague and that he has dedicated his *Principia philosophiae* to her. He will wonder if the man remembers what the boy once experienced in Prague, in a garden, among roses.

And, being of the Kin of the Weerde, he will live long enough to fight in most of the wars of the Age of Reason that Cartesian dualism will usher in.

But for now it is a summer evening and Miles Godric is earning his reprieve; forgetting all else to stand, wounds stinging in the surface change of stature and feature, and laugh, and anticipate the next battle.

HISTORICAL NOTE

The young René Descartes shared a common preoccupation of the European scholars of his time – contacting the hypothetical organization known as the Rosicrucians. His desire did not outlive his period of service in Maurice of Nassau's army in 1619, however, during the winter of which his diary records singular dreams.

It seems probable that he was in Prague after the capture and sacking of that city, after the Battle of the White Hill in 1620. Michael Maier's connections with that centre of neo-Platonic experiment are longer and better documented. The mysterious vanishing of this European scholar and author is reported to have taken place in Prague in 1622.

Upon Descartes' return to Paris at the height of the Rosicrucian scare, he was himself widely assumed to be a member of that invisible college, and could only counteract this by making himself available to the public and therefore, after a manner of speaking, visible. In his later writings he continues, to say the least, to distance himself from the hermetic world-view.

TO THE BAD

Brian Stableford

———————

I think I ought to write the story of how my sister Cecilie went to the bad. Some of you will probably think that I have gone to the bad too, for simply wanting to write it, but that is one of the reasons why it ought to be written.

No one in the family had the least suspicion, while we were growing up, that Cecilie would one day go to the bad. When we were children, I was always the naughty one; Cecilie was always good. After a while, that kind of contrast came to be expected of us. Our mothers would shake their heads and fondly lament that it was always the same with a litter of two unless they were identical twins. They were always looking out for us to disagree and be different and because Cecilie was always so anxious to please, I was inevitably cast as the rebel. It wasn't all my fault.

Not that I could see this at the time, you understand; at the time I thought it all came naturally to me: the breakages, the sins of omission – even, oh horror of horrors! – the lies and the *indiscretions*. It's only hindsight that allows me to see that it was all a kind of *game*. I was unwittingly nudged into being a living illustration of all the things that kids of our kind shouldn't do and shouldn't be, so that I could be patiently redeemed and straightened out. My childhood was made into a lesson from which Cecilie and I were both supposed to learn what we need to know in order to get by. It would have been a neat trick if it had worked, but it didn't.

The trouble was that this approach to our sentimental education made me question things, and there were some questions which never did get answered during the straightening-out process. I came to understand well enough about sins of omission, and lies, and the overwhelming necessity to be *discreet*, but there were other things about which the doubts remained. One of them, as you will have guessed, was writing.

I first sat down to write a story when I was eleven years old. It was a science fiction story about men on Mars – Yuri Gagarin had just orbited the Earth for the first time and I was hung up on the idea of space and conquering the universe. At first, the adults assumed that I was just doing my homework, but when I told Mother Thalia what I was really doing she asked Father John – my actual father – to have a quiet word with me.

'It's just not our way, Francis,' he told me, gravely. 'Writing is one of *their* things. It's necessary for you to go through the motions at school – that's all part of *fitting in* – but it's not something you can bring home. It's not something we ever do on our own account. Writing, you see, is a kind of indiscretion in itself. It *preserves* things, and there's too much danger of revealing something even when you don't mean to. *Our* arts are the performing kind, which leave no material traces: music, singing, dancing. Cecilie is a *lovely* singer – you could have learned to play an instrument, if you'd only put your mind to it. You still could.'

'It's a science fiction story,' I assured him, earnestly. 'It's not about *us* – it doesn't matter a bit whether the people in it are our kind or theirs; they just have adventures.'

'That's a dangerous way to think, Francis,' he told me, soberly. 'It always matters whether people are our kind or theirs. *Always.* Forgetting that is the greatest of all indiscretions.'

I abandoned my story, and decided that I would be a *real* astronaut instead of a science fiction writer. I must have nursed that ambition for a year or more before I finally became reckless enough to mention it to Mother Heloise. It was Father Valentine who was delegated to explain why it was just as bad as wanting to be a writer.

'You're old enough now to think about this sort of thing *realistically*,' said Father Valentine sternly. He was the oldest of the co-husbands, and he always seemed scrupulously stern. 'The world is becoming hazardous for people with secrets to keep, and we have to be very, very careful in selecting appropriate niches for ourselves. It's best to avoid anything which involves being closely scrutinized. Can you imagine what an astronaut must go through in terms of medical examination and testing? We can alter our appearance inside as well as out, but we couldn't be certain of passing for human under *that* kind of scrutiny.'

I saw the sense in it. I understood what he was telling me. Even then, though, I began to see corollaries of his argument that disturbed me. Father Valentine was oblivious to those corollaries, but Father Valentine had been born in 1830 and to him – as to the great majority of our kind – bureaucracy and medicine were just newfangled nuisances which threatened our best-kept secrets. He couldn't see that doing our utmost to avoid all the kinds of scrutiny to which the humans had begun to subject themselves was a strategy which could only work for a little while longer, and served to cut us off from certain benefits which the humans obtained from their new skills. He couldn't see that we ought to have our own legion of doctors, studying and refining an up-to-date kind of medicine for our kind. He couldn't see that in telling our children to stay well away from any contact with X-ray machines or blood tests or operating theatres, for fear of being *indiscreet*, we risked cutting ourselves off from something very valuable.

Cecilie dutifully took not the slightest notice of the science lessons we had at school. She was a good girl, easily clever enough to appear conventionally dull. I was the rebel, too clever for my own good, who couldn't help being interested. It didn't help matters that I always seemed 'young for my age' to my fast-maturing classmates; if there's one thing the average bully hates more than a smart-arse it's a precocious smart-arse. I assume that the bullies had a good laugh when the family pulled me out of school at sixteen, as soon as they could get us out of the system.

In spite of the differences between us, Cecilie and I were very close. We were bound to be, I suppose, given that we were the only kids in a household of eight adults. Mother Lucrezia had had a three-boy litter fifteen years earlier, but by the time Cecilie and I were able to take notice they seemed to us to be uncles rather than brothers, and they soon passed on into the network.

When our turn came to be passed on – to begin our 'real education', as Father Raphael put it – there was some talk of splitting us up, but we protested and all four mothers came in on our side. I think their most telling argument was that Cecilie would be a 'stabilizing influence' on poor unreliable Francis. Oddly enough, nobody took the trouble to explain to us exactly why we had to pass on. I presume that the mere fact that it was customary was considered explanation enough; our

great respect for tradition is, after all, one of the things
which is supposed to make us superior to those wild-
hearted humans.

I remember thinking that I was very clever when I
worked out the logic of it. It was like a flash of illumination when I first saw that those who are perpetually in
hiding must always have hiding places in reserve; they
must always have somewhere else to go when discovery
threatens and it must be somewhere they know, somewhere where they can fade into the background. It isn't
enough for one of us to be part of a single household;
our links to other groups, even other families, must be
many and complex. So for thirty or forty years – three
or four times as long as we spent in *their* schools,
learning the geography and mechanics of *their* social
world – we visit our Kin, learning the geography and
mechanics of our hidden and parallel world.

Ours was a small-town household in the north of
England, so it was virtually inevitable that we should
be passed on to Kin in the capital city. Mother Lucrezia's
litter had been passed on along the same route thirteen
years earlier, but things had changed since then. London
in 1967 was not quite the same place that London in
1954 had been.

Our aunts and uncles in the wicked city weren't nearly
as protective as our mothers and fathers had been; we
were there to learn after all, and they had no intention
of wrapping us up in cotton wool. We went out a great
deal, together and separately. We made a great many
connections, with the other kind as well as our own. It
wasn't just Cecilie and myself who absorbed something
of the human *zeitgeist* – there were other youngsters of
our own kind around, who were just as fascinated by
the fashions and the music and the ideas of the day.

In the beginning. I was the one who was curious and excited about everything we did and everything we discovered. I was the one hungry to find out what was *going on*. Cecilie was nervous and intimidated, and took time to come out of her shell. As the months went by, though, the situation changed dramatically – and Cecilie changed far more than I did. However interested I was in all the things that were happening I always remained an observer, an outsider. I never lost the consciousness of being apart from it all. I didn't think of my apartness simply in terms of belonging to a different species; I was certainly no human-hater. I guess it was simply an attitude of mind. I still fancied myself as a pioneer of sorts, as an *explorer* of the vivid and confusing wilderness of sex-and-drugs-and-rock'n'roll (and it *was* all one thing, to those who were a part of it). Cecilie was different. Cecilie, once she had learned to love the life, loved it with all her heart. Once she had loosened up, she threw all her energies into whatever was happening. She went to the bad. She went *native*.

It wasn't obvious to her, or even to the aunts and uncles we were lodged with, that what she was doing was going native. Father Valentine would have seen it immediately, but Father Valentine had come to seem to us – and even to our adult hosts, although at least one of them was old enough to remember Queen Victoria's Golden Jubilee – to be a boring provincial stick-in-the-mud. You see, we didn't think of the things that were going on as a purely *human* thing; in many ways, they seemed more *our* sort of thing: the music, the dancing, all the performances and displays and trips (which blew our minds in exactly the same way that they blew human minds, and made all our physiological differences seem trivial . . .).

Cecilie was far better prepared to take her place in

that kind of culture than I was. I was a doubter and an explorer; she was more adept at fitting in – and she had such a *lovely* voice. It was a time and place extremely and fatally hospitable to talented singers – especially if they could be beautiful. That's one of the corollaries of our talent for fitting in, of course; we can make ourselves dull, but we can also make ourselves beautiful, if we want to be. It must have seemed entirely natural to Cecilie that in adapting herself to an age of beautiful people she must make herself beautiful. In fact, it was a sad mistake.

The aunts and uncles didn't mind her singing with the Firestreaks at first. The bass player was one of us, and they thought that it was good for her to *mix*. How could she learn to fit in and hide herself away, they reasoned, if she didn't mix?

Aunt Darya had a quiet word with her when it became obvious that she was sleeping with Ray McHale, the Firestreaks' lead guitarist, but she took that meekly and reasonably enough. Uncle Shilaq had us both on the carpet when we arrived home too stoned to know what day it was, but it was water off a duck's back. We *knew* it was all OK – and the aunts and uncles seemed to know it too, deep down. They were understanding people; they didn't tell us what not to do, the way Father John or Father Valentine would have done; they only told us to be careful. They didn't see any real problem in what Cecilie was doing with the Firestreaks. After all, it was only music, only performing, and our kind are born to perform.

The alarm bells didn't begin to ring loudly until some time after the Firestreaks cut their first single, when it became a minor hit. A minor hit meant publicity, and the first rule of our existence is, of course, that all publicity is bad publicity and good publicity is worst.

All of a sudden, Cecilie's photograph began to pop up here, there and everywhere in the newspapers, and she even made it on to the TV. Everybody watches TV, even in the frozen north.

When Father John and Father Valentine came down to see us it was obvious that they were hopping mad – and not just with Cecilie. Their real wrath was reserved for the aunts and uncles who'd let us 'run wild'. They knew it had to be the fault of the aunts and uncles because they took it for granted that it couldn't be *theirs*. They'd brought us up so carefully and so *well*, hadn't they? In a way, facing them was fun, because it made us part of a conspiracy with adults – the aunts and uncles – for the first time in our lives. We looked upon the whole thing as a freak of nature, like a sudden storm, that had to be meekly endured while it was happening, but could be forgotten as soon as it went away. We listened stoically to Father Valentine's legendary lecture on the perils of fame, but we didn't really hear a word.

Father John wasn't quite so predictable, and I couldn't help being interested in some of what he said.

'These are bad times for our kind,' he told us, soberly. 'Things are changing far too rapidly. You're particularly vulnerable to the tide of change because you're young, but you mustn't let yourself be seduced by visions of unlimited possibility. At the end of the day, there are only a handful of possibilities which really matter: survival or extinction; the long, lazy afternoon or the coming of the Dark. The most difficult thing you have to learn in life is to keep a proper balance between hope and anxiety. It's an unpleasant lesson to learn that the proper balance has more anxiety in it than hope, but that's the way it is, and always will be.'

I was still a sucker for a well-hung argument, but it

didn't mean a thing to Cecilie. She was hooked on hope by now, and anxiety had been banished from her soul. She wanted to *live*. To her, at that particular moment in time, it seemed that only the humans really knew how to live, and not all of them: only the *young* humans; only the beautiful people. Cecilie was already a beautiful person and then some; she had advantages mere humans didn't have. Surely it must have been one of us who invented the mini-skirt – humans just don't have the legs for it!

The Firestreaks never reached the very top. Maybe it would have been better if they had, and maybe it was unjust that they didn't. Cecilie really did have a *lovely* voice, and Ray McHale was as competent a guitarist as many who achieved greater things, but they didn't have a real writer on the team, and they didn't get the kind of material that could sustain them for long. Personally, I think it was a bad career move to enter the Eurovision Song Contest and a worse career move to come second, but that's life.

It was the infamous affair of the centrefold which really screwed things up. I never did discover how Father Valentine got hold of a copy; I'm pretty certain that none of the family had a subscription. If I had to bet on it I'd hazard a guess that it was one of the men in the village who got the magazine, and his wife who gleefully recognized Cecilie in spite of all she'd done to alter her bodywork. Either way, it was the end so far as the family was concerned. Father John came to fetch us home, and it was pretty obvious that if and when we were put back into the network we would probably be bound for Siberia or Patagonia.

I was surprised and hurt when it became clear that the mothers held *me* to blame for it all. They had allowed us to stay together so that Cecilie could exercise a benign influence upon me, and they naturally assumed that the influence had unfortunately flowed in the wrong direction. I pleaded my innocence in vain – but at least I had the sense to ride with the punches. Cecilie didn't. Cecilie ran away. She went back to London to live with Ray McHale, and she left a note to say that if anyone came after her or tried to interfere with her chosen career, she'd complain to the police and the *News of the World*. The police probably wouldn't have taken any notice, but the *News of the World* certainly would – she was, after all, a fading pop star who'd once posed in the nude for the kind of magazine they put on the top shelf at W. H. Smith's.

Cecilie wasn't ever any threat to our security – not really. She only wanted to *live*, after the fashion she'd adopted as her own. She was a product of the times: times when there really didn't seem to be any limits; times when joy and extravagance were sanctioned by everyone except us. Cecilie was only doing what all our kind have done ever since mankind first appeared: pretending to be human. She just pretended a bit too hard, that's all.

'No one will hurt her, will they?' I said to Father John, when it finally became clear that the break was absolute.

'This isn't America or the Dark Ages,' Father John assured me. 'We don't have cousins with daggers hidden in their long black cloaks. But there are worse things than being assassinated. She's cut off from the family, and the fact that she did it to herself won't make it any easier to bear when she needs us.'

'When she needs us,' I told him, 'she'll come back. And we'll take her back, won't we?'

'If it's as simple as that,' he agreed, 'yes we will. But

if she really does become famous, she'll have to stay away. We can't stand too much scrutiny, you see. Our private lives are too different – it's difficult enough to cope with the village gossip and the Government's data-gatherers.'

The next time I saw Cecilie – the last time I saw her – I did my best to persuade her to drop it all. I knew it wasn't going to work, but I had to try. By then, she was a whore through and through. She had contrived to make herself even more beautiful, and she regarded her beauty as pure commodity. She'd left the Firestreaks and abandoned Ray HcHale, and she was determined to make it on her own, any way she could. And she did.

I don't suppose she's a star exactly, even today, but she's well on her way to being a household name. TV has made her face familiar to millions of people. She fits into her chosen scene very well – as well she might, given that she had a lot of early practice in the dubious art of following convention. I don't know how lonely she is, but I don't suppose it matters to her. Not much. How many others are there just like her? I could name three, and guess at one or two others – but it's interesting, in a way, that there might be many more. Our kind are so good at hiding, at fitting in – nobody knows how many of us there are in Britain, or Europe, or the world.

Once, I wanted to write a science fiction story – this one strictly for our own consumption – about a future time in which human beings have become extinct but nobody knows, because the world is still ludicrously overpopulated with our lineages, all of them pretending fiercely to be human and defending their secret to the death from *everyone*. I know it's silly, but ... I know that I have to forget the other stories, and concentrate on this one. I know that I have to finish it with a lesson – a *moral* – because that's the only hope I have of excusing the fact that I've written it. For what it's worth, though, those of my readers who are utterly horrified by the mere fact of its existence are overreacting. If it were ever to fall into the hands of human beings, they'd just think it was science fiction, and pretty dull at that – not a monster or a mad assassin in sight.

The lesson we might try to learn, I think, is this: we've reached a threshold in our career as a species and things will never be the same again. Even the Father Valentines of this world already know that, but it hasn't quite sunk in. They think of it as decadence and corruption, but it isn't. The point is that the humans now have lots of things which are genuinely valuable but which we're reluctant to share. It's not just medicine and the possibility of setting off on all the great science-fictional adventures, like conquering the universe and becoming immortal – I'm sure we'll figure out a way to jump on those bandwagons eventually. It's seemingly trivial things like excitement and well-being and quality of life. We think we have those things already, by our own standards, but I'm not so sure.

I think that what we have to learn from my sister Cecilie, and all the others like her, is that there are some aspects of modern life which really have to be *lived* to be appreciated, and not just *performed*, hollowly, by way of imitation. I'm not arguing that we should blow our cover and try to become full partners in Planet Earth Enterprises (Incorporated or otherwise). I'm not even saying that we should condone what my sister Cecilie's done, or copy the particular ambitions which drew her away from her family and wider Kin. I'm just saying that we ought to look a little longer and harder at what the humans of today are doing and try to figure out what might be in it for us. If it's left to the humans they'll only louse it up, but we could really do it *well*, if we were only prepared to try.

Maybe we could be really beautiful people if only we could loosen up a bit, and think a little more about living our lives and a little less about concealing them. Maybe that isn't such a silly and shabby ambition to have.

This story is dedicated to the bad; I have a sneaking suspicion that they'll be the only ones who can possibly understand.

A STRANGE SORT OF FRIEND

Josephine Saxton

I only remembered much later that my first impression of Serena had been, 'She looks a bad bitch – must avoid her!' This intuitive flash must have slid out of reach immediately, because it was not long afterwards that I found my place at the canteen table was somehow always next to her. This, I think, helps to illustrate what I want to say, which is that the mind creates its own realities. One minute you know that something is true and real, and the next minute your world is broken open like a chocolate egg, containing very little except crumpled paper. Love, hate, happiness, misery – what am I telling you? This only: a kind of confession really – that for a while I truly believed an extremely preposterous thing. I look back with astonishment at how gullible I was.

Let me fill in some background to the story; let me tell it my own way. Bear with me if possible; picture me stopping mid-sentence with my mouth open and the words stopped, pondering in bewilderment how utterly idiotic even the most intelligent, cultured, sensitive human being can sometimes become when under suffi- cient stress. I apologize if my statements sometimes seem inflated and egotistical, but I was brought up to believe in my better qualities; it was instilled in me by two excellent people that a belief in the self, the better human self, is not egotism but applied objectivity. I have of course learned not to voice these aspects of myself. Now for Serena, whom I thought to be a 'bad bitch' and who became my friend, someone I valued and loved, and who . . .

We had both begun working at the depot within a couple of days of one another, and neither of us had ever worked in such an environment before. Tentatively, we exchanged notes as to what two educated, intelligent people of mature years could possibly be doing in such a place. Her story had elements like my own, its outer parameters tallied. We had sufficient in common to feel 'at home' in a dialogue. I think we were both alienated in those surroundings at that time, and welcomed the exchange. This was in the tea break and the half-hour at midday. We also walked home together most of the way; she lived not very far from me. So far, so ordinary and normal.

What transpired later seems completely incredible when I look back on it or rather, it is incredible that at this time I could have believed my eyes. The mind leads a life of its own I have concluded, and if it wants its hapless owner to be led astray by ideas and visual mistakes, then it can achieve a whole changing of the world. Take such jokes too far of course and 'madness' ensues, and the joking mind cannot return to a normality generally agreed upon. I was deceived for a while into contemplating the reality of something utterly bizarre, which is quite interesting if not pathetic. I am more cautious now about my perceptions of the world, especially where people are concerned. I am, in fact, more withdrawn from life altogether.

Anyway, Serena was there in my life, a somewhat eccentric and dilapidated working woman, someone I could talk to from among the generally tedious crowd which stolidly remained unsullied by reading, thinking or intellectual exercise of any kind. We had some things in common, and while her views of painting and literature were always rather odd, at least she could pick up on references, instead of answering with a blank stare.

Our views of the workplace matched; we hated it, and would leave just as soon as we had got ourselves straight and saved some money, although she was vague and without ambition. I wanted a sum to live on while I wrote my film script of the life of Aleister Crowley. I had a contract and a small advance, not enough to live on for long. It was to be a low-budget movie which nevertheless aimed to get itself seen and make money. Living here in Leamington, where Crowley was born and where there is much secret interest in his work was a head start, or so it was thought. There was a film company attached to the nearby university, composed mainly of semi-professionals.

Meanwhile, gathering material in some of my spare time, I and Serena and many others were parcelling up orders as fast as lightning and not being paid much for it. We became grey-faced with fatigue; I bid goodbye to the last of what had once been beauty, telling myself that it did not matter. We worked in a warehouse which was alternately overheated and then freezing, when the huge doors at the end opened to let out the forklift trucks loaded with the fruit of our labour. Most of the workers including myself had a couple of vile colds, followed by hacking coughs. Not Serena; she seemed unusually immune to normal ailments, although she did mention some symptoms which I took to be menopausal. We made a poor-looking pair of drudges tracking home in the evening; the feeling of life at that time with the October nights bearing darkly down was Victorian lower class, although thank heavens I had a nice house with a hot shower and central heating or I think I might have died of wretchedness.

Serena never felt the cold, always complained of the heat. She had breathing problems at times, and made unfortunate sounds almost as if she had a cleft palate which she never excused and I ignored. Her manners left much to be desired but I concluded that she had not been brought up well. She was from some East End area of London, but her accent also had a strange country roll. At least I had someone to talk to and although she had a queer comprehension of what she read, at least she read. Excepting the presence of Serena I would have suffered a severe anomie. I cannot endure soap operas, nor any television for long, a fact which is often interpreted as a sign of madness. Perhaps it is.

I was at a trough in all my relationships except for Leon, a partner perhaps rather too young who lived with me, and had a steady job in computers. Serena too was in a rut except for Gary, whom she always referred to as her boyfriend, a term which grates on my nerves. He was out of work, had hardly ever worked. He had huge fines to pay to do with motoring, dud cheques, non-payment of all kinds of things. A parasite. He was easily less than half her age, far too young, and from everything she told me rather odd to say the least. I thought he sounded autistic or schizophrenic as he rarely spoke except to express a wish for death, but she found this restful. He sometimes went through manic phases, so the diagnosis was unclear. Odd anyhow, and not likeable. Leon, seeing him at a dance, said he gave him the creeps. I assumed that Serena fulfilled some kind of motherly role towards him, although she boasted of their sex life from time to time. I never discuss mine. When it is good it is good, and when it isn't it stops. I despise people who discuss something shared with another, I deem it a betrayal. It is a measure of my loneliness at that time that I forgave her many peccadilloes which in my more gregarious phases would have repelled me completely.

Serena was not just unconventional but downright weird – to me a mark in her favour. I seem at various times in my life to make friends with weird people; they warm to me and I to them. I am a painter and I write poetry sometimes (my interest in film-making was a later craze, as things transpired), and at an early age absorbed the idea of being an outsider, a Bohemian. I was an adopted child and used to wonder if my real parents were talented, as my adoptive parents were not, although they were clever and kind. I find ordinary people boring, and they often dislike or mistrust me. I have little to say to the Person in the Street. And folk wisdom I do not find illuminating. If a person is described as 'really nice' or 'the salt of the earth', I find myself yawning. I exist very well on a salt-free diet.

But the fact that she was 'different' was not my first attraction to her as a friend. My first impulse was compassion, an empathy towards her which moved me to want to help her, to make her help herself. From the conversations we had, I discovered that she was apparently on a pathway to self-destruction. I on the other hand was looking after myself and my health, had a nice place to live, kept my act together as well as possible and made sure I ate properly and dressed well enough to please my ego – the ego I think a necessary entity which enables one to get through life, and is not something to be lost lightly. Serena apparently didn't have one, or else it took the form of what might be selflessness, the obverse aspect of the same thing.

When she first came to work she had just arrived in Leamington, and owned only one pair of shoes with

holes in them and very few clothes decades old in some
cases. She was sleeping in the old car she and the
boyfriend owned, and used public toilets for her bathroom: a derelict, virtually. She had been living in some
broken-down country cottage somewhere, and had come
to Leamington because a couple of her children were
living here. I discovered that they were what I would
call 'anarchist' although they were truly more chaotic
than anarchistic; there comes to mind a dirty kind of
girl with hennaed hair in rat-tails, with illegitimate
children, living in horrible rented flats with a crew of
unsavoury males drifting around. Their mode of living
was post-hippie cliché, the lifestyle without the ideal-
ism. They never paid for anything if they could help it,
any of them. They were not creative, thinking people,
just messy and incompetent.

Why didn't I suspect something was up when she
first said in a loud enough voice for several to overhear,
'I'm a Christian, as a religion it's never been bettered.
I'm a believer I am, although I never go to any church, I
wasn't brought up to church nor nothing, it's just a
feeling you know?' No person who actually is a Christian ever says so like that, it is unchristian behaviour.

'I detest Christianity,' I countered, instantly wound
up. 'It is a religion of blood, pain, denial. It has caused
untold mass destruction of peoples and cultures, it has
repressed females, it spreads darkness and misery everywhere. It is hypocritical.' I don't pull punches, which is
perhaps why I have few friends, but what I liked about
Serena was that she was the same. Always said what
she thought, or so I believed then.

'Yes, but what about the light side? What about
eternal life? What about the message of hope and universal love?'

'Bullshit, all bullshit. Simplistic junk designed to put

the masses to sleep so they won't notice what's going on.' She snorted at that, a horrible raucous snort, and sprayed crumbs as she replied.

Serena was an ugly woman, with deep, dark grey grooves from the corners of her nose right down to her jawline, which was hard. Her eyes had no whites to them, and one seemed slightly off-focus, giving her a shifty look, although her eye contact was piercingly direct from under drooping eyelids. Her front teeth were a denture which sometimes slipped; her laugh was hard, false-sounding, each syllable beginning with a pronounced 'h', a sort of bray or bark which annoyed me dreadfully at times. (I admit to being over-sensitive about many things, perhaps I should have been a critic, for I find fault too readily.) Her hair was naturally fuzzy although she was very white; it looked like a bad perm. Her figure had gone and she slouched, so badly at times I wondered if she was slightly deformed. Her legs were unshaven, the hairiest I have ever seen on a woman, and her feet were totally without grooming, horny and with ugly, uneven nails. She looked at least twenty years older than her true age, and I felt sorry for her, indeed.

This was why I befriended her; I could never resist helping the unfortunate or the sick. My heart goes out to such people, or it did; I have since learned to act differently, more in accordance with a saying of Gurdjieff, which is: If you help people, they will hate you for it. Always true, but I was weak and I enjoyed the feeling of being a beneficial and encouraging influence, self-indulgent I know, although truly I felt my spirit to be behind the impulse.

She admired my skin and I told her about moisturizers, face-packs, night cream. She didn't bother with things like that, she said, Nature took care of everything.

'Nature is a killer, and, furthermore, doesn't give a damn about middle-aged women who have done what Nature requires of them. You've got to look after yourself.'

'God will look after me if Nature won't,' she countered. 'I only believe in the Good, I don't recognize Evil, there's no such thing. There is only the Light, there is no Darkness.'

'God and a course of vitamins and maybe some Agnus Castus,' I told her in cynical tones. 'And furthermore, there can be no light without darkness, that at least must be obvious, otherwise everything would be grey!' My short leash was strained. I had thought myself at a nadir, but that was the beginning of a descent.

I told Leon about her and he agreed with me that she was certainly in need of help, by the sound of it. He considers himself enlightened, a feminist, and always made the right responses to my litany. I had always felt that I could trust Leon with my deepest thoughts and feelings, and that he was a person of true integrity. I now believe there is no such thing: anyone can be corrupted. This is a world ringed with darkness that is always waiting to encroach.

Around that time, by what seemed to be no more than coincidence, synchronicity as I shall reveal, I went to interview a woman who lived in Leamington and who professed to be a witch. She had posed as a scarlet woman for quite a few years, and was a devotee of Mr Crowley. I had met her at parties a few years previously, when she dressed in exotic, tarty clothes; satin camiknickers with suspendered stockings, spike-heeled sandals, laced corselettes, bits of lace shawls, bright red hair swept to one side, amazing make-up with brilliant red lips, plenty of jewellery, feather boas – pure theatre, although she walked around at all hours in this get-up, and was one of the features of the town. Leamington has numerous eccentrics, but at that time she stood out. She had great courage, great beauty, great style and a huge crowd of lovers.

When I went to see her however, that phase was past. She was dressing very dowdily in horrible old clothes, topped by a dirty blue beret with all her hair shoved out of sight, and no make-up at all. She was not beautiful but she had charisma, and had kept the numerous lovers. She told me she was in disguise, and that when a magician reaches a certain level of skill, the outer image must be sacrificed. At one time Mr Crowley had gone around in sky-blue knickerbockers, with a magician's staff and a cloak, but in later life he dressed very quietly to the point of being invisible. I had known that of course, but I was impressed with her following suit, and the calm certainty with which she spoke. I was dubious about her magical powers, but not about her belief in herself.

She calmly told me a great many other things too, which I listened to with growing incredulity. I regarded it as nourishment for my film script. In my mind I had flights of inflated dreaming about the film, in which it was a great success and a whole new career opened up for me. I had a brilliant inspiration while sitting talking with her, that Alexei Sayle would play Mr Crowley; there was an astonishing resemblance I thought. But I am wandering off the story. What this remarkable young woman – called Joan – told me seemed bizarre in the telling, and compulsively rich in interest.

She told me that she had read a secret diary written by Mr Crowley which told of some remarkable discoveries he had made in the course of the practice of magick. He had proved beyond doubt that there was another race of beings living amongst us who were not human but which passed for human, because they could change their shape. These creatures were far higher than us in their thinking and philosophy because they not only knew the great true secret, which is that Good and Evil do not exist, being only concepts instilled into the human mind to put bonds upon it, but that they lived above this human nonsense. They were a more ancient race than human beings, had developed separately from us and had ideas and aims which the human mind, unprepared, could barely comprehend. He had met several of these beings and said that a few had helped shape human history, but that mostly they remained in disguise for their own purposes.

The way Joan told me of Mr Crowley's discoveries did not make them sound mythic, but real, very real. Of course I was very aware during the interview that magic, or as her mentor would have it, magick, is a concentrated application of the power of the imagination and nothing more. There is no such thing as superhuman power, nor telepathy, nor is it possible to communicate with spirits or demons, simply because there are none.

There is the Dark, though. This is my personal name for something I have always felt the presence of out there somewhere, or just behind my left shoulder, metaphorically speaking of course. I do not know what it is but I feel it, and fear it. Something destructive, alien; it does not of course affect me, in fact I put such numinous feelings down to an allergy although to what I have been unable to detect. Cow's milk, chocolate, sherry, cabbage and coffee have all been suspected but nothing is proven. There is of course a rational explanation, being that the feeling of the Dark is in itself irrational. I spoke to Joan about the Dark, and she smiled mysteriously and said that Mr Crowley knew about that too, but she would not or could not expand further. She did expand upon his skill in time travel and bilocation though, talents I had never heard attributed to him, although sorcery in general is supposed to confer these powers.

I began to have ideas about making the film work on two levels; Crowley's personal biography, and a kind of fantasy with effects, taking him to multiple times and spaces. I later abandoned it of course as it was outside the scope of the movie, and too expensive. I also went off the idea, which seemed banal when taken out of the presence of the compelling Joan. I only wished to write a script about a remarkable and strange genius, not to promote magick as if it were a true phenomenon or come up with some trashy fantasy, for there had been too much of that. Mr Crowley, genius, was also deluded.

I asked Joan what these creatures who lived among us were like, and she told me they were much like us a lot of the time, but that when they reverted to their own true form they were frightening to those who had no stomach for strange things. They were definitely not human and, although shaped roughly as we are, have descended from another branch of evolution altogether. I found this an interesting and fantastical idea and asked her if she had met any. She knew several; she had taken them for lovers and spoke lasciviously of their powers of endurance, their sheer greed. She said that in bed they were not imaginative, but were without morals or inhibitions, which made up for a lot.

I felt ashamed at being secretly excited at her descriptions of their marathon sexual excesses, at the same time thinking that she was very odd, even slightly unhinged. She had taken large quantities of various drugs since her teenage years, and I wondered if this had permanently changed her mental outlook. And yet she was so ordinary in some ways, so pragmatic, so pleasant.

During our interview she went into her little kitchen and prepared vegetables for an evening meal, and offered me a slice of excellent home-made cake.

My friendship with Serena progressed. I do not make friends easily, and was delighted to have found a new one. She was getting very tired working at the depot, seemed depressed, and took a few days off work. I was out shopping with Leon one Saturday afternoon and suddenly decided to take her some flowers. I had the feeling that it was probably years since anyone had taken her flowers. Filled with the delightful feeling that comes from doing a good deed, I bought two large bunches of mixed blooms, wrote a card, and we went to ring her doorbell. Her boyfriend answered, and stood there staring at us with empty grey eyes, saying nothing. At my prompting he focused sufficiently to usher us up the stairs of the very run-down building, once a lovely Georgian house but now housing grim shops at street level and having badly converted flats above, and showed us into their bedsitting room.

I was horrified at the smelly slum, but behaved as if visiting a well-kept house; I gratefully sat down, declined tea, and offered my flowers to the figure lying in the utterly filthy bed. She lay under torn and greasy coverings with her bush of hair spread on a grey pillow, looking quite dreadful. When she saw the flowers she barely reacted, but, as if remembering her manners, smiled and held out a hand. I saw her whole arm naked, and was amazed to see the thick hair growing almost up to the shoulder, just like a hirsute male. Her smile was strange, with closed lips, for some of her front teeth were in a glass on the arm of a foul old armchair by the bed. She invited us, in a hoarsely hollow voice, to sit down but I said we were in a hurry to get to the shops before they closed. She was evidently relieved at that. The boyfriend just stood there like a mute, staring not even at us but at the wall.

I wished her a speedy recovery, although she had not offered to explain her illness nor had I asked. Somehow I dared not, or felt I should not, that a kind inquiry would be intrusive. She looked ancient, and not just lined in the face but almost toad-like in texture. I thought as we went down the staircase with its rolls of dirt and slicks of grease, that she too probably suffered allergies. I did not regret my gift of flowers, though. Leon and I did not discuss the visit until later, in the pub.

'You certainly cultivate some weird friends,' he remarked after drinking a half pint in one long draught. 'I've never seen such a shambles. Who the hell is she?'

'I don't know really, she comes from East London somewhere originally; divorced, five adult children, spent two years in a peace camp after her divorce, and also spent her share of the matrimonial loot on gigolos, as far as I can make out. She's had hundreds of men, so she says. Thought she would catch up on finding out more about sex after her divorce. Hard to believe to look at her.'

'Incredible. What a dump they live in. That guy's a bad lot, and I'm never wrong on first impressions. Wouldn't trust him at all, a really odd type.'

I agreed with all that, although his belief in his capacity for correct first impressions is laughable. We changed the conversation, but we were both a bit shaken. The atmosphere and the décor of the place had been grimly horrible. Even the pub seemed quite hygienic and pleasant after that, and it is in truth a rather sleazy dive, with occasional marked overtones of the hells of Hieronymus Bosch. I am not an imaginative type of person, I do not fantasize like many people I have known, I do not daydream, in fact, I hardly dream at night. A more creative and agile mind might have jumped to conclusions immediately, but not me. Note that I had diagnosed Serena as possibly having an allergy, and that I had suggested she take Agnus Castus, a herb known to stimulate female hormones. It seemed obvious to me that she needed not only that but possibly medical treatment and vitamins, and that was before I saw her ill. But of course, 'Nature was looking after her', and this irritated me and made me think her arrogant.

On the way home one night I suggested that she come with me for a drink before going home. She said she could not be long because Gary hated her to drink, he effectively guarded her and fretted if he did not know where she was. I told her it was time she asserted herself more, and she agreed. It was in this way that she was introduced to several of my acquaintances, my own territory.

It was not long after that when Serena began to have trouble with her boyfriend Gary. It seemed to me from her descriptions of his behaviour that he was becoming manic, even dangerously so. They were having terrible quarrels, and he was becoming a changed man. He had more energy, never slept, had begun to eat a great deal of meat and disappeared at night not saying where he was going. She was in a terrible state of nervous tension and looked harassed at work, although not so very strange as she had when ill in bed. She asked my advice.

From the descriptions of his behaviour which she gave me, I deduced that Gary needed medical help – was possibly dangerous. He threatened her with knives, pushed her about and paced the room all night raving about his energy, his future, his marvellous plans for setting up in business and making a fortune. Serena said that hardly anything he said was in sequence or made sense and that he contradicted himself continually.

I directed her to a clinic where a psychologist could be consulted free of charge, and when she had been she told me that she could probably have Gary sectioned – put in a secure ward – possibly indefinitely. For someone who could say that a few weeks before he had been her boyfriend, she seemed curiously unemotional. She talked about love, and loving people, quite a lot but I never saw any real evidence of love in her relationships. This is of course usually the case with people who boast of their own loving nature; such people don't really give a damn about anybody but themselves.

Two days later Gary had left her and gone off in their car with another woman, a younger, plumper, silly woman who had fallen for his ravings. He had taken a lot of Serena's things, and put the contents of her fishtank down the drain and broken the glass, and had also absconded with some money. She retaliated by telephoning the insurance company where she had just paid a year's insurance and cancelling the deal, obtaining a refund. I praised her for her spirit which at that time seemed undaunted. She seemed determined, and spoke of a new life, a fresh start, cutting out dead wood. I had tutored her in these sentiments and impulses over a number of months.

The next day at work Gary turned up and gave her a beating until the manageress threatened him with the police. Everyone who worked with her felt sorry for her, I most particularly. I arranged to meet her in the pub that evening. I was deep in giving consolation and advice when Leon turned up. He did not look pleased at her presence, but after a couple of drinks joined in with the supportive litany. We got her to laugh, and in my somewhat euphoric state of charity, for once the sound did not grate upon my ears. I suggested that we all go for a long walk the following Sunday. She needed fresh air, exercise and company, I decided. She must not sit brooding. She had moved out of the ghastly flat, and was living in the spare room at her nephew's flat. She was virtually homeless and friendless; I and Leon, would look after her. I told her, now that she had only herself to look after, she must open a savings account, but also spend some money on clothes for herself.

On Sunday morning she arrived on time, and I could not help commenting on the change in her appearance. She looked healthier, younger, altogether more cheerful. She did not slouch so much, her whole muscle structure looked in better shape. She was not at all what you might call attractive, but she was almost presentable. I had, to my own shame, felt ashamed of being seen in the pub with her before. She looked cleaner, smoother, lighter, as if a burden had dropped away, which of course it had. Her Gary had been dragging her down for almost three years. We all three set off along the canal bank, in bright sunlight, at a deliberately brisk pace. I wanted to drive out her blues with exercise. We did upwards of six miles before lunch, which we had at a pub.

I was elated. All three of us seemed to be getting along so well, in mental accord about so many themes which our lunch-time beer evoked. We laughed a lot, and again I was not so irritated by her donkeyish expressions of mirth; they seemed more normal. People stared a little at the three of us I thought, but this always happens to strangers in country pubs.

Walking though, she did not last out long and asked to rest while we went on, because her feet hurt. She was wearing the same awful pair of once bright yellow shoes over nylon socks. I vowed to find some sticking plasters somewhere; perhaps a little shop would appear. In fact, about a mile further up the canal bank there was a Sunday market and I bought a packet of plasters straight away, and felt triumphant. I was like a mother duck with a lame duckling; I even contemplated buying her some decent wool socks, but Leon said that was going too far.

On the way back we found her lying in the sun and difficult to rouse, very torpid. And looking like an old tramp too, I could not help thinking privately, but my compassion still ran high and I presented the plasters, waiting for praise and thanks like a child. They were not forthcoming. She took off her shoes and socks and I had to look away, for her feet were such a horrible sight. I have never seen such neglected feet, all horny and rough, gnarled, the toes bent, the nails unkempt and unclean, more like the claws of some strange bird than human feet. She patched up her sore spots and we walked further, until in the heat of the afternoon we rested in some shade by a wood.

I had been listening to the birdsong for some time, enjoying the lift to the spirits which cheerful sounds convey. Serena then told us that this was her first ever country walk, she had never done anything but stroll. She seemed unaware of the beauty of her surroundings and indeed, the birdsong ceased when she laughed at something. There ensued one of those strange silences which sometimes occur on a hot afternoon in the country. I remember feeling a little thrill of fear at this quiet and looking at Leon for his reactions, but he seemed not to notice anything; he chewed a blade of grass as town people will, as if some distant browsing gene were jolted into action. There was a charge of hyper-reality for a short while, an experience which I believe is probably quite common but not spoken of because it is not understood.

Just then a beautiful dragonfly came by and my spirits rose higher. When Serena's hand shot out and captured it expertly, unfeelingly, I could hardly believe my eyes, but just gave a small strangled cry of horror. I saw her face, her small, dark eyes glittering, her mouth open, her narrow tongue actually hanging out with concentration. 'She's mad!' I recall thinking, and got up quickly to try to dispel the atmosphere which had gone bad. Leon laughed and congratulated her on her skill, and I said nothing. My sympathies were with the dragonfly entirely and I walked on ahead in silence, the two of them trailing behind. I walked very briskly to recharge my mood; I detest gratuitous cruelty, any cruelty.

The other two were out of sight for quite a while, and I feasted my spirits on the sight of baby swans, various wild flowers, clouds, the renewed birdsong, a squirrel. By the time I had rested and they had caught up with me, the two of them laughing and cheerful, I had repressed the horrid sight of Serena killing an innocent creature, and one which is quite rare at that. I did not want to quarrel with her, and although I often chided her about her self-neglect, I never criticized her actions. I had no close female friend but her at the time and I valued her company; apparently I was prepared to compromise, to overlook faults and failings. Probably, if this were not done, there would be few friendships of any kind, for people are frail.

We all went out drinking one weekend, and got somewhat plastered and overly genial. On these occasions behaviour changes radically, in my case it is almost as if some other personality emerges, which has only been waiting for the alcoholic key to free its madness. We set up a watchword for the weekend, a catch-phrase, and I originated this, which was 'Outrageous'. Anything we said or did was OK so long as it was Outrageous. We were hardly truly outrageous, but we did make a lot of noise in restaurants, laughed a great deal, hurled jocular insults at various passing souls in the pub – known to us of course, not strangers – and generally caroused.

People were attracted to me that weekend; I lost my invisibility, which I have cultivated over a number of years, and became more as I was when a student. But you need others to do this kind of thing with, and then I had the two of them, for Leon too seemed lighter; usually he is a rather gloomy soul, sunk into himself, and he drinks heavily. So I found all this a great and lovely relief, to have my lover and my friend, to waste a little time for a change, the three of us together, in companionship, with some understanding of one another.

Of course you will easily have guessed what happened, and why my whole narrative is threaded with hostility and bitterness. I have struggled with these negative feelings and even now, a year later, I feel great waves of hatred, pain, loss. Serena managed to entice my Leon into bed with her; I had gone to bed early and he had gone out with her, and they came back to our house and she stayed the night.

It is interesting how the mind can both know and ignore a fact at the same time: I had heard strange sounds in the night, having been woken up twice, but had not allowed myself to register what I heard. Although how I would identify the groanings, whistling and hissing sounds with sexual activity it is difficult to say, for I have never imagined that anyone would or could make such sounds to express pleasure. At one point in my half-dreams I thought the central heating had been left on and had air in the system; another time

I thought I heard a neighbour's Rottweiler, which I fear, killing a smaller animal, perhaps an unfortunate cat. I put my hands over my ears – you cannot rescue a cat from a Rottweiler even if you are dressed and properly alert – and slept again, uneasily.

Leon told me quite casually that Serena had stayed when I got home later that day, taking an attitude of enormous surprise that I should mind at all. After all, we were all three close friends now, what did it matter? My suppressed horrors had already been confirmed first thing in the morning, for there were traces of her in our bathroom, a strong, female animal smell on my personal towel, not a normal or healthy smell, not quite musky; a bit like rotting pears, but undoubtedly Serena. I stuffed it into the rubbish bin, choking back sobs of pain and disgust. It was not so much that I had lost Leon, but that I had been cheated by Serena; she had become more friendly with me in order to get nearer to him. And the two of them had cut me out of the three-sided friendship which I had helped create for us all. I felt like a small child as the parents' bedroom door slams in its bewildered face.

I was in shock for a day, then began to break down little by little. I realized painfully the profound implications of their careless and stupid act. Everything had changed, and could never be the same again. My short-lived bliss was over.

The whole incident seemed to create a change in my personality, to spark off something very deep and awful in me. I was in dreadful pain day and night, an emotional and spiritual hurt which bled over into the physical realm; my heart pounded in series of palpitations, my muscles ached, my eyes were shot through with sharp pains and at the least mention of her name my whole system was as if flooded through with a hurtful poison; my body became a massive twinging thing, panting with misery, catching its breath with great gasps of agony which I could not control. I made great efforts to control these reactions; I thought I would go mad.

Leon was out a great deal, he would march out with a bottle of wine in one hand and, so to speak, his cock in the other, flaunting his right to do as he pleased no matter what I felt. When I protested that people who lived by exerting their rights rather than exercising their sensitivity were grossly unpleasant people, he just stared at me uncomprehendingly. It was as if he had been hypnotized, possessed, was under compulsion. He said he was not in love but Serena was. I told him, you are brewing up hellish trouble for yourself: she is hardly presentable, what will you do on occasions such as the office parties which you have to go to, take her as the girlfriend? His answer was stubborn silence.

I began to detest him, to despise myself for having got mixed up with such a *schmuck*, and yet I clung on to him as if he meant life and breath. This triumph of illogicality was almost a madness, in fact, I lost my reason several times over the next few months. He made my life a torture, I even felt genuinely suicidal. I felt so betrayed that I thought I would never again totally trust another human being, and that would mean loneliness and lack of love for the rest of my life. The future gaped at me like a black hole. The Dark loomed.

We fought too, verbally and physically; I became a harridan almost overnight; my nicer nature died, and I wanted to kill. I was haunted with terrible desires, frightful images; I wanted to cut Serena's face, disfigure her, a strange impulse as she was already ugly. It riled me terribly that my lover should have been stolen by a creature with no loveliness; it was more insulting, more hurtful than if he had taken a beautiful lover, someone irresistible. I dreamed up tortures for her; the dark side of my mind had completely run amok. It was like being possessed; this incident had broken open a side of my nature which was almost unearthly in its nastiness. I hated myself and tried to control it, and matters became worse. I wished gang rape on her, any awful fate I could dream up, that would be hers. I clenched my whole being a dozen times a day in total and utter ill-wishing − I wanted her to experience every last bit of humiliation and pain which I was experiencing; every wave of pain I had, she would have in return. I wished slow deaths upon her, and slowly died myself. I have never been so ill and yet so filled with energy. My eyes sparkled, my muscles were toned, I danced everywhere; I flew, I burned up the hours on adrenalin caused by fear of loneliness and hatred of the two treacherous friends, who had cut me right out of the lovely triangle I had created. The more I screamed at Leon's retreating back the more I thought about the disagreeable aspects of our years together; I reassessed his behaviour and the state into which I had sunk, and began to hate him. I could see that in a way, both Serena and Leon had done me a favour for showing me what awful people I had treasured. And yet they were all I had: Leon had been a jealous lover and chased away all my other friends. I was alone, I felt I was howling like a wounded wolf in the middle of a cold desert.

I lost weight. Still I speeded along, running through my jobs and creating endless possible scenarios for the film about Mr Crowley. But when the time came for discussing the scenarios I was suspicious of the motives of the other people involved; I lost control, I ranted, disgraced myself, I wept and stormed out, accusing them of stealing my material. I trusted not one person in the world any more, I wanted no more friends if this was how it turned out. One night I found myself in the pub and Serena was there, and I followed her out and gave her a beating, making her weep.

'You're not human, you vile bitch, what you have done to me I do to you. I have wasted years on Leon, valuable years; I never thought he would behave so stupidly and cheaply or do anything so gross, screwing a horrible creature like you in the next room! I wish I had never met you, damn you! Go away, nobody here in Leamington needs you, we were all happy before you came. You call yourself a Christian, damn you – if you want to be a Christian I'll crucify you personally! Don't you know that to be a Christian you have to satisfy God, not yourself, you stupid bitch!'

All this to an accompaniment of blows and pushings, she did not retaliate, just whined, a strange noise that excited no pity in me at all. I knew later that I should have been ashamed of such behaviour, but instead only regretted not hitting her harder. I sneered to Leon about her professed Christianity and he was astonished. He replied that she was no Christian but had told him she was completely atheist. He suggested that she had told me she was a Christian to wind me up, but in my paranoid state I felt she had said this as part of a disguise: she was hiding something, I knew it.

But Serena looked well, younger, healthier. She laughed a lot. At work we did not speak but kept our feud secret from the other workers. I felt depressed when I was not madly angry, I swung from one extreme to another. She seemed quite balanced while at work, but when I saw her in the evenings, in the middle distance, she was dressed like a young girl in silly tight clothes, a large hat, make-up; very tasteless but celebratory and signalling sexual activity. I noticed that she had depilated her legs and arms, and seemed better washed. Her fingernails were cleaner but those awful feet were displayed in cheap sandals. She had taken my advice and got herself some new clothes; in poor taste, wearing Indian house-sandals in the street. Nobody ever wears these out of doors in Leamington and certainly not the Asian women who introduced them.

I often heard her boasting about her wonderful new boyfriend and clutched my hands together to prevent myself from running at her with intent to murder. I had no one to tell my pain to, no other close friend. I vowed never to try to help another person again as long as I lived. My charity was at an end.

One night by mischance she was sitting at the same table as I in a pub where I had gone for a rare pint of Guinness. I had stopped drinking because it fuelled my rage. I looked up in utter alarm and embarrassment to see her there, grinning, dressed in see-through Indian pyjamas, the kind that would only be worn in an Indian movie. She just did not realize the impression she was making, which in some ways was an advantage, because she was behaving like a glamorous twenty-year-old, and full of self-confidence, which has its attractions even in an ugly person. We stared at one another. I had not meant to speak but something blurted out of me.

'You may have stolen a lover, Serena, but you have lost two friends. Love does not last, friendship might have.' She gave a strange little twisted grin and I saw her false teeth shift in her mouth.

'I would still be your friend if you would let me. I love people.'

'You never were my friend: all the friendship came from me, you only came near me to get at Leon, I see that now. And as for loving people, I think you know nothing of love, nor of people. You are not human, you are weird, I mean bad weird, no conscience, like a psychopath or a goddam alien. You don't function as a human being at all.' At this point something very strange and frightening happened. I shall never forget what I saw.

Something happened to her eyes. Those strange eyes with no whites were momentarily obscured by a membrane, not unlike the membrane which draws across the eyes of a cat when it is ill. Simultaneously her hand, looking very clawlike, came up to her mouth and, right there in the pub, she removed her upper set of false teeth, revealing a row of yellowed fangs distinctly inhuman in shape. The corners of her mouth drew up and back to reveal how far these incisors grew, and I saw that her gums were almost black like those of some dogs. I felt myself reeling with shock, sounds grew distant. The membrane over her eyes slowly drew aside once more, and I knew I was gazing into eyes which were quite definitely not human. She spoke, and her voice was hoarse and heavy, deeper than usual.

'I am Weerde all right, but not as you think. All my family are Weerde. What you don't know is that you are Weerde. You don't know who your parents are, do you? I at least know mine.' She returned the false human teeth to her mouth, gave out a horrible coughing noise and picked up her pint of beer. Nobody else seemed to have noticed anything at all, and she looked at me and smiled and smiled over the top of her glass. Her eyes spoke now, telling me that she had my lover; I could forget him, she was offering him delights of which I knew nothing nor ever would.

I thought then, for the first time in connection with Serena, of what Joan had told me about the ancient race living among us. It was as if a mental curtain had been lifted; I told myself that I had been hypnotizing myself into not seeing what was there because it did not fit within my parameters of reality. I believe that this happens a great deal: we simply refuse to see things because they would disturb our world too much, so it wasn't at all crazy. My world was disturbed at that frightful moment, and I felt all reality shattering inside me like a windscreen hit by a stone. I punched my hand through the obscuring shards and saw a monstrous cloud of darkness approaching, its jaws open to feed on the world. There would soon be nothing left, for if one preposterous fact could be seen to be true, then so could a thousand, and in half a day the universe would be inside out. From this comes the peculiar blindness of those people, many of them scientists, who pour scorn on anything remotely fantastic. They express their terror that we live in a fragile construct which at a gesture from something outside 'normality' can atomize the world, and us with it. I knew all this, in a kind of slowed time, a drowning sequence which spun the film of my life and beliefs to be looked at again, a replay with more insight.

I saw with horror that Mr Crowley might not have been deluded, that his magick might have been a true science and his calling up of demons a fact, and that even if magic is an extreme use of the imagination, this very imagination is a thousand times more powerful than most dreaming humans could themselves imagine. My entire rational universe fragmented, and in its place there appeared a world populated by witches, Yeti, Loch Ness monsters, sorcery, shape-shifting, ghosts, bogies and singing mice. I felt both crazy and illuminated.

I stood up, and without saying anything or knocking over my glass, or revealing my horror in any way, I left the place. When I was outside I ran and ran, supressing a scream, and flew into the house, slamming the door behind me. I think my eyes must have stared and my

hair stood on end, and I know I panted with lips drawn
back, out of sheer terror, disbelief and also the impact
of certain knowledge of the Impossible. I knew I was
not going mad, I had no doubt. I called out loudly for
Leon, and he emerged from the bedroom where he was
packing a case. He was leaving me.

'Don't go! She isn't human, she's weird, she'll eat you
alive; you'll be tainted, awful things will happen! She's
using you, she has no feelings, don't go, please Leon . . .'
I babbled these time-worn phrases into a face set
against me.

'Do me a favour,' he said wearily. 'Put another record
on. If you really want to know, Serena has more feelings
than you have. I've never had good sex in my life until I
met her, I know that now. You are as cold as a lizard,
you don't give me anything or do anything for me. Just
get out of my way, OK?'

I didn't say another word. I caught a glimpse of his
eyes, and knew he had changed. I called what I saw
possession, whereas an hour before I would have swallowed that word and said he was simply feverish. I
kept out of his way, and when he had gone with a
classic slamming of doors, I felt only relief. He had
destroyed my love for him, only proving, maybe, that it
was not very strong, I do not know. I rushed around
opening all the doors and windows to let out the smell
of him, and of her, which clung to him. I got out the
vacuum cleaner and the dusters and cleaned the place
right through, and felt slightly more calm. There was
something else still bothering me though.

As I polished a mirror I focused on my own face. I
grinned at my teeth, peered under my eyelids, pulled at
my ears, scrutinized my skin. I looked perfectly normal:
there was nothing odd at all. I stood there a long time
in front of the mirror, thinking. Were there a lot of

Them? Had her boyfriend been one too? Her whole family?

I decided to go and visit Joan again, and did so the next day. She was not there, her friend told me, she was in a mental hospital. She had been sectioned there some weeks previously and would not speak to anyone.

It was at this point that my universe began to re-create itself again. I had been mentally and emotionally undermined by the whole series of events, in need of help myself perhaps. At such times one can begin to see and believe things which are untrue. I have conveyed just how powerful such delusions are: for example the awful sight I witnessed when Serena removed her false teeth in the pub. My mind undoubtedly filled in that ghastly hole in her face with those strange, animal teeth. It was symbolic of the sort of feral person I had seen her to be, that was all. And for a brief while I had thought that Mr Crowley was a real magician, as if there could ever be such a thing! I had been ill, I had had a narrow escape, several in fact; from Leon, from Serena, from a psychotic episode. I feel somewhat stabilized just from writing all this down.

Leon I do not miss. He was part of a phase. I do not need a treacherous male in my life. I see Serena infrequently – I work elsewhere now – but in the street we sometimes pass and I shudder, not because I think her to be some ancient life-form, some weird subhuman branch which neither Darwin nor Kammerer even dreamed about, but because she is what I first thought her to be: a bad bitch. A bad, bad bitch.

RAILWAY MANIA

Michael Fearn

I found the box tucked down the side of one of the gravestones at the cemetery in Chapel Le Dale. It was quite clearly a new addition, because I often came to pay my respects to the graves of the navvies who had been killed building the railway, and this was at the side of one of a small group of graves which were set a little apart from the rest. It was a newish, small, olive-green tin box, probably army surplus.

There has always been a link between railways and churchmen. I suppose I am just one in a long line of what must seem to be rather dotty old clerics who, too heavenly minded to be of much earthly use, spend their time with the dwindling evidence of this country's great railway past, which is certainly greater than its present. Fortunately, those who are acquainted with me will know that I have my feet firmly anchored to the ground. I haven't had a locomotive named after me like Bishop Eric Treacy, but my zeal is none the less, for all that. A psychologist once explained the railway hobby as the need to be part of something that is running to schedule in a world of growing confusion. That may be his explanation. I just like trains.

So it was with anticipation that, having taken morning service in Skipton, I set out in the car for what was probably going to be one of my last afternoons beside the *Long Drag*, as the Settle to Carlisle line has always

been called. I am getting on a bit now and they're going
to retire me soon, but when I get out into the wildness
of the Ribble Valley I feel nineteen. Besides, there was
a steam special to be photographed on Ribblehead Viaduct. It was going to be a good afternoon, and I had
barely shaken the hand of the last member of the con-
gregation when I was into the vestry like a shot and out
of the back door. The drive to my favourite part of the
line via the cemetery took place in brilliant June sunshine, but I didn't kid myself that once I got to the
viaduct I wouldn't be freezing cold.

On that winter morning of 1866, we are told that the
bells rang in Appleby, when the House of Commons
passed the bill granting the Midland Railway Company
the right to build a railway line from Settle to Carlisle
over the northern Pennines. This was the railway which
many said neither could, nor should be built. It was a
product of the Midland's desire for its own route to
Scotland. Unable to secure satisfactory agreements with
the London and North Western Railway to use the
route over Shap, James Allport, the Midland's Manager,
had drawn an imperious pencil stroke on a map between Settle and Carlisle, saying: 'We'll build our own
damned line!' It was a railway built in a fit of pique, an
access of *folie des grandeur*. Six-and-a-half thousand
men had been involved in the building of it, and now it
was threatened with closure: part of the problem, in my
opinion, caused by employing accountants to run railways, instead of railwaymen. I simply had to spend as
much time there as I could.

I confess that I shouldn't have, but yes, I fished the
box out from its niche beside the headstone, and opened
it. Inside there was a perfectly ordinary pad of note-
paper: the kind with the cardboard back that always
falls off. It was filled to the end of the last-but-one

sheet with as close to a Victorian copperplate hand as
it is possible to render in blue ball-point. I put it next to
my sandwiches, tape recorder and camera on the front
seat of the Mini, and drove as close to Ribblehead Viaduct as I could.

I was right about it turning out to be a perfect afternoon. I climbed as close as possible to the line, then I
sat down and opened the box once more. That was the
point at which my day changed completely and even
though I was shortly surrounded by others of the railway fraternity, they certainly might as well not have
been there. I began to read.

> I remember quite a lot of what I have written down
> here, even though I was only a youngster of eighteen at
> the time. Some I was told and much I can guess, for I
> am almost twice the age that Uncle Sam Inskip was
> when he saw the men coming.
>
> One member of the party was a young man in tailcoat
> and stove-pipe hat. He carried with him a map which
> he consulted from time to time, having the manner of
> one who would have berated the very limestone and
> earth for being different from what his map showed, if
> thus provoked. A slightly older man of stooped and
> clerkish appearance carried other rolled-up documents.
> There were three other men, obviously labourers, who
> were carrying sticks.
>
> I remember that it was a kind day for September, high
> clouds and bright sun. Every so often, Sam told us, the
> party stopped and one of the labourers hammered into
> the ground a stake half the height of a man. It was banded
> in alternate hoops of black and white. I caught sight of
> the men several times myself as I was out tending the
> sheep, and I recall thinking that it was a miracle that
> they had even got so far, dressed as they were.

'Skiving off, Vicar?' I heard, and looked into the rubi-
cund and friendly face of Ted Longstaff. I had noticed

at second hand that some of the local railway group had been arriving for the past half-hour or so, and had set up photographic and sound equipment. Ted was a railway buff of many years' standing, and I could not be rude. I had to talk to him for a while, discussing the inconsequentialities that fellow enthusiasts chatter about. We exchanged reminiscences of the last days of steam on the *Thames–Clyde Express* and the *Waverley*.

I feel as well disposed to my fellow man as the next chap, probably better than some, but I did wish that Ted would go away. You see, the railway enthusiast in me had realized that I was reading a firsthand account of the marking-out of the line in 1866, and the clergyman in me was beginning to feel a little cold. This account was recent, and it was written on a pad which still carried the modern price label from the sub-post office in Clapham. Surely a work of imagination? Anyone who was present at the scene described, even as an adolescent, now had to be over a hundred and forty years old. Ted sensed that I was preoccupied and walked away, muttering under his breath about how I could be out there anyway on the only day of the week when my kind did any work, so far as he could see. I read on.

> When they reached the edge of what we thought of as our land, Sam stood, checked his shape, and walked down diagonally from the cottage to join the men at a stand of trees which was a particular favourite of his.
> 'Good day, gentlemen,' he shouted, and I knew that he would be very careful to sound neither too brusque nor too cultured. These humans are so sensible to the slightest inflection and we did not see many people here to practise on.

'Humans!' You can imagine what I felt now. Actually no, I don't suppose you can.

This is the conversation as my uncle told it to us later that day.

'Good day to you, farmer,' the young man had replied. 'Is there some way in which we can help you?' There was something strange about the young man's accent.

'Aye. You can start by tellin' me who you are and what you're doin' on my land.'

'My name is Charles Stanley Sharland. I am a surveyor attached to the staff of Mr John Crossley, the Chief Civil Engineer of the Midland Railway Company. We are marking out the route of the new railway line from Settle to Carlisle.'

'Railway line . . .'

'Surely you must have heard that the Bill received the Royal Assent on July the 16th last?'

'I heard summat o' th' sort. But they'll never build a line through here: it's ower wild for that.'

'Progress, my good sir!'

'You're not from round here, are you, lad?'

'No, sir. I have the honour to come from her Majesty's colony of Tasmania.'

'Isn't there enough for you to do out there without coming and poking your nose in round here where it's not wanted? And you'll be wantin' them trees out of your road, I suppose?'

'Most certainly.'

'Then I'll ask you to spare that one.' Sam pointed to the tallest.

'Why that one in particular?'

'To hang you and all the engineers of the Midland Railway upon it, for daring to come here at all.'

Sam turned on his heel and stormed back up the hill, towards the cottage. The marking-out party continued.

This, of course, was the clincher. Either it was a very good piece of historical research or it was an actual, firsthand account. Sharland *had* led the staking-out party from Settle to Carlisle in 1866, but had become famously snowed in at the inn at Gearstones, near Ribblehead. He had been forced to tunnel out to continue with the work, but this was surely far earlier in the year. Possibly an unrecorded, previous attempt? Sharland had died in Torquay at the age of twenty-six without ever seeing the line completed. His clerk had died locally of influenza, and there was a story that he had continually shouted out in his delirium about being unwilling to go back to Ribblehead because a 'weird man who wasn't really there' had kept trying to get him to throw himself from the valley sides. I whimsically noted the biblical parallel of the Devil suggesting to Christ that he throw himself from the pinnacle of the Temple, and continued my eavesdropping.

> Great grandfather Josiah Inskip was a hundred and sixty at that time, and in human terms he looked seventy. He was the only remaining member of a Stasis-faction group which had come here for peace and isolation after their part of the Tame valley had vanished under a cotton mill. He used to tell us youngsters that we shouldn't be bothered here, but even if we were, we ought to remember the trouble that was caused when humans arrived, and never to trust them a single inch. He used to sit by the fire, smoke his pipe and spit. I always thought that was disgusting, but I never would have dreamed of telling him. The grate was always black-leaded by mother Rachel until it shone, but no one ever visited. It often seemed to me that we had taken to human ways just that little bit too much. Such things do not normally matter to Weerde.

Weerde? What were they? From the writing style, there were no grounds to assume that the writer did not know what an adjective was, or that they couldn't spell.

I remember that day's events bitterly and well, for they were directly the cause of my having to leave on my wanderings a good while before I was ready. This is something no Weerde likes to do, for it is a period full of danger and risk for us, and we must be fully prepared by our fathers, womb-mothers and by the rest of the group.

An armchair on either side of the fireplace formed the arms of a squarish U whose base was the oak settle, which Rachel shared with Jessica, Sam's womb-sister. Even though she was my second mother, I could recognize that Rachel was a well set-up lass of fifty-three who looked thirty in human terms. She had been sufficiently influenced on her wanderings to insist to Sam that they be 'married.' This they had done in Garsdale. The others were out and the offspring were playing in the lengthening shadows. Their shouts reached us through the open door. I am quite sure that if the adults had realized I was there they would have made me go, but they were too preoccupied. It is strange how such times can come back to you across the years, so clearly.

'But we aren't a group of filthy Darkcallers! Why should they take over our land to build this monstrous thing? It was for the very reason of these humans and their pernicious need to cover every inch of the land with their created *things* that we were hounded out of Greenfield. It's as if they don't believe they exist unless they're constantly littering the ground with the proof . . .'

'Josiah, it simply is not that desperate a situation.' Rachel rose, and knelt down before the fire, placing the poker between the cast-iron bars and lifting the coals. A small plume of sparks rose. 'The railway in the city takes very little room, and here it would be noticed even less.'

'Very well, father,' said Sam. 'Have you any suggestions? I confess that I found it a shocking trial to have to play the yokel for the surveying party.'

'Something must be done. You've had your wandering years, Sam, and you've seen humans, but you haven't seen what they can do to a place in months.'

Uncle Sam heeded his father's words and organized us well that night. Not only did we remove the markers that the party had put out in the morning: he had us fill in the post-holes. The southbound party found their work undone.

Have you ever been so utterly convinced by the authenticity of something you have read, that you did not question it for one moment? Everyone who has read at all has at least one piece of writing that they come back to again and again because it is a real, created thing. Whether the events it describes are completely fictional or not, either the writer's skill or the emotional impact of the content has a life of its own. All I can tell you is that I heard a rushing sound passing by twenty feet below me and I knew that this would be the special: 4472 *Flying Scotsman*, one of Sir Nigel Gresley's supreme creations pulling a rake of restored, varnished-teak LNER coaches, but quite frankly at that moment the date was 1866 and I didn't even look up.

I should explain that it did not go well for the Midland Railway. *Why* should I explain? If you are reading this I am almost certainly dead, so what difference can it possibly make? Maybe I was not so far from my original calling, with faith dulled into a round of routine observance, as I might have liked to think. Call it a finicky attention to detail. The Midland's application for an Abandonment Order in the light of the difficulties they faced was turned down by Parliament: the land-owners and the farmers had now got behind the idea of the railway, and if they had to have the thing at all they really thought it would be a good idea if it happened as fast as was practicably possible.

The account went on to tell of how Sam took his sheep to market and heard that there was quite a lot of excitement about the line. It was said that it would be the making of the entire area. It would open up the border country to the rest of the world. Leeds in two hours! London in five! Then came a most remarkable passage:

> Being Weerde, he was able to circulate around the busy market and be even more inconspicuous than a human who does not wish to be noticed. We know enough about human perception, having shared a world with them (albeit for a few short ages), to know that they sometimes seem to look straight past us without noticing that we are there: a phenomenon which we have used to our advantage upon numerous occasions.

It would be a truly stupid cleric who ignored the fact that there are inexplicable things in the world, but such was the realism of the account that I find myself (in this rather donnish and mannered report of the events) at a loss to see how I failed to realize more quickly what I was dealing with.

> Sam listened. A viaduct at Ribblehead, just below our group's house. A tunnel at Blea Moor. Damn these humans! This was as good as putting up a beacon to the Dark! Farmers from Horton, New Houses, Selside all seemed to agree that there would be much to be gained. Sam came home with a heavy heart. By the time I met him at the junction of Cam beck and the nascent Ribble, he realized that he was going to have to take charge of events. Then came the evening that excluded me from the group as surely as if the Midland Railway had dragged me out with one of their locomotives.
>
> 'Rachel, I tell you we shall have no peace. You may be more familiar with these trains than I, but the more machines there are the more chance there is of the Dark being called.'

'And I tell you, Samuel, that these people are the sons of their mothers just as our Thomas and Ruth are!'

Josiah stirred by the fire, and shifted in his chair. We all looked at him with affection, habits or no habits. He really was beginning to revert now. It would not be long until he found it too much of a strain to take human shape. The very reason we were here was for isolation, and we did not wish to start a yeti-bigfoot-sasquatch rumour in these parts, as aged Weerde who found shape-stabilization difficult had in certain other parts of the world.

The argument continued. It was quite obvious to me that even the threatened presence of large numbers of humans was going to cause trouble. Discussions were common in the Inskip group, but this was an argument. I suppose the fact that I was subject to the hot and intemperate mood swings of a rather difficult adolescence might explain what happened next. What the humans were doing to us already was making me uncontrollably angry.

'I think they should be allowed to build their railway.' The words had escaped with the same lack of conscious control as an unexpected sneeze.

Sam turned slowly round from his seat opposite Josiah and asked:

'What's that you said, Davy?' He looked as though he knew all too well, but was hoping that I would be able to reassure him. Matthew, my own father, was a taciturn individual, and I was far closer to Sam than to him. He simply shifted on his own stool and looked uncomfortable.

'Let the boy have his say,' Josiah rumbled from his chair, and I found myself the centre of attention. I remember feeling so hot that I wished the fire were further away.

From behind me, my father's voice asked:

'Now, David, what do you mean?'

The people I loved most in the world were all looking

at me with expressions which ranged from concern to hurt bewilderment, and I felt quite out of control. There was a long, silent pause in which I could hear the fire logs spit.

'I think we should let them carry on, and call the Dark, and then they will take them off and we shall be left in peace again,' I blurted.

'You'll not talk like that in this house!' Sam roared. 'Have you any idea of what you are suggesting?'

'Sam, he's only a youngster. He's a year or so yet from his wandering time ...' Jessica tried to calm the situation down, but Sam had been roused, and it was too late.

'He should have thought of that before he chose to open his mouth. He's only here as the eldest of the children: not as a full member.'

'All the more reason to let him off,' my father said.

'Matthew, I know he's your boy, but you must see that we can't ...'

I couldn't bear for this to go on any longer.

'Stop it!' I yelled. 'If you mean that we risk calling the Dark, I don't believe they're real! They are just an excuse a lot of old men and women give for never doing anything!'

Of course, I did not mean any of this, but it was too late. Sam told me to leave. The others could probably have changed his mind, but I really had gone too far. I know that many young humans leave home after disputes of this sort, but it really is not the way with us. We know that we will leave, but we leave in order to return. We also have what has always been called the *ceremony of return*, which takes place on the day the Weerde youngster leaves. The hours spent with each adult member of the group, listening again to the tales and advice culled from their own wanderings are followed by time alone with everyone in the group, even the smallest. They will be adults when one returns (or they may have left on their own wanderings) and all personal disputes and animosities must be settled. All debts must be paid. Some of the old ones may have died, so all things must be said. I was denied that solace. None of this could take place for me.

I know that this caused as much grief in the group as it caused me, for I did not actually go far. Shapes were too unstable to go out into human society for some time, and my Kin had to begin to live on their own livestock and whatever scant crops they could force to grow on such inhospitable heights. Great grandfather had chosen this location for isolation, not horticulture. From the Saurians we had learned the science of stone, and the memory of Earth's oldest race was strong. The death and burial of Josiah on Batty Moss showed Sam the way of it, and he took charge. Much of the rest of what happened I have from Jessica, who refused to isolate me completely, and who would meet me by arrangement in Ingleton or Garsdale on shopping trips every so often. It was in the December of 1869 that Thomas ran into the room where his father, Rachel and Jessica were in conversation.

'Father! There are hundreds of men on the Moss with big things with legs on them and . . .'

'Calm yourself, Thomas. I shall come directly.'

'There was no need to elaborate, or to chide his offspring for exaggeration. There were, indeed, hundreds of men on the Moss. They had what were quite obviously drills, and several holes had already been bored.

The humans did not know why, later in the day, a new charge-hand came to take over the location of the drill, and no one could have said that they remembered much about him. From that moment onwards, they had no luck with their drilling, and it became clear that their drills were going down into twenty-five feet of mud and peat, and that no stable foundation could be found. The drilling party became discouraged and some of them began to feel very agitated.

In the bitter, knife-like north-east wind and louring

cloud there was scant need to inject another factor of discomfort to encourage the desertion of the illiterate navvy. Men who could carry bags of sand up and down sheer valley sides all day could not countenance the additional illusion of there being wild beasts at the edge of their vision. We are shape-changers, and know what humankind are really frightened of better than they do. We have had the time to find out. Work had to be abandoned for the next few days until a priest of their ridiculous god could be brought in to purify the site.

No, to be honest, I was not shocked by that. One thing you have to develop in my calling is a broad back – especially in these days when there seems to be a special case for what I was trained to believe was a moral or religious absolute. Perhaps there is something in the psychologist's ponderings about railway enthusiasts, after all!

This being, this Weerde, continued his narrative.

It was a small town of wood, this Quebec, as the navigators called it, the shanty town where the three hundred men and their families lived who were to build the viaduct at Ribblehead. It had this name for they were forced to scale heights daily just as terrifying as those faced by Wolfe. Yes, I have to admit that I lived in Quebec for a short time, and worked with the men there. This is why it was hardly surprising to me that whispers started from a quarter that no one else quite understood, to the effect that the viaduct was to be built on bales of wool. That was all that was said to be available locally to soak up the groundwater, otherwise the viaduct would sink as soon as it was raised.

This legend is still current, and I have heard it quoted as truth by very knowledgeable railway historians. Each of the piers of the viaduct, actually built on concrete for one of the first times, emerged from the floor of the Moss caged in a wooden framework. The 'bog carts' with a barrel for wheels delivered the materials to the site, and every sixth pier was made thicker so that if one fell, it would only take another five with it.

My Kin were forced to rely upon shadow and reflection; upon suggestion and innuendo. The Welsh masons and Irish labourers were a fertile ground for such seeds: moralistic and dissipated by turns. The life of Quebec was that of any frontier community. Justice was rough and ready, and stories ran like wildfire. Drunkenness was a way of life, and venereal disease so rife that Mrs Garnett of the Manchester Missionary Society paid a visit to attempt to instil some moral rectitude into the hearts of the navvies. They were too busy with the Helm wind, typhoid and influenza to take any notice.

The sound would stay for ever with those of us who heard it, of a Welsh mason who could lift three men, crying for his Ma as he was sucked into the bog of Batty Moss or Dandry Mire. The clay slides that buried whole gangs in the workings for Blea Moor Tunnel became a speciality of Jessica's, as she told me, for all the Inskip group had come round to the idea that if they were to retain any degree of privacy or make sure that yet another area of the planet were not converted into a veritable lighthouse for the Dark, action had to be taken. We had learned well from the Saurians.

Men fell and were blown from the bridge. Quite often this happened without Weerde intervention, but there were stories of grey, semi-human figures coming upon various navvies unawares. The common ground in these accounts was that the figures always suggested suicide as a means of making an end of the undoubted, extreme discomfort. They would also prey upon the minds of men already disturbed to suggest that they were not much men to have subjected their families to the dire inconvenience of Quebec life. The navvies worked often in conditions of intense cold, and humans who are suffering from exposure are very suggestible, even to the point of going to sleep and not waking up, on command. Wouldn't their families be better off without them, or happier at least in Leeds or Manchester, where they could get a decent factory job? My group would have been quite happy with mass desertion: death was not a necessity, merely absence.

One who survived said it was as though a voice had said to him that it would simply be easier to stop trying to hang on and point stone blocks at the same time. He had seen out of the corner of his eye a figure whose approach had startled him. He had staggered and fallen, only to be held by his braces snagging against a support.

'I felt a hand push me, you see. It just seemed the right thing to do like. My hands were frozen anyway, so I fell. When I was caught by my braces I thought "there's lucky", all cool like, as if nothing had happened.'

The rumour about the wool had some basis in fact in the end because Sam had driven his entire flock of sheep into one of the holes for the piers as a last, desperate spoiling measure. Humans were so sentimental about animals. Surely this would stop them. No. The viaduct was finished in 1875, but by that time there were no Weerde at Ribblehead. There were also two hundred of the navvies and their dependents in the cemetery at Chapel Le Dale.

I can control my anger no longer. I am David Inskip, the Weerde who was forced from his home too early by human folly, and my age is one hundred and forty-seven human years. When a Weerde has given you his name, you may know that there will be a reckoning. I no longer care whether anyone finds this account, which I shall leave on my father's grave. It has served its purposes: it has clarified my thoughts and made me feel better. It is also the only memorial to my Kin.

Humans! You are on this world for so short a time
and your values are nonsensical! How can you know
the true worth of heart, of stone, of love, sharing and
years? How can you understand that the Dark is a
ravening brood that must one day return towards the
world you have stolen from us and see your works as
evidence of your presence? The Dark will come. They
will feed. We will *all* perish for I, like all my race,
curse the fact that through living with you our shape-
changing nature has made us so like you that some
of us, particularly some of our young have em-
braced your glittering trash and shunned their true
nature.

I look now at the cemetery at Chapel Le Dale, for I
know that twelve of the graves contain bodies of a
different shape: bodies who occupy the ground with
understanding, not mere oblivion. Yes, we have grown
to be like you to a degree which is mortal to us. We
cannot grow great again whilst constantly trying to
adapt to the dangers which you pose to us. My group
all died from your influenza in the end.

It has always been one of my regrets that it was not I
who weakened the Tay Bridge in 1879 when it broke in
a storm and the Dundee train fell into the river. What
was accomplished there by proven human incompetence
I have managed to reproduce over the years. My first
success was when I returned for the first time to the
neighbourhood of our group home and found an un-
inhabited ruin. It was I who set the signals to clear and
gave two light engines the road to proceed to Carlisle in
1910, where they were caught on Ais Gill summit by
the Glasgow express, which they should have followed.
So satisfying that it was Christmas Eve.

Quintinshill in 1915 was perhaps my greatest
triumph. A simple matter to arrange for a telegraph
message not to be sent: one almost had the feeling of
sculpting a disaster from the basic stuff of chaos. Four
trains, including a troop special from Liverpool. Over

three hundred dead. Very fitting, although loss of life was only ever a means to an end.

I set the trap points to derail the Penzance express at Norton Fitzwarren in 1940. I caused the driver to over-run the signals at Lewisham in 1957. I have scrambled a good few signal wires in my time, but I am quite happy for others to take the public credit.

Many years have come and gone, and I am now very old. I have wandered your world. How could I come back to a home which you had ruined and to a family whose quietness and peace you had ruptured? My hate is cold and it has matured. As I watch one of your trains struggle across the land where my father's sheep ran, I know that I am going to Folkestone where you are digging a vast tunnel under the sea for more of your trains.

When I finished the account, I put it back into the box. I was seated alone by the side of the tracks which David Inskip had hated so much. All the others had gone: I hoped that they would simply think that the batty old Reverend had finally cracked.

I don't suppose for one moment that you can con-ceivably imagine what it is like for the vicar of a very comfortable little parish in rural England to be faced with the blood-and-bones struggle of good and evil in the world. Even stating the problem in its fundamental nature like that seems ridiculous in the late twentieth century, when our lives have become so predictable and controlled. This was an issue of faith: an issue such as I, a dotty railway parson, had not had to face in forty years. I knew that there was evil here, but certainly it was not at all one-sided. Was there actually a greater evil against which protective steps had to be taken?

For the form of it, I repeated the prayer of exorcism over the tract, now back in its box. Somehow, amidst that scenery, only the Latin would do: *In nomine patris et filii* ... I then said the Lord's Prayer, and was jerked back to reality by a pronounced drop in temperature (but it was only the wind) and the rowdy, southward passage of the two-coach multiple unit to Settle.

There was also such a weight of time, and desperate loneliness. The Weerde. Earth's oldest living race. Whether any of this is true or not, I am firmly convinced that David Inskip was exactly who he said he was, for since that day my own researches have tied up loose ends in the Settle–Carlisle story which have never been solved any other way. I was left with one final dilemma: his threat to the Channel Tunnel. He had reason to loathe railways, and there have been several accidents during its construction. I doubt that we shall ever be able to prove him responsible. The box is buried again but I am afraid I shall not tell you where.

The fact that you are reading these observations means that I am dead, for they are part of the papers lodged with my will and the notes of an unfinished book on the line, which I was writing myself. A superb way of avoiding any responsibility, and I was always rather good at that.

BLIND FATE

Liz Holliday

Teiresias stared into the darkness of the cave. She was there, he knew it: Sphinx, curse of Thebes, riddler, throttler of men. The enemy he had never met. He saw her as a patch of warmth on the cold stone at the back of the cave, heard the slow rasping of her breath. The still air was heavy with her scent. It filled his throat, thick with the complex undertones of old age, and overlaid with the stink of rotting human blood and flesh. There was something in that smell of rain on slate, of crushed flax seeds and beeswax; something familiar underlying it all that he could not quite place however he struggled.

He heard her turn in her sleep, smelled the slight change in her odour as she woke.

His heart thrashed wildly in his chest; the blood sang in his ears. She was an Ancient One, and therefore as different from ordinary Kin as the Kin were from humans, if the Songs of the Lines were to be believed.

He feared her. Suddenly, he could no longer deny it to himself. He stepped back into the strong light at the mouth of the cave. His chiton wrapped itself around his legs, threatened to come loose from the fibula that pinned it at the shoulder. Trying to hold it up he trod unwarily. Bone crunched under his foot, loud as the snapping of a dry twig.

Her head came up. Light glinted like fire in her eyes. His fingers were suddenly like jelly. His chiton slipped

203

through them, until it was held on only by his girdle. The rough wool chafed his skin. Better to think of that than the approaching Ancient One, than the prospect of failure, than the loss of his name to the Songs of the Lines.

Fear filled his mouth with thin bile. Unable to swallow it back or even spit it out, he let it spill out over his chin. Hide hissed on rock. Claws clicked on stone. No wonder the humans could not answer her riddle, he thought. I doubt they could even speak their names.

Yet I am not human. I am Teiresias, and I am sent by Zeus. I will not be silent.

Something huge and shadowy was making its way to the front of the cave. Teiresias closed his eyes, and though he could not shut out the clatter of her talons or the awful, complex smell of her, it was enough to give him back his voice.

'Come forth,' he tried to shout. His voice cracked, and he tried again. 'Come forth and face me.'

The thing that moved forward into the half-light hardly seemed human. Perhaps she no longer cared. She towered over Teiresias, twice the height of a man. He stared up into her face, all thrusting muzzle and tiny eyes. Blood caked the golden fuzz of her skin, the ancient dugs that sagged against her belly. The Sphinx shook her head, and the heavy mass of her hair settled like wings folding against her back, all matted with grease to her knees.

'So,' she said softly. Her breath seared Teiresias like furnace heat. 'Another has come to hear my riddle, and to die.'

'I heard you ate the flesh of men, Aunt,' Teiresias said, trying to hide the desperation in his voice.

'I know you. I have always known you.' The Sphinx brought her head up and tilted it as though she heard a noise. She said, 'You have the taint of Kin about you, Nephew. And to what degree are you my nephew?'

'I am Teiresias, who the men of Thebes sometimes call seer. And I am of the line of Eueres and Chariclo, which owes its allegiance to Zeus, First Father of the Kin, whom the humans call father of the gods. My name is sung in the Songs of Lines for the deeds I have done.' Teiresias managed to get the ritual reply out without stumbling. The sun seared his back; he imagined that the Sphinx's talons, raking him, would burn as badly.

'And I am Sphinx, known also as Kassmia in the Songs of Lines. I am most ancient, and I do the bidding of the First Mother, Hera; she whom the humans call Most High Goddess.'

She moved slowly towards him. In all the world, there were only her eyes, cold as the fixed stars, bright as fire. They held him. He watched in awe as she came near. Her odour overpowered him. He tried to retreat, but the rock wall bit into his back, into his palms.

'Did you think to kill me for Zeus's pleasure, Nephew-of-Another-Line?' Teiresias felt his eyes go wide, smelled the metallic odour of his own fear and knew he had betrayed himself. Sphinx touched his face with her hand; her skin was rough with callous, greasy with ingrained dirt. He moved his head aside. Her fingers stroked the soft flesh of his throat. 'Did great Zeus not tell you of the pact between my line and yours before he sent you to face me?'

His breath burned in his throat. 'No,' he whispered.

'In the earliest days my brother Typhon, already of great age, fought Zeus.' She glared at Teiresias. Her breath quickened, and he smelled the odour of triumph on it. 'Typhon disarmed him and hamstrung him with his own weapons, then fed him a poison which made him unable to sleep, unable to concentrate. Thus bound, he was unable to sleep the healing sleep. Typhon had been afraid however, that Zeus, winning, would use the poison on him in revenge. For this reason, he gave me the antidote to guard.'

She stopped. Teiresias waited. The silence was broken only by the rustling of the leaves on the cypresses that cloaked Mount Phikion, the scurry-and-stop of a shrew deep in the cave. It was unbearable. The Sphinx's eyes, gold flecked with blood red, filled up his sight. He began to speak, knew what she expected him to say. He refused. For fully a hundred heartbeats he was able to refuse, though he wanted to scream, wanted to die rather than look in those eyes. He knew he smelled of fear and acquiescence; the stink of the losing beast in the battle.

Sphinx let her finger score his skin gently. Teiresias felt a trickle of blood run slowly down his neck. Beheading, he thought; the death of the brain: damage we can never heal. 'Well?' asked the Sphinx.

'Zeus sent Cadmus, the human founder of Thebes, to you. With him was my forefather Eueres. They pleaded with you in the name of Zeus and in the name of the humans, whom they called mortals. You refused.' He hesitated. Whatever he said, she would kill him. The taint of it came off her like sweat. He saw her mouth move in the beginning of a snarl. 'Finally,' he said, quickly, 'they pleaded with you in the name of Hera, the wife Zeus has acknowledged before the humans. You relented then, but not before you had extracted promises from human and Kin alike: that they nor any of their Lines would seek to kill you.'

'So it was spoken before the Council,' Sphinx said. 'And let it be so,' she continued, in the words of the ritual.

'And let it be so,' Teiresias agreed.

The Sphinx touched a talon to the sticky blood on his neck then sucked it off, slowly. When she had finished, she smiled. Her teeth were etched round with crimson. 'What business have you here, Nephew-of-Another-Line?' she asked.

'Zeus bids me say this to you,' he said. 'It is his will that you leave Thebes. If King Laius falls, it will be to the detriment of the Kin. Therefore he has commanded Hera to give up her quest for the return of the human Chrysippus.'

He had no warning. The Sphinx lashed out. Her claws caught him across the chest, ripped himation and flesh alike. He screamed in pain, moved aside too slowly, as if he were human. It was too late: she had him pinned against the bare rock. There was too much pain. He could smell his own blood, fresh and raw, and his own fear. From the Sphinx came the smell of excitement, a kill to be made; sexual arousal. He felt himself sliding into unconsciousness: remembered Zeus, who was so much more to be feared.

The Sphinx bent her head to his chest and began to lap at the blood that welled there. Her tongue was cold and rough, and sometimes her fangs touched his flesh. Vomit bubbled up into his mouth, bitter as wine vinegar. He spat it out, and it stained the orange rock dark. The rock wall bit into his hands and back and buttocks as he trembled against it, tried to hold himself up with his spread arms.

He would die, he knew it. Tears burned acid trails down his cheeks and slid into his mouth. He would die, and with him his place in the memory of the Kin; there would be only the oblivion of death, or whatever worse thing waited there. It was worse than he could contemplate.

He clung to the pain, and through it tried to think of Zeus with his complex odour of morning dew and fresh turned earth, bull's blood and the acrid tang of lightning. He has commanded me, Teiresias thought, I may not fail.

He had commanded Hera also, Teiresias thought; he had to concentrate, to remember why Zeus had sent him there. Zeus had commanded Hera never to make use of the humans' oracles again. She had used them to frighten Laius, so rumours in the Kin went. The oracle had told him that any son of his would kill his father and marry his mother. Laius had reacted in a very human, typically unexpected way by having the child exposed on the hillside. It was something they did regularly, though not to royal heirs.

I saved him though, Teiresias thought, in case we could use him. Him with the spike through his ankles, that parched night in summer. So I named him Oedipus for his swollen feet and took him to Corinth. For this, among many other things, my name is sung in the Lines. Many other things.

That gave him courage, so that he was able to look at the red stained face of the Sphinx when she lifted it and said, 'Hera requires Chrysippus. He was hers before ever the human stole him. Zeus may not command me in this.'

Teiresias turned his head away with difficulty. The Sphinx pressed close up to him. He saw blood-swollen mites crawling in her hair. The acidic smell of them made his eyes water.

'I understand, Aunt,' he said at last. He ran his tongue over dry lips. 'I wished only to warn you that your depredations cause these humans to call on prophecy and oracles, and try all manner of spells to be rid of you. You know what that may mean.'

'Riddles, Nephew? I thought you did not like them.'

He could hardly breathe. The Sphinx's weight pinned him to the wall. Her breath slowly rasped, counting out, he imagined, the last minutes of his life.

He took a breath, managed to speak again. 'What I

mean is no riddle. We have the histories. What once was may be again.'

'Say it.'

'We've worked so hard to make these people rational, to do away with dreaming. Yet still they dream, and now you turn their dreams to darkness.'

'Ah, to darkness. The rational begets insanity. A riddle wrapped in enigma born of paradox. Yet I thought you hated riddles, Nephew, you and all your Kin: say it.'

'If I must. They will call the Dark upon themselves. And when it devours them, what will become of the Kin then?'

'We will be passed over, as we were before. Or we will be eaten also. Either way, the waiting ends. No riddle there, Nephew.'

It came to Teiresias then that she was quite mad; that all she had done had been designed to force the humans into occult practices. There would be no reasoning with her.

'If you come again, Nephew, I will kill you, oath or no. I have Hera's love; I have my place in the Songs. Do you understand me, Nephew?'

'Yes,' he said. He hardly dared breathe, could hardly hear her breath for the thought that he might yet live.

She pushed him aside as suddenly as she had captured him. He crashed against the ground. Pain jolted up his arms and spine, and across his shoulders. He hardly cared. He levered himself to his feet, and stood swaying in the half-dark, knowing he should run, staring at the bones and hair that littered the cave floor, unable to move.

He heard the Sphinx take a step towards him; she still stank of triumph and decay. He moved back, though agony burned in his muscles.

'Don't go yet, Nephew,' the Sphinx said. She smiled at him. Light glinted on her teeth. 'You have not heard my riddle.'

'I do not need to, Aunt,' Teiresias said. 'I see now you have no need of further answers.'

'Nevertheless,' she whispered, 'what is it that alters thus: in the morning it goes on four feet, in the afternoon on two and in the evening on three, and yet is weakest when it has most support?'

'What?' Teiresias said. He stared up into her black eyes, cold as the Dark. He searched in his mind for some answer he could give her. Nothing came. Nothing overheard or learned by chance would answer: nothing in the histories, the genealogies, the Songs. No chance conversation with a human, who might be expected to invent answers to nonsense questions as they invented tales to explain the world to themselves.

'Can't you answer, Nephew?' the Sphinx asked. 'Then you shall die, as any human would!'

'By the oath my forefather made, Aunt, don't do this — '

Teiresias saw her taloned hand lash out. He tried to move, but he was too slow: too slow, and in too much pain. Light flashed on her claws, and then the world exploded into redness and pain. He screamed.

He brought his hands up to his face. Through his agony he felt blood and jellied slime. The darkness was blacker than a moonless, starless night; he felt as if he might fall forwards into it and be lost for ever.

Beyond his screaming, something laughed. There was a sharp shove in his back. He stumbled down the hill, into the cool of the cypress trees.

Behind him, there came the voice of the Sphinx: 'If you come again, have an answer for me, Nephew. For my oath's sake. I'll give you further clues: this creature speaks with one voice, though its tongue is quicksilver, Mercury-ruled, and changing ever; it sleeps often, but its body is iron, ruled by Mars and changing never. What is it?

It had begun so long ago. Sphinx, sleeping without changing in the quiet of her cave, dreamed of that beginning; dreamed in the manner of the Kin, of what *had been*; though she had tried, she had never found the way to dream in the manner of humans, so that memories and desire and fear melded and became strange.

She dreamed of Prometheus, torchfire staining his golden hair crimson as the humans clustered around him in the night, listening. The chirruping of the cicadas counterpointed the shuffling of the crowd, the soft susurrus of their breathing. Sphinx stood among them, watching them and watching Prometheus, for this was in the days when she could take the human shape.

The wind from the ocean mingled salt with the bittersweet scent of ripening oranges and the scent of burning pine, but beneath that she could taste the humans' fear and excitement, heady as wine. The small hairs along her back stood up, fingers tingled, every part of her alive with his nearness.

'Friends,' he called out. His voice was smooth as oil, with just a sharp hint of command beneath it. 'You know that some of us who walk among you can change our shape at will. Our bodies are strong. You know this in your hearts, for you call us gods.'

Prometheus raised up his arms. Even at this distance, he smelled of oil and sweat and honeysuckle. Sphinx trembled with desire. She remembered trembling; in her sleep her claws stretched convulsively and she whimpered deep in her throat, remembering what had come next.

'You must not call us gods,' Prometheus said, and only the cicadas broke the silence in the stadium, as if a thousand people held their breath at one time: the god spoke heresy. 'We are fearful creatures, and we are afraid of the Dark. It will come upon us, so we say, and devour us all, raiding in the night, eating our souls. And it is you we fear, dear friends. For those who are eldest among us say it is the humans that will bring these raiders down on us all.'

He paused for breath. His skin glinted in the torch-light. Silence filled up the sultry darkness.

'So we keep you in ignorance, like cattle or goats. We walk among you lying by a failure of truth, lying by implication. Yet I tell you, when it comes you humans will be our hope. By the bright fire of your minds you will find a way to fight, when all my Kin can do is hide in the shadows.'

His eyes were wild, earth-brown flecked with gold. The scent of him, salt tang beneath honeysuckle, roused Sphinx as he roused the humans: as he always had, no matter what shape he took. She wanted to go to him, draw him off into some quiet place; they would make love in the human way, then sleep the changing sleep together, and when they woke join again in the manner of the Kin – if it were safe. In true shape the scent would be that much stronger ... she felt her mouth go dry with desire. But it was never safe. It was one reason why they had decided to reveal all to the humans, against the wishes of the Kin.

'By the bright fire of your minds and hearts, I call upon you to stand with me against the deluge!' Prometheus cried out. His voice echoed slightly. 'Will you stand with me?'

The humans cried, 'Euoi, euoi,' until the hillside rang with their shouts. Sphinx found herself swept along in a rising tide of brightly coloured himations; the clamour of running feet and harsh, quick breathing filled her ears, as the odour of exultation and poorly hidden fear filled her mouth. They made him a crown of myrtle leaves to wear, and spread laurel branches for him to walk on.

So they went from the hill into the city. Moonlight silvered the pale steps of the Temple. Firelight flickered within. The air reeked of spilled blood and roasting flesh, but over it all was the dull scent of animal fear.

The humans fell silent. Prometheus walked up the steps into the temple.

Zeus was waiting there, with others of the Kin.

Sphinx, in the cave, whimpered as she slept. She should have known, should have known, should have known.

The humans had run screaming in terror: this was part of Zeus's intention. They made the Kin into gods, if they were aware of them at all. That their gods sometimes walked among them, and them all unknowing, had been a matter of rumour and supposition to them.

Zeus in glory was another thing entirely. Already growing ancient, he was taller than a human and broad in proportion. He was dressed in white, and crowned with myrtle. All around him younger cousins of the Kin stood, bearing torches and rods of purifying fig and mallow.

They were young, these children Zeus had chosen, she thought contemptuously: not more than forty, any of them. She could tell, for their scents were simple things, without undertone or resonance.

Sneering, she stood her ground among the rushing humans. The copper taste of their fear overlaid the mingled scents of burning verbena and cedar. They were like stampeding horses, she thought, flesh in flight from what it could not understand.

After a time all became quiet.

Later, in the Caucasus Mountains, Prometheus began to scream. Sphinx heard those cries in her dreams, nightly. The humans said that Zeus had chained him to a rock there. They said that Zeus sent eagles each sunset to tear out his liver; that by morning it had grown back.

Sphinx knew better. It would take longer than that to grow an organ. And she had seen the fury in the First Father's eyes. He would take his revenge bloodily, and in person.

No eagles would fly at his bidding over the Caucasus.

Teiresias stumbled through the trees near the road to Thebes. Exhaustion and pain had almost driven him into unconsciousness. He felt blood crust his face, his hands where they covered his eyes, the massive shallow wound on his chest. The crust was constantly forming, constantly breaking to let fresh blood seep slowly out, sending tiny thrills of pain through him; they were all that kept him conscious.

In all the world there was only pain. Sometimes he paused. The forest was rank with aromatic olive and lemon-scented cypress, and the sweet, sickly smell of juniper. Its silence was oppressive; birds and animals all fell mute before Teiresias. In the distance though, he could hear the slow clopping of donkeys on their way to the agora in Thebes, and the shouts of the farmers who drove them. The scent of the olives and raisins and oily sheep fleeces they carried drifted up to him, all mixed with the sweat of the farmers, the stink of mead and garlic on their breath.

They were human, but they lived in the normal world, a world where there was something other than pain in the eyes and chest, and the rank odour of your own blood and flesh and fear. He envied them.

A branch lashed his hand where it covered his face, caught his torn cheek below the socket of his eye. He screamed with new pain.

He would have wept, but he had no tears to cry. Instead he vented his anger on the air and on himself, screaming aloud and tearing at his clothes, his hair, his damaged face. He had failed; had failed, and his name would be taken from the Song of the Lines: nothing he had done would last beyond his time, not even his children would remember him . . .

He collapsed, at last, into spasmodic, dry sobbing. Afterwards, he found that he had burrowed into the cypress and olive leaves that littered the floor. He chewed some of them into a wet ball to make a compress, then pushed it into his eye sockets. It eased them somewhat; still, he wished he had a bit of willow bark or a few laurel leaves to chew: anything to take away the pain.

He breathed deeply, allowing himself to fall into the first stage of the change sleep. In his vision, he saw himself whole, with eyes to see. It would take a long time, he knew that, and he would be weak when he awoke. Such damage would be hard to repair.

Yet he had to hurry. The Thebans would make spells and sendings, consult oracles and auguries: there would be all kinds of foretellings and dangerous occult practices. Zeus was right. They would bring the Dark down upon them all.

The humans said Prometheus – Prometheus, the old lover of the Sphinx, he remembered – grew a new liver every night.

The humans were fools.

Prometheus was still screaming. It seemed to Sphinx that she could hear his screams, no matter how far away he was, whether she slept or whether she woke.

In her dream she heard Zeus laugh as he carried out the punishment for the hundredth, the thousandth time.

She would not think of that, would not think of the time when Hera had forced her to watch, with Zeus all unaware of their presence. She would not think of his blood blackening the dark stone, nor the begging in his eyes, nor his screams.

Sphinx half awoke, thought drowsily of Hera, for whom she was doing this, and whose love she would surely earn.

She remembered a time before that, when she had watched the First Mother as she bathed. The pool was fed by a little stream that fell over a few rocks and was dashed into shards of crystal; it smelled ice cold, its cleanness accentuated by the scent of the sweet bay trees, with a sound like the shattering of glass. Yet she was most aware of Hera's scent, a scent of sun-heated clay and burned almonds; and her breathing, which was light and rapid. She knows I am here, Sphinx thought, and her desire was almost painful, a fire in her groin.

She dismissed the slave wordlessly, and walked forward.

Hera came out of the water towards her. Her hair, red as flame, lay in heavy coils across skin as pale and smooth as alabaster. Water clung to her in glistening droplets, dripped slowly down her breast, reached her nipple and fell, unregarded, into the pool with a tiny plash. Sphinx wanted to gather it up with her tongue, to lick Hera's cool flesh: to feel the water that had touched the First Mother's body in her mouth. To drink it down and make it part of her.

'Come here, Kassmia,' Hera said.

'Don't call me that.'

'It's what they will call you when they sing your names in the Lines. Or do you not wish them to remember how you tried to destroy Cadmus?'

'That's finished with. Besides, he was only human.'

'Indeed,' said Hera. She walked up on to the bank. Her soft footfalls darkened the pale grass, crushed narcissus and daisies. Dying, they released a bitter-sweet ephemeral odour. Sphinx stared for an instant, then looked away; but the image was burned into her eyes: Hera's nipples scarcely darker than her skin, the shadowy triangle beneath the flat curve of her belly.

How young I was, Sphinx thought, half out of the dream.

Hera touched her on the shoulder. Her fingers were cold from the water, yet they seemed to burn Sphinx's flesh where they touched. She shivered. She smelled her own desire and Hera's mixing together like the headiest wine. Sphinx turned as Hera swept her hair away from her neck, kissed her inaccurately on the delicate upcurve of the shoulder.

'How young you are,' the First Mother said.

'I am older than you.' Sphinx answered her, though desire bade her be silent. 'You should not forget it.'

I never, Sphinx half muttered near wakefulness. *I never dared.*

'Oh, I do not,' Hera said. 'But you must remember how much less age counts than breeding, you who are born of the lesser Lines.' Her hands drifted down, found the soft curve of Sphinx's breast, the hard upthrust of her nipple. The fine linen of the chiton chafed gently against her skin, gave off an odour of the quince and black peppers in which it had been stored. Sphinx stood still as stone, refusing to move, hardly breathing at all. Hera's fingers worked at the clasps that held the robe together at the shoulders.

The top of the chiton fell forward, over Sphinx's girdle. Hera laughed, then bent her head to kiss the slope of Sphinx's breast. Her tongue trailed fire over the bare skin; Sphinx stared straight ahead of her, but all the while her hands wound rhythmically through the wet coils of Hera's hair.

The First Mother fumbled with her girdle. When she was unable to untie the knot, she knelt and bit through the cord. It parted with a soft snicking noise. The chiton fell around Sphinx's feet like a sea of cloth.

Hera pulled her down on to it. 'Gold on blue,' she whispered, and stroked the tiny sun-gilded hairs on Sphinx's arm. Her fingers were as gentle as afternoon rain. 'You really are delightful.'

Hera smiled at her, red lips stretching back from blunt human teeth. Her hand slid on to the harsh curled hair between Sphinx's legs.

'Do not.' Sphinx said, even as her legs parted to the First Mother's questing fingers. She felt her eyes go wide and quizzical.

But oh, we did, we did, Sphinx thought, watching the dream. Her breath caught in her throat at the memory.

In the dream, her hand capped Hera's, moved it away. Hera laughed.

'Why do you want this, now?' Sphinx asked.

'Because you are mine,' Hera answered her. 'And I take what is mine.'

'I am myself. Long have I walked apart from the Families, among humans. This is well known.'

'Indeed. Yet alliances have been made, not always wisely. What has been noticed by one may be noticed by others. You should walk more carefully.'

'Threats, cousin?'

It wasn't like that! Sphinx whimpered to herself. They had made love, there among the wet, scratchy grass, in the dappled sunlight. Hera had been tender and fierce, the scent of her filling up the day, the complex geometry of her body an unfolding delight to Sphinx. Afterwards they had had such a sleepy, strange conversation, full of sorrow for Prometheus bound to his mountain, and promises for the future, if only Zeus did not realize Sphinx had helped Prometheus.

'A warning, *cousin*. Zeus is insane in his anger, and he is right. If the humans knew what we are, they would call disaster down upon us all. Or simply kill us. And if Zeus knew you had helped Prometheus, that is what would happen to you.'

'He would not!'

'He would. As he will kill Prometheus when his anger has run its course. But you should not fear, cousin. He need not find out. Of those who have his attention, only I know. And I will not tell. Not while I am happy with you.'

Sphinx stared at her. In the dream, Hera's eyes were hard as stones, unsoftened by the love Sphinx remembered there. She looked away. 'Yes,' she said.

'So you are mine. And that which I want, I shall have.'

'Yes,' Sphinx said again.

Her eyes flicked open, all at once in the half-dark. Her heart raced. 'No!' she said aloud. 'It wasn't like that!'

They had made love. Hera had told Sphinx she loved her, that Prometheus would be released in time. That he would be welcomed back into the family. But only if Zeus did not find out about Sphinx's involvement. Let him discover that, and he would believe they colluded against him. He would kill them all, rather than allow it. Sphinx had shivered in Hera's arms, until her gentle words and caresses had soothed her. It was all right.

Hera told her. Only Hera knew, and she would never say. She loved Sphinx, and she was sure Sphinx loved her too. Was it not so? Sphinx murmured that it was, it was. And so Hera had promised to protect her, and Sphinx had said she would do anything, anything at all for Hera, who loved her.

Her talons clicked reflexively on the stone. How could you dream of what had never happened, of what could never be? It was almost human, she thought. She had sought this, desired it, but now she saw that it was most terrible.

Change memory, and you changed the past. That was why the Kin had the teaching Songs and the genealogies. That was why they strove to be included in the Lines of the Names.

But the humans: it was as if they remade the world from moment to moment, forcing it to change in their image. Their art reflected things which could not be seen, their music feelings that had never been spoken. They asked questions of the world and bade the world answer. It gave up its secrets to them, and in return they made it new. Something came from nothing, and what *was* shifted at every moment. How else explain the tales they wove around the exploits of the Kin? How could there be any safety in that? Prometheus had been fascinated by them. He had thought the Kin's hope of safety lay in what he called the bright fire of their minds.

Salt stung her eyes. It smelled a little like him. She had never seen him again.

Heat woke Teiresias. His swollen tongue moved spasmodically over his lips. He could hardly move, and his breath came harsh and ragged. And so he lay there in the stink of his own sweat and urine, so much stronger than that of the cedar mulch that cradled him. The darkness was absolute. He tried to open his eyes. The lids would not move. In panic, he touched his face with his hand. His fingers encountered outcrops of cheekbone, chin and nose. No pain, he thought; no pain in chest or arms or face. But still he could not see.

The flesh beneath his eyes had healed over, but roughly, so that it felt like ploughed earth to his questing fingers. He probed his eye sockets and found skin grown flat across them, like the surface of a tambour.

Later, he reassured himself. They will grow back and I shall have sight again, and see the hills and the water and the vast sky. I shall.

He clambered to his feet. He was weak. He realized that he did not know how long he had slept. It would take days, he thought, to do all this. He staggered, and leaned against the twisted bole of an olive to support himself. The body was wrong.

He considered this, and explored his body with shaking hands. Breasts like melons sagged without muscle to support them almost to his waist. There were hardly any hips to speak of. Reluctantly, he slid his hand beneath his ruined chiton. His penis was a mere scrap of flesh, and behind it a vaginal slit opened to his probing fingers.

He took a deep breath, and then another. Panic rose in him, but he forced calmness on himself. Panic had done this to him: panic and pain. He would sleep again, and this time his intentions would be firm set in his mind, and there would be no error in the Change.

She, Teiresias thought through the haze of thirst, I am a she now.

She could not sleep here again. The Sphinx might find her, or some wandering shepherd, or . . .

She forced calmness on herself. There were Kin in the city who would take her in.

The himation lay somewhere at her feet. She bent to find it, and was caught up in the sensation that the world was turning beneath her feet. Her hand caught at the cracked bark of the olive tree in time to save her from falling. After a moment she was able to lower herself to the ground. Her scrabbling fingers found the himation. The cloth was greasy, and bits of leaf and mulch clung to it.

Teiresias draped it over her shoulders, ignoring the smell of old sweat and sweet decay that came off it. She threw one short end over her left shoulder. It did not feel right. The cloth bunched against her neck chafed, and she felt it slap against the backs of her legs as she walked. She tried again, but she could not find the fibula no matter how her fingers searched over the mantle.

In the end she gave up. With her hands stretched out in front of her, fearing at any moment to walk into a tree, she set off south to the city.

Teiresias reached the agora in Thebes by mid-afternoon. Her mouth was full of the dust of the road; sweat stuck her chiton to her back, trickled down her face across eye-wells she dared not touch, and yet still she thirsted. She stumbled on in total darkness. The sphere of her perception had drawn in until she could barely distinguish the thick odour of the humans from that of their animals, nor pick out male from female, foreign metic from slave or citizen.

This, she thought in a moment of lucidity, this is how it is to be human: blind in all my senses. Then the euphoria of dehydration took her again, and there was only the scuff, scuff of her feet on the road, the insistent beat of blood round the body, the rubbing of wool against her legs as she walked.

Somewhere a flute was playing, and people were conversing; but the sounds were far away, and as inconsequential as the humming of bees. The aroma of roasting meat hung in the air. It came from a sacrifice at the Temple: the beast had been fed on barley for days before it had been slaughtered. She could tell from the smell of the flesh. So, she thought, I am better than the purblind humans after all. She laughed to think of it, and again when she realized that the humans were falling silent at her approach, as silent as the beasts in the forest.

Thus she came to the steps of the fountain house. She made her way up them, through the arched colonnade of the stoa, guiding herself by touch and sound.

The stone was cold and damp, a smell as sharp and clean as any mountain lake. It was all she could do to stop herself from falling to her knees and licking it.

She staggered slightly as someone pushed past her. Her flailing hands touched flesh and fine linen. There was a small gasp, and someone's heartbeat grew quicker. She knew that if she did not drink soon, she would faint.

'Water,' she heard herself croak.

A man cursed her coarsely. Someone hushed him. Then it grew quiet, except for the chaotic sounds of many people breathing, the shuffling of sandal-leather on stone, the tantalizing chatter of nearby water.

After a moment, she felt someone take her arm. She was pulled along, and then the human – yes, human by the smell – tried to guide her hand into the cascade. She shook the person off, and plunged first her head, and then her whole body under the water.

Her lips stung at its coldness, and at first she could

not swallow it down. Slowly, her throat accepted it. It burned and bloated in her belly. Her head sung with icy pain. Still she stood in the fountain with the water parting over her head, soaking hair and flesh until her whole body tingled. But then her lips pulled back hugely from her teeth, so that she thought she would split open. The water she had drunk spewed out of her mouth, hot and acidic, and fouled the floor in front of the fountain.

There was a flash of pain, a clatter of stone on stone. She stepped away from the fountain. Her feet echoed slightly on the floor, so that she knew there was a space clear all around her. The odour of fear and anger was so thick she could almost touch it, and she heard the pounding of many hearts, counterpointed by much quick breathing. She caught their fear, felt her own come up to greet it, the scent bitter as hot metal. For all the water she had just drunk, her mouth went dry again. She heard a scuffling sound quite close to her, and was about to speak when another stone caught her hard on her breast. She covered the sore place with her hand.

'Look at the hag,' a voice called out.

Another stone bit into her side, then another and another. 'Whore more like!'

She turned to run despite the darkness, but her out-stretched hand found a pillar of the fountain. She turned again and tried to run, but there were hands everywhere, pushing and pulling her.

'Doesn't make more than half an obol a day, I'll be bound!'

'And them she turns to stone!'

Something jabbed at her side, shoved her hard against the back wall of the fountain house. She turned again.

'Kill the abomination!'

There was sudden silence. Then Teiresias laughed. The sharp sound cut through the heavy air like a sword through flesh. Another stone caught her in the ribs. She gasped at the sudden pain.

'See what punishment the gods have sent us now!'

'Do I appal you so, you brave Thebans? Do I? I, poor, blind Teiresias?' It amused her mightily.

Hands pulled at her, tried to take her down off the steps. She shook them away. Weak as she was, she could still do that to the humans.

'Listen to me,' she screamed into the darkness and the silence. A small part of her heard the edge of panic in her voice, and knew the humans would never notice it. 'Listen to me! You may not kill the Sphinx, for she is the servant of Hera. Yet mighty Zeus has sent me, that I may rid you of her!'

Someone shouted that they should take her to the Temple, so that the gods themselves could decide her lot. The cry was taken up by many others. She allowed them to take her then. The darkness closed in around her, and the human stink of them, and she was led through the streets amid shouting and clapping, and given over into the hands of her enemies: the priestesses of the Oracle in the Temple.

Gravel rattled on stone. It roused Sphinx. She stared across the darkness of the cave. There had been dreams, such dreams since the nephew had gone. A dream such as a human might have, that changed reality and left nothing certain. That dream she remembered, though the others had fled like the tatters of morning mist on water.

She pulled her arm from under her head. It hurt. All her limbs were stiff, and her stomach ached with hunger. Thin bile filled her mouth. She felt as though she had cried for a thousand years, that she would drown in tears. She rubbed her eyes with the heels of her palms. The sound came again.

'Hera be with me now,' she whispered to herself; and then, even more quietly, 'Prometheus.'

The sound came again. A smell of human came from outside, of worked metal and leather, and fear. Always the fear.

She crept silently towards it, taking care not to disturb the bones and animal pelts which littered the floor, nor to trip over the discarded armour and weapons she had collected.

'Come forth,' a voice shouted. 'Haemon, nephew of Jocasta queen to Laius, King of Thebes, challenges you!' There was a pause. Sphinx wondered how long his nerve would hold. When he began again, his voice was higher, straining up towards breaking point. 'For the honour of those fine warriors and athletes, citizens and metics you have foully murdered, I challenge you! Let none say that Haemon of the Royal House of Laius is a coward!'

Nephew, Sphinx thought. Her nephew Teiresias, come again to taunt her. He would learn, as all the Kin would learn, that she was not easy prey.

She heard his breathing now, rapid and light; and there were others with him. Coward, she thought, and spat on the floor.

A slight figure stood below the cave entrance. He was in full armour. Sunlight gilded his helmet and shield, and glinted on the curve of his sword. Behind him, the cypresses cast black shadows against the orange rock. A slave stood near them carrying the nephew's spears, and on the path far below the mountain, another waited with his chariot. That accounted for the human smell, Sphinx decided.

The nephew had slept the sleep of healing and of change. Perhaps he thought to trick her: a new appearance and slaves to mask his smell.

She smiled. He was brave and devious this nephew, as befitted a member of the Kin. Or perhaps he feared Zeus greatly. She would teach him to fear her better.

'You cannot deceive me, Nephew. I have the scent of you now!' It would not do to let him know that she did not, that all she could smell was his slave. It would make no difference in the end: he would die like a human, after all.

'Come forth and face me!' he cried. The point of the sword trembled, then described a tiny circle in the air. Sphinx stepped out of the cave. She imagined the effect she would have on him, bright and shining as she was, vast with age and great with power.

'Answer my riddle,' she demanded, and stepped up close to him, brushing aside the sword. He stared at her. His face was very pale, the eyes large and staring. Insolence, she thought, to come to her in human shape. The stink of them was all over him. 'Answer, *human*,' she said, putting all her contempt into the single word.

His throat worked as he tried to swallow. She stroked it gently, like a lover.

'Why are you doing this?' he asked.

'For love of Hera. But you know this. I do what I must. As you do.' It was a challenge, and she knew he would recognize it as such, no matter that he had come to her in human guise.

'I don't understand,' he said.

He feigns innocence well, Sphinx thought. She smiled at him. He stepped backwards. 'You will play one game too many, Nephew. You know well that Laius has that which belongs to Hera.'

'My aunt's husband makes all lawful sacrifice to the goddess, and all libations are poured at the proper time. All honour to Hera, and to Zeus the father of all!'

'Even so, she shall have more. Laius shall give up his paramour Chrysippus, and then I shall have completed my last duty for the First Mother.'

'No.' There was flat denial in the other's eyes.

'Oh yes. And when Hera sees him, she will realize she never truly loved the boy. She will realize he is but human, and will love me for ever.'

'It cannot be. I do not understand what you are saying, but you should tell her ...' his voice tailed off. Sphinx caught a brief tang of fear from him. The point of the sword dipped. He straightened it carefully, and began again. '... Tell her that Chrysippus is dead.'

'You lie, Nephew. You come to me shaped as a human, and you lie. You may not fight me, nor can you answer my riddle. How could you? You are no human, and do not have their bright fire burning in your brain to answer riddles! And now you think you will drive me out with lies!'

Sphinx heard her voice rising, the words falling out of her mouth faster and faster. A shower of spittle flew through the air, spun in the sharp light and disappeared. She took a deep breath, and forced her voice lower. 'They will not do, these lies and deceptions. Your name will be forgotten. I shall see to it, when I am Hera's chosen one – '

The other began to back down the hill. 'I do not wish to fight,' he said. His voice was as high as a boy's. 'You are the chosen of the goddess, as you have said. She has forbidden us to fight you. Yet shall I – '

'No,' Sphinx screamed. 'You will answer my riddle. I thought of it myself! Myself, as a human might!'

Even as she said it, a memory flashed through her mind: firelight danced across Prometheus's face, warmed her hands: they had been travelling. An old man had come to share the fire, bringing food and wine with him. They had swapped tale for tale, song for song; but in the end he had bested them with his riddles. They had parted in the morning, friends; but it was from that time that Prometheus had become obsessed with the mystery of human creations, with their riddles, tales and art. And Sphinx, Sphinx had become obsessed with Prometheus.

'Listen,' Sphinx said, 'what is it speaks with one voice, but in the morning goes on four feet, in the afternoon on two and in the evening on three, and yet is weakest when it has most support?'

The boy – her nephew, she told herself; ignore his smell, it had to be the nephew; hadn't he said as much, in his devious way – was almost in the shadow of the trees. She leapt at him. The slave screamed, and she heard him drop the spears. Her fingers tangled in the nephew's armour. He fought back weakly.

'Well, Nephew?'

'I don't know, I don't know, I don't know,' he said. His face was wet with tears. The sudden smell of urine and excrement mingled with the coppery odour of his fear. His pulse skittered arhythmically. ' – but he's dead and I don't know what you want me to say, I don't – '

Sphinx bit down on his neck, silencing him. Warm blood fountained over her face. It tasted salt and human and good.

Teiresias felt herself begin to sway in time to the clapping and stamping of the priestesses, and the clicking of their finger-cymbals. Their breath was rapid and light, and she knew they would soon enter the prophetic frenzy. The heat was stifling. The incense burning in the fire-bowl made Teiresias feel light-headed, as if she were floating somewhere in the cool, dark space she had made her own. If she could stay there, she would be safe, would be able to remain herself through whatever indignities the humans would heap on her. Her hands began to clap in time to the cymbals, as if they were not under the control of her mind.

Soon, she thought, soon it would be over. They had brought her here, to the temple of Apollo, and they had fed her honey and barley, and given her wine and the sacred water to drink. They would sacrifice her. She knew their ways. They were human and they were mad, and in their madness they worshipped things which were not.

The incense hissed and spat.

They will call down the Dark upon us all, she thought. They would have to be dealt with. She would have to deal with them. Later.

A scream cut across the chant. We will all be sacrificed in this mad rite, Teiresias thought, I no less than they. The Dark will eat their minds, and time will eat my name, and I will be forgotten at best in the Songs of the Lines.

There was silence for a moment, and then the voice began to howl and moan. The smell of excrement filled the chamber.

The priestess is in ecstasy, Teiresias thought. The Kin told tales of it. The smell of incense was suddenly undercut by the sweet smell of sickness and the musky odour of excitement.

She heard the rapid drumming of hands and feet on the floor; drumming without rhythm. Noises came out of the dark at Teiresias; little animal noises made deep in the throat, and great howls she had not thought a human throat could shape.

Cloth slapped against flesh. Footsteps slowly crossed the room.

'Speak, Sibyl!' The priestess cried. 'Let us hear the words of the god!'

The animal noises slowly stopped. They began again, and slowly took on the shape of words: 'A black bird flies up out of the hand of the hero. "Life or Death" he asks the Sphinx. The Sphinx which is not the Sphinx watches him, watches it, and does not answer. Her eyes are the eyes of the god. What does she see? No man knows. Her heart is wild with rage. Blood falls from her mouth and waters the roots of the black cypress trees. They wither.' The Sibyl stopped speaking. Teiresias heard her vomit. The room filled up with the smell of decaying fruit.

The priestess spoke: 'Hear while I interpret the words of the – '

' – Weep Thebes, for those trees are you,' the Sibyl interrupted. 'The hero holds in his hand a bird. "Choose," he says to the Sphinx, "life or death?" But she says to him that the fate of what he holds lies in his own hands. He kills the bird, Thebes, as you have killed your future, and all the ground is covered with blood and stinking bones.'

'Enough,' the priestess said at last. 'The gods do not demand our tears. Listen to the meaning of the Sibyl's words: the fate of Thebes is in our hands, as the hero's life is in his hands. Life or death, it is for us to choose. The gods demand sacrifice, as they ever have. Yet they are not cruel, despite our foolishness. They do not demand an innocent, like the bird, but a blood sacrifice of purification. And they have sent to us one fit for their purpose. Thus may the evil be expelled from our city.'

The priestess had made the oracle mean what she needed it to mean for her own purposes, Teiresias realized. If the Sibyl had something different, still the priestess would have demanded a purification. None of the Kin were capable of doing as much. The humans lived in a quicksilver world, one which they tried constantly to shape to their own desires. It was a terrible thing to contemplate, and a fascinating one, she thought. It would drive you mad if you let it: as it had driven the Sphinx mad, trying to be what she could not be.

It was not the way of the Kin, Teiresias thought. They preferred simple problems, simple solutions. Such might yet save her life.

'I speak,' Teiresias said. 'I, who have been sent by Zeus to rid you of the Sphinx. Listen to me: in this city, there is a boy called Chrysippus. He is the beloved of Laius your king. Yet before that, he was the beloved of Hera, consort of Zeus. He has been most unwise, or Laius has. Hera is angry because he has spurned her. Therefore she has sent the Sphinx to do you harm. Return him to Hera, and all shall be well.'

A wild cry went up all around her.

The priestess took Teiresias's face in her hands. She stroked the skin that covered her eyes with calloused fingers. Her breath stank of garlic and the laurel leaves they chewed to poison them into prophecy.

'You are no true seer,' she said. 'Chrysippus is dead. He went up to the mountain soon after the monster first appeared. He gave himself to her, and she killed him for it. He was no answer to her riddle, though he left another behind him.'

'Then you will have to find another answer: though none may please Hera, you may satisfy the Sphinx.'

The priestess turned away. 'Let there be blood sacrifices and purification. Let the gods be appeased!' she cried out.

They will kill me, then, Teiresias thought. It was certain. The humans were not rational, but they were determined. Their minds are like their bodies, she thought. They never change.

She seemed detached from her body, watching what they did with silent amusement. Then she thought she heard the Sphinx speak: *Its tongue is quicksilver, Mercury-ruled, and changing ever; it sleeps often, but its body is iron, ruled by Mars and changing never. What is it?* A human! Teiresias thought it over again and again, as they draped a chiton of fine black wool over her and pleated it in the male fashion. They wound strings of black figs around her neck and in her hair. She laughed when they told her. Black figs! The sign of the male sacrifice: they wanted to pretend she was Chrysippus, was Laius.

They led her out of the *cella* and into the *temenos* of the Temple. Teiresias smelled the blood and burned flesh that clung to the great open-air altar. She thought of knives, stained red by the blood and the firelight.

The sound of flutes pierced the air, and the jangle of finger-cymbals.

The priestess cried out. 'See the *pharmakos*! Oh great god Apollo, witness our sacrifice. Witness how we send our evils out of the city. Let Thebes be purified. See the *pharmakos*!'

They pushed her out of the Temple grounds then, and into the agora. Something swished in the air above her, then bit into her back. She heard her own cry even above the sound of the flutes. There came another blow, and another.

The priestess called out, 'See how we beat the hag with fig and mallow switches. Listen to the music of the flutes. See how we purify the city. Witness, all you citizens. Witness!'

Citizens and metics and priestesses crowded around her. Their screams and shouts and rapid breathing counterpointed their punches, and the musk of sex came off them like sweat. They harried her through the city streets. The only thing that mattered was to listen for the sharp swish of the priestesses' canes, and to brace herself for their bite. She stumbled along, forever falling forward into darkness that offered no sanctuary. By the time they left the city walls, she could hardly walk: every step brought on new agony as the cuts on her back opened and stretched. When she finally understood that they had stopped, she fell to the ground and would not, could not, stand.

They came at last to the foot of Mount Phikion. The two priestesses who were dragging her along dropped her. The flutes fell silent. While the priestesses debated, the heavy sunlight slowly dried the blood on her back.

She lay in the olive- and lemon-scented darkness until she heard footsteps approach, and the soft huss of breathing. She looked up, hoped she was staring at the human's face; and that *that* scared her witless.

'Stand, *pharmakos*,' one of them said at last. Teiresias tried to pull her arms underneath her, to haul herself to her feet. Too slow. The priestess kicked her in the ribs. She got to her knees. The chiton tore away from her back, tearing off the new scabs. She gasped.

'We have considered long, *pharmakos*. In the way of things, we should kill you. We should burn your body, without making libations of your blood, and we should scatter the ashes to the wind.'

'I hope,' Teiresias tried to say, though her mouth was swollen and bloody, 'I hope you have a sharp knife; and that your city is ready for more devastation, for this will not please Zeus.'

'Nevertheless, a sacrifice must be made.'

Yes, thought Teiresias. More pain, more suffering.

How like a human. She could hardly think. 'What will you do when Zeus is angry with you? He did send me, you know. What will it be like, to have the hatred of two gods in your city?'

The priestess smelled old and desperate. She grabbed Teiresias by the shoulders and pulled her to her feet. The pain was almost enough to make her pass out. 'Nevertheless, we shall have sacrifice. But not as I have said. The monster wants blood. Let her drink yours, and all our evils with it.'

Of course, thought Teiresias. She could smell her own fear, but still it was a better chance than a knife of metal. If they knew that they would think of some other death for her, she was sure.

They dragged her to the mountain. Her back burned as if a torch had been played lightly over it. There was nothing in the world but pain and fear, and the Sphinx waiting for her. She begged the priestesses for unguents, and they laughed at her, and told her to stop wasting time.

Since they expected it of her, she tried to fight them as they took her toward the cave, but feebly.

A little over halfway up the mountain, she stopped. They pushed her forward, but she said, 'Let me go alone. I promise I will go. Am I not consecrated to this? Have you not, with your own hands, dressed me and fed me and beaten me for this moment? Only let me go alone, for if I disgrace myself I would not want you to see my dishonour.'

They agreed. She tried not to show her relief by any sign gross enough for a human to read. She waited until she heard them make their way back down to the path; and then a long moment more, savouring the absence of heartbeats and breathing, the lack of human stink. Then she groped her way forward, feeling her way through the maze of cypress trees. She fought fear and pain every step of the way until she smelled the cave ahead of her, and it was too late to do anything but stumble forward.

The Sphinx was there. She smelled old and mad, and not at all afraid.

'See I return, Aunt,' Teiresias said. Her voice was too high, too full of pain and fright.

'And changed, I see. Yet without your eyes. Would you not see your doom coming upon you?'

'No doom, Aunt. I have the answer to your riddle.'

'What might that be, child?'

'Humans; they walk as you have said, and their bodies never change: though you are wrong; their minds change less than you might think.'

The Sphinx bellowed with amusement. Teiresias heard her hand smash up and down on the rock as she laughed, a thin wheezing like the hissing of water thrown on a fire.

'And do you think,' she said when she stopped, 'do you think you are the first to solve this? You, rather than all the bright-fire humans?'

'No,' Teiresias said, and thought: I thought I was safe. Safe! A warm stream of urine trickled down her leg; the smell of her fear was stronger than she had ever known it.

'Who told you the answer, Niece? Which fool human did you beg?'

'None. I found the answer for myself.'

The Sphinx screamed. The sound echoed and re-echoed, like thunder in the mountains. Teiresias heard her move, tried to get out of the way. In the darkness she moved in the wrong direction. The whole of the Sphinx's weight landed on Teiresias, who fell backwards. She screamed as her damaged back crashed against the ground.

'For this, I will kill you, Niece.' Her hands grasped Teiresias's throat. Teiresias fought for breath. The Sphinx squeezed. There was no breath in her lungs, just growing pressure and no breath at all: she clawed at the Sphinx's hands.

At last she managed to say one word: 'Songs.'

The pressure eased. Teiresias took one deep, gulping breath. Then the Sphinx lifted up Teiresias's head, and banged it against the ground. 'Speak,' she said.

Teiresias coughed. A thin line of mucus ran out of her mouth. She wiped at it, then raised herself up on her elbows. With difficulty she managed to sit up. She knew the Sphinx would smell her fear, hear the banging of her heart and the too-quick hammering of her pulse. There could be no pretence.

The Sphinx said again, 'Speak.'

'If you kill me,' Teiresias said, staring into her private darkness. It was hard to remember what she was saying. 'If you do, who will tell your tale to the family?'

Wrong, she thought. Not mention family. She tried again. 'Who will tell Hera what you have done for her?'

'You are cunning, Niece. I thought that other was you, you know. He said he was Jocasta's nephew, but I thought he was you. I am old and easily confused, I know this. But I do love her. Hera. She used me at first. I hated her, for she held Prometheus's fate over me. But when she had had enough of me, I found I had not had enough of her. I need to be of service to her, for it's the only way I know to love her. If I let you go, will you swear to tell her all this tale, even to your own degradation?'

'And let it be so,' Teiresias said in the formal manner; she wanted to give the Sphinx no reason to doubt her.

'And you will honour to the letter the oath your mother made?'

'And let it be so,' Teiresias said again, thinking: and let it be so that I have failed, that the Songs of the Lines will speak of me thus, that Zeus will show me his anger. Only let me go.

'And let it be so, then,' the Sphinx replied. 'You may go, Niece.'

Teiresias forced herself to stand. The pain in her body was very great; that in her soul no less so. She tried to remember how the land lay above the little shelf of bare rock outside the cave, but she could not concentrate. Then just as she started to move away, the Sphinx said. 'Wait, Niece. I hunger. What shall I do?' She sounded amused, and vengeful. Kin were Kin after all; and humans were not.

'I believe, Aunt, that there are some humans on the road below,' Teiresias said. 'Though I am not certain. Perhaps you should look?'

As the Sphinx went down the hill, Teiresias crawled away into the trees. The shadows were cool, like slipping into a cold pool on a hot afternoon. She made her way slowly, savouring the silence and the earth and lemon smells of pine and cedar and olive. She found a place that seemed safe, deep in the old heart of the forest.

She was numb with pain and failure. Her oath to Zeus was broken, and also the promise she had made to herself. Worse, she was oath-bound to tell the tale of both in front of the Kin's witnesses. Her name would not be lost or even reviled. It would simply be a thing to amuse the Kin in days to come.

Yet she lived. There could be reparation. Trying to hold that thought in her mind, she lay down. As she slipped into the healing sleep, the cries of dying humans came to her on the wind. She smiled and slept.

*

Thebes was a memory Teiresias was glad to leave behind her. She stood on the hillside overlooking the narrow defile that led from Daulis to Delphi and contemplated her best route. To cross it would be difficult, at least in human form; but it would still be quicker than going round by way of Delphi. Her sight had almost returned, though when she felt her face there was still a thin film of skin covering her eyes, so that she saw everything through a red veil. Her wounds had healed easily enough. She had not dared try to turn again from female to male; it was a difficult change and she wanted to be safe in a Kin house before she attempted it.

She would go to Zeus, she had decided, and tell him that Hera had set the Sphinx on Thebes. His anger would be terrible; it might even break that branch of the family. But rotten wood deserves to be broken. Besides, she had seen the rituals of the Thebans. She had smelled the power of them and she feared them. They had to be stopped before the Dark came down upon them all. Personal happiness was not too great a price to pay.

She heard the clatter of a chariot approaching from Daulis. The way was narrow, and there were already two travellers on the road. She would not be able to get by; besides, as a woman travelling alone she was at great risk. It was not respectable for her to do so, which meant she was prey for any man. Instead, she settled herself to wait, hidden in a small stand of olives.

She could hear them clearly, despite the distance, and see them less well. The one coming towards her from Delphi was on foot. The other was a passenger in a chariot, with a slave for his charioteer. There would be no room for them to pass. It would be tolerable sport, if they had no better sense than most humans.

'Stand aside,' the man in the chariot cried. He was finely dressed, his horses well caparisoned and better bred. Teiresias smiled. She could hear the swift pace of their hearts beating, smell their bodies preparing to fight. Human arrogance would make folly, as it usually did, she was sure. As she expected, the other man did not move.

'I move for none but my betters,' he said, 'And I acknowledge no betters but the gods and my own dear parents. Now have done and let me pass.'

'Certainly I shall not,' the other replied.

Teiresias stood up to see better. The charioteer drove the horses forward. At the last moment the other man stood aside. The chariot moved between him and Teiresias. He screamed in agony. When the chariot moved on, Teiresias saw that his foot had been crushed. It was a bad wound, and worse for a human, who could not heal himself, she thought.

To her surprise, the human stumbled after the chariot. It had not yet picked up speed. He hurled his spear at the charioteer and without waiting to see the result, hauled the other man out of the chariot. They fought for a few moments, but the finely dressed man was clearly unused to fighting, and he had become tangled in the reins when his charioteer collapsed beside him.

Teiresias watched, bemused, as the man with the damaged foot tied him to his horses' harness. Then he plied the whip until the horses leapt forward.

The man from Daulis began to scream. It seemed to Teiresias that she could see his flesh shred and his blood speckle the stone, hear the bones break on the rocks. It brought back memories too painful to bear, and yet she could not look away.

The other man, the supplicant from Delphi, sat and tended his foot. Then he got up and limped towards

Thebes. Teiresias thought that he was brave. Brave and foolish: such humans might have been made to be used. She stood up and retraced her steps, and intercepted him where the path opened out at Daulis.

'Hail Broken Foot,' she called to him from the shelter of a stand of wild orange trees.

'Who calls me thus, hag?' he said when he reached her. 'I am Oedipus, son of Polybus King of Corinth, and of Merope his queen. Stand aside and let me pass.'

The harsh noon sun burnished the fittings of his armour, and made the sweat gleam on his shoulders and face. He did not smell at all afraid, or even put to much exertion by his fight. Close to, she could see the old scars on his feet, smell the almond undertone to his scent. It reminded her of the night she had taken him from the hills outside Thebes. Ah, thought Teiresias: Oedipus, you were made for me to use.

'Indeed I shall, Oedipus, for I know you honour no mortal above your parents.'

'Indeed I do not, and only the gods above them. How do you know this of me? Speak!'

'I am blind, but I know what I know.' It was the kind of vagueness the humans admired. Teiresias continued: 'And also that the oracles have said you will kill your father and marry your mother.'

It was a calculated risk. Almost, Teiresias thought she might have to fight him. He stood still as a statue in the road, while his scent told her of the battle that raged in him.

At last, when she thought she had ruined all her chances with him, he turned and spat on her feet.

'I do not fight women,' he said. 'Not even hags. Begone from me before I change my mind!'

Teiresias did not move. Oedipus pushed past her. 'I am a better seer than the Python of Delphi,' she said. 'I know of a way you can honour your parents and go to Thebes a saviour. Will you listen to me, who meant you no harm?'

'That is no fit question. What man does not aspire to be a hero?'

'So. I have seen your bravery, Oedipus, and I know your will is strong. I tell you, on Mount Phikion near Thebes there is a monster called the Sphinx. She has been sent by Hera to terrorize the Thebans, for they are weak and foolish. Kill her, and you will be a hero in Thebes, and they will speak your name for ever!' How strange, Teiresias thought, to offer as an inducement to the human that which all the Kin desire.

Oedipus looked long at her. She refused to look away.

'Show me where this Sphinx is, and I shall kill her and cut her body into seven pieces, and take her head into Thebes in triumph.'

'Indeed you will not, for no man may kill the Sphinx. Yet I will tell you what all there know. She will ask you a riddle. If you answer her badly, she will throttle you and eat your body. But if you give the right answer, she will destroy herself.'

'This is no certain battle then. Why should I not simply kill her with my sword?'

'Hera has decreed that you may not,' Teiresias said. It was true enough, she thought. Alone of all of them, Hera and her branch of the Kin sought direct dominion over the humans.

She stared at the ground, and watched Oedipus out of the corner of her eye. He was a big man and swarthy with it, but he would be no match for even the youngest of the Kin. He frowned slightly, and seemed about to speak. 'The Sphinx is her chosen servant, after all,' Teiresias continued quickly. 'Besides, she is a mighty monster and I doubt you could kill her if you wanted to. Which you should not, for then the Thebans will hate you as one who has subjected them to Hera's greater wrath. But listen: I can tell you the answer to her riddle.'

'Speak or be silent, hag,' Oedipus said. 'But be quick about it.'

'This is the riddle: what speaks with one voice, but has four legs in the morning, two in the afternoon, and three in the evening, yet is weakest when it has most support?'

Oedipus frowned. He paced a little. Then he stood in front of Teiresias, and thumped the butt of his spear on the ground. 'I don't know. Tell me!'

'Man,' said Teiresias. She watched Oedipus. He frowned, and looked up the hill. Then he turned back to her, his eyes narrowed slyly.

'Good,' he said. 'It's very clever. You may go.'

Teiresias did not ask him to explain the riddle. She doubted he understood it any more than she did. He limped slowly up the hill. His feet sent little clouds of orange dust up from the path. She let him get some way distant. Then she called out, 'Oedipus! We are not yet done.'

He turned and stared at her. She held him with her eyes. After a moment he made his way slowly back.

'Do you not wish to know how I am certain I am right, Oedipus?'

'Oh very well then. Tell me.'

'I have tried this answer, and she has told me I am right. Yet she did not kill herself.' Everything about him, the way he stood, his odour and his expression told Teiresias that he was furious. Spear raised, he strode towards her. She held up her hand. To her surprise – and she suspected, his own – he stopped. 'And so I have listened to the Oracle,' she said, 'and I have thought of another way. Do you have the liver of a hero? Will you try it?'

'Tell me,' he said, grasping at her arm; and so she did.

Teiresias watched as Oedipus prepared to challenge the Sphinx. The cave loomed above them, a dark blot on the pale stone. They were downwind of it. She had taken special care to make sure it was so.

The human's back was straight, despite his lame foot. His voice was strong. Sweat made the muscles of his shoulders gleam in the pale sunlight. Yes, thought Teiresias, she needed no oracle to see how it would be between them when she came back to him in some more suitable form. His fingers clutched tight around the wren she had caught and given to him. He smelled of oil and the dust of the road; there was no scent of fear on him.

'Be careful with that,' she said more sharply than she had intended. 'It is of no use to us dead.'

The bird fluttered uselessly. Oedipus stroked its head with the tip of one finger. It was an oddly gentle gesture to come from so violent a man, Teiresias thought, and wondered how it would feel to be stroked thus by him.

'If I die, you will tell my mother and father that I perished with their names on my lips and honour to them in my heart?'

'I shall,' Teiresias said, and spoke the words of the ritual in her thoughts: *and let it be so*, for the human had given her back her honour and her hope of a place in the Song of the Lines.

He smiled at her with blunt white human teeth. Then he turned and hobbled up to the cave entrance, making much of his limp and using his spear as a staff. She heard him make the challenge, saw the Sphinx come out. For one moment, she thought he would run.

She could understand that. The elder was huge, a blackness that could blot out the daylight, blot out hope.

'I, Oedipus of Corinth challenge you, Sphinx. I will answer your riddle, if you dare to tell it to me,' he said.

The Sphinx stood for a moment, as if testing the air. Even at this distance, Teiresias could smell her, rank and ancient, complex as the Song of the Lines itself. She had to fight the impulse to run. The Sphinx screamed her challenge.

Oedipus's answer echoed back from the sheer face of the mountain: 'Man. Man: when a baby he crawls, when an adult he walks, when old he hobbles with a stick.'

He had teased out the riddle in the days it took them to walk back from Daulis.

As she expected, the Sphinx threw herself on Oedipus in a rage. He was ready for her though, and stepped nimbly aside. He jabbed at her eyes with the spear, forcing her to keep her distance. In his other hand, he held the wren; Teiresias heard its doomed twittering clearly.

The scent of almonds and musk mingled with that of the Sphinx. How is it, Teiresias wondered, that he fears her so much less than I do? Perhaps the humans with their blunted senses are sometimes better fitted for their tasks.

'I am the chosen of Hera,' the Sphinx said. Her voice was low, little more than a hiss. 'If you fear the gods, you may not kill me.'

He will kill his god, Teiresias thought. She found that her heart was beating fast in her chest: blood rushed in her ears. He will kill his gods because I have told him to.

'I honour the gods above all mortals, even including my parents. Yet I say that I challenge you,' Oedipus said. The smell of human fear and Kin came to Teiresias. 'Like for like. You owe me an answer, monster. Here, then, is my riddle: is what I hold in my hand alive or dead?'

There was silence. Teiresias, Oedipus, the Sphinx: all were still. She cannot answer, Teiresias thought. She cannot. The moment stretched out. I could run, Teiresias thought then. I could.

'You are a fool,' said the Sphinx at last. 'This is no true riddle. How may I know the answer?'

The fate of what he holds lies in his own hands. Teiresias heard the words in her mind as clearly as she had when the priestess spoke them. She began to tremble as she plunged into the memory of what had happened to her after that.

She stared straight ahead of her, hardly focusing on the Sphinx or on Oedipus. The Sphinx would tear him to pieces, then come after her. She would eat them, flesh and bone, as time would eat their names. All memory of them would be lost to time.

'I cannot,' the Sphinx cried out. She dropped to her knees and covered her head with her arms. 'Sweet Prometheus, I cannot see the answer.'

Your fate lies in your own hands. Yes, she thought. The humans were fools, but that did not mean they could not sometimes speak the truth.

Oedipus stood watching the Sphinx uncertainly. He began to make a stabbing motion at her with his spear. The Sphinx looked up at him. He aborted the motion. 'Will you pledge to leave this place for ever?' he asked. 'Will you go, without harming anyone who lives here, or any of their possessions? Pledge now, and I will let you live.'

Kill her, Teiresias thought. Kill her now.

'I will not,' the Sphinx snarled. She leapt towards

Oedipus. Her legs drove her forward, past his spear. 'I will crush you, human. You are nothing, and your name will be nothing. Your parents will forget they ever bore you.'

She slashed at him, tearing through his chiton, through flesh, almost to the bone. He screamed. The bird fell dead and forgotten from his hands, a small bunch of dark feathers. He and the Sphinx circled each other, warily, assessing.

Fool human, Teiresias thought. She meant to run, but she could not force her eyes away. Thus Chrysippus had died, thus Haemon, and how many others, their names lost in their deaths. Bright fires extinguished by the night. *Your fate is in your hands.* Mine also, she thought; a chill slipped down her back. This is how it is for humans, she thought, as she realized how she had changed the memory. No wonder the Sphinx had been fascinated by it.

She stepped out of the trees.

'Stop,' she called. Neither did so. 'You will change nothing, Aunt,' she said. The Sphinx halted, and turned to look at her; Oedipus likewise.

'You may not oppose me,' the Sphinx said. 'Remember your bond.'

'I do not intend to,' Teiresias said. 'I only mean to say this: you cannot learn to change the world by killing him. None of us can. Not you, not Hera, not Prometheus. We can only watch them and wonder, and avert their worst calamities.'

'I can,' Sphinx cried. 'I can. Prometheus did. He did. You are young. You did not know him.'

'I do not need to. I know what we are, and we are not human.'

'I will be, though,' the Sphinx replied. As Teiresias watched, she began to try to force a change upon her body. It was much too fast and she was much too old. Still, the muscles loosened, the bones shifted in their sockets.

Oedipus moaned in fear. 'Avert your eyes, Mortal,' Teiresias said, trying to sound as she thought a human would expect a god to. 'This is death for you to see.

He stood gazing at the Sphinx, eyes bulging, mouth lolling open. Teiresias pushed him roughly to the ground.

The Sphinx writhed and screamed. Her body flopped uselessly this way and that. Once, she was still for a moment, and stared at Teiresias out of eyes that retained a trace of sanity. Then her mad fit continued.

Like a priestess in ecstasy, Teiresias thought. When at last the Sphinx fell to the ground and was still, she stood over her. So it ends, she thought, and went to help Oedipus to his feet. But as she moved away the Sphinx touched her on the ankle.

'Niece,' she whispered. 'Kill me, Niece.'

'I may not, Aunt,' Teiresias replied.

'All bonds are broken, Niece. All debts repaid.' She shut her eyes. Tears leaked out of her closed lids. 'I still smell him, sometimes. Prometheus, on the mountain. He smelled of honeysuckle and salt, and when I cry I smell him.'

'Don't, Aunt,' Teiresias said. It seemed to her that her heart would break. They would be so much saner without the fire of the humans to taunt them. 'You should be happy with what you are, not strive to be what you cannot.'

'Kill me, Niece. It's all there is left.'

Yes, Teiresias thought, as she picked up Oedipus's spear. And again, as she plunged it into the heart of the Sphinx, yes.

As they went back down the mountain, Oedipus said

to Teiresias, 'I thought you called the Sphinx "Aunt". I thought you called me "Mortal".'

'You think too much,' Teiresias said. 'Or perhaps you dreamed it.'

He nodded, and stroked her face with the side of one heavy thumb. 'Shall I see you again?' he asked.

'Perhaps,' she replied. 'Your fate is in your own hands.' It was suitably vague, suitably human.

Later, in Thebes, when she saw that he had married Jocasta, and had realized that the man he had killed on the road was his true father Laius, she thought of that moment. And when she went to him to tell him that, she said again: *Your fate is in your own hands.*

But he did not seem to listen.

A CHANGE OF SEASON

Storm Constantine

———————

He only ever saw the seasons change from the inside of
trains. Now, the summer was fading into that frowzy,
tired sort of interim period – the Earth masquerading
as an overdressed and sadly declining middle-aged
woman – before a brief spurt of harsh colour led the
unforgiving winter in by the nose. The land rushed by
beyond the dust-veiled window, and he rested his head
against the glass. The urge to travel, to devour the
miles, was fading inside him, as the colour faded from
the land. Soon, he knew, it would diminish beyond
recognition and he could settle down for a while. But
first, a final roaming into unfamiliar territory; a time to
step down from the train, vacate the arteries of the
body, investigate the organs themselves.

The station was small, the air cold and ripe against his
skin. It seemed the summer had left the north already.
He was the only person to get off the train in that place,
and was given a sour up-and-down glance as he sur-
rendered his ticket, by a gaunt individual with a look of
inbreeding about him, skulking in the inspector's booth
beside the station gateway. The traveller did not bother
to smile or speak. As he sauntered out into the empty
street beyond, adjusting his backpack for comfort,
a familiar sense of unreality stole across his senses.
These are cardboard buildings, cardboard props for a

second-rate drama. He walked towards the sun where it was high in the sky, a solitary figure in an uncluttered scene. He felt as if this was the ending of something, not the beginning. He would walk away out of existence. Yet his boots made a solid satisfactory sound against the road and his flesh felt real and comfortable about his bones. He was a good performer.

It was not really a town, more a village, and a forgotten one at that. The sense of history was faint, although he was aware that people had lived in this place for many centuries. It had never witnessed any events of importance, he was sure, being no more than a receptacle for a few mundane souls who moved from womb to grave with less purpose than animals or perhaps, he thought charitably, the *same* purpose as animals. The place looked empty, but he knew that, had he walked in the other direction, he would have come across the heart of it: the lone, under-stocked supermarket, the row of pubs, a small cinema showing films considerably out of date. This conviction was not the product of some psychometric skill, but merely a familiarity with towns of this type. You had to look hard for the romance in this country. Abroad, little towns seemed to possess a bustling other-life, like insects below the grass; there were often mysteries to uncover, mysteries that could be cherished like gems unexpectedly discovered in a rock that had seemed uniformly grey. Here, the social structure demanded a different kind of behaviour – upright, polite, mannered – but that usually meant the mysteries, when they were coaxed from hiding, were all the more delightful and perverse.

He wanted to walk out on the moors – there was little to interest him in the town – and sniff the air for exciting perfumes. There might be a solitary stone manor squatting in the furze, where deranged family members feuded with sanity. There might be a cottage where a lovesick desertee mulled over the painful intricacies of the past. There might be a farm, with buxom daughters and leery sons, where a traveller might weave a little mischief for a while. The moors seemed the proper setting for such scenarios. If he walked, he was sure to find something to pass the time. The richness and variety of the human race enchanted him; he was not repelled by weaknesses or failings and was tolerant of most behaviours, even the least endearing. In fact, difficult people interested him far more than those whose conversations and ideas inspired the spirit, or whose physical beauty constricted breath in the throat. He sought out the unusual, observing behaviour with cool yet committed interest.

He had been travelling for many years; he had lost count of the exact figure. He had visited most countries where it was easy to gain access and several where it wasn't. He wore a wide-brimmed hat that shadowed his eyes, shutting out the history of the world, if not his own history, to the casual observer. Sometimes he would play the role of the enigmatic stranger, dark and impenetrable; at other times he would be the world's fool, the travelling jester, and at these times he might play an instrument or tell stories. Some countries reacted more favourably to this persona than others. In England he observed the code of reticence and became the withdrawn one, the stranger on a train. Few people sat next to him on his travels, but those that did he generally wanted to communicate with. Now, at least for a while, he wanted to feel the bones of the planet beneath his feet. He would walk the moors and see what the future exposed to him, or exposed him to. He was never frightened.

It was moist country, rich with the fecund smells of earth. Hills swelled towards the horizon, punctuated by the moving pale dots that were sheep. The sky was a high, bleached blue and once out of the town, a waspish wind scoured the land. The traveller walked in an appreciative daze. He had a feeling in the sinews of his flesh that something intriguing would soon be offered to his senses. He saw some people with dogs striding through the heather; he heard the pixie call of excited children. The polished hides of parked cars burned in the distance, winking glares where they caught the sun. These things did not call to him. He was aware of the timeless ambience of this land. Perhaps the things he saw and heard were simply ghosts, or echoes, of high summer that would fade into the approaching cold.

He found a cluster of houses nestling in the cupped hands of a valley. The road that led to it was hewn into the land itself, its high banks thick with seeding grasses. There was a deep, loamy smell as if some elemental creature was breathing hard beneath the soil. He came to a crossroads where a black and white sign pointed towards the houses and said, 'Little Moor'. Little more than what? wondered the traveller, smiling to himself. The other roads, it would seem, led to nowhere.

The houses of Little Moor surrouned a small post office and general shop, as if they had been drawn against their will to this lone node of communication with the world. Near by, a white building protected the rise of a hill, and there was a sign proclaiming it a boarding-house and inn. Shiny cars were parked outside, beneath an ancient monkey-puzzle tree. Whenever possible, the traveller avoided the comforts of official hostelries, preferring to inveigle his way into private homes where there was more to enjoy. He liked a captive audience. Still, it was sometimes necessary to patronize the gathering spots of any community he visited, in order to strike up acquaintances. Picking his benefactors wisely, he seldom had any difficulty in securing lodgings. Women were intrigued by him, although the most subtle often hid this, and men considered him a 'character' who was interesting to talk to. Children he resonated with on a completely different level – their own – so he was also popular as an avuncular entertainer. His personality was entirely unthreatening, despite his air of mystery.

As a preliminary investigation, the traveller went into the post office to purchase a soft drink. The interior of the shop was stuffed with merchandise of the most unlikely variety. A mature female in powder and cardigan held court behind the old glass-topped counter, and there was a squinting crone sitting on a stool next to a bead curtain that obviously led to the living quarters. The silence caused by his entrance suggested these two had recently been involved in a dispute; it was more than the cautious silence reserved for strangers. The postmistress looked at him hard, ready to purse her mouth into disapproval, so he took off his hat and smiled. She visibly smoothed herself.

'Shut the door!' said the crone. 'Open doors let the air in.'

'Mother!' said the postmistress, in tolerant embarrassment as the traveller shut the door more firmly. 'What can I do for you, sir?'

The traveller voiced his requirements in his most velvety tone. He was charmed by the fact that the thick green bottles of sweet refreshment were stored in the cellar to keep them cool.

'Won't keep you a moment,' said the postmistress, dodging through the bead curtain, with an owlish backward glance that he guessed was meant to be sultry. A stillness descended into the shop and the traveller could hear the low buzz of a motorbike far away.

'Don't get paid for this!' said the old woman unexpectedly. The traveller smiled at her inquiringly. 'I count the post,' continued the woman, 'count it all, every one. No pay for it.'

'Oh.' The stillness became rather stiff. Did it really take this long to fetch a bottle from the cellar, he wondered? Perhaps the postmistress was applying a further layer of powder to her nose for his benefit.

'Here she comes,' said the old woman. The traveller thought she meant her daughter, but the door opened behind him and another customer came in. 'Hallo dear!' said the old woman, in a tone of some affection.

It was a girl, maybe seventeen or eighteen years old. She carried a large wicker basket which was hung over one arm and pressed tightly against her body. She wore a long dress in a faded floral print and scuffed sandals. Her arms were bare and, he could see, rather scratched, as if she'd been playing with a boisterous kitten.

'Hi, Mrs E.,' she said, and put her basket on the counter. She gave the traveller only the shortest of inspections. Here she comes, indeed! he was thinking. This was the lure, the gem in the heart of the rock, he was sure of it. After years of practice he could sniff out items of interest very quickly. Her long, abundant hair was the most beautiful shade of dark red; probably dyed, but enchanting none the less. Her face, admittedly, was plain but her eyes were wide and contained the hidden shred of 'otherness' he had trained himself to spot. The postmistress breezed through the curtain, clutching the bottle the traveller had ordered, her mouth pasted with a fresh gout of thick, red lipstick. She smiled airily at the girl. 'Hallo, Lily, love,' she said, and then redirected her attention to the traveller. 'Staying in

Lil'moor, are you?' she inquired brightly, as he counted out his change.

He couldn't help smiling at the unintentional pun and was tempted to answer, 'Well, I will if she's amenable,' but opted for, 'It's a lovely spot. I hope to stay here, yes.'

'We get a lot of tourists,' said the postmistress. 'Where are you staying? At the White House?'

'I haven't decided yet.'

'There's no decision to it,' said the girl, quite coldly. 'It's the only place for tourists around here.'

'In that case, my mind is made up,' said the traveller, putting the bottle into one of the pockets of his long coat.

'Want me to open that for you?' asked the postmistress.

He shook his head. 'No thank you.'

'You're not one of those people that use their teeth, are you?' The postmistress touched her throat provocatively. The traveller put on his hat. 'I always carry a bottle opener with me,' he said. 'Good day to you.'

Outside, he waited for the girl, Lily, to emerge. Of course, she spent considerable time chatting to the postmistress and her mother. He sat down on a convenient boulder and opened up the bottle, swigging idly as he waited. He never wasted an opportunity. He knew through past encounters that it was best to act on impulse or else regret at leisure. It was his duty while roaming the world to cram as much experience into his life as possible. He wanted to taste every fruit there was on offer, even if it was sour. More than anything, he liked to experience the effect he had on other people.

Eventually, the bell above the post office door made a muffled 'ting!' and the Lily Maid walked out into the sunlight. She paused for a moment and squinted up at the sky. Her basket was laden with tins and she had bought a couple of oranges that had the wizened appearance typical of small-store produce kept long on the shelf. When she realized she was being observed, she assumed an almost guilty expression as if she had been seen doing something shameful. She nodded curtly, hesitated with a half-open mouth as if about to speak, and then began to walk away up the road. Once, she looked back. Satisfied, the traveller stood up, threw the empty bottle into a waste-bin outside the shop and headed for the White House.

He would take a room there for a night a least. The interior of the place was all polished dark wood and horse brasses, with a token grandfather clock ticking in the hallway. A notice-board advertised church activities in the area. He could not remember having seen a church near by. It was necessary to ring a counter bell for service; clearly the White House was not crammed with business at the moment. A man, an ex-military type, came through from a room at the back. The traveller assessed him swiftly; retired, wife somewhere else in the building, hearty group of local friends, perhaps the father of a difficult child who had grown into a difficult adult. He did not fall prey to the traveller's charms at all, however well directed they were, and maintained a stiff, unwelcoming mien as his new guest signed the register. The traveller's appearance was perhaps not typical of the usual White House clientele and it was likely he'd only been permitted to stay there because trade was slack. The proprietor would undoubtedly prefer to fill his inn with family holiday-makers and respectable moor-walkers. The traveller's attire and long hair probably suggested untold dissipations to this conventional creature, who would also scorn all males who had not enjoyed army life at some time. Enchanting

delusion! The traveller envisaged many interesting encounters to be had with the landlord; his name was Mr
Eager.

'Dinner at six-thirty!' he said. The traveller imagined
a peremptory gong would be rung at that time, and woe
betide the listless guest who ignored its summons.

His room was comfortable, if not a little too flouncy.
Mrs Eager would also be flouncy of course, for the
décor was her signature. The traveller would strike up
a friendship with her, to the disgust of her husband. He
wondered whether the Lily Maid ever came to the White
House. His first impression of her suggested she was
not the type to drink out in pubs. Once he'd made the
acquaintance of Mrs Eager he might be able to find out.

At six-thirty he presented himself downstairs just as
Mr Eager was about to bang the anticipated gong with
a little felt-covered hammer. He nodded cheerily to the
landlord who, surprisingly, went quite red about the
neck and face. The traveller wore new black jeans and
an open-necked black shirt, which revealed the white
hollow of his throat, the place where it looked as if
someone had gouged a hole in the soft, bloodless flesh
with a knuckle. His long hair was tied firmly back at
the neck and he had willed himself into a pleasing state
of suave, groomed, aristocratic vagueness. He defied the
landlord to call his appearance disreputable; he would
be faintly patronizing with the man tonight as a lesson.

After dinner, during which he had made a point of
ingratiating himself with Mrs Eager (who was all that
he had decided she should be), the traveller took a pint
of beer out into the White House garden and sat against
a wall where a late-blooming lilac hybrid exuded its
scent behind him. Gradually, as the evening thickened,
other guests drifted outside to sit at the wooden picnic
tables, and locals also began to arrive. Car doors

slammed, a few children made an appearance. Then there was a glimmer of white, and the Lily Maid herself walked into the garden, dressed in pale cotton and wrapped in a fringed, woollen shawl. She sat down alone at one of the tables and self-consciously fiddled with her hair, kicking the bench with her feet.

Delightful! thought the traveller, how unbelievably opportune! He had not imagined she would come this close to him so soon, although he knew the seeds of interest he'd planted must have taken root, and wondered whether he should approach her right away. No, perhaps a minute or two of observation first . . . He watched her, savouring the moments before contact was made. She seemed so fey, so fragile, almost awkward. Once or twice she nodded and smiled at people she knew, but no one made a move to join her. A moth fluttered above her head and landed for a moment on her hair. The traveller shivered with anticipation.

Presently, a young man came out of the White House, carrying two full glasses. He sat down beside the girl and placed a drink in front of her. They did not speak but simply sat there, side by side, looking into the dusk. The traveller suppressed a *frisson* of annoyance, even though he'd known it was unlikely the girl would be alone. Her partner was hardly more than a boy, pallid and scrawny, his hair unkempt and the starved curve of his jaw like a blade. He wore old, frayed jeans and a huge, shapeless jumper full of holes. He and the exquisite girl lifted their glasses in unison, drank, did not speak.

The traveller had finished his beer. He stood up, cradling the empty glass, and walked towards the lit garden door of the pub as if to purchase another. Just as he was within reasonable speaking distance of the Lily Maid and her companion, the girl began to say something. He could not hear the words, but the boy nodded distractedly.

'Hallo there,' said the traveller, and they both turned their heads in his direction. He smiled and gestured towards the pub with his glass. 'We meet again!'

At this point, if there was no sign of welcome, he could carry on walking without loss of dignity. The girl frowned at him and then smiled wanly. She leaned towards her companion and began murmuring in his ear, dismissing the traveller from her attention. The traveller walked past without pausing and went into the bar. He did not feel annoyed, only mystified. He employed a careful choreography when intruding into people's lives and yet on this occasion it appeared his first movements, which were often the most devastating, had somehow failed to arouse. He was puzzled by this, and checked his appearance in the mirror behind the bar. Mrs Eager, oblivious of his mood, was happily chatting into the air around his body as she filled his glass.

He had obviously made a mistake. Some people were immune to his allure because of an innate lack of imagination. It was pointless to bother with individuals like that; too much work. He'd simply made an error of judgement. He looked around the bar. Perhaps someone else? What he saw did not inspire him. Tomorrow, then, he would be moving on. A pity. His pique was destined to last no more than a few minutes.

'Don't you?' Mrs Eager said.

The traveller shook himself into the present. 'I beg your pardon?'

'I said how much I love this time of year; the smells, the feelings, don't you?' She waved dangerous, lacquered claws in the air. She smelled of heavy, oriental scent, which failed to conceal the clinging aroma of flesh past its prime.

The traveller nodded. 'Yes,' he said. Mrs Eager, he was sure, would also be an amateur poet, and perhaps ran a small writing circle in the village. She would have been easy prey, if he'd been interested. 'Could I ask you something?'

She puffed up with pleasure. 'Of course!'

'The young couple out there; a girl with red hair and a shawl, the pale boy, do you know them?'

The question was obviously not the one Mrs Eager had anticipated. Her face had fallen a little. 'Oh, you mean the Winter twins?'

'Twins? I don't think so.' Even as he said it, he realized he was wrong. Of course they were twins.

'Well, they're the only people who fit that description,' said Mrs Eager. 'Why?'

'I met the girl – Lily? – earlier today.'

'Mmm.' Mrs Eager leaned conspiratorially over the bar. 'They . . .'

He wouldn't let her say what she wanted to say. 'What are they drinking?'

Mrs Eager jumped back abruptly. Later, she might wonder with her poet's mind why his softly spoken words had made her feel as if she'd been slapped across the face. 'They usually drink cider,' she said. 'Are you buying for them?'

He nodded. Mrs Eager worked the pump with a pursed mouth. 'What's that scent you're wearing?' he asked her, smiling.

He wasn't normally so obvious in his manoeuvres, but realized there was little point in trying to deny how deeply Lily Winter had aroused his interest. Her resistance called for dramatic measures. Carrying the drinks on a metal tray the traveller went back out into the garden. He would not have been surprised if the twins had already left, but they were still sitting together at the table. Lily was leaning down to fuss a mongrel dog with a madly wagging tail that had come to sniff around her ankles.

'Mind if I join you?' he asked, sitting down. The twins looked at him with some surprise and the dog slunk away. He put the drinks down in front of them. 'I hope you don't mind. I feel like a bit of company and I'm afraid you' – he wagged a finger at the girl – 'are the only person I've met around here.'

She laughed without reserve, a reaction he hadn't expected. 'Hardly *met*!' she said. Perhaps she felt safer with her brother there. The evening light suited her. How could he have thought her plain?

The traveller shrugged and grinned sheepishly. 'I know, but everyone else in this place is . . .' He pulled a face.

'We call it a pre-graveyard,' Lily said, nodding. 'I know what you mean.'

'You're Lily Winter, right?' So far he hadn't yet looked at the boy. She didn't seem too pleased he'd found out that much about her; perhaps because there were other things to discover, which she feared he'd also picked up. 'And you are . . .?' she asked, a little coldly. He told her.

'Are you foreign?' she asked. 'No, of course not. Are you a gypsy, then, or something? What an unusual name.'

He shrugged again, offering no further explanation.

'This is my brother Owen,' she said, gesturing to her companion, 'or did you know that too?'

The traveller shook his head. 'No. Pleased to meet you.' He met the boy's eyes for the first time, expecting territorial surliness, and found to his relief he was merely looking at Lily's eyes again. Uncanny: a mixture of caution, amusement, and a certain cynical awareness of his purpose. He realized, half unpleasantly, that these two somehow *knew* him. Was this a disadvantage or not? The boy was more presentable than he'd first thought as well. How fortunate to find these creatures here; their acquaintance might provide more experience than he could have hoped for.

'He lurked outside the post office for me,' Lily said to her brother, flapping a hand at the traveller. She did not deceive him. She and Owen had undoubtedly discussed the matter already. Owen smiled.

'I do not deny it,' said the traveller. 'As a contrast to the hags in there you were like a goddess!'

The twins exchanged a secret glance, but it did not altogether exclude him. They were willing to play, he felt. He experienced a delirious moment of weakness as if the performance was not his but theirs. It was a strange and unfamiliar sensation, but not unpleasant.

'Are you on holiday?' Lily asked him, drinking from the glass he had given her but keeping it low to the table. Her eyes smiled at him over its rim.

'A travelling holiday,' he said. The twins both made noises of interest, so he began to relate some stories about his experiences, a few of which were fabrications and distinctly less interesting than the truth.

'So, are you lost now?' asked the boy. 'This is nowhere. How did you end up here?'

'I never know how I end up anywhere. I just keep moving. It's the best way, I find. Sometimes I discover wonderful things. I don't look for them, I just make myself receptive. How did you end up here?'

'We live here,' Lily said.

'You don't seem typical of the natives.'

She made a careless gesture. 'Well . . .'

'Our mother was an outsider. We inherited the house,' Owen said.

It was perhaps rather an odd way to put it, but at least it implied they lived alone and might have spacious accommodation. The traveller had the distinct impression that Owen was thinking the words: 'Wasn't that what you wanted to know?' but was aware he might be projecting his own desires on to these people, reading more into their behaviour than was actually there.

'So what is there to see around here?' he asked, taking a drink.

'Nothing!' the twins said in unison. They laughed.

'There is always something,' the traveller said, 'anywhere. Always something.'

'Don't count on it,' Lily said. 'What sort of thing are you looking for?'

He shrugged. 'Just places of interest.'

'Monuments, ruins, that sort of thing?'

'Yes, that sort of thing. I like history.'

'Oh, there's plenty of that here,' Lily said. 'History. No present though, and certainly no future. Nothing changes.'

'Sounds idyllic.'

'Depends on what you like, I suppose,' she said. 'Living here gets very boring.'

'If you don't like it, why stay?' he asked. 'Couldn't you sell your house?'

'We could,' Owen said, 'but if we went to a bigger town, we'd have to work. Our income is enough for Lil'moor. We don't want to work for anyone.'

'I can't say I blame you,' the traveller said. It was a sentiment he shared.

'You're staying here, then?' Lily said.

'For the time being. I acted on your recommendation.'

'It was hardly that!' she said. 'What do you think of the Eagers?'

'I don't think Mister likes me. She seems all right.'

Lily nodded. 'They've only been here five years. Now they think they own the place!'

'They do a lot,' Owen said, which implied criticism rather than praise.

'She started all this church business. Fêtes and things,' Lily said. 'It's absurd. Lil'moor doesn't even have a vicar of its own, but this man comes out from Patterham now and again. More regularly since Mrs Eager took him in hand, I think. The old dears like it.'

'I didn't see a church,' the traveller said.

'Oh, it's a way out of the village,' Lily told him. 'Almost as if Lil'moor was bigger at one time and has just shrunk away from it. You'd like it; it's very old.'

'We could show it to you,' Owen said. Lily looked at him sharply and then smiled.

'Yes, we could. Do you want us to?'

'It's very kind of you.'

'It's just something to do!' she said, and stood up. 'Well, come on then.'

'What? Now?' The traveller was taken aback.

'Better by moonlight,' Lily said. 'Come on.'

There was no moon, but the clear sky lent a ghostly radiance to the land. As they walked together up the middle of the road, the traveller again experienced a feeling of being helplessly overwhelmed. Lily appeared to have undergone a dramatic personality change. Gone was the reticent, innocent reserve of their encounter in the post office. She chattered the entire time they walked, mainly about other people in the village.

'They don't think much of us,' she said.

'Why drink in the pub, then?' he asked.

'Because they hide the fact they don't think much of us,' Owen said, 'but we still *know*. They might think they don't want us around but they'd be disappointed if we weren't. We're part of this place.'

'I don't care what they think,' Lily said.

'You must get lonely sometimes,' the traveller said. The thought of them living alone together in isolation suddenly made him feel uneasy.

'Oh no,' Lily said. 'Never.'

'We have a car,' Owen said. 'We drive to places, don't we, Lily?'

'We drive to places,' she said. The traveller was beginning to wonder if they were not rather simple in the head.

The church was really quite unremarkable and not as old as the twins had suggested. Its most significant feature was that it had been built in such a bleak spot. It was surrounded by gravestones that were kept in check by a dilapidated fence. Several tired-looking yew trees provided the traditional vigilance for the dead. It was a place where lone spectres might walk, but there were none in evidence tonight.

'It's locked up,' Lily said. She was wearing her shawl low on her arms, and the traveller could see her skin was pimpled with cold. The three of them stood against the fence, looking at the graveyard. It seemed they had made rather a pointless journey.

'Let's show him the ringstone,' Owen said to his sister.

'That's a good idea.'

It seemed rather staged. The traveller was unsure what to expect, but wondered whether he was about to be on the receiving end of a joke. They went through a lych-gate that seemed unnecessarily imposing, or part of an older structure. A straight gravel path ran up to the church doors, and appeared to circle the building. The traveller was bemused to see there was a TV aerial sticking out from the church roof.

'It's round the back,' Lily said, running into the shadow of the church.

'We often come here at night,' Owen said.

'I thought you might,' the traveller replied. They were just children.

The ringstone was nothing more than a listing gravestone, its engraving long weathered into nonsense. 'This is it,' Lily said. She was leaning on the stone, her white hands gripping it at the top.

'And what is it, exactly?' asked the traveller.

Lily and her brother started laughing. The traveller felt decidedly uncomfortable. 'We must join hands around it,' Lily said.

'How pagan,' the traveller observed, unimpressed.

'Oh, probably,' Lily agreed, 'but it's a custom.' She held out her hands, waggling her fingers. 'Join hands.'

Reluctantly, the traveller complied. Lily's fingers were icy cold, Owen's warm and dry. 'Do we have to make a wish or something?' the traveller asked. He felt absurdly awkward.

'No, we circle,' Lily replied. She pulled on his arm.

I can't believe I'm doing this, the traveller thought, stumbling round the stone. I have no control over these people, they are wild. 'Whose grave is this?' he asked.

'Don't know,' Lily said. 'It's not important.'

He suspected that circling the ringstone was a custom traditional only to the Winter twins and strongly hoped no stray dog-walkers from the village would come along to observe this ridiculous ritual. 'That's enough,' he said after a few minutes, pulling away from their hands. They did not object.

'Tomorrow we could take you somewhere else,' Owen said.

They escorted him back to the White House and cheerily waved goodbye, promising further entertainment the following day. The traveller was not sure of his feelings about Owen and Lily Winter. In some ways they annoyed him, and Lily was not at all like he had imagined her to be. She should have been a shy virgin whom he could have gently initiated into the ways of the world. He now suspected that she was not a virgin at all. How disappointing. There would be no scholar's bedroom with bookcases full of slim volumes. There would be no delicate watercolours on the wall, painted by her own untutored hand. The scratches on her arms, which he'd fondly thought she might have incurred playing with a favourite cat in some secluded, scented garden, had probably happened while she'd been fixing her car or something equally mundane. Still, she and her brother were unusual people even if not in the direction he'd hoped.

Mrs Eager was still hovering around the bar cleaning glasses; it was not as late as he'd thought. She offered to make him some meat sandwiches, which he gladly accepted, and while she did so he sat down in the guests' lounge to read a local paper. Mr Eager sauntered in, pushing out his belly, and attempted to be sociable. He asked the traveller whether he played golf.

'I'm afraid not.'

'Hrrm, hrrrh.' The landlord was either clearing his throat or playing for time. 'Sitting with the Winters, were you?' he said eventually. 'Rum pair, rum pair.' Mr Eager shook his head in perplexity. The traveller made no comment. 'Bit of square-bashing wouldn't harm the lad . . .'

'They seem very young to live alone,' the traveller said.

'Tch, yes!' said Mr Eager. 'The mother died two years ago, but they keep the old place up. They're looked out for around here.' He glanced at the traveller in a knowing, slightly threatening manner.

Mrs Eager had come into the room, carrying a tray.

She had obviously overheard her husband's remarks. 'Mrs Winter was a very private person,' she said, offering the traveller a plate of sandwiches. 'She came here when the twins were babies. Had a little money, I think. She always kept herself to herself and never mentioned what had happened to her husband, but she was a good woman. The twins have run a little wild perhaps since she died, but grief can do funny things to people, can't it? You spent the evening with Lily and Owen?'

The traveller nodded. 'Yes, they're very quaint but I enjoyed their company.'

'We look out for them here in Lil'moor,' Mrs Eager said. 'We have a close community.' Her concern explained why she'd seemed a little frosty with the traveller earlier on (perhaps she'd imagined he had sinister designs on the Winters), but it was certainly at odds with the way the twins thought they were regarded in the village. Poor waifs, they lived in a fantasy world. How would his intrusion affect it? He hoped to find out very soon.

At lunchtime the following day the traveller had a visitor. He had been hanging around the White House in the hope that Lily and Owen would turn up and was therefore surprised, and even a little disappointed, when Owen arrived alone. The boy was wearing the same tatty clothes he'd worn the previous evening but had apparently brushed his hair. His flawless skin looked shockingly clean against the oily wool of his jumper.

'Lily's busy,' he said. 'I've got the car outside. I'll show you around.'

The Winter car was a big, rounded vehicle upholstered in aromatic leather, with walnut interior trim. It smelled of age and Owen was quite dwarfed by it, sitting behind the steering wheel like a child. He drove, however, with the habitual terrifying confidence of the young.

'Lily's making a meal,' he said, as the car bowled along one of the lanes leading from Little Moor. 'A meal for you. For tonight.' He grinned at the traveller.

'That's nice. Where are you taking me?'

'A ruin. That's what you want, isn't it?'

'Drive on!' The traveller poked his hand out of the car window, letting his fingers run through the whipping grass of the steep hedgerows.

'You could cut yourself,' said Owen, 'lose a finger. Are you afraid of blood?'

The ruin, like the church, lacked the antiquity the traveller enjoyed sensing in old buildings. It was simply a small house on the moors, a crofter's cottage set back from the road, gutted and forlorn. He tried to hide his disappointment from Owen who appeared quite proud of the place.

'Wait till you see it properly,' he said. 'It's quite remarkable.'

The traveller followed the boy from the road, and a few sheep bustled away from the empty house as they approached it.

'Is this a place you and Lily visit often too?' the traveller asked.

Owen wrinkled his nose, his hands deep in his trouser pockets. 'Not really. It doesn't have the mood for regular visitors. You have to respect the feelings of these places, you know.'

'I see.' It was becoming clear to the traveller that these two children, deprived of stimuli, had invested their landscape with a rich personal symbology. He wasn't sure whether this was endearing or exasperating; he would have to wait and see.

The door to the house was missing, leaving only a black hole. 'Look at this,' Owen said. The traveller looked inside. All of the floors had gone, even the ground floor, so that the whole building had become a kind of dark well, littered with rubbish and pale plants. 'It's bigger inside than outside, you see,' Owen said. 'That's very unusual. Come round the back. There's a way in, I'll show you. You must feel it inside.'

The ground around the house was swampy and strewn with animal droppings. The traveller picked his way through the mulch without much enthusiasm. The house appeared taller from the back than at the front; the basement was at ground level. Owen ducked into a hole which seemed to have been frenziedly torn into the wall; bricks covered a wide area of ground near by. The traveller wondered whether Owen and Lily were responsible for it. Hesitating only for a moment, he followed the boy inside.

The traveller had to concede that Owen was right about the place; it did seem larger than it had appeared from outside, but he knew that was an illusion. Pigeons were roosting in what remained of the attic rafters and the moist, peaty ground was white with their guano. There were signs that people came here regularly. Crates were bunched together to form a makeshift table, their surfaces marked with candle wax. It was as if occult rituals had been conducted there. The traveller swallowed thickly, and the taste was sour. He hoped he was wrong.

'Feel the atmosphere,' Owen said, in a whisper. 'Just be still, and feel it.'

The traveller felt nothing. If this was the Winter twins' temple, its ambience left him untouched; but then it would.

'What am I supposed to feel?' he asked.

The boy looked at him sharply. 'We thought you were like us,' he said, and then shrugged. 'Close your eyes. Wait.'

Sighing, the traveller did so, and then opened them again quickly. By his side Owen Winter was standing with his head thrown back, his eyes peacefully closed, his lips slightly parted. The traveller realized the boy was really quite beautiful. He looked like a dying saint or someone inviting a kiss. Not realizing he was being observed, Owen reached out and took the traveller's hand in his own. 'You will feel it through me,' he said. The traveller felt nothing, nothing other than the warm pressure of living fingers. That, at least, was not un- pleasant. My dalliance with these waifs will be short, he thought, but not without refreshment. Owen sighed and released the traveller's hand. 'Well,' he said, blinking. 'Did you feel it?'

'I felt only you,' the traveller replied.

Owen smiled, 'I think you are too cold or something. Let's go.'

They spent the afternoon tramping around the moors, visiting several other empty cottages and farm build- ings, but none of these were treated with the bizarre reverence Owen Winter had displayed for the first house. Some of the places were indeed interesting, and the weight of the centuries there pressed down upon the traveller like a welcome blanket in the thick of winter. Owen's behaviour was erratic. At one moment he appeared almost scholarly, talking about the history of the moors, while at another he might sound positively deranged, alluding to ghosts and unexplained phen- omena. The traveller was genuinely confused as to whether the boy was slightly mentally ill or just deliber- ately contrary. It was impossible to tell. He could not believe this innocent was involved in any occult prac- tice; he was simply an immature romantic looking for mystery. And don't I do that myself, in a way? thought the traveller. Owen did not attempt to touch him again.

In the late afternoon they got back into the car and Owen drove them home. The traveller was intrigued by what the Winter house might be like. It could be large and look haunted with ivy over the eaves, or small and cottagey hugged by climbing roses. He dismissed the possibility of it being nothing more than a grey semi-detached house, bought by the mother from a district council. The reality, however, was none of these.

It was a detached house, though not large, situated on a winding lane where family homes were widely spaced. It was surrounded by tall evergreens, but had no name. It had rather a raddled appearance. Owen parked the car in a muddy drive at the side of the house, and when the traveller got out, he could see a distorted wire chicken-run behind the house where a few ragged birds were scampering up and down. There was a kennel and a chain but no dog, and a bare clematis hugged one of the walls. The back door was painted in an unsightly and flaking turquoise colour. Owen scraped mud from the soles of his pumps on a piece of metal by the door and, out of politeness, the traveller did likewise. Then they went inside.

The back door led straight into the kitchen which was steamy with the smell of cooking food. Pots bubbled on an old gas stove. The traveller took off his hat and put it down on the large, farmhouse table. He looked around himself with interest. The walls were bare brick except for one that had been inexpertly white-washed; splashes of white marked the brown tiled floor. Bunches of herbs hung from one of the roof beams, but were so dusty it did not look as if they were used for anything. Three crates of apples under the table gave off an overripe smell; one of them was occupied by an elderly cat asleep among the fruit. A group of new kitchen units against one of the walls was the sole

concession to modernity but, white as they were among
so much dark and earth, they looked absurd and out of
place. Their Formica surfaces were already scored by
cutting-knives, and the scratches had been stained
brown by tea. At one time, someone had begun to turn
this dilapidated house into a home, but the job had
never been finished and there was no sign of recent
work. Strange. The twins' mother must have lived here
for about fifteen years.

'Hope you don't mind the mess,' Owen said and went
to open a door, calling 'Lily!' into the space beyond.

The traveller stood in the middle of the kitchen, bom-
barded by the images before him. His home, when he
returned to it, would never be allowed to sink into such
disarray. How could a person be comfortable in such
chaos? It mystified him. He was beginning to think of
home more often now. He sat down on a wooden chair
by the table and Owen said. 'No, don't sit there. Go into
the parlour.' He gestured to show the way.

The parlour was surprisingly comfortable; a woman
had put her mark here. Perhaps the mother had begun
renovations in this room. The walls were covered in
framed embroidered samplers and a large, welcoming
fire was burning in the huge stone hearth. Again the
walls were of bare brick, but in this room it was simply
rustic, a decorative effect. A beautiful old Persian rug
covered most of the floor, but around its edges the
boards gleamed with honey-coloured varnish. The traveller threw himself into a well-padded chair and Owen
offered him some wine. 'Home-made,' he said. 'But you'll
like it.'

The traveller was not prepared to disagree, although
he had a refined palate which objected to brutality.
Owen poured out a glass of pale liquid from what
appeared to be a crystal decanter. 'We make it from

apples,' he said. The traveller was pleased to find the wine tasted of fairly well-bred sherry. Then Lily came into the room. She looked enchanting, wearing a simple, long black dress, her hair held back with a silky scarf. She had painted her lips with a smudge of pale lipstick and her lashes were spiky with mascara. The traveller's heart warmed. He wished she had been with them for the afternoon.

'Did you have a good time?' she asked, sitting down on the arm of the traveller's chair. He burned with the proximity of her body. She smelled of soap and floral scent.

'Yes, it was very interesting,' he said.

'Did you show him the house, Owen?' she said.

Owen sat down on the rug at their feet. He nodded.

'What did you think of it?' Lily asked the traveller.

'I suppose you mean your little church,' he said.

Lily laughed. 'Well, it's not exactly that!'

'I think I disappointed your brother. I wasn't sure how I was supposed to react.'

'I wasn't disappointed,' Owen said. 'We only wanted you to go there. You weren't supposed to react.'

'Why did you want me to go there?' the traveller asked. He thought he might as well enter into the spirit of their game.

'We wanted to show you to the land,' Lily said.

'Oh.' A dark misgiving touched the traveller's heart. He did not approve of the implications in those words.

'Anyway, the food's ready now,' Lily said, jumping up. 'We'll eat in here, shall we?'

The meal was wholesome if rather sloppy. Lily and Owen kept up an inane chatter the whole time, plates balanced on their knees. When everyone had finished eating Lily piled up the plates in the hearth and refilled the wine glasses. Her cheeks had become slightly flushed. She curled up on the floor by the traveller's feet and, twirling her glass in her hands said, 'When are you going home?'

He smiled down at her. 'Soon,' he said.

'Where do you live?'

'My family has a place further south.'

'And you're going back there?'

'Yes.'

Owen was lying on his stomach in front of them, his chin in his hands. 'What do you do? Do you work?'

The traveller paused. 'I will do, I expect.'

'You're rich, aren't you!' Lily said, pleased with her deduction.

The traveller shrugged. 'My family has money, but that's no excuse for being lazy. Besides, I will have a family to help support eventually.' He wondered why he was telling them even this much. Why? It was the first occasion he had ever opened up to anybody during his travels, including those times he'd spent with distant Kin. Perhaps he was satisfying a need; the journey time was nearly over. Perhaps he was throwing coins at destiny. Perhaps.

'Oh,' Lily said, having digested this information. 'You have . . . a girlfriend or a wife, then?'

The traveller leaned back in his chair and blinked at the ceiling. 'I will enter into a marriage when I return home.'

Lily giggled. 'What a funny way of putting it.' A silence came into the room.

'I'm not married yet though,' the traveller said, and sat up straight again with a sigh. He held out his empty glass to Owen. The boy gave him a studied, calculating look that went on for a few seconds too long before he got up and refilled the glass. Lily extended a cautious hand and traced a pattern on one of the traveller's boots. 'You are a very strange man,' she said.

'How strange?' he asked.

'Well, we don't like people much, but you are different. We like you, don't we, Owen?'

'That's why we showed you things, invited you here,' Owen said. 'We like you.'

'I'm flattered.'

'Do you like us?' Lily asked him shyly. She did not look up at him but the traveller could see the colour had deepened around her face. Her little ears had gone scarlet. He reached out and put a hand on her shoulder.

'I think you know the answer to that,' he said.

'We have many secrets,' Lily said. 'We think we can trust you.'

'People here think we're witches,' Owen said, 'but we're not.'

'We are very close,' Lily said. 'We always have been.'

The traveller got out of his chair and sat down on the rug between them. He gently pulled Lily against him with one hand and reached out to stroke Owen's hair with the other. 'Don't tell me,' he said. 'It's not necessary.'

The traveller woke up alone beside the fire. He lay for a few moments reliving the delicious experience of Owen and Lily Winter: their hands, their young eyes, the impossible slimness of their bodies, their utter submission to his pleasure. They had obviously experimented together for a long time. Where were they now? Had they stolen away to indulge in a more private communion? The traveller considered that, for tonight at least, it would be best if he returned to the White House. The clock on the wall told him it was not yet midnight. He sat up and pulled on his clothes, noticing that Lily and Owen's garments were still mixed up with his own. Wherever they had gone to they had gone there naked.

Strange and lovely children. He wondered how long he should stay with them. He did not want to encourage a dependence, which he suspected was a risk, but neither did he want to leave this abundant orchard right away. All too soon the time for travelling would be over. He would be given new responsibilities and commitments. There could be no more sampling the world's fruit then.

The smell of apples, very strong and slightly sickly, drifted in from the kitchen. The traveller went out there, stretching, looking for his coat and hat. All the lights were off and he did not know where the switches were. It was very dark and the house was making comfortable, sleepy sounds, wrapping him in its perfume of apples and cooking. It no longer seemed unhomely to him; its mess was comfort. His coat was lying over the back of a chair.

As he shrugged himself into it he looked out of the window at the dark garden. He saw pale shapes moving about and heard a sharp, high-pitched giggle. The twins were out in the garden, naked in the chill; naked beneath the stars. The traveller stood by the window to watch them, an affectionate smile on his face. They were so beautiful, like sprites, slim and white. They ran around a sundial, round and round. He wished he could scoop them up, put them into his pocket, and carry them home. He would like to have such wonders in his own garden one day. You have your secret little wild things, he thought, and I have mine, but tonight mine are heavy, heavy. He sighed and thought of his mother's face, one straight finger pressed against her pale lips. 'Never speak, never speak of what you are. Trust only your Kin, for the Kin stay together, and those beyond the community are a danger to all.' Her words echoed through his mind, words that had been with him since childhood so long ago.

He forced himself to look away from the window but just as his head turned, an odd movement caught the edge of his vision. He pressed his face against the glass, his mouth open. His fingers were flat against the panes.

Twirling, dancing, long-limbed sprites, they were attenuating even as he looked, their muscles flexing outwards. They were blurs upon the dewy grass reaching out for one another with fingers like blades of frost. Changing shape.

We thought you were like us . . .

He could not believe what he was seeing and the gristle cracked in his own face as he stared.

We have secrets . . .

Yes, yes! You shouldn't exist, not here, not alone.

Our mother was an outsider . . .

The traveller ground his forehead against the glass with a groan of pain. Look away, look away. Forget! Impulsively, he smacked the flat of his hands against the window and the sharp, sudden noise of cracking glass splintered the night air. The twins froze, caught like animals in a glare of light, looking in at the house with the startled eyes of feral animals. Loners are not tolerated. Loners unwittingly betray. They must be culled!

Lily walked up to the window and put her fingers to the glass, touching the place where his brow pressed the other side. Her small breasts nudged the panes. She looked very brave. She could not guess what was on his mind. She thought he was afraid. 'It's all right,' she said. 'Really. It's all right.'

'It is not!' the traveller said, through clenched teeth.

She looked puzzled, throwing a glance behind her to where her brother stood uncertainly by the sundial. The traveller's throat had filled with fluid. He blinked at the pale wraith outside. 'Keep moving,' he said thickly. 'Sell the house! Go away! Keep moving!'

Lily frowned. 'It's all right,' she repeated. 'We often dance outside like this. There's a wall round the garden. No one can see we're undressed.'

Perhaps he was wrong. Perhaps he'd seen nothing but a pair of children enacting a private rite of their own. The glass was old, warped. He backed away from the cracked window.

'No,' Lily said, her brow puckering, 'don't go. Please don't go.'

He knew he had to leave. If he left now he could convince himself his sight had deceived him. If he stayed they would show him their secrets, all of them. They had promised as much. Now he was afraid of what he might find out. He did not want to be the keeper of unwanted knowledge, for the keeper defers to a higher authority eventually and then the time would come when a stranger would arrive in Little Moor, someone whose function was to eliminate dangers from the world. The traveller could not bear to think of that. If they *were* like him, the Winters did not know what they were; they were innocent. The people in the village looked out for them. They might be safe unless another of his kind came by.

'We want you to stay with us,' Lily said urgently, patting the glass with her fingers. 'Stay for a while. We will make you happy.'

'I know,' the traveller said, standing in the shadows. 'You already have.' He backed slowly towards the door, feeling behind him for the handle. Outside the air was sharp with the promise of frost. He inhaled deeply, feeling the needles in his lungs. Then he walked briskly away towards the White House. Nobody followed him.

The train sped south, casting a flickering shadow over

the yellow cornfields, recently harvested. The traveller stared out at the dying season, his cheek pressed against the glass. The winter was coming now, coming fast. Up north, in the hidden valleys, on the bare moors, in the timeless pockets of life where very little ever changed, the secret people thrived. They could be very different, these people – outcasts from the human race, eccentrics, grievers, loners – an infinite variety of separate souls. The hard season would come to Little Moor and in the moonlight wraiths might dance in the snow, pale as the winter element, timeless creatures. He remembered the warmth of their hearth, the warm of their flesh. He remembered nothing more.

GOING TO THE BLACK BEAR

Colin Greenland

———————

'This is a song I wrote about the war, it's called *A Letter from Kenny*.' She played the intro looking down at the bare board floor with the beer stains, then when she started to sing she lifted her head. They didn't stop talking though; they didn't want to hear about the war. They were just loggers and quarrymen; all they wanted was Brenda Lee or Connie Francis or some of that country music. She sang over their heads into the smoky air of the bar-room. The season was over; all the vacation cabins were locked and shuttered, the colours of fall had faded and gone from the trees. Tomorrow she'd head out for Bangor, find the Black Bear; they were cool there, they had the Kingston Trio, Phil Ochs. Bob *Dylan* had played the Black Bear. Tomorrow she'd try for Bangor and after that she'd quit. Go back home.

She sang the chorus, sang it louder. They had to listen. There was one guy, a young guy over in the booths, sitting on his own. He was listening. She sang it to him.

I'm still waiting for a letter from Kenny
To tell me when he'll be coming home . . .

He was kind of a nice guy: he had real nice blue eyes. They seemed to shine through the smoke, brighter than the beer lights at the bar. He didn't look like a logger. He had a jean jacket but he had a white shirt on, like from India or somewhere, with a little embroidery on the collar. Maybe he'd been in the war; maybe that was why he was listening. Maybe that was why he was sitting on his own, not talking to any of the log men. He wouldn't stop looking at her. She gave him a special smile. Maybe he had a car, maybe he was going somewhere towards Bangor. He wasn't from around here, that was for sure.

She finished the song and some of the people clapped. He didn't clap. She was disappointed. He just sat there drinking and smoking and watching her. He was amazing, so blond and tanned and everything, she thought he was a lifeguard up from Florida or maybe all the way from the West Coast. Everybody was talking about the West Coast, everybody but her had gone there this summer; she was up here at China Lake playing for truck-drivers. Couldn't get much farther from San Francisco if you tried. She did the short set. All the way through *Pretty Boy Floyd* she kept thinking, Please don't go.

He didn't go.

She came down from the stage, between the tables and into the crowd, holding her guitar up so it wouldn't get hit. She hated this part, when the gig was over, down on the floor with the people. They all knew her now, but she didn't know them. They didn't mean any harm, she just couldn't handle them. She smiled and said thank you, didn't look at any one of them too long.

'That was real good, honey,' said Myra from the bar, passing her a Michelob. Then the juke-box came on, pretty loud: the Drifters, wiping her out of the air. She was history. She drank deep, wiped her mouth. She went along past his booth, caught his eye.

'Hi,' he said.

'Well hallo,' she said. She smiled and he smiled too, sort of. She hung around there a second, another second;

he had to say something else or she had to walk on by. He gave the slightest nod at the empty seat opposite, kept looking at her. His eyes were steady as blue stones. She found herself putting her guitar in the window seat and sitting down facing him.

So that was that.

She drank fast, she was thirsty.

He spoke then. 'You ready for another?' he said.

His cheekbones were like gulls' wings. She wanted to fly on them. He was drinking an Old Milwaukee, straight out of the bottle like the logging men. She had one too. She flexed her shoulders, rubbing her back against the partition. 'I curl right up when I'm playing,' she said. 'Like a caterpillar or something.'

Most guys would think that was cute, he just sat there like an Indian. Well, he was no Penobscot, not with that hair.

'You have a name?' she asked him.

He kept looking at her a while before he answered; something was going on in his eyes like he was trying to remember his own name. It would have been kind of spooky if he hadn't been so beautiful. She could watch him a long time, she thought.

'Tom,' he said.

'Hi, Tom,' she said. 'I'm Stephanie. I guess you know that, right?' She reached up and traced the letters of her name backwards on one of her fliers Myra had taped to the window.

'You're good,' he said.

'Well I'm glad you liked it,' she said.

She drank some more beer. He didn't say anything. Usually guys tried to impress her, they wanted to put the make on her right away. Like the guy last night in Augusta who wanted her to be a star. 'Stephanie, you've got it,' he kept saying. 'You got the message.' Nobody that she didn't know had ever watched her as hard as this one, yet now he wasn't paying her any mind. She was pleased and insulted both at the same time, and ashamed of herself for being insulted. She was sure he was a veteran, some of them were kind of remote and confused in themselves. That would be a pity.

'Did you like *Letter from Kenny*?' she said. 'I saw you listening to that one. Were you there, in the war?'

He considered, rubbed his hand over his jaw. His nails were worn right down. He moved like he was real tired, like a much older guy. 'Wars,' he said. She thought he nodded.

They didn't like to talk about it, that was cool too.

They went out back and sat on the hill, suspended right up above the lake. 'It's so beautiful up here,' she said. She saw the stars in front of them reflected down in the water, black water in the spaces in between them. Pretty deep, she supposed. She asked him, 'What sign are you? Scorpio, right? I bet I'm right.'

There was enough light from the windows of the bar for her to see he was looking wary now, like he was afraid she was going to lay some heavy trip on him. 'I'm Aquarius,' she said. Even if they didn't know anything they could usually relate to that. 'Well I'm Capricorn really, but I have Aquarius rising,' she said. Then she got frightened because she didn't usually tell men that and she wondered what she was saying. She made a D major and strummed it softly, so as not to have to say anything.

His cigarette burned down and he flicked it away. It fell through the cooling night like a dying firefly. It seemed to fall a long time, like it was going to land way down in the lake.

'I guess you're who you want to be really,' she said, conceding. 'I mean, you're not from around here, right?'

'No,' he said at once.

'Where are you from?'

He gave her a slow look, and took a drink. 'Just now I'm wandering,' he said.

'Like me,' she said. 'I'm from Boston. I'm on the road,' she said. She could never say it without feeling like she was reading the words off something, like they were true but she wasn't supposed to say them about herself. 'Tomorrow I'm in Bangor: were you ever there? Did you ever go to a place called the Black Bear, a bar up in Bangor, called the Black Bear?' He shook his head.

'That's a good place,' she told him. 'That's where I'm headed.'

Not looking at him, looking across the dark shoulders of the trees at the white lights and the red lights creeping down Highway Three, she picked the melody of *Mining for Gold*. To her surprise he started to sing.

> *We are miners, hard rock miners,*
> *To the shaft house we must go . . .*

He sounded different when he was singing, sad and husky like he really did have the rock-dust in his lungs. She turned and looked at him again. She wondered if he was someone she should know. 'You're really good,' she said, 'are you a singer?'

'I can sing,' he said.

'But on the road, I mean, in clubs and stuff?'

The idea seemed to amuse him. 'No.'

'You should! People should sing, in their lives, not just people like me who get paid to sing . . . Sing some more,' she said. 'Do you like Bob Dylan?'

But just then with a big hiss of brakes and a low rumble from its empty bed, a log-truck pulled into the parking lot. Stephanie felt exposed, she didn't want to play sitting there with the headlights scything round the place, the engine coughing and hawking in the broken night. She sat still as Tom was sitting, with her hands still on the strings until she heard the driver jump out of the cab and go into the bar. When he slammed the cab door it sounded like something finishing. There was dew on the grass, her dress would be wet. She stood up and felt it. She stood with her arms down by her side, holding the guitar off the grass by the neck. 'I should go in,' she said. It sounded like she was apologizing to him for something. 'Got to get up early, get the good rides.'

He sat there like some old statue, arms round his knees. His white shirt was a pale glow in the light coming down from the bar.

'I love your shirt,' she said softly.

He said, 'Come with me.'

Her heart jumped in her chest. 'You going to Bangor? Or Belfast would do.'

He said, 'Sleep with me tonight.'

Her head spun like a firecracker. Man, he was cool. He was so cool her throat seized up that minute. She wanted to smile but she froze right up. She wanted to say yes, but how could you say yes when he just came out with it like that?

She never made love with men she didn't know. She always said no to the truck-drivers, no matter how sweet they were; the big old men in their big old trucks. But she knew one thing, she wanted to be free. Everybody had gone off to the West Coast this summer to be free – well she could be free right here in China Lake. If you couldn't be free, like right now, then it wasn't freedom at all, right?

She said to him, 'I have to get to Bangor tomorrow, anyway.'

He said, 'OK.' He looked like he'd been carved out of wood.

She stood up. She stood over him. She was ten feet

tall, and she felt herself growing bigger every second; she was shooting up into the sky. 'I have to go and get my stuff,' she said, 'say goodbye to Myra.'

He said, 'OK.'

Still he hadn't even touched her. She was so big she was going to burst. She gave a little shaky laugh. 'Well, stand up,' she said.

He stood up. He was tall, not too tall. Just right. She held her face up, wanting him to kiss her. He lifted one finger and put it gently on her lips. She closed her eyes and gave a little shiver: he was the coolest man she'd ever seen, she wanted him now, on the wet grass. His finger smelled of tobacco and something else she didn't know, a scent like some strange kind of animal. Maybe he was a hunter. He was still enough to be a hunter, he had a hunter's eyes that didn't blink, ever. She kissed his finger. She loved him with her eyes. 'Hold this for me?' she said, giving him her guitar. Now that was really free, trusting him to hold her guitar for her, her *guitar*! She went running back inside, skipping up the back stairs light as a willow leaf.

His car was just some old Pontiac, nothing fancy, cracked plastic seat-covers bleached by the sun, a pair of jeans on the back seat, gum wrappers, empty packs of Chesterfields. Smells of cigarettes, old hamburgers and fries, smells of man. Stephanie felt shy suddenly, sat with her feet up against the dash, her long skirt pulled tight around her legs. She watched the road, up and down, up and down. Wherever the road went the pine trees went too. They looked like ranks of stern black sentries. Beside the road they loomed over huge boulders, thirty-foot boulders that just sat there like someone had dropped them.

The big trucks went grinding by. That was a good word, a good line. With their banks of lights on top and all down the sides they looked like big pinball machines, towering over your car, grinding out of the deep forest. Stephanie tried to think of another line for a truck song, but she was too nervous. She looked sideways at Tom, so he wouldn't catch her looking. His jaw made her think of a hard blade, like a snowplough, like he was part of the car now, pushing through the trees. She looked round at her guitar in its cloth case on the back seat with his spare jeans tucked under it so it wouldn't slide off the seat on the curves.

A sign said WALDO COUNTY. Someone had scraped out the second O.

'How far is it?' she asked.

'First place we see,' he said.

She felt nervous a moment, thinking, Well, what did he mean by that? Was he staying close by or did he mean he was going to pull off and start in on her right there at the roadside?

He drove past a big firebreak without stopping. She calmed down. Free, she reminded herself. It's cool. Beside the road is cool too, she imagined, in the country anyhow.

'What kind of tree do you like best?' she said.

'Tree?' he said.

'Yup.'

He looked around like he'd never seen the trees before, never seen them up and down the road and all around everywhere.

'Redwood,' he said. 'Oldest tree in the world.'

She thought of California where her friends had gone. She looked around. 'I see oak, I see pine – nope – we're fresh out of redwood.' He didn't laugh. She shifted in her seat, sitting up more.

'Can we have some music?'

He looked at her, like he thought she was strange. 'Sure,' he said. 'You sing us something.'

'No,' she said. 'You.' She put her feet down and felt the peeling edge of the plastic under her with the tip of her finger. 'I've been singing all night.' He sang.

They dressed Kenny up in a uniform –

'Hey!' she said again, in surprise, delight.

And they sent him off over the sea . . .

He remembered the whole thing, every word. Sang it really well too. It should have sounded funny, a man singing it, about another man, but it didn't.

That song wasn't written down anywhere. It wasn't even on anybody's tape she'd ever sung on.

'Ahh, you saw me before some place, right?' Stephanie said.

He shook his head. He blew out smoke in a long plume as if he was about to speak, but he didn't.

'You remembered the whole thing just hearing it once?' she said. 'That's incredible. I mean, that's really amazing, you know?'

They crested another steep hill. She put out her hand and patted his arm just above the elbow, suing for his attention.

'I think you've seen me before!' she said.

He signalled and she dropped her hand. Her hand remembered the feel of his arm through the cloth. It felt soft sort of, like a kid's arm, nothing like a lifeguard's muscle at all. Probably she'd been romanticizing him in the dim light of the bar. She did that, she knew: romanticized men.

He was swinging the wheel round, turning off to the right down a deep gully. Suddenly she felt vertigo, as if he was going to tip them both down a big hole in the ground. The road was a switchback, just a logging road cut out of the hillside.

'Down here?' she said. It was dark down here.

He didn't answer.

It's cool, Stephanie reminded herself.

The road curved, climbed again, fell. She saw the lights of a town off through the trees, like neon snowflakes in the distance. The Pontiac bounced, she clung to the handle over the door.

'So,' she said, 'you know any more songs? You write your own songs?'

He threw her a sidelong glance, gave the smallest shake of his head.

'Oh you should, you have a good voice, you know.' Her voice sounded small over the engine sound. 'Everybody should have their own songs, like for when you're feeling happy, you know, or when you're kinda down ... like the blues ...'

He wasn't responding. She looked out of the window. Stiff black trees replaced each other endlessly along the road. There was something down there, she could just make them out among the trees as they came round a bend: hard-edged shapes, were those houses there?

Tom was slowing right down.

They were some mobile homes, away back under the trees. In a second she'd be able to see clearer. Logging camp, she guessed, only now it looked more permanent than that. The headlights showed aluminium siding, ribbed and dented: old paint, wintergreen, brown streaks smeared across it. Pale pink curtains at a window. Over the mutter of the car engine she heard a dog bark once, saw black shapes stirring restlessly behind chicken wire, saw their eyes give back the headlights, red and orange.

The trailers looked ancient, long ribbed things with round ends, sat there in the mud like tanks, like some kind of invasion craft. They had cables hooked up to a generator somewhere. She could see blue TV light stirring through the curtains of the one nearest the road. There was a car up on blocks, and some kind of engine lying on a couple of planks in the mud with a tarpaulin half over it. Kids' toys lay around, garbage of all kinds: she couldn't see what, she didn't want to. Everything she could see looked dirty, neglected, like you wouldn't want to touch any of it in case it gave you diseases.

She asked him, 'Is this it?'

Lord, she hoped it wasn't.

Tom reached for the key and turned the engine off.

Stephanie's heart thudded hard and low. He hadn't put the brakes on, they were rolling slowly and silently past the camp down the gradient of the road. He was staring out of his window at the trailers as if he wanted to know who was home, and thought he could see right through the walls if he stared hard enough. Stephanie looked away to the left, up the road, down the road. Nothing but trees. Nothing but black needles. But when she stared into the dark she felt like something she couldn't see was staring back. She looked up at the treetops, the black sky, but she could still feel it staring at her.

The car crept on down the road, twigs and rocks crunching under the tyres. Tom was sitting stiff as a shepherd dog, just staring into the camp. One of the camp dogs was starting to whine, setting the others off. The car felt thin as a paper shell suddenly, no protection at all from anything. 'Who is it, Tom?' asked Stephanie, her voice sounding high and squeaky in her ears. He didn't turn from the window. Nor did he stop the car. She could smell the strange smell of him again, real strong.

'Cousins of mine,' he said.

She swallowed. The dogs were barking; a light went on in one of the trailers.

'We going to stop?'

His hand found the key again and he gunned the engine back into life. 'No,' he said determinedly, and they were gone, surging down the hill, leaving the place behind, out of sight in a second behind the trees.

The feeling that something was staring lingered a way down the hill, then quickly dwindled to nothing. Stephanie felt relieved, ashamed of herself, of her imagination. She wasn't free at all, she was spooky as a Radcliffe girl at a reefer party. Goodness sakes.

She wouldn't look at Tom. She looked out of the window.

A half-mile further down they took a fork and soon came back out on the highway. She saw an orange gas sign standing up above the trees; meat trucks growling up the gradient; a pick-up loaded with churns; a tan VW van broken down, a fat guy in a windcheater with his head stuck in the hood, a frightened-looking woman with a permanent and rhinestone glasses in the passenger seat, gazing hopelessly into every car that passed. Tom drove on by.

They pulled in at a motel. 'You folks are lucky,' said a fat old man in an eyeshade, struggling up out of the basket chair where he had been drowsing in front of the late show. 'I was just about to close up for the night.'

He beamed widely, showing bare gums, turning a dog-eared register towards them and taking the cap off a ballpoint pen. 'Mr and Mrs – ?'

She looked at Tom.

'We ain't married,' he said softly, flatly.

She saw the old man stiffen like a startled chicken. She looked at Tom warily, astonished herself. Cool was cool, but you couldn't go letting it all hang out like that in front of some old country boy, he'd probably call the fuzz. But the old man was laughing soundlessly, his shoulders shaking. He winked and gestured at Tom approvingly with the pen. 'What are ya, brother and sister, is that it?' He winked, mugging at Stephanie. 'You're his sister, right?' He nodded, smiling broadly, loving every minute. ·

She grabbed Tom's arm and squeezed it. 'Yes,' she said firmly.

The old man thought this was even funnier. He wheezed and slapped Tom on the shoulder as he gave him their key, directed them across the yard to a clapboard cabin.

'Go on with ya!'

Stephanie turned the light on, but Tom turned it off again. He bore down on her, herding her on to the bed. She dropped her backpack. In the sick, pale light through the drapes his face looked intent, heedless, blind. She felt herself swelling again, this time beneath him, her breasts rising up to fill his hands. She was full of herself, filled with hunger for him, with his hunger for her. His mouth was hot, the back of his neck hot where she clasped his mouth to hers. Was he sick? Did he have a fever? He was fiery, furious, writhing in her arms. She clung to him as to a frightened horse: they plunged and reared together, sweat coursing down his sides. Veins stood out in strange patterns on his neck and forehead. He cried out in a language she did not know.

In the morning she woke feeling sore, ragged, proud. She could smell him on her, all around her in the sagging motel bed. She turned to him but he was not in the bed beside her. She almost cried out, she felt so desolate, so deprived. The power of the feeling frightened her. Then she saw him sitting in his pants and no shirt, backwards on a chair at the window, smoking a cigarette. Naked, daring, Stephanie got out of bed and put her arms round him from behind, kissed the back of his neck. He hadn't opened the drapes. He was staring through the gap between them as if there was something special he was hunting, moose or deer, up the ridge behind the yard. She nestled her cheek against his, peering over his shoulder. There was nothing there she could see, just brown trees. It was broad day out there, she'd slept half the morning away.

'Well hallo,' she said.

He reached up a hand, patted her bare arm. Didn't look round. She felt sweaty, stale. 'I have to shower,' she said. 'So do you.' She pressed her fingertip against his naked shoulder. His skin was still warm, as if he had been working hard. 'Does this place run to breakfast?'

His voice was low, steady. 'I want you to come with me today,' he said.

'I have to get to Bangor today,' she said.

He looked at her then. His blue eyes were opaque, preoccupied, her problems were nothing.

'I can go that way,' he said. 'I have folks there, some-place.'

It was fine. Still something made her hesitate. Not that she didn't trust him, only – only something.

'Well, OK, only I have to get to Bangor today, then I can maybe get a gig at the Black Bear tomorrow. You know where that is? The Black Bear?'

His face was impervious as the face of the Angel Gabriel. He looked at her like a big shot record producer she met once at someone else's show. 'I'll take you to Bangor,' he said.

'Well, fine,' she said, uncomfortably.

She wished he would come and talk to her while she was in the shower, but he didn't look like he would think of it and you couldn't just ask. She dried herself on the little scrap of hard towel, then dressed in her road shirt and jeans. The old man was pottering around in his singlet and overalls; he chuckled and greeted them courteously, made them a pot of coffee thick as creosote.

'You sleep OK, little lady?' he asked, treating her to another exhibition of his gums. He seemed to think she and Tom were staying there expressly for his entertainment.

She sat in the car with the door open, her feet sticking outside, tuning her guitar. She looked at the motel, she saw those were blueberry bushes around the cabins. Usually that would have cheered her up; today she was not so happy. She wondered very much where they were going. And she had a problem: she didn't like a man to take her for granted, but she didn't want to start a fight and spoil their last hours together. He was someone special, she was already writing a song about him – two songs – in her head.

He came and got in the car, started up. She put her legs inside, slammed the car door. She kissed his cheek. The late morning sun was the colour of corn oil through the raw branches of the trees. A rustbucket pick-up came clanking and squealing past them as they bumped out on to the road. Stephanie held the guitar upright on her lap, trying to keep the head from banging on the windshield as they bounced and swayed.

Tom glanced at her. 'Put that thing in the back seat,' he said, coldly.

'Tom? Are you mad? What's wrong, is something wrong?'

That wasn't very cool, nagging him like that. It upset her when someone spoke slightingly about her guitar.

'Nothing's wrong,' he said. Either he was mad, or he was sick. He sounded short of breath. His face was dark, dark shadows under his eyes and over his cheeks.

His hair that was as blond as cornsilk looked dark too, and coarser, maybe it was greasy. Maybe sex made his hair greasy.

She lifted her guitar carefully over the back of the seat, trying to reach the cloth case with her hand, her fingers, she couldn't do it. She abandoned it and sat round straight again, facing the front. She reached up and touched him on the cheek. His beard was strong, he hadn't shaved this morning.

She saw then where they were headed. Off the highway, back up the logging road. Back up towards that place where his cousins lived. In daylight it looked perfectly normal up here, pine, oaks and maples, pigeons flying overhead, road signs all dented and scratched up from buckshot, nothing spooky at all.

At that moment they passed something dead, something quite big, it looked like. Stephanie glimpsed a staring eye like a deer's, four spindly legs at bad angles, a great deal of crimson blood. She flinched.

'I'm going to have to leave you for a while,' said Tom suddenly. His eyes looked haggard, unfocused. There was sweat on his face like last night. Suddenly she was aware of the powerful heat coming off him, filling the car.

'Tom, what is it? Are you feeling OK?'

But he shrugged off her hand, muttering. And then they were at the camp. He stopped the car with a jerk, reached his arm across her to open the door; he was bundling her outside.

'Tom? Tom, please!'

The last thing she saw of him was his grey face looking up at her through the dusty window of the Pontiac as he slammed the passenger door, looking up at her open-mouthed, his head lopsided like he was under water.

'Tom! Tom, wait! My guitar!'

She stood holding her hand out grabbing at the empty air, watching the Pontiac weave back on to the road and roar away uphill. She cursed in alarm and shock. He had her guitar, she had to wait here, couldn't move from this spot until he came back. No, she wouldn't think what if he didn't. She was despondent at her own helplessness.

A bad smell hit her nostrils. There was a cage of goats next to the cage of dogs, both ankle-deep in filth. The dogs were climbing on each other, rearing up against the wire with their whole bodies, trying to get at her. She didn't much care for dogs. She also had that sensation again that something she couldn't see was staring at her from somewhere. She looked around, combing her hair frantically back from her face with her fingers. She looked into the encampment, over the blackberry bushes.

There were babies watching her, children, two, four, six of them. They were practically naked, streaked and spotted and blotted with dirt, their noses running. They all had huge nostrils. Stephanie came round the bushes and approached them. The eldest looked to be a little girl about eight, skinny as a post, her hair matted in tangles and tufts. She had an unravelling sweater that hardly reached over her dirty little pot belly, and a skirt the colour of mud. Her feet were bare.

'Whatcha want?' said the little girl, screwing up her eyes.

'Nothing,' said Stephanie. 'I don't want anything.' What was she going to say? 'I just have to wait here a while for someone.' It didn't sound good, even to her own ears. She looked nervously at the trailers. The door on the nearest one was open; it looked dark inside, she couldn't see anyone in there.

'Who you waitin' for?' asked the little girl. There was something funny about all their heads, their skulls were very long, as though they had an extra bit on the back. Their eyes were all the same colour, the ones close enough to see. They were a sort of yellow colour, like a glass of beer.

'You waitin' for that man?'

'Yes,' said Stephanie. She didn't know where to put her hands. He'd left her here without her pack, without a thing. Goddamn him!

'Who was that man?' asked a little boy, his hair cut so short he was almost bald. Stephanie took a breath, trying to breathe through her mouth, trying to shape up to all this. She still had the feeling she was being watched. 'Well, he's your cousin, I guess.'

This meant nothing to them.

'His name's Tom,' she said. They just stared.

There was a black dog with them, some kind of crazy mongrel mix. The girl pointed to it, it was bigger than she was. 'This is Dory,' she said. 'She's a dog.' She looked up at Stephanie as if for approval.

A young woman came to the open trailer door. She was wearing long, wrinkled yellow woollen underwear under a grubby mauve nylon dress and dirty sneakers on her feet, laced with string. She held her hand to her face, propping up her hair, which was flopping out of a home permanent. It had been violently bleached and was growing out dark. She had the same nose as the kids. And her eyes were yellow. Goodness sake, these were genuine hillbillies, just like Woody Guthrie sang about, that were in Oklahoma. Or was it Kentucky? Even as her disgust faded Stephanie began to feel sorry for them. She saw herself back in Boston at the Blue Jar: 'This is a song I wrote for a hillbilly family I met up in Maine . . .'

'Nadine,' said the young woman, 'you best tell Carter.'

The eldest little girl ran off behind the trailer.

'Hallo,' said Stephanie, with a sympathetic trust-me smile.

'What you want?' said the woman.

'Your cousin Tom just brought me,' she said. 'He'll be back in a little while. He had to go off somewhere, I don't know where he was going, he didn't say.'

She heard herself babbling and stopped abruptly.

'Don't know no Tom.'

'I don't know his other name,' said Stephanie apologetically. 'Blond hair. Beautiful shirt, white shirt. Drives a Pontiac, it's brown, with orange hubcaps. He said he's got cousins here.'

The woman was no older than her, yet some of the kids were probably hers. She was standing there behind them as if she'd go for an axe if Stephanie moved any closer. She was looking at Stephanie like she was the nut, as if she had two heads, as if she was some old dinosaur that had crawled out of the woods. Probably they were all retarded. Jesus, what a terrible life.

The woman didn't seem to be worried. 'You have ta come in,' she announced, as if it were a fact of life. She disappeared inside her long immobile mobile home. Taking a deep breath, Stephanie stepped up after her, Dory and the kids following.

Inside, the sense of invisible eyes on her did not decrease.

The first thing she saw was an unmade bed, a greasy quilt and comforter tumbled on it. There was an ashtray spilled on the quilt, an empty beer can lying at the foot of the mattress, up against the footboard. The place smelled of cigarettes and beer and animals, obviously it wasn't just Dory that slept in here. There were Coke bottles everywhere, paper sacks bulging with un-considered garbage, piles of newspapers, some of them old. So old they were brown. Alongside the bed was a chest of drawers, two drawer fronts missing, limp clothes dangling out. You could see no one had cleaned the windows for years.

It was horrible that anyone should be so poor as to have to live like this. The government really should find them proper homes. She wondered how long they had been living here, for ever it looked like. Where had they come from originally? Maybe their parents had been transients, she wondered if they knew any songs. She couldn't see a banjo, an accordion, even a kazoo. Nothing but the TV flickering on the chest. A woman in lace and a man in buckskins were arguing playfully on the porch of an airless frontier set. *If you think I'm marrying you, Mr Grace, you can think again!*

'Sit down,' the hostess said.

Stephanie sat at the head of the table. The kids immediately took the rest of the seats, Dory too, squashed up on one chair with one of the babies.

'My name's Stephanie,' said Stephanie.

They all sat looking at her, three of them sitting in the same attitude: right elbows on the table, sucking the edges of their hands. The table was littered with dirty plates, an oily black handgun, a ketchup bottle, a mangled Red Indian doll of bright red polythene with one leg missing. No child claimed the doll. Stephanie sat tight, not wanting to touch anything. Everything smelled just awful. The woman was opening a cupboard under the sink. 'You want some coffee?' she said.

'Yes please,' said Stephanie. 'That would be very nice.'

There were clattering footsteps. Nadine was back. She had brought Carter with her. Carter was very tall.

He stooped, avoiding the electric heater on the wall above the door. He didn't look so old either, though older than the nameless woman at the cupboard, plus he was almost bald. He wore a black cord shirt with the sleeves rolled up, a pair of jeans that had once been blue. He had the yellow eyes, the gaping nostrils. What hair he had was a dark grey that looked like motor oil rather than age. It hung down in straggling hanks from little asymmetrical patches around his head. It did not disguise the shape of his skull. The woman's husband or her brother? Or both?

When he smiled Stephanie saw his teeth, and wished she hadn't.

'This is her,' said the woman, rising from the floor, her hands still empty.

'You must be Carter,' said Stephanie.

Carter said nothing, nodded, smiled vacantly. Stephanie wondered if there was something seriously wrong with him, but his eyes were very steady on her, unblinking, inscrutable, like Tom's eyes. Hurry up, Tom. Behind her the TV made a squeaky burst of helter-skelter discords, slithering strings, racing brass.

'I don't suppose you get many visitors way out here,' said Stephanie.

Carter spoke. 'Not too many.' His voice was high and musical, like a child or a whimsical old woman. He went to where the woman was standing in the kitchenette and put his arm around her, pinning her arms to her sides. 'Get our visitor a drink?' he said, not taking his eyes off Stephanie. ·

The woman was indifferent to his grip. 'I was just goin' t'make coffee . . .' she said, lethargically.

'What a shame,' said Carter to Stephanie. 'We're all out of coffee. You'll have to have a real drink.'

He fetched out an unlabelled bottle of something clear

as water and thumped it on the table. Stephanie looked at it, looked at the icebox. 'Maybe a Coke, if you have one.'

The couple looked at each other as if they didn't know what it was. Stephanie would have said water but she didn't trust their water. 'I don't need anything, really,' she said. 'I'm fine.'

Carter leaned in front of Nadine and poured an inch of the colourless spirit into a plastic glass. It had a chipped decal of Donald Duck on the side. Stephanie smiled weakly. Be free. The drink smelled of nothing, nothing at all. She took a sip, inhaled sharply and choked, her throat gripped by claws of fire.

'Good, heh?' Carter said.

He did not sit down, stood leaning on the sink with his arm around the woman, smiling his hideous smile. Stephanie took another drink. This time it went down pretty easy. Her throat was completely numb already. 'I mustn't drink too much,' she explained, 'I have to keep a clear head for tonight, I have a date. I mean a gig. In Bangor, at the Black Bear. Maybe you know it?'

Carter leaned forward again. He topped up her glass.

'I'm a folk singer,' she said, drinking. She smiled bashfully at the children around the table, at their probable parents. 'Some of us think it's terrible the way the old songs are just being forgotten, like the old Kentucky miners' songs, maybe you know – ' She drank, nodding. 'And blues. Nowadays it's all Tin Pan Alley, right?'

She smiled. They didn't understand her.

'The Hit Parade. You know? Some guy in an office writing songs for money.'

She drank.

'It's chaos now!' she said.

At some point during this she thought she had turned around in her chair and watched TV for several minutes. She had a distinct memory of doing it, of watching two men chase each other through an obvious studio swamp and pointing it out, laughing. She remembered doing it, but she did not know when she could have done it. She was sat facing the table again now, the way she had been all along. Perhaps she had hallucinated it, the way people said you did when you took drugs. Perhaps the drink was drugged. Her glass was empty. The children and their dog were sitting motionless, staring at her. Her body was quite relaxed. There was a warm fug in the trailer; it wasn't unpleasant at all, nothing was watching her, there wasn't anything out there. It seemed to have got dark outside pretty early. Where was Tom? Where was her guitar? Her glass was full.

She saw Carter standing in front of her, drinking a bottle of Coke. She finished her drink. So did Carter. Then he held the bottle horizontally between his hands and broke it in half. He snapped it just as if it was made of sugar. Stephanie cried out, no one else reacted at all. Something outside scratched on the aluminium wall, scratch scratch. Those newspapers, she remembered, seeing some by the door. Some of them must be older than the trailer. Some of them were brown as old leaves. Her head was whirling. Carter grinned, letting the big chunks of glass fall spinning from his hands on to the table, clatter to the floor among the garbage. His nostrils gaped like drains. His hands were completely uninjured. He wiped them on his hips and went outside.

The woman went past Stephanie's chair, pushing her hair behind her ear. She opened a drawer in the chest and pulled out something long and white. She held it up to show Stephanie. It was a long white dress, shiny like satin, like a wedding dress. It was soiled like everything round here. Where the hell was Tom? Why was the woman showing her her wedding dress? Were they even married, the two of them? 'Pretty,' Stephaine said, humouring her.

'Put it on,' said the woman.

'Me? No.'

'You hafta,' the woman said. Stephanie could see her thinking before she spoke. 'Carter says the women hafta wear the dress.'

In terror Stephanie slammed down her glass. She grabbed hold of the seat of the chair. 'No! No!'

The woman picked the gun up from the table. She handled it loosely, as if she thought it was some kind of kitchen utensil.

'Ya hafta put it on,' she said.

Stephanie stood up. Time jerked. She was changing into the dress, there with them all watching with their yellow eyes. The dress was tight and smelled of cheap soap. 'You're not going to shoot me,' she heard herself saying. The woman said nothing, just stood there with the gun stuck on to the end of her arm. Stephanie was trying to fasten buttons behind her back. Her fingers were frankfurters. She was very drunk and very scared. The woman pointed the gun, motioning her to go out-side.

They were all out there, women and men both, in bib overalls and shapeless mud-coloured dresses, bizarre make-up on their faces, lipstick and eye-shadow in the wrong places. Their heads were long and their eyes were yellow and their noses were snouts. Carter was with them. One of the other men had a flashlight; there was a fog, you could hardly see the trees all around. Stephanie's eyes prickled as if the fog was irritating them. Perhaps she had been watching TV in the trailer all afternoon and night had now come.

'Tom!' she shouted. 'Tom!'

Gently they ushered her through the wood. The children followed, Dory pattering alongside. From behind the next trailer Stephanie could hear a noise she recognized, fear focusing her senses, as a grindstone. It was the continuous scraping sound of someone pedalling, stopping as if to check the blade, pedalling again.

The shed was older than any trailer in the world. There was a rotten old well beside it too, under a sumac bare as a bone. The well-cover lay cracked in two in a drift of red leaves. The shed was half-collapsed, inside it had ancient junk, farm stuff, chains, scythes. The place was lit by rows and rows of candles, big black ones standing in catering-size syrup cans and oil cans, soup cans, dogfood cans. There was a powerful ammonia smell, like industrial cleaning fluid. Stephanie saw bones on the dirt floor. She looked away.

Carter's twin brother climbed off the grindstone and came towards her around the block that stood in the middle of the shed. The block was waist-high, long and completely empty. Its wooden top was scrubbed raw. It looked quite clean apart from some dark stains. When they stretched her out on it Stephanie tried to pull away. She was shouting and screaming. They held her head. She could see small tendrils of dark fog curling through the holes in the ruined roof.

The women daubed paint on her face. They were chanting low, mumbling something all together in the back of their throats. Their hair was matted with dirt into slabs like tobacco. Stephanie was beside herself. She heard herself sobbing, whining, pleading, but they were holding her tight by the wrists and ankles. Suddenly Stephanie jerked her head free and vomited straight out sideways, clear liquor and clots of motel eggs and doughnuts. They grabbed her again, someone cursing. She heard high, thin voices laughing wheezily, felt them tug as if they were trying to pull her in quarters. She thought of the Coke bottle. She was breathing hard, snivelling, puke in her nose, she thought she was going to throw up again.

The chanting continued though it sounded faint, even half-hearted like prayers at high school, as if they were only doing it for Carter's sake, or someone's sake, because they were told to, because they always did. When she saw the knife Carter was holding, a big chopping knife with a long pointed blade, she made a shrill sound and shouted sharply, 'Oh, God, no!' In disgust, appalled that this was all life had held for her. She felt moisture seep up the fabric of the white dress. Her bladder had let go.

'*Escouriath nemeth hi jevelion!*' shouted Carter.

There was more, nonsense language, what he was shouting didn't mean anything.

A man took a handful of Stephanie's hair and pulled her head back over the end of the block. Upside down she could see the women, their painted faces like clowns pretending to be whores. She could see Nadine picking her nose. The blade was cold on her throat, then hot as it pierced the skin and blood began to seep out along it, spilling down both sides of her neck.

When the creature came in it slammed through the doorway, sending jars cascading from a high shelf and snapping one of the posts with its shoulders. It cleared the block lengthways at a spring, candles flying in all directions, and knocked Carter to the floor. Stephanie saw it pass over from underneath, it was like a long dog with long hair and no tail. Above it the dark clouds were writhing in at the holes in the roof. Then, abruptly, her head and hands were free. She jerked up away from the thing that had landed on the floor behind her snarling, gnawing savagely at something. Carter was shouting, gurgling. People were moaning, yammering in high voices.

Stephanie kicked out and freed her feet, slid from the block, banging her hip. The din was incredible; Dory and the newcomer were fighting. Stephanie could see them, their bodies surging and slamming down beyond the far end of the block. Dory was getting the worst of it. She was squealing, a horrible, thin sound like air rushing from the valve of a rubber tyre. The creature was standing up on its back legs, Dory hanging from its mouth. It was cuffing her savagely. There was a gun-shot, incredibly loud; Carter's woman was shrieking, waving her gun around. The thing threw Dory aside and lunged at her.

Stephanie turned to flee. The babies were at her feet, reaching up to her with little white hands. Suddenly the shed was filled with black dogs – someone had opened the pen. Some of the dogs seemed to have breasts like a human woman, more like chimpanzees than dogs. Stephanie kicked out, shrieking, and fought her way outside. She flung a glance back over her shoulder as she fled. They were all going for it, heedless of its strength and size. Some of them were on fire. She ran into the road, crying, sobbing incoherently, blood splashing from the cut on her neck and dripping down her white dress and around her bare feet as she fled through the fog. Blackberry bushes loomed. She swerved and ran out into the road.

'Tom!' she shouted. 'Tom!' There was no one about, only confused screaming and howling at her back, behind the trailers. Gasping, she staggered up the road.

Up around the bend there was a car parked, facing uphill. A brown car, a Pontiac. She ran up to it, sobbing and swearing. It was just left there like he hadn't even been anywhere. All the windows were closed. There was no one inside.

She grabbed the driver's door handle. The door opened and she fell inside, blood dripping on the seats, slamming the door behind her, banging all the locks down. His clothes were on her seat, white shirt, jacket and jeans; she was kneeling on them. She crawled into the back seat, found her guitar and held it up in front of her like a shield; there was nothing else. She could see his shoes and socks on the floor by the pedals. Nothing happened. No one came after her.

She pulled his jacket around her shoulders. It smelled of him. She rubbed her face, smearing blue paint on her hand. She clapped her hand to her cut. It felt long, but not deep. If she held her chin down, maybe it would hold closed.

She panted and cried and shivered. A dog ran out into the road from the bushes and she shrieked. It looked around in all directions excitedly and dashed straight back in again. She could hear a muffled, heavy crashing as if the shed was being pounded severely with a big, soft weight.

Stephanie felt she was about to throw up again. She looked around, wound down the window fast and vomited out of it. Then she wound it up again and collapsed back in the seat. Her head was pounding. Adrenalin or no, she was still extremely drunk. Poisoned. She tried to stay awake, but her eyes kept closing. She was jerking herself out of a series of dreams, Nadine trying to strangle her, a big, jolly fat man with a face like Santa dangling a length of something dripping cockroaches in her face; she was a little girl again and her mother was beckoning her to follow her along the crossbar of a goalpost. Eventually, still holding her guitar, she slept.

She did not know how long she was asleep. She only knew her eyes were open again and the sun was hammering at her eyeballs. The sun was high, and Tom was standing there holding the car door open.

In the silence Stephanie could hear the TV still playing in the deserted trailer. A woman's voice was excitedly recommending Kolynos. The sound was way over there, but it drilled into Stephanie's head. Her throat was dry from the drink and sore from screaming. She nearly screamed again with shock. Tom's face was covered in dark brown blood, it was caked around his mouth and on his hands. 'Tom! Tom ...' she croaked.

He leaned in over the driver's seat, took the guitar away from her and put it in the front passenger seat, on top of his clothes. He looked into her eyes like a veterinarian looking at a pet. He looked like he hadn't slept. He was wearing a plaid shirt that was too small for him and a pair of greasy jeans torn in the crotch. He took hold of her head gently, spanning her paint-smudged face with his dirty hand. He turned her head to the left and then to the right. It hurt. Blood seeped from her cut. He touched her neck and she flinched.

She kept saying, 'Where have you been?'

He didn't reply. He was a soldier. He let go of her and sat down in his seat, shut the door. His head and shoulders blocked out the sun. He lit a cigarette and started the car. The engine noise made Stephanie's brain throb in her skull. She could smell the strange smell of him, the blood on him. Now he was here his presence seemed to fill the car; she couldn't think what to say, what to think. She was wearing his jacket. Her clothes were left behind in the trailer. She looked back among the trees as he drove down the hill. Nothing was moving there.

'They tried to kill me, Tom!'

Her voice sounded foolish and feeble. She was starting to cry again. She swallowed hard, trembling.

'Are you hurt?' she said. 'You're all – '

He shook his head, not looking round. He wasn't
hurt or else he wasn't saying. He wasn't saying anything. Stephanie felt a surge of panic.

'What was that thing?'

It was like a creature in a dream. Flashes of drunken
memory, like stills from a movie, scrambled, meaningless. It was all like a dream. She had heard the TV
chirruping, a crow calling harshly, echoing above the
noise when he started the engine. Underneath everything was a big hollow space that nothing in the world
would fit.

'Bear, I guess,' said Tom around his cigarette.

'No. No. Tom, it wasn't a bear.'

'Wolf, then, I guess.'

It was because of her he was making like he didn't
care, because she was a stranger. She was ignorant of
things that happened in the backwoods. Life and death
were different there and he wasn't even going to try to
explain it to her. She wanted to scream at him, 'Why
did you leave me there?', and she was too afraid of him
now. He wasn't cool, he was made of stone.

The big, dark space moved away, closed itself off;
they left it behind. Stephanie felt exhausted, she felt
numb. She looked at the back of his head. He looked
like someone she didn't even know.

'We going to the cops?' she asked, very quietly.

He didn't answer. Maybe he didn't hear. She couldn't
say it again.

The bright day opened wide above the road.

Stephanie sat up and reached for her guitar. She
pulled it to her over the back of the seat. Her backpack
was in the trunk, but she didn't dare ask him to stop so

she could get it. Her cut throbbed. She shut her eyes and her head spun. She opened them. 'I need a doctor,' she said. Her voice shook. It was her last demand.

He pushed the gearshift. Sitting forward, she could see his hand. His nails on the stick were long, thickly rimmed with brown.

'I'll take you to Bangor,' he said.

He turned his head and smiled at her, a tight, meaningless smile of dried blood cracking around the white stick of his cigarette. She felt a wave of cold come from him over the back seat. She could feel it against her skin, the cold.

'I have folks in Bangor,' he said.

ANCIENT OF DAYS

Charles Stross

———————

There were less than two weeks to go until Christmas, and flakes of snow were settling silently on the window-sill. Sue leaned against the wall next to the casement so that her breath formed patterns of condensation on the glass. The red glow of the newly lit street lights turned the falling snow to blood, drifting down across the deserted alleyway behind the lab. She blinked slowly. Was it her imagination or was there a new shadow behind the dumpbins? Holding her breath so that it would not fog the glass, she stared out of the window. The shadow disappeared and she breathed out. Then she undid the catch and swung the window open in invitation. 'You're late,' she said.

The shadow reappeared in front of her, resolved into the shape of a man shrouded in a donkey jacket against the cold. 'Rush hour traffic,' he said, his voice somehow deadened by the softness that settled on every surface. 'Help me in?'

Sue extended a hand. He took it and levered himself up and over the sill. He swung himself into the room and dropped to the floor, looking around as he did so. 'You're wet,' said Sue. 'Did you bring any equipment?'

He nodded and held up a small briefcase. She looked at his face. Something wasn't quite right. 'You look strained,' she said as she shut the window.

He nodded tiredly. 'I am not as young as I used to be, Sally. If you knew what I had to do to get here – ',

'I can guess, and as for the name I'm called Sue,' she said, a trifle too sharply. He stared at her for a moment then nodded and forced a smile. The shape of his cheek-bones turned it into something hollow and unconvincing.

'Please accept my apologies then – Sue. It's late and I've got a job to do and we've all been under considerable stress recently – '

'Accepted. Just remember who it was who laid their neck on the line to get a job here . . .'

'It is noted,' he said curtly.

'No it's not!' she flashed. 'This unit is licensed to work with pathogenic organisms. They wanted a blood sample and insisted upon giving me a series of vaccinations – '

'Ah, I'm sure it hurt.' He shook his head, oblivious to the finer points of immunological stress. 'But in view of what you found that's immaterial now, isn't it?'

She turned away angrily and busied herself with an untidy pile of papers that sat on the desk in the corner by the centrifuge.

'Believe me when I say that this could be the greatest threat we have ever encountered,' he said softly. 'Greater than any ancient encounter with half-glimpsed horrors . . .'

She nodded slowly, wondering if she had it in herself to forgive him the slight. 'You might have a point,' she said. 'But only time will tell.' She rummaged through a drawer in search of a paper-clip, bound the documents together, and slid them out of the way. Then she walked to the battered metal locker and removed a creased lab coat. 'Let's make a start on it, shall we?'

Kristoph grinned and removed his donkey jacket. 'Let's,' he said. He opened his briefcase and pulled out a pair of disposable plastic gloves. 'Now who shall we apportion the blame to? How about some animal rights activists? Or shall we make it look like an industrial job this time, do you think?'

Kristoph was not his real name. He had no real birth certificate, although he had carried several. He was much older than Sue, and he had lived through interesting times. He had lost a large part of his heart on the Eastern Front, so that fifty years later he still wondered if he could ever be whole again: he had survived the decades since the war by auctioning his soul at Checkpoint Charlie, running jobs for the Stasi and the CIA and another less familiar Organization. With the collapse of the Wall he had been set free to wander, and finally to turn his hand to Family business. As he prepared for the job in hand he whistled a half-forgotten marching song to himself.

'Will you stop doing that?' asked Sue.

He glanced up from his kit and caught her eye. 'Why?'

'Anyone would think you were an old Nazi,' she said.

'Oh.' He glanced down again so that she wouldn't see his smile. *Now* he remembered what the tune was. 'Time flies,' he said, clipping the briefcase shut. Then he stood up. 'How long have you been here then?' he asked.

Sue walked to the window and stared out of it again. 'Two years,' she said, 'but that's only in this job. I had to go to one of their universities to qualify for it. My family – '

'Demonstrated a laudable degree of foresight,' opined Kristoph.

'In this day and age anything else condemns you to life as a menial. Times have changed. If you want to get ahead you've got to play by their rules. The net's too tight.'

Kristoph, who knew better than she, held his silence.

'I've heard all the old tales,' Sue continued. 'My parents are really keen on them. But things aren't the same, are they? It's hard to maintain a sense of . . . community . . . while all around us . . . '

Kris stood up. 'I think you'd better show me to the offices. We don't want to start too late; this could take all night.'

Sue turned slowly, looking around as if she had forgotten where the door was. When she opened it she glanced swiftly down the corridor outside. 'Clear,' she called over her shoulder as she slipped out of the basement laboratory. Kristoph looked around curiously as he followed her through the deserted passages of the department.

The concrete floor was scuffed and dirty and the whitewashed walls had seen better days. Fluorescent lights flickered overhead, casting what Kristoph saw as a gangrenous blue-green glare across the crowded bulletin boards. An ancient ultra-centrifuge keened to itself in a shadowy niche as they hurried past. Sue pushed through two pairs of fire doors and turned a corner on a concealed staircase. 'Meet me in room D-11 if we become separated,' she said. 'It's two flights up. There's a walkway from the corridor opposite it to the Geophysics block if you need a quick getaway.'

'I don't think that will be necessary,' he said quietly.

'You know there are security guards?' she asked, pausing on a landing halfway between floors.

'Whatever makes you think we'll encounter any trouble?' he replied, looking her straight in the eyes.

She appeared to be slightly flustered. 'Nothing,' she said. 'I just thought you spook types always liked to know a way out of a tight corner – '

Kris held her gaze for a moment then nodded. 'The

ones you read about are the ones who get caught,' he said. 'Don't worry about me, Sue. I can take care of myself.' He waved a hand in an abrupt cutting motion. 'Carry on. We haven't got all night.'

Presently they arrived outside a locked door. 'This is it,' she said.

Kristoph bent over the lock for a couple of minutes, fiddling with a set of fine-tipped pliers. 'You've got to be careful to leave all the *right* signs,' he murmured. 'Otherwise the Polizei get suspicious. Is there a vending machine anywhere near here?'

'Sure,' said Sue. 'Why?'

'Get me a cup of coffee please,' he said. 'White, no sugar. We're going to be here a while.'

The lock snicked open and he turned the door handle as she walked away. The room within was darkened. He pushed the door open and reached around it for the light switch, every nerve straining for signs of potential trouble. But there was nothing amiss: it was just another night-time office, plastic covers drooping over the copier and word processors. He breathed out slowly, willing the muscles in his arms to relax as he looked around. There were papers in every in-tray, filing cabinets full of pre-publication data: he rubbed the skeleton keys in his pocket. The soul of a research group lay exposed to his midnight fingers, so prosaic an institution that it seemed ridiculous to connect it to some hideous, numinous threat to the survival of the Kin. But that was what Ancient of Days had said – and Kris knew full well, with the bitterness of experience, that when Ancient of Days spoke, everyone listened.

Kris went to work with a precision that was born of long experience. First he closed the venetian blinds; then he switched on the photocopier and went to work on the first of the filing cabinets as it warmed up. His briefcase he placed upon a nearby desk, opening it to reveal two reams of lightweight copier paper: *Why bother with toys like Minox spy-cams*, his trainers had once explained, *when any well-run office provides all the tools you need?* He whistled as he worked, in an effort to forget the snow on the window-ledge. If it wasn't for that damned snow, with its burden of remembered horrors preying on his mind, he might even admit that he was happy.

There was a knock on the door. Kristoph spun round then relaxed, recognizing that it was Sue: a slight catch in her breath and the way she shifted her balance on the floor outside gave her away. 'Come in,' he said, turning back to examine the suspension files in the top drawer of the first cabinet.

She opened the door. 'Your coffee,' she said, placing the cup next to his case. 'Any idea how long you'll be?'

He yawned, baring teeth as white as those of an actor in a toothpaste commercial. 'You tell me. If there's not much to lift from the project files, then . . .'

'You're in the wrong cabinet for the research data,' she observed, looking over his shoulder. 'That's all Departmental admin. The interesting stuff is filed in the drawers marked Homoeobox Research Group. Funded by the Human Genome Project, natch.'

'It's all Greek to me,' said Kris, turning to the indicated cabinet. *Greece, yes . . . and the partisans in the hill country . . .* he stamped on the memory. *Maybe I've been around too long*, he thought bleakly. *The generation gap is widening all the time.*

'I shouldn't worry about it,' she replied, sitting down in a chair in front of one of the word processors. 'Change overtakes us all. This shit is so new it's all developed since I left school.'

'How long ago was that?' Kristoph asked, picking out the first file and carrying it across to the copier.

'Ten years since I took A levels,' she said, 'then a BA degree, MPhil and research for the past two years. I'm in a different field, though.' She rolled her chair round, craning her head back to stare at the ceiling. 'Polysaccharide chemistry, not ontological genetics. They've made huge breakthroughs in the past ten years, you know. How long is it since *you* were at school?'

Kris laughed. 'I was never at school,' he said, stacking papers face down in the feeder tray. 'At least not as you know it. I learned to read and write in primary school with the other children, but then the dictator's men came. Ideology was in the driver's seat, and there were secret police – night and mist – and identity papers to contend with. We couldn't move as freely as we did before all this modern nonsense. I went into the army at sixteen because I was a young fool and thought it was a good way to get away from home, to lose myself among millions of other young men; I didn't understand about humans then.'

He fell silent for a while, watching the sharp-edged shadows moving on the wall behind the photocopier. *I don't think I should have told her that.* 'We suffered in that war,' he said quietly. 'I don't know how many died; there's no way of telling. But all through that area – the pain – '

'Then you must be, what? Seventy years old?' Sue asked. She wasn't spinning the chair any more: she was staring at him, her face a sharply pointed question, hungry for answers. 'And still, you – '

'Still,' he said. 'I'm not even settled down with a family. If I was human I would be an old man, now. Retired to tend my bed of roses.' Abruptly, he leaned forward and grabbed the stack of ejected documents, stuffed them back into their file and returned them to their drawer in exchange for another bundle. 'They created the roses, you know? The humans. They bred them, from earlier plants.'

'I know,' she said. 'Just as now they're trying to re-design themselves to fit their own desires. It's an interesting preoccupation . . .'

Kris shuddered at the sight of her expression. 'Pass the next file. What's your real name?' he asked without looking up. She told him.

'Well,' he said, running his long, thin tongue along his lips as he stared at the control panel, 'you would do well to remember who you are, Sue, and think carefully about where your loyalties lie. We're letting them play with fire, and you are sitting very close to the hearth. There are those who would say that if you were to be burned it would be only your own fault.'

She walked away from him, towards the window. 'I say that as a friend,' he added. 'There are other groups at work as well . . .'

She turned round then, and Kris felt himself frozen by the black spike of her gaze. He stared back at her unwaveringly. Something very ancient and very chilly passed between them and he made a small gesture with his right hand, a relic of an upbringing in backwoods Silesia. Behind them the photocopier whined on, un-attended in its shadowy corner. 'You don't know what you're talking about,' she said, her face relaxing into a shape that was both alien and intimately familiar to Kristoph. 'Believe me, genetic manipulation is perfectly safe,' she added, baring inhumanly sharp teeth at him. 'You can tell that to Ancient of Days. It's safe as stones as long as we're in control. Safe as stones . . .'

Later, as soon as it could be arranged, five strangers

gathered in impromptu committee. There were no validated safe houses available in the city at present, and Ancient of Days had insisted upon full security precautions being observed: therefore they met in the place normally maintained for serious emergencies, where interruption was unlikely.

The city sewer systems were more than a century old, and a lengthy programme of refurbishment had been under way for ten years now. Old brick-lined tunnels crumbled gently beneath the pounding wheels of trucks and cars, and the new prefabricated concrete sewers bypassed them completely. The original maps were in poor condition, many of them lost during the war, and the old lore of the tunnel-walkers had dwindled as a result of modern career mobility, but there were still some who knew where the ancient tunnels ran. One of those summoned to the conference had spent years in similar tunnels under Bucharest; and another had been around when they were built. And tonight, two nights after Kristoph's twilight raid on the research group's offices, they were about to meet.

Slime wreathed the sewer, forming a tidemark three-quarters of the way up the rotting brick walls. Five metres below the streets of the city it was completely dark, and Kristoph was forced to stoop over his lantern in order to keep his head from brushing the ceiling. Jagged black shadows danced along the tunnel behind him like a retinue of silently mocking mimics. Once a pair of close-set red eyes gleamed at him from an outflow: Kris nodded at them as he shuffled towards the meeting place. There was no telling where Ancient of Days might cast her eyes and ears. He pushed onwards, ever deeper into the maze of fetid burrows beneath the city, wading knee-deep in ancient effluent. His thoughts were grim.

He arrived at a dead end. A pile of rocks and mud had collapsed through a hole in the ceiling, blocking off the tunnel ahead. Cracked and rotted timbers poked out of the heap, and a pool of black mud had gathered at its foot. Kris paused, then reached out and pushed down hard on one of the exposed timbers. With a gurgling sigh the water around his feet drained away; whirlpools swirled briefly about his ankles as he braced himself against the powerful current leading to the concealed grate. Presently the floor was dry – dry enough. Bending down he felt through the mud for a projecting iron ring and pulled up on it. The trapdoor was ancient but well-maintained, and he let it swing shut above him as he descended the steps below. Now there was no need for a torch. Ancient of Days had passed here before him, and where she walked darkness was not permitted. Kristoph shivered, not from cold but from awe and a faint dread. He had met generals of State Security and deputy directors of Central Intelligence, and he had worked with assassins and spies and defectors and the other shadowy predators of the cold war jungle; but none of them possessed even a fragment of the legendary power which Ancient of Days controlled. And never before had she taken a direct interest in his affairs, to the point of requesting his attendance . . .

He looked around. He stood on dry stone flooring at the bottom of a high, narrow room similar in shape to an oubliette in a medieval castle, except that it was considerably larger and there was a door set in one wall. It was a modern door, plywood and aluminium, and it was as jarringly out of place as a plastic denture in the jaw of an Egyptian mummy. He shook his head disapprovingly then reached into a pocket for the key he had been given. Then he unlocked the door and went through.

'You can leave it open,' she said. Kris's head snapped round and he froze, staring at the woman who stood in the corner of the room behind him. 'We're expecting three more guests,' she added.

'Who are you?' he asked.

'Call me Helena.' She came forward, out of the shadow cast by the weak light bulb that hung from one corner of the ceiling, and Kristoph realized that she couldn't possibly be Ancient of Days; for one thing she was far too young, even though she bore the marks of encroaching middle age. Her left cheek was scarred by a patch of psoriasis, an angry red margin around a silvery, scaly patch, and with a sudden jolt Kris realized that she might actually be *human*. 'Don't worry. I'm not as ... human ... as I look.' She rubbed the back of one gloved hand against her cheek. 'There are two others coming, then Ancient of Days herself. You brought the documents, I take it?'

Kris glanced round, taking in the rest of the room. It was furnished, albeit sparsely, with camping seats and an upturned tea chest as a table. It was also very cold. 'I'd prefer to leave that until the others arrive.'

'Very well then,' she said, thrusting her hands into the pockets of her coat, 'it can wait. I hope you appreciate the gravity of the situation – '

'Lady, I'm the one who turned over the office,' he said with heavy irony. 'I was on the Kennedy assassination committee; I set up spy swaps during the fifties. Before that, I was site officer on Operation Silver. Trust me, I'm a professional.'

She laughed, which was not unexpected, then abruptly looked away, which was. 'Bullshit. Spy stuff. Fun and games.' She turned back to him. 'This is the real thing,' she said intensely, 'you'd better believe it! This is so important that – '

He held up a hand and she stopped. The noise of

hands and feet descending a ladder was clearly audible. 'We have company.'

The new arrivals didn't wait around. Both of them came through the door, then stopped and stared at Kris and – whatever her name was – Helena. 'Ivan Salazar and David Jakes?' asked Helena.

'Yeah,' said the shorter one, removing a yellow construction-site helmet and running a pudgy hand through his thinning hair. 'I'm Dave. That'n's Ivan.' The taller one stood with his hands thrust deep in the outer pockets of his trench coat. Kris stiffened, automatically focusing on the bulge in Salazar's right pocket. 'Sorry we're late.'

'Any trouble?' asked Helena.

Ivan slowly pulled out his right hand. It was empty, and Kristoph relaxed slightly. 'Not much,' Ivan said in heavily-accented English. 'Not much *now*.' He grinned sharkishly and Kristoph looked back at his pocket. *Must be a .22*, he thought. *Anything bigger would show. Now where have I seen him before?*

Kristoph looked back at the tubby American and unexpectedly realized that he was being stared at. The man had exceedingly cold eyes. 'No offence,' he said, 'but we ran into some identity verification problems a while back. Ivan hasn't had time to change yet.'

'Did you deal with the problem?' asked Kris.

Ivan nodded. 'He terminated it,' said Jakes. 'He terminated it so efficiently that half the police department are after him.'

Kris looked round and caught Helena's eye. She shook her head very slightly and shivered. 'The person you've all come here to meet should be arriving any time now. I hope you don't mind waiting; she's a bit slow on her feet these days and likes to take time to look her visitors over in advance.'

'Huh.' Ivan stared at the plywood door, irritated by his treatment but trying not to let his resentment show. 'Now you've introduced us, how about telling us why we're here? I mean, this four-star accommodation is all very flattering, but – '

Salazar chuckled to himself, a warm, throaty sound. 'Guess, man,' he said. 'Just guess.'

'Are you corporate?' Kris asked, raising an eyebrow. 'If so, from which entity?'

'Ah.' Jakes shook his head. 'We're not here to talk about peripheral business. It's bad practice. Observe compartmentalization at all times. We are all Family, it's true, but we might be on different sides – '

Kris spat on the floor. '*Human* sides. Always building walls between each other. Huh.' He turned to Helena. 'How long until She arrives?'

'Not long now,' she said. 'In fact – '

The door opened. Ancient of Days stood waiting. Nobody moved: the sight of her condition was too shocking.

'Holy shit,' whispered the one called Dave. 'I had no idea – ' He took a step forward.

Ancient of Days raised a warning arm and spoke. '*Wait. Come no closer. My condition is of unknown aetiology and may prove to be infectious to your kind. Please make yourselves comfortable – *' one obsidian pupil swept the room; a scale-encrusted nostril flared in remote amusement – '*insofar as that may be possible. We have much to discuss.*'

Kris could hold his peace no longer. 'What's happening?' he demanded angrily, meeting her huge eyes full on. 'Why weren't we told things had gone this far? The situation may be irrecoverable!' Then he stopped, shuddering in his boots as he realized what he had just done. Ancient of Days looked down upon him and for an endless instant of terror he could hear his heart stand silent, the blood in his veins freezing as he waited for her response to his presumption.

'*That is not yet the case. But, be that as it may, you are now needed here urgently. Please listen carefully; you will have your turn to reply. What I called you here to tell you about is a matter long overdue, and one that should have been dealt with years ago, before the humans reached their current dangerous state of power.*' She looked round at those who were gathered to her, then refocused on Kristoph. '*I must start by asking you a leading question, in order to judge how much you need to know at this stage. Tell me, how much do you know about genetics? And what, in particular, do you know about the so-called "Human Genome Project"?*'

A welcoming house ... a hot bath ... a lover's arms. After the raid Sue went home and tried to lose herself in the eternal present, far away from the grim shadows that Kristoph had raised by his passage. But there were a number of obstacles; Eric, for one thing, couldn't let things be, and for another thing she couldn't help wondering just what it was that Kristoph had been sent to look for.

Eric entered the bathroom as she was rinsing conditioner out of her hair. He sat down on the closed lid of the lavatory and carefully shut his book before he turned to face her. 'What is it?' asked Sue, switching off the shower attachment. Unlike Eric, she didn't read many books when she was home; only people.

He looked at her and smiled. 'Just wondering what it was all about this evening. Was it really Family business?'

It was characteristic of Eric, an ill-timed curiosity that pried into hidden corners just when she most wanted to leave them alone. She'd become used to it in the eight months they'd lived together, and expected it to drive them apart over the next few years. This relationship was an anomaly, after all; neither of them were mature by the standards of their people, who were traditionally promiscuous, and their intimacy was more a consequence of their isolation than of any convergence between them. 'No,' she said, and then, on second thoughts, 'I'm not sure. The man they sent – he said he was called Kristoph, but I don't believe him. He's some kind of spook, can pick locks and knows how to burgle an office and make it look like someone else's fault. He was hunting for something in the HGP contract notes but I think he didn't know quite what he'd been sent to get.' She sank back in the bath and shivered, then reached out to run some more hot water into the tub. 'He was really creepy, you know? And the stuff he was spouting – '

Eric put his book down on the window ledge, carefully avoiding the patch of condensation that trickled down one corner. He always seemed to be carrying a book around the house with him, but never seemed to read from it; she had speculated whimsically that he made himself invisible when he was reading, as a defence against being disturbed. 'Where is this Kristoph from? Who sent him?' He leaned forward and picked up the conditioner bottle and began turning it over in his hands, inspecting it as if he expected to discover a hidden message embedded in its soft pink plastic.

'I don't know who sent him, but I expect it was some hard-line oldster shit. He kept referring to the *Dark*: you should have heard him going on! "Take care, sorceress, lest they send for the Witch-finder General and burn thee at the stake!"' Her voice deepened an octave and her cheeks sagged into nascent jowls as she delivered the injunction to a wisp of steam that hovered over the shower fitting. 'They're still living in the prehistoric past, Eric, not the New Age crap the humans keep spouting on about but the real thing – ' she yanked the plug out angrily.

Eric watched in silence as she sat up and let the water drain around her. She saw him eyeing her breasts as they sagged slightly, no longer buoyed up by the fluid around her. 'Any thoughts on the matter?' she asked, trying to conceal her anxiety. 'Come on, don't just sit there!'

Eric passed her a towel. 'Thanks,' she said, standing up and wrapping it around herself. The air on her skin felt cold even though the room was half-filled with steam.

'I think we ought to investigate this carefully,' he said. There were times when she hated his imperturbability; just this once it was a shred of comfort. 'It sounds like the kind of intrigue that could affect us if we ignore it – the old wolves still have teeth.'

'Huh.' She shook her head and stepped out of the tub. 'Will you stop speaking in tongues and give me a straight answer for once?' She reached out and gently cupped his cheek in her hand. 'What's worrying you, love? All the old stories coming back to haunt you?'

'No, it's not that.' He stood up, accidentally dislodging her hand in the process. 'It's just a nagging feeling I've got.' His face hardened slightly so that the soft, pampered look of the mathematics professor was eclipsed for an instant by some harsher, more primal expression of his identity. 'Maybe we should look into precisely what the HGP group are working on for their industrial grant. I doubt that the Ancients would be interested if it was harmless to us. But there might be something we can spot which your spook wasn't educated to identify. Something that will put the programme in an entirely different perspective.'

Helena, assistant to Ancient of Days, nevertheless didn't live in the tunnels along with her mistress; she had a daylight identity and a job that payed the bills the night-blind humans levied in return for warmth and peace among them. After the meeting broke up she found herself inviting Kristoph back to her house; she deliberately refrained from exploring her motives. Kristoph, for reasons of his own, accepted the invitation.

Perhaps it was the remembered chill of the news that Ancient of Days had borne, or perhaps the central heating was malfunctioning; in either case, the hall felt cold as she took off her coat and hung it behind the door. 'Something to drink, perhaps?' she asked as he patiently scraped his boots on the doormat. 'Or some coffee?'

'A drink would be great.' Kristoph unbuttoned his coat and hesitated a moment before hanging it on the door. She heard him test the Yale lock before he turned and followed her into the living-room. 'You live here alone?'

She shrugged and bent down over the sideboard. The stereo was still switched on and the room filled with the faint strains of Vivaldi. Two tumblers of Scotch appeared, followed by ice from a small refrigerator. 'I like to keep the world at a distance,' she said, turning to pass him one of the glasses. 'I'm no lonelier than I want to be.'

'And how lonely is that?'

'You're here. There've been others, but none of them cared to compete for my attention with Her.'

'Ah.' Kristoph sat down at one side of the sofa, then

glanced at her inquiringly. She took a mouthful of burning spirit in order to cover her indecision, then quickly sat down next to him.

Presently Kristoph asked, 'Did you choose to serve Her, or did she choose you?' He stared into his glass and swirled the thin layer of liquid around until the bottom was exposed. 'I mean, I wasn't aware that she has any tradition of priestly attendance . . .'

'She doesn't. And to answer your question, I didn't choose to serve her and she didn't choose me. It just happened.' Helena stared at his glass for a moment in fascination. 'Are you going to drink that?' she asked.

'Eventually. I'm sorry, it's just a bad habit of mine. One of my acquaintances said I was like a cat; I play with my food. That was some years ago.' He stared moodily at the window-sill. 'I try to cultivate my private eccentricities. They're a kind of defence, if you will, against this modern habit of living in crowds. It strikes me that the bigger the city you live in, the more anonymous you become. It's as if it's an infectious disease, and the most common side-effect is loneliness.'

'Perhaps you're right.' She rubbed her cheek reflectively. 'I certainly don't know of many other Kin living in this man-swarm. Perhaps that's why She asked me to help her. She needs eyes and ears among the humans, you know. They used to be easy to deceive, but now their intelligence is as good as or better than anything we have –'

'No it isn't,' he said. 'Please believe me, their intelligence people know *nothing*.' He said it with a degree of venom that made her tense instinctively before she realized that it was not directed at her. 'I'm sorry, Helena. I've been alone among them for a long time – perhaps too long. The time when it was possible to live exclusively among Kin-folk is long past.'

'It lends a certain tension to life, doesn't it. There

have been times when I've gone months without seeing another Weerde face. I felt like I was going crazy, you know, like that patient of Freud's . . .' she turned and stared at him intently.

'Steppenwolf. Yes, I knew him well.' Kristoph tossed back what was left of his glass and stared at her. 'It's late, Helena. Would you mind if I stayed the night?'

'That's why I invited you here,' she said, her face tingling with anticipation. 'It's very cold outside, even though the war's over. Can you think of anywhere you'd rather be?' Kristoph was of a certain age, as was she, and even if he didn't understand what it was like to be single and unmated at eighty years of age, there was time for plenty more opportunities ahead.

'I can't,' he said, a strange roughness edging into his voice. 'I've been searching for a long time now – ' He glanced away, suddenly shy. 'I don't know you, but I feel as if I've known you for years,' he tried to explain.

'In the morning you must tell me where you've spent your life,' she said. 'Then maybe we can think about the future.' They stood up simultaneously and came to-gether in an endless, clinging embrace. 'But first – ' she kissed him. Gradually, her face relaxed into its primal form, her cheeks flowing and her teeth expanding to grate against his lengthening jaw as she felt something vital return to her. A flame of desire that had been bottled up behind an alien mask for too long had finally discovered its own identity: and by the time the two lovers raked the clothes from each other's backs, an onlooker would have seen nothing human about them. But that was as it should be, for neither Helena nor Kristoph were – or ever had been – human.

Two days after the raid and, astonishingly, nobody had noticed Kristoph's carefully laid trail of clumsy clues. In fact, none of the staff so much as noticed the unlocked filing cabinet or the opened door. It might as well have been a non-event. Sue, who had been steeling herself for vans with swirling blue lights in the rainy night and a plastic tape cordon around the premises, didn't know whether to laugh or cry. Instead, she took the first afternoon off with a well-rehearsed migraine and followed it up the next morning with a headache. Nothing too serious, though. Working in a lab with biohazard stickers on the door meant that any serious symptoms could land her in an isolation ward, exposed to an examination that she was not prepared to undergo.

Eric worked on the other side of the campus, in a cramped office in the Department of Mathematics and Computer Science. How he'd ever got into academia still mystified her; a knack for passing exams, he used to say, smiling faintly when she probed for an explanation. Nobody took any notice when she stopped by his office on her way in to work that afternoon, looking pale and a trifle nauseated. A lecturer carrying on with a post-grad was nobody's business but their own, after all, and stranger things had been known to go on in university staff rooms.

'Up to a rummage tonight?' Sue asked, sitting in his favourite visitor's chair and idly stirring the papers on his desk. 'We could go on to a restaurant afterwards – '

Eric pulled open a desk drawer and withdrew a black plastic case. 'No trouble at all,' he said. 'You think it'll be safe?'

'Sure,' she said. 'I swallowed enough of the buzz-words to ask the right questions. We'll say it's about a grant extension for your department, and we've got to dig the right names out to put on the letter. How's that?'

'I've been doing a bit of reading around the subject,'

he said, gesturing at a fat book balanced on one end of the desk. 'Developmental genetics?'

'Figure a mathematical slant on it,' she said, shrugging. 'Otherwise, be yourself.'

'Hah. OK. We'll leave the copying for some other time. But for now, are you sure you can remember just which drawer it was that your visitor took a particular interest in?'

'Pretty much so, yes. He was after HGP-funded stuff, specifically anything to do with Geiger-DESY Research and a Doctor MacLuhan. He didn't seem to know why, but he photocopied everything in sight and shoved it in a briefcase. I couldn't tell you what the notorious Doctor was up to, though; I've never heard of him, he seems to be some kind of industrial connection . . .'

'Hah. Thicker and thicker, my dear Watson.' He sat up and spun his chair round to face away from the desk. 'How are Geiger-DESY connected with the Department?'

Sue thought for a moment. 'If it's anything like the way industrial funding goes elsewhere in the field, it's a simple directed research project. In return for a first shot at information from the Homoeobox Research Team, Geiger-DESY pays a huge whack and provides equipment. The university pays for the staff and gets the kudos while the company get the patent rights. How's that sound?'

'And what line are Geiger-DESY in?' asked Eric, thoughtfully. 'I thought they were into drugs – '

'There's not much difference these days, I mean, the times when they used to go out in pith helmets and poke around the jungle in search of some new wonder plant are all but dead, aren't they? It's all molecular modelling and receptor-affinity analysis. As often as not they start out with a complete biochemical description of a problem and work backwards towards isolating a genetic –' she stopped, realizing that she'd lost Eric a while back. 'Well,' she concluded, 'it's no surprise that Geiger-DESY are into the Human Genome Project. That's where everyone's expecting the next big therapeutic breakthroughs to come from.'

'Like a cure for AIDS?' asked Eric.

'That, and other things,' she acknowledged. 'When the Human Genome Project is complete, they'll have a total map of the human genetic structure. They'll be able to play with it, working out what causes what and how it acts not as a blueprint so much as a *program* for generating human beings. If you insert a bug in the software you get a malfunction – AIDS is a bug in the immune system, spliced into the program by viral reverse transcriptase – but, equally, if you've got a faulty computer program you tackle the problem by trying to debug it, not by hitting it over the head with a blunt instrument like a drug.'

'I think I see,' said Eric. 'One other question, though. What's a homoeobox when it's at home, and why's everybody so interested in it?'

'Ah, well, you do pick the easy ones, don't you?' Sue stood up and looked out of the window. There was nobody outside. She flicked the lock on the door then turned and faced him. 'Watch.'

Slowly, her face began to flow. At first it simply looked as if she was relaxing, all her muscles slowly slackening: but gradually the process accelerated, until it was as if all the underlying tissue was falling away from the bones of her skull. Cheeks sagged then began to stretch as cartilaginous flaps brought her jawbone forwards. Eric watched, petrified, as her lips pulled away from her gums – *'Stop it!'* he hissed at her, glancing hastily at the door. 'What do you think you're –'

Sue raised her hands to cover her face. 'Don't worry,' she said, 'there's nobody about. I checked first, I swear it. Look, you asked me a question. *That's* your answer.'

'Pardon?' Eric stood up and checked to make sure that there was nobody outside the window.

'It's a little-known fact that humans, ants – even us – share most of the same genes. What differentiates us is the homoeobox: a complex of genes which are, I guess, *meta*-genes. They control how, why, and when other genes are switched on or off; the flow of control in the genetic program, so to speak. What's the difference between a blood cell such as a lymphocyte, and a muscle cell? Or a neuron?'

She lowered her hands and Eric saw that her face was back to normal again. He smiled with embarrassed relief. 'Please don't do that again in public. Someone, a student, could call at any time . . .'

Sue shrugged. 'They didn't. Look, what I'm getting at is this. The stuff Kristoph was looking at, it was all to do with research on mapping the homoeobox. Got that? The one section that tells a human foetus that it's to grow up into a human being and not a gorilla or a flatworm. We're not the only people working on it, but – '

Eric turned round. 'I think I've heard enough. Will there be anyone in the office if we go there now? I mean, right now?'

'It's anyone's guess. Hey, what's the sudden hurry?'

Eric shook his head. 'I've got a feeling that this could be bad. I think I know why Kristoph was sent to look through those files, and if I'm right it could be very serious indeed. In fact if they're doing what I think they're doing and we don't stop them right away those clowns could land us all in a real mess.'

The department office was open but nobody was in

when Sue and Eric arrived there. One of the word processors was switched on, and it looked as if whoever
was using it could return at any moment. 'Act as if this
is something you do all the time,' Sue murmured as she
opened the unlocked filing cabinet drawer.

'Is there any particular reason why you think I
wouldn't do that without being told?' asked Eric, standing behind her with a conspiratorial air.

'Not really,' she remarked, slightly nettled, 'you're
blocking my light. Here, I think this is what we want.'
She opened the folder and turned over the contents.
'Doctor MacLuhan, Suite Four, Geiger-DESY Research
Foundation Laboratories. What he's asking for – looks
like a breakdown of one particular sequence, doesn't
it?' She flicked more pages. 'No, that was last month.
This month . . . applications with respect to polymorph-
ism, phocomelia, *regeneration* – '

'That's it,' said Eric. 'Phocomelia, isn't that when, you
know, like thalidomide – '

'Failure to develop limbs, yeah.' Sue made a quick
note of MacLuhan's address then slid the folder back in
the cabinet. 'I'll bet you anything you care to mention
that this is what caught Her attention – '

She turned round. One of the departmental sec-
retaries, a woman Sue recognized but couldn't put a
name to, was standing in the doorway staring at
her. 'Hallo,' said the woman, 'I thought you were off
sick?'

Sue slid the drawer shut and smiled at her, then
carefully turned the smile into a wince. 'I was,' she said:
'I had a migraine.' She rubbed her forehead. 'You know.
But professor Sampson wanted an address out of the
files so I figured – ' she shrugged.

'Oh, that's quite all right,' said the secretary, sitting
down. She looked up at Eric, who was standing beside

her desk with one hand behind his back. 'Can I help you?' she asked brightly.

'It's OK,' said Eric, 'I'm with her.' The woman nodded then turned back to her screen.

Sue beckoned surreptitiously, and Eric followed her out of the room. 'What's that you've got in your hand?' she whispered once they were outside the door. Eric slowly brought it into view, then uncurled his fingers so that she could glimpse what he was holding. Then he dropped the lock-knife back into one of his jacket pockets and set off down the corridor at a brisk walk. Sue hurried to catch up. *Eric*, she thought grimly, *you and I have got a lot of talking to do*; but she also had a feeling that his caution might be justified. This was not a time for half measures.

The orange glare of street lights filtered through the windows, casting a rippling shadow on the wallpaper above the bedstead as it passed through the cloud of cigarette smoke that hung motionless in the air. The bed was occupied: Kristoph lay on it, chain-smoking Benson and Hedges and staring at the ceiling. He was naked, and the sheets lay in tatters beneath him. He sensed a presence near by and tensed, then turned one eye towards the door. Helena was standing there, a bottle in one hand and two glasses in the other. She too was naked, and smiling.

'*What's so amusing?*' asked Kris, in a language that he had used so little of late that it came haltingly to his tongue.

'*It's nothing*,' she said, putting the glasses down beside the bed. '*It just looked . . . I don't know. It was the cigarette that did it. I'm too used to looking at people through human eyes; seeing you as you are is –* strange.'

She climbed on to the bed and squatted, adopting a pose that would have been very uncomfortable if her joints had been of human articulation. Her long tongue lolled from one side of her mouth as she regarded him.

'*I find it that way too.*' Kristoph couldn't pull his eyes away from her nakedness. '*I had nearly forgotten what my own kind looked like, other than in a mirror.*'

'*It's over now. You've found me.*' She reached out with uncanny agility and snagged a glass, then filled it from the bottle. It was a whisky tumbler and the bottle was red wine, but somehow such considerations seemed petty to Kristoph. The sensations, the tingling beneath his skin and the heat of his ardour, had taken him by surprise. Not an unpleasant surprise, but a surprise none the less. It had been a long time since he had mated with another of his species, and he was astonished to discover that it was far more pleasant than he recalled. But then, he was of an age to be bonding, and such changes should be expected. Helena extended the glass to him and he took it; their hands stayed in contact for longer than was necessary simply to pass the wine.

'*The waiting is over. I had almost given up hope of meeting one of my own age and predicament. That there could be others –*' he shrugged. It was considered desirable among the Weerde to form group relationships.

'*At least we can continue the search together,*' she said, nestling up against him. '*If in your wanderings you should meet anyone –*'

'*Hah.*' A short barking cough that was the same in any language. '*A sad fantasy. I thought my solitude was the product of my travels, and now that I've met you you think your loneliness the consequence of your stability! Is there no happy medium?*'

Helena considered this for a while, then gulped back her entire glass in a single mouthful and said: '*No.*' She extended a hand and Kristoph passed her a lit cigarette. *'What do you suppose we should do? Settle here among the humans, or travel at large within their world in the hope of finding partners before we fully come of age?'*

'Neither seems very hopeful,' Kristoph remarked. He sat up and leaned close to her, then fell silent. She nipped gently at his ear to get his attention.

'What of the woman who showed you into the office?' she asked. *'The one who works for the university?'*

'She's too young,' said Kris. *'And she is already living with another of us. It's strange how the young behave, isn't it?'*

'They're closer to the humans than to us,' Helena suggested. *'Imagine if you were one of them, born in the past forty years. The Ancients go on about the dark history of our people, how we were foredoomed to live amongst those we mirror in the flesh and how dangerous it would be to invoke any kind of solution to our problems from outside – the universe is a dark and fearful mystery, shrouded in ancient death – yet the young, the young live with television and credit cards and research.'* With each of these words she lapsed back into English, for her primal tongue held no equivalents to them. *'Everything they are raised with tells them that the Ancients speak nothing but senile nonsense. It is not merely that they have no respect for the Ancients, but that they speak a different tongue altogether. It is no longer possible for them to separate themselves from the humans – '* she broke off.

Kristoph stubbed his cigarette out on the ashtray beside the bed. *'What did you just think of?'* he asked.

Helena stared at him. Her eyes were huge and dark, with no visible whites around them. *'I think that it would be a good idea to pay these two youngsters a*

341

visit,' she said thoughtfully. '*I would like to meet them. And besides, I have a certain sense that if we don't they might become embroiled in something that will not be good for them. What do you think?*'

Kristoph threw his head back and poured a glass of wine between his sharp white teeth. '*If you like,*' he said. '*When shall we go?*'

Helena twisted and rolled off the bed, then rose to a crouch. Her spine slowly began to straighten. '*As soon as possible,*' she said slurring as she fought to control her shifting vocal chords. '*My sense of urgency is great . . .*'

As soon as the door swung open, Sue realized there was something wrong; *it smells strange.* 'That was a lovely meal,' said Eric, behind her. She held out a warning hand and entered the hallway, switching on the light as she did so.

'You can come on in,' she said. 'I just thought I smelled something . . .'

'Gas?' he asked.

'You can't be too careful. But no, it wasn't gas.'

She hung her coat up as he closed the front door, then she switched on the living-room lights and walked straight in. 'Hallo,' said the balding man with the gun, 'did you enjoy your meal?'

'Oh shit,' she said, starting to back away. 'Hey, Eric – '

'Don't move,' said the other one, the tall thin man standing behind the door. 'You move, you get hurt.'

'Ah.' Her stomach felt like lead and her knees were about to give way.

'Hey, what's going – ' Eric, standing behind her, looked over her shoulder and saw the man with the gun. 'Shit,' he whispered.

'That makes it unanimous,' said the bald one. 'Won't you come on in? I'd like it if you'd sit on the sofa – there – where I can keep an eye on you.'

Slowly, with exaggerated care, Sue sidled over to the sofa and sat down. Eric followed her. She could see him out of the corner of her eye. *I hope he doesn't do anything stupid*, she thought. Then, *how do I stop this happening?*

'That's good,' said the bald one. 'That's real cool. Now maybe we should have a chat, you know, loosen things up?'

'Who are you?' Eric asked in a low voice. 'What do you want?'

The tall one strolled over from the doorway to stand behind the seated man. '*You know who we are*,' he said, in a language which sent shivers of recognition down Sue's neck. '*We come to talk sense.*'

The man in the chair shrugged. 'You'll have to excuse my partner,' he said: 'he can be a bit blunt. Someone you might have heard of – one of your neighbours in this city – called us in to do a service. Ancient of Days. Perhaps you've met her?' He cocked his head, looked slightly disappointed when neither Sue nor Eric responded. 'A shame. She's very – impressive. Anyway . . .'

The tall one pulled his right hand out of his coat pocket. There was a small black pistol in it. He pulled his left hand out of the other pocket: it was holding a cylindrical object. He began to screw the cylinder on to the muzzle of the pistol. 'You'll have to excuse him,' said the seated one, 'He's a bit nervous.' He blinked at them: 'the police don't like him very much. Anyway. Where was I? Ah yes. We owe you one for showing the point man in, where the files were held. However, you don't seem to have got the message: this is *not* a matter you want to get involved in. Oh no. In fact, you should do your best to forget about it, unless and until Ancient of Days sends for you. Is that understood?'

'I understand,' said Sue. Suddenly her mouth was dry, but it was a dryness born of anger: she found that she wanted to spit. 'I understand that what I see is a bunch of superstitious fools chasing around in the dark preparing to kill – yes, that's it, isn't it? That's what you do for a living – to kill a harmless scientist because some clapped out fruit cake thinks human genetics research is going to conjure up the devil . . .'

'*Wrong*,' said the seated assassin. 'You understand nothing. You cannot possibly remember what it is we face; you will be nameless to history if you insist on giving aid to the *humans* in pulling down everything we have tried so hard to preserve!'

He raised the pistol and Sue unconsciously stopped breathing and steeled herself to jump; but before she could move there was a flash of light reflected from the gunman's face and a voice screamed '*DOWN!*' in her ear.

She rolled forwards and tried to hug the carpet. She heard three muffled spitting sounds overhead, and then a crashing of glass and heavy objects as the tall assassin fell, knocking the television set off its stand.

'Idiot,' snarled Kristoph. 'Were you *trying* to get yourself killed? Why didn't you duck?' Then, gently but urgently, 'Oh, see what he's done. Quickly, fetch a towel. Now!' Sue heard footsteps hurrying, doors banging, then a low moan behind her. She rolled over and sat up and saw Kristoph bent over the back of the sofa, gripping Eric – collapsed across it, his eyes closed – by one shoulder, both hands wrapped around an upper arm from which a huge, dark stain was slowly seeping. 'A towel will do but a compression bandage or a torniquet would be a lot better and I need one or the other of them in a hurry,' Kris muttered. 'Otherwise he may bleed to death all over me.'

She remembered standing in the bathroom, watching blood trickle and swirl down the white porcelain sink as the rushing water numbed her hands. She remembered ransacking the cupboard for bandages and finding nothing but a small tin of Elastoplast, suitable only for grazes. And the towels were all pink, the same colour as her vomit when she heaved up her entire meal into the toilet. Then a strange woman was holding her by the shoulders and saying "It's all right, the bleeding's stopped and it's a clean puncture" as she slowly led Sue through into the living-room. Eric wasn't on the sofa, but his blood was. Unaccountably, she began to cry. After all, it wasn't she who'd been shot, was it?

After a while she realized that she couldn't see the bodies. 'Wh-what happened?' she asked, trying to dry her eyes and realizing as she did so that her blouse was ruined, spots of blood everywhere on her right sleeve.

'Don't you worry about it,' said the woman, 'everything's going to be all right. Your friend is in bed, Kris is stitching his arm up – he's done it before, he says – he's going to be OK. A flesh wound.'

'We've got to get him to hospital – ' Sue began, before she comprehended how foolish her words must sound.

'Don't you worry about it,' said the woman. 'I'm Helena, by the way. I came here with Kris. Is there – ' she stared at the bloodstained sofa – 'anywhere else in this flat where we can go? Apart from the bedroom or the kitchen?'

Sue didn't think to ask what was wrong with the kitchen. 'The back bedroom,' she said automatically. 'We can – I need to – sit down . . .'

'I'll say you do.' Helena took her by the arm as she stood up again and stumbled through the hall to the spare room. When she got there she collapsed on the bed and curled up and began to change, so that Helena was hard-put to get her clothes off her. But that was OK. It was only a little more than she'd bargained for, after all.

Shock and exhaustion forced Sue into a deep sleep. Helena sat beside the bed, watching the shifting form that lay there, its flesh slowly crawling in an unconscious attempt to shut out the outside world. *I can't even look at my own kind without seeing them through the eyes of a human,* she realized. *How much worse must it be for one of these, raised in a modern city and exposed to their education, their entertainment, their friendship all their life? Our ancestors would barely recognize them. Worse, they would barely recognize the ancestors* ... She shook her head in sympathy and stood up. Then she left the room, closing the door behind her as she tracked through the hall and into the main bedroom. Kristoph glanced up as she entered, then continued to wrap his makeshift bandage around Eric's shoulder.

'She's taken it rather hard,' Helena commented.

'I'm not surprised,' said Kristoph. His voice was rough, as if he was fighting an inner battle and did not wish to be disturbed.

Eric rolled his eyes. 'Ah – it's not easy,' he whispered. 'This mess ... we were going to come looking for you ...'

'Lie still. How is he?' she asked Kristoph.

'I've seen worse. Small calibre bullet, went clean through the quadriceps. I think he froze when the flash went off, otherwise he'd have been down on the floor with her and this wouldn't have happened. Nicked a vein, but no arterial bleeding. Knowing how we heal, you should be fine in a few days,' he said for Eric's benefit. 'The real question is what happens in the meantime,' he continued under his breath. 'Depending whether those bastards were here of their own accord or at someone's command.'

'We can fetch two tea chests for the bodies,' said Helena. 'Then we ditch the sofa. Nobody's called the police so we may be able to conceal it – '

Kris looked at her coolly. 'That's not what I meant.'

Helena sat down on a low stool in front of the dresser, then turned to face Kristoph and the bed. 'You know I've served Ancient of Days for sixty years. It wasn't necessarily through choice.' She paused and looked at him, but he made no response. Eventually she continued.

'I was twenty-two when the call came. My family told me what to do, and in those days one obeyed. Reluctantly, but – I grew up a farm. I was told to go to the city and present myself to Her. I didn't want to; I was afraid, and perhaps a little rebellious, but not too much so. I did as I was told, in the end. When I met her, She told me what I was to do. It seemed she had a servant before me, her eyes and ears among the humans, who had gone insane or died. I was to take his place. She hasn't been able to walk among them for a very long time – over a century, I think – and so she needs a set of proxy senses, preferably young, which can be exposed to the swirl and rush of the human civilization above her head.'

At the other end of the bed, Eric yawned and shut his eyes. Kristoph glanced up. 'I'm listening.'

'I gathered news,' she continued. 'I read all the literature and newspapers. I arranged for Ancient of Days to have a colour television, supplied by cable – not that she watched it. I dare say the images it brought to her were simply incomprehensible. Her curiosity is vast, but she needs me for the *feel*, the idea of what it's like to live among the humans. She hasn't ever seen an aeroplane except in pictures, has never ridden in a car. This degenerative condition of hers is quite recent, but she refuses to summon anyone who might be able to treat it. I think she wants – '

'She wants what?' asked Kris.

'I don't know. It's just that I thought ... she wanted me not as a pair of eyes but as a mind, to understand what was going on in the world. You understand that; you've lived among Them, haven't you? But last time she was on the surface she rode in a horse-drawn carriage and there were new gaslights along the streets. And I don't think she quite understands how far things have changed, or how fast.'

'Hence the pet thugs,' Kris speculated. 'Yes, that would explain a lot. In which case, these two – ' his gesture encompassed Eric, and the wall behind which Sue lay sleeping – 'have a more valid perspective on the world than she does, at least with respect to the humans. Doesn't that follow?'

'I don't like that line of reasoning,' Helena said uneasily. 'It's what it leads to ...' *My destination barely five minutes ago*, she chided herself. How long had these flowers of doubt been germinating? The dusty towers of the city had never struck her as a fertile soil for new ideas of any kind, much less for thoughts of treachery. *She needs me, but how can I possibly serve her? If my loyalties belong with anyone, they should lie with the young. It's not for me to decide. Maybe –*

'I think we should take these two to visit Ancient of Days,' she said slowly. 'They might be able to resolve this situation where I could only fail. In any case, it was her servants who died here tonight. She should be informed; at least, if you mean to involve your friends that you told me about.'

Kris stared at her. 'Do you really think so?'

She met his gaze. 'Yes. Otherwise she will assume the worst and act accordingly.'

'And you think it isn't already too late for that?' he asked. 'That her thrashing around doesn't offer a threat to the continuity of the race? Come on. If that's what you believe, I want to know – '

But to her shame she had to glance away; and when she looked back at him the time for second thoughts had long since passed.

Times changed, Kris thought as he waited for the phone to ring, but people never did. That was the root of the problem. A glass of whisky sat among the shadows next to an overflowing ashtray, the last cigarette in the pack balanced burning on its rim. The faint howl of a descending jet cut through the night and rattled the windows in their frame as he stared out across the city. A ringing tone cut the air; he forced himself not to pick up the receiver. It gave out a second ring before the answering machine cut in. The voice at the other end of the line was faint, as if its owner was shouting down a buried pipe.

'Hallo, is this – '

'THIS IS SUSAN SPEAKING. I'M SORRY I CAN'T COME TO THE PHONE RIGHT NOW, BUT IF YOU'D LIKE TO LEAVE A MESSAGE, PLEASE SPEAK AFTER THE TONE.'

' – Oskar speaking. Call me back.' *Click.*

Kris picked up his cigarette. He felt a little ill at the prospect of what he was about to do, but he couldn't see what alternative there was. For Helena, sure: for these two kids who'd gotten themselves into a whole lot more trouble than they'd dreamed of, too. For the pair of hitters Ancient of Days had sent round – but they were beyond sympathy, beyond regrets. No, it was the fact that what he was about to do was irrevocable that made him sick with worry; him, who'd seen men eating each other on the Eastern Front and other things too terrible to talk about.

He picked up the phone and began to dial, careful not to enter any wrong digits. Oskar picked up the phone on the fourth ring. It was three in the morning in Berlin and Kris could visualize the crumpled beer cans on the floor, smoke curling beneath the ceiling, the smell of oil from the black metal machine parts scattered across the newspaper pages on the sofa. 'Hallo?'

'Oskar, this is Kris. I have a candidate.' His mouth was dry and his throat burned from the cigarettes, but that wasn't why his heart was pounding.

Oskar grunted. 'After all this time? Are you sure?'

'You better believe it. The location is – ' he gave directions. 'You'll need to bring tools. And watch out, you'd better be clean. It's already gone critical; we had a *securitate* airhead trying to scare the canaries earlier this evening.'

'A *what*? They must be crazy!'

'No way. He was travelling under falsies, ID of Ivan Salazar from the Langley entity, but that wasn't his real name at all. I fingered him on a liaison job oh, years ago. He was one of us, but shit sticks if you roll in it for long enough. I figure he's one of the ones who skipped out after they fragged the Ceauşescus during the coup, maybe figured he could cut it as a wet operative for the Families. Anyway, it's really hit the fan this time. We're talking a Hummingbird situation, got that?'

There was silence from the other end of the line as

Oskar absorbed this information. 'Yes, but which side are we on?' he finally asked.

Kris froze. 'The winners,' he said slowly and deliberately. 'Spread the word. We've got a Hummingbird situation, here and now. Get the wagon rolling then hop the next flight out of Tegel. We need you on the job.'

'Check,' replied Oskar. 'The fuses are burning. Good luck and goodbye.'

The phone went dead, but Kris didn't put it down. The sound from the buzzing receiver was unlocking memories from his childhood, stories he'd been told by his mother about what happened to his uncle Hans in the terrible night of the first Operation Hummingbird, Uncle Hans with his proud brown uniform and Stormtrooper strut who had vanished in the Night of the Long Knives, never to be seen again. *Is this how it happens?* he wondered; *must the young always eat the old?* His palm sweated as he squeezed the smooth plastic of the receiver. *It wasn't always like this among our people. There was a time when the gap wasn't so wide. It didn't have to grow this way, did it?*

But he'd set the wheels in motion and now there was only one way out – and death was an integral part of the process.

Helena was clearing up in the kitchen when she sensed somebody standing behind her. She straightened up and thrust a blood-stained wedge of kitchen roll into the waste disposal then rolled off her soiled rubber gloves before turning round. It was Sue, looking pale but collected and wearing a thick dressing gown that was too big for her. 'How do you feel?' she asked.

'Not bad, considering.' Sue breathed deeply. 'Mind if I ask your name again? I didn't catch it before.' She looked around distractedly, but not down, never down.

She looked as if she was trying to walk on air. Helena was still a long way from finishing.

'That's all right; my name's Helena,' she replied. 'And you're Sue. Are you sure you ought to be up? That was –'

Sue waved a hand. 'I'm tougher than I look. And so is Eric, I think. He'll be fine and so will I. But he –' she looked at the body lying on the mat of newspapers Helena had spread on the floor – 'he's not going anywhere. I think we deserve an explanation.'

Helena sighed. 'You're not getting one here. I'm in this over my head, I just tagged along for the ride.' She laughed self-consciously. How could she possibly justify what she was doing on the kitchen floor? Then she frowned. 'Look, I'm not explaining this very well, am I? Kris and I thought you could – could do with some help. We weren't expecting things to have gone this far, not yet.'

'Uh huh.' Sue nodded, finally glanced down, then turned and fumbled in one of the cupboards above the work surface. 'I need a drink. How about you?'

'That's –' Helena paused – 'a kind offer.' She rummaged in the cupboard for a minute then found two tall glasses and filled them half-full with rum. It wasn't Helena's favourite spirit, but she took it all the same. 'You've been very lucky so far. Ancient of Days probably doesn't realize how isolated she is. The oldest ones –' she took a sip of rum – 'seldom do.'

'Who is this Ancient of Days?' Sue asked. Helena looked at her sharply.

'Exactly what Her name implies. The one I – help me – am sworn to serve.' She took another sip, then a mouthful of the neat spirit. It burned in her stomach, like the dull fire of revenge. 'One of us, left over from a former age. She serves the Kin by searching out threats to

352

our collective survival. But in latter days she's become unreliable.'

'Hence ... this?' Sue asked. 'You mean she thought she could simply order us to kill all the scientists working on homoeobox structure and the rest would lose interest or be too frightened to continue working in the field?' She finished on a note of disbelief.

'That's about the size of it,' Helena admitted.

'What does she think they are? A bunch of medieval alchemists?' Sue downed her glass in one gulp and slammed it on the work top. 'Jesus Christ!'

Helena didn't say anything.

'It's a complete sack of shit!' Sue exclaimed. 'Scientists don't work like that, hiding dingy secrets from each other and bolting at shadows! All it would take would be two, maybe three suspicious incidents and we'd have every police agency in Europe breathing down our necks. What does she think she's *doing*?'

'Protecting us,' Helena said drily.

Sue glared at her. 'And what are *you* doing?'

Helena sighed. 'Protecting you, I think. Times change, and the Ancients can't adapt. For most of our history responses which worked a millennium ago have been equally valid today. But not any longer. You – your generation – are our future. You don't need to exist on the edge of human society, you can slot right in with them! But in the process ... ' she shrugged.

'But what's in it for you?' Sue looked agitated, uncertain whether to be grateful or suspicious or angry. 'Why are you helping us? You said you were sworn to serve her! What are you doing here?' She sounded close to hysteria.

'Cleaning up after the party,' Helena said calmly as she bent down and picked up the electric carving-knife again. It was strange how little blood there was, she noted. Weerde tissue fluid clotted far faster than human, and the bullets had been low-calibre. 'For what I'm doing now, the punishment would have been forgetfulness,' she added. 'To have one's very name expunged from the memories of all who one held dear, to be cast out into the wilderness on pain of death, there to wander through the empty forests until even the memory of speech faded and one was nothing more than a beast.' She glanced up. 'But that doesn't mean very much to your generation, does it? You've grown up among the urban *sapiens*, after all, and they do things differently.' She shook her head. 'I wish I knew where it was all going.'

Sue didn't reply, but a moment later Helena felt her crouch down beside her, and there was another pair of hands to help expunge the evidence of the crime.

Oskar caught the red-eye shuttle out of Tegel. It was delayed three hours by snow, and when it lumbered into the cold dawn sky the outline of the redundant Wall was clearly visible on the ground below. Less than two hours later he was landing in the city. Somebody was waiting for him.

Howard was already in the country, running a high-value, high-risk shipping agency from a motel bedroom near Milton Keynes. When his brokers discovered he was gone they were furious: but not as furious as they were three minutes later when the Special Branch broke down their door. But Howard wasn't around to care. Now he was a truck-driver called Mark, and within a day even his fingerprints wouldn't match those on Interpol's files.

Fiona got the call when she returned to her lodge in the Pyrenees after a good day's skiing. She fobbed off her current boyfriend with a tale of an elderly aunt and a stroke, made an air connection out of Toulouse, and caught the Chunnel link from Paris.

Frederico didn't head for the city. But then, that wasn't his goal. His target was in the Vatican. There were a hundred others in the Organization who, like him, weren't heading for the city; but all of them had targets. And when they reached them, the targets would die.

It was agreed within the Organization that a purge was long overdue. It would have been sensible to have held one during the turbulence of the Second World War, when it was already becoming obvious who was trustworthy and who was unreliable, but back then the Organization had still been weak, a compact of like-minded Weerde who understood the ways of the modern human world less imperfectly than their forebears. Therefore the Organization lay low, recruited individuals disaffected with the way of the Families, and waited.

Times changed. The war ended, and with the falling of the iron curtain came opportunities for expansion and re-entrenchment. The Organization made very good use of them. The Ancients, however, were oblivious to the fundamental changes in the world at large; their response to the Cold War was identical to their response to the British and Spanish Empires, the Romans, Alexander the Great ... it was a practised response, and it had worked before. Unfortunately, some times changed faster than others.

Eric opened his eyes and blinked until the ceiling swam into focus. *Bullet wound. I never thought it would hurt like this. More like ...* he tried to clear the bloodstained drill-bits from his mind's eye. He felt weak, *drained*, but fine, except for the bruising ache in his left arm. He

tried to sit up and the arm almost exploded; he gasped
and forced himself to hold still until the pain passed.
Then, very carefully, he propped himself up against the
headboard and began to explore the damage inside.
Torn muscles grated against one another, sending
surges of pain up those nerve trunks that had not been
severed by the bullet. A fibrous matrix of clotted blood
had spread through the tissue around the ruptured vein,
holding cells in stasis while the complex machineries of
his immune system went to work. Already the first new
cells were infiltrating the mass, spreading along the
boundary of ripped flesh and commencing the job of
reconstruction. Eric concentrated: without guidance the
wound would heal badly. There might even be a scar.
He was still tired and his head ached, but it was essential that he –

'Aha, he's awake. Aren't you?'

Eric opened his eyes again. 'Very probably,' he said,
speaking so quietly that it was almost a whisper. 'Who
is it?' *As if I couldn't guess.*

'I'm Kris.' He sat down at the foot of the bed, stretching the quilt. 'If it wasn't for me you'd be dead.'

Eric tried to sit up properly. 'I suppose I should be
grateful, but it would help if I knew what was going
on.'

Kris nodded understandingly. Eric looked at him and
wondered what it was he didn't like about this man.
This Weerde, he corrected himself. *One of my own
kind. But he looks more like a wolf!* The thought was
distinctly uncomfortable. There was a hot tingling in
his arm as the muscles began the slow process of knit-
ting together again.

'What is it you want to know?' asked Kris.

'Well – ' Eric struggled, at a loss for words. 'What all
the fuss is about,' he said finally. 'I can understand an

Ancient becoming interested in the homoeobox data, but her response seems rather excessive, wouldn't you agree? It's not as if it can achieve anything, after all.'

'I don't know,' Kris said. 'It *used* to work ... three hundred years ago, against alchemists and would-be magicians.'

Eric snorted disbelievingly. 'Come *on*. What does she think this is? The Middle Ages?'

Kristoph didn't say anything; he didn't need to.

'All right then, be the smart guy! See if I care. Thanks for saving my life, by the way.' Kris raised an eyebrow as Eric rolled his feet over the side of the bed and sat up experimentally. 'There's more to this than one out-of-control Ancient and a couple of former secret police-men,' Eric added as he waited for the dancing black spots to clear from in front of his eyes.

'True,' Kris stood up. 'Here, let me help you. I think you lost a fair bit of blood.'

'Yes, I can't say I'm looking forward to cleaning the sofa – ' Eric stopped talking as he stood up, taken aback by his own astonishing irrelevance. He wobbled a bit, but the black spots didn't come back and he was able to shuffle around after a fashion. *I must be crazy*, he thought, floating. *This isn't me here, is it?* His arm burned like a torch. 'Tell me about everything in particular.'

'There's an Organization,' began Kristoph. 'It's been around since the twenties, waiting for something like this. It's probably happened before, but each era creates its own orthodoxy, doesn't it? Maybe some such group is where Ancient of Days came from originally. Some bunch of plotters who were afraid that their elders were going to give them away to the Roman secret police.'

Eric shuffled over to the chest of drawers and

fumbled one-handedly over the chair in front of it. 'Dressing gown,' he muttered. It seemed a much more concrete concern than any ancient tale of police and thieves. He berated himself: *Your future depends on this!* But somehow it didn't seem like an immediate problem; more like a light farce, seen through a few too many layers of cotton gauze. *I must have lost a fair bit of blood.*

'Here. Like I said, we've been waiting. The signs have been around for a long time. Crocodiles seen in the sewers under New York, Yeti sightings in Tibet; the breakdown in human family structures in the developed world –'

'You make this Organization sound like a bunch of shamans steaming over the entrails of the Sunday Times crossword,' Eric winced as he tried to ease his damaged arm into a baggy sleeve. In the end he gave up and wore the robe over it, tucking the cuff of the empty sleeve into the belt. 'I mean, are you trying to tell me they deduced from all those signs that some of the Ancients were liable to go loopy within the next few years?'

'Something like that,' Kris assured him. 'There were no overt signs of loss of control – not until recently – but little things were slipping everywhere. All those signs were warnings of a certain ... malaise. Now its unmistakable. Their responses have become so inappropriate that I'm afraid there's no alternative to action.'

'What are you going to do to them?' Eric asked with false levity, pausing in the doorway. *I feel drunk,* he realized. *The truth will set you free! And isn't that better than wine?* He glanced over his shoulder at Kristoph, who stood behind him holding an unlit cigarette in one hand.

'What can we do?' Kris replied. There were quiet voices coming from the kitchen. 'There's one thing you can be certain of,' he said, striking a match. The shadows it cast across his face gave him a calculating, lupine expression: 'we're not going to do anything to them that they wouldn't do to us first if we gave them the chance.'

Eric felt himself go cold everywhere except his arm, which was feverishly hot. Suddenly, despite his injury and blood-loss and the intoxicating sense of his own survival, he felt entirely sober. An atavistic urge, from god-knew-what recess of his hind brain, made him want to bare his teeth and snarl. Instead, forcing himself to do the right thing – *come on, Mister Cool!* a part of him sneered contemptuously – he went into the living-room. It was unlit, but the street lights were bright enough to let him see that there was a dust-sheet flung over the sofa and a rug on the carpet, and the vase of flowers was gone from on top of the television. He walked over to the windows and looked out across the street, then fumbled with the latches and pushed one of them open. A chill breeze cut through his dressing gown, swirled past him and numbed the stench of blood and gunpowder.

'What do you think?' asked the quiet voice behind him. He didn't turn round.

'I think –' he paused, seeking the words with which to express his anger, his *rage* at this violation of his carefully maintained humanity – 'there is no precedent for the current situation.' He stared down at the streets, watching the traffic scurry and hum along in illuminated columns far below. 'We're a conservative people, aren't we?' The word *we* hung strange and heavy on his tongue. 'But the world we live in is undergoing eruptions and upheavals. And when conservative peoples are placed under such a stress they tend to ... well, look at the first Russian revolution.'

The breeze was beginning to work through to him. He was still weak, and his arm ached; he couldn't summon the resources to keep himself warm. He reached out and pulled the window to until only a slit was left open. 'Is this happening everywhere?'

'It is,' said Kris. 'Maybe you're right, maybe there hasn't been an upheaval like this since the – since the ancient times, the days of legend and darkness. The old race. But someone –' his voice faltered, and in a flash of astonishment Eric realized that he was pleading with him, pleading for his approval, his understanding – 'someone has to look to the future! And you are the future, more surely than any conclave of Ancients.'

Eric turned his back on the window. Kristoph had lit his cigarette, and in the darkness the glowing coal resembled an ancient saurian eye. 'But where does that leave you?' asked Eric. 'If your organization takes credit for this killing, where can you go from here? Where is your thought for your own future?'

Kris blew a thin plume of smoke from his nostrils. It swirled lazily about his head then drifted towards the door. 'I suppose we'll have to be the scapegoats, the nameless ones who will be driven from the present to atone for the sins of the past. Doesn't that sound right to you? Something's got to go, after all.'

'Not if you succeed. The whole thing sounds so extreme –'

'You're uncomfortable with the idea of killing, aren't you?' said Kris. He began to button up his coat, preparing for the cold of the streets outside. 'Listen, I've got to go out now, to arrange for some waste disposal. But there's something you should remember, professor, when you go to work in your warm office next week

and sit in your comfortable chair behind your tidy desk.'
His face began to slide into another, ancient shape; or
else the shadows cast by the city lights were shifting
across his cheeks. 'Remember you're a predator, professor, one of a long line of free-ranging killers. And
remember that one's natural instincts can sometimes be
very hard to ignore . . .'

Presently, Eric struggled to his feet and walked into
the kitchen to see what was going on. Sue and Helena
were just finishing with the knives and moving on to
the bin liners. They both looked up, then Sue had her
arms round his neck and was kissing him, tracking
bloody stains across the front of his garment. 'You're
doing well,' she whispered in his ear. Louder, 'has Kris
gone for some boxes then?'

'That's quite likely, I think.' Helena rose and peeled
off her gloves again, shaking them out carefully. 'Ah, I
don't think we've been introduced. Have we?'

'Eric, Helena,' said Sue. 'Helena stayed to help clear
up,' she added, letting go of him as he glanced around.
But Eric wasn't dwelling on the mass that occupied the
centre of the floor. 'I can see we've got some socializing
to do,' he said. 'It's a long time since either of us have
met anyone who wasn't – entirely – human. Still,' his
expression became unreadable, 'do you suppose Kristoph will be long?'

'No, I don't think he will,' said Helena. She smiled
sharply. 'He said he had one more job to do, then it's all
over and we can just lie low, "go to the mattresses" as
the mafia call it, until everything dies down.' She put
the knife and the gloves in the sink and turned the tap
on them.

'Then it'll all be over,' said Sue, an expression of
relief dawning on her face. She turned back to Eric and

hugged him, burying her face in his shoulder, all petty irritations forgotten for the moment. 'I'm so glad it's finished.'

But she was wrong. In fact, it was only just beginning.

Epilogue

THE LADY AND/OR THE TIGER: II

Neil Gaiman and Roz Kaveney

———————

Lamb stopped reading. His head hurt and he had a cramp in the back of his leg. He had read enough. He checked his watch; dawn must be breaking by now. Chepstow was asleep in the armchair in the corner of the room. Lamb stared at him, wondering if he were truly human, if any of us were.

The Librarian's eyes opened.

'So, Mr Lamb.' He looked at Lamb inquiringly.

'So what comes next?' Lamb said. 'Something bursts through that door behind us, and tears my throat out?'

'Not necessarily,' Chepstow said. 'It all rather depends on you. Why don't you open the desk drawer?'

Lamb pulled it open; inside the drawer were a revolver and, next to it, a pair of white gloves.

'You need not take the gloves,' said Chepstow. 'And if you take the revolver, you may do with it what you will; we give you one bullet and that is all the help you will get from us.'

Lamb hesitated.

'You were a marked man long before you came to the Library,' Chepstow said. 'You have disturbed what you looked at. They were watching you long ago. You may, if you wish, take the gloves, and stay with the Library; it may not be the life you planned for yourself, but it is life. If not, well, one of the tokens of white gloves is that we have washed our hands ...'

'It's not enough,' said Lamb. 'The knowledge is not enough, and that is all I would ever have. There's more than that.'

'Ah,' Chepstow said. 'The woman.'

'Who shot her? Who was it? And what was she? Was she trying to get away from them? Or was it one of these damned factions, wiping out a member of another? Now that I know this much I have to know the rest. I have to find out who killed Caroline.'

'And then?'

'I'll kill them.' Lamb paused. He stood up, and closed his eyes. 'Once her face was done with changing, she looked so calm it was almost as if she was alive. She was still beautiful, you know, when I left her lying there.'

'It is,' said Chepstow, 'at least conceivable that she is beautiful still.'

Lamb opened his eyes, and looked at him.

'The Weerde are, after all, rather hard to kill,' Chepstow said. 'And the person who was following you did appear to be female, not that that means very much.'

Lamb paused.

'Thank you,' he said, and began to walk the length of the long underground room, one step at a time.

'Take the revolver,' Chepstow urged. 'You may need it still.'

Lamb shook his head. 'What's behind the door, Chepstow?' he asked. 'Is there ... is there anyone there? Really?'

'That question is not one I could presume to answer, sir. I am afraid I must leave the matter with you.' The Librarian of the Conspiracy stood up and walked to the other door, and opened it. 'If I do not have the opportunity of seeing you again, sir, may I say it has been a pleasure. Goodbye.' And he was gone. The lock of the door snapped shut behind him.

Lamb stood alone, and he waited in the silence beneath the earth. He thought about Caroline. He remembered her perfume, remembered it so vividly that he imagined he could smell it now. He looked at the revolver on the table, and the gloves. Then he walked back to the table, and made his choice.

There was a gentle tap on the door. Lamb went to answer it in a joyful decisiveness, although he truly did not know which to expect – the lady, or the tiger.

THE WEERDE WAS DEVISED BY MARY GENTLE AND NEIL GAIMAN, AND EDITED BY MARY GENTLE AND ROZ KAVENEY:

Neil Gaiman is co-author of the bestselling apocalyptic fantasy *Good Omens*, with Terry Pratchett, but is better known for his work in the comics medium, particularly for his ongoing dark fantasy *Sandman*, which has won lots of awards. He comes up with quite a few of the ideas for Midnight Rose, while other people do the real work: Alex Stewart did all the heavy lifting on *Temps* (also published in ROC), and Mary Gentle and Roz Kaveney had to get their hands dirty with *The Weerde* and the forthcoming ROC anthology *Villans!*

Mary Gentle is known for her science-fiction novels *Golden Witchbreed* and *Ancient Light*, and most recently for the Renaissance technoBaroque fantasies *Rats and Gargoyles* and *The Architecture of Desire*. She edits for Midnight Rose Ltd, and reviews for *Interzone*. She has and MA in seventeenth-century studies and continues with unrelated research. In her spare time she runs around a lot, swordfighting, and shooting people in laser-gaming events. She is a born-again red-head

Roz Kaveney is probably best known as a journalist and reviewer writing on science fiction, comics and other topics for the *New Statesman*, *Foundation*, *City Limits* and *The Sunday Times*. At one time or another she has read for most of the SF lists in London, and edited the two *Tales from the Forbidden Planet* anthologies. In what would otherwise be her spare time, she is an anti-censorship and civil-liberties activist.

Exploring New Realms
in Science Fiction/Fantasy Adventure

Titles already published or in preparation:

The Day It Rained Forever by Ray Bradbury

Myth-maker extraordinaire, Ray Bradbury has created in his writing a world of uncanny beauty and fear. In this collection of twenty-three classic stories there are the gentle Martians of *Dark They Were and Golden-Eyed*, the killers of *The Town Where No One Got Off*, the sweet sounds of *The Day It Rained Forever* and much more. Glowing with luminous images of past and future, they resonate with the unforgettable mixture of nostalgia, fear and wonder that make him a science-fiction writer like no other.

Of Time and Stars by Arthur C. Clarke

A Tibetan monastery hires a giant computer to list the nine billion names of God – with terrifying results. A bored housewife encourages her laboratory-bred serving ape to take up painting – and astonishes the art world. A lunar exploration mission stumbles across a sentinel left by an ancient space-faring civilization. *Of Time and Stars* collects eighteen of Arthur C. Clarke's classic stories. Full of humanity, humour and solidly scientific speculation, this volume includes *The Sentinel*, the story that inspired *2001: A Space Odyssey*.

The Neverending Story by Michael Ende

Imagine an enchanted book, one so steeped in the magic and mystery of a distant land that you want it to go on for ever. Bastian, a lonely boy of ten, finds just such a book, *The Neverending Story*, and hides away to read it. There he learns about Fantastica, a remote kingdom ruled by a childlike Empress, now on the brink of death. Without the Empress, the whole future of Fantastica is in danger and all its creatures will follow her to the grave. Can Bastian set things right and save Fantastica from its fate? His quest, a bewitching blend of legend and adventure, will transport you to the magic place where dreams really can come true.

Exploring New Realms
in Science Fiction/Fantasy Adventure

Titles already published or in preparation:

Echoes of the Fourth Magic by R. A. Salvatore

When a U.S. submarine is drawn off-course by the murderous magic of the Devil's Triangle, Officer Jeff DelGiudice survives the terrifying plunge through the realms. But his good fortune has a shocking consequence. He finds himself stranded in a strange world awaiting its redeemer. Now Jeff must face his destiny – in a dangerous, wondrous quest to lead humankind's children back to the realms of Light.

Shadowrun: Secrets of Power
Volume 1: Never Deal with a Dragon
by Robert N. Charrette

The year is 2050. The power of magic and the creatures it brings have returned to the earth and many of the ancient races have re-emerged in a world where technology and human flesh have melded into deadly urban predators. For Sam Verner, living in the womb of the Renraku conglomerate was easy, until his sister disappeared. Now he wants out, but to do so he has to slide through a world where his first wrong move may be his last . . .

The Earthsea Trilogy
Wizard of Earthsea · The Tombs of Atuan · The Farthest Shore
by Ursula Le Guin

In a land beyond time there lived Sparrowhawk, the greatest of the great wizards. Following a succession of magical feats, each greater and more daring than the last, Sparrowhawk, the legends say, entered his boat, turned his back on land, and without wind or sail or oar moved westward over sea and out of sight . . .

**Exploring New Realms
in Science Fiction/Fantasy Adventure**

A Gift Upon the Shore by M. K. Wren

Rachel Morrow and young Mary Hope, isolated at Amarna on the remote Oregon shore, seem to be the sole survivors of the nuclear holocaust, their lives given purpose only by Rachel's mission to preserve whatever books are left.

Until Luke appears – filling Mary with need and desire, both for him and for the Ark, the organized community from which he comes. Yet the encounter threatens everything she and Rachel believe in – for the Arkites are a strict, patriarchal society who think all books but the Bible are evil and who have no place for dissenters. Then Mary becomes involved in a bitter conflict with Miriam, the icy beauty who vows to destroy her precious legacy – even if she has to kill to do so . . .

**Exploring New Realms
in Science Fiction/Fantasy Adventure**

The Soul Rider Saga
by Jack Chalker

Titles already published or in preparation:

Cassie did not feel the Soul Rider enter her body . . . but suddenly she knew that Anchor was corrupt. Knew that the Flux beyond Anchor was no formless void, from which could issue only mutant changelings and evil wizards . . . Flux was the source of Anchor's existence! The price of her knowledge is exile – the first confrontation with the Seven Who Wait for the redemption of World . . .

**Exploring New Realms
in Science Fiction/Fantasy Adventure**

BATMAN™ IS BACK IN ACTION!

Batman™: To Stalk a Specter
by Simon Hawke

Gotham City Blackmailed!

Drug Lord Caught by U.S. Commandos! Desiderio Garcia to Stand Trial in the U.S.! The headlines – and the authorities – are jubilant, but not for long. For Garcia has a deadly would-be rescuer: the superassassin known as Specter. And Specter's reign of havoc and horror has already begun. The people of Gotham City are held hostage and destined to die by the thousands unless Garcia is freed. The people's only hope lies with Batman's bold and dangerous plan. In a war with only one winner and one survivor, he's going to make himself the archkiller's target, matching his enemy weapon for weapon, deception for deception – and with good for evil!

BATMAN™ CREATED BY BOB KANE

**Exploring New Realms
in Science Fiction/Fantasy Adventure**

SHADOWRUN™

Secrets of Power
by Robert N. Charrette

Titles already published or in preparation:

Volume 1: Never Deal with a Dragon

Volume 2: Choose Your Enemies Carefully

Volume 3: Find Your Own Truth

Where Man Meets Magic and Machine . . .

The year is 2050. The power of magic and the creatures it brings
have returned to the earth and many of the ancient races have re-
emerged in a world where technology and human flesh have
melded into deadly urban predators. For Sam Verner, living in
the womb of the Renraku conglomerate was easy, until his sister
disappeared. Now he wants out, but to do so he has to slide
through a world where his first wrong move may be his last . . .

**Exploring New Realms
in Science Fiction/Fantasy Adventure**

Chronicles of the Kings Tramp
by Tom De Haven

An exciting new trilogy!

Titles already published or in preparation:

Book One: Walker of Worlds

Book Two: The End-of-Everything Man

Jack, a Walker, is in danger. He has learned a secret; he has earned an enemy. Jack must flee the world of Lostwithal. He must flee to Kemolo. The secret he carries could mean the end of all the worlds, not just his own. But Jack cannot violate the Order of Things, not even to preserve it. Jack, a Walker, must walk the worlds.

**Exploring New Realms
in Science Fiction/Fantasy Adventure**

Temps
Devised by Neil Gaiman and
Alex Stewart

At last, the cutting-edge of Superhero fantasy!

Danger: Talent at work

To the tabloid press the Department of Paranormal Resources is a scroungers' paradise, issuing regular girocheques to a motley collection of talents with questionable results.

But for the 'Temps' who place their bizarre abilities at the service of the State in exchange for a miserly stipend and a demob suit, life with a very British League of Superheroes leaves everything to be desired . . .

Temps begins a startling new series in which a team of gifted Psi-fi writers explore a strangely familiar world of empaths, precogs and telepaths – with hilarious and terrifying results.

Contributors include: Storm Constantine, Colin Greenland, Graham Higgins, Liz Holliday, Roz Kaveney, David Langford, Brian Stableford . . . and many more.